DEDICATION

For my husband Karl and our two daughters, Kayla and Abbey. You are the loves of my life. Your patience and support will always be with me and I cannot thank you enough for letting me have my time to write. In the end, if you are proud of my work, then I've accomplished an important goal and my soul will be satisfied. At least until I begin writing my next book!

AKNOWLEDGEMENTS

Special thanks to someone I've called my "number one and only fan" during the two years in which I started and stopped writing this book. Jeanette Dwyer, you were kind enough to read this, chapter by chapter, draft by draft. You encouraged me when I thought I would never finish it, and then politely nagged me until I reached the point of publishing. If not for you, this novel would probably have remained a skeleton in my computer. Thank you!

And to all the African-American slaves who have long passed, I owe a tremendous debt of gratitude for allowing me to spin a story that could well have been true. This book acknowledges their sacrifices during one of the darkest periods in American history and will hopefully contribute in some small way to our nation never forgetting the lessons we learned.

"Whenever I hear anyone arguing for slavery, I feel a strong impulse to see it tried on him personally."

~Abraham Lincoln~

TABLE OF CONTENTS

Prologue, Olivia

My name is Olivia, and I'm a cancer survivor. Well...that's not entirely true. I've never been sick. Honestly, what I survived was my mother Emma's cancer. As awful as it sounds, it was actually because of the cancer that I survived her. When her long battle with the illness resulted in defeat, my struggle to win her love and approval ended. I finally overcame the burden of her contempt for me. You see, in spite of her Southern white upbringing, Emma's rebellious daughter chose to marry a man named Anthony—who happened to be gloriously dark-skinned. Black.

Just a week ago Mother was buried on such a golden morning that it seemed to mock the somber occasion. I grinned at the irony. Later, as if paying penance for my irreverence, I received the honor of sorting through the clothes and personal things in her closet. Daddy was horrified at the thought of having to deal with this heartrending detail, so leave it to my thoughtful siblings to assign the task to me. Fair enough, I suppose, as I was the only grown child who didn't rush back to South Carolina to help out during Mother's illness.

In her enormous closet were several identical boxes stacked neatly on shelves above her designer clothes. I rifled through several of them, pausing to look at everything, trying to understand why she held on to such an assortment of memorabilia: ticket stubs, playbills, bits of wrapping paper, invitations to social events she could not possibly have enjoyed. The opera, animal rescue charities...Mother hated the opera and despised four-legged creatures, for God's sake!

Then, in one unremarkable box, I uncovered what appeared to be an old leather journal among frothy layers of silky fabric. Its worn cover housed pages that were distinctly yellowed by the passage of time. It smelled musty, yet curiously sweet.

Gently I pulled out the antique volume and opened it to the first page, sending an envelope sailing to the floor. Reaching down to retrieve it, I recognized Mother's handwriting. Perfectly shaped letters meticulously spelled out my name--Olivia.

An unusually cool breeze wafted in through the open window, so I found one of Mother's sweaters to pull around my shoulders. The familiar scent of her Chanel N°5 still held to its fibers and suddenly I felt her presence. She was holding on to me, something she seldom did in my years as her grown child due to both the geographic and the emotional distance between us. I shuddered as I unsealed the envelope and lifted out a letter…

"My Dearest Olivia,
I leave to you this journal, passed down from generation to generation in my family. It was kept by Marianne Witherell-Richland, who would be your fourth great-grandmother. She began writing several years before the American Civil War. Your grandmother gave me this book when I was a teenager and reading it for the first time, I was intrigued by the friendship of Marianne and a slave girl named Willa who lived with her family at Heavenly Plantation.
Marianne wrote about her life on the rice plantation, not far from Charleston. She often reflects on the injustices committed by members of her family—our family—against their slaves. Some of the wrongs were simply horrific, making slavery ever more an appalling stain on the history of our family and our South Carolina homestead. I'd always felt that slavery was wrong, but was more convinced after reading the journal, until something terrible happened to me."

Okay, here it was. After all those years I'd discover the inner-workings of my mother's mind. I took a deep, lasting breath and exhaled slowly, feeling both elated and terrified. I wanted to know her better, but feared that whatever she revealed would not make me understand her any more than I did. I might even regret the knowledge I'd gain. I contemplated my situation for what must have been several minutes and decided to continue reading what my mother wrote…

"At one point I no longer cared about what slavery did to African Americans. While I couldn't begin to justify what our ancestors did, suddenly it ceased to infuriate me the way it had. I became numb. And then a certain kind of hatred grew in my heart. It began to gnaw at me and it never stopped.
It is obvious, Olivia, that I have always detested your relationship with Anthony. I know that you suffer because of my prejudice, which I am sure you think is completely unfounded. I acknowledge the unfairness of my behavior and am so sorry. My hurt has cost me a valuable relationship with you, Olivia. I've been powerless to change how I feel about him, even when I realize that it is wrong. There is simply too much emotional scar tissue remaining from a secret I've hidden all my life.
Olivia, when I was in college I often went to the library late at night, alone. I loved the solitude. Loved being there all by myself, surrounded by the great works of literature that often inspired me. One particular night, I walked back to the

sorority house with my thoughts still wrapped up in a Shakespearean play. It was Othello; I remember it all too clearly.

I didn't hear the man approaching me from behind until suddenly I was pulled close to him. His hand covered my mouth, threatening to carve me up with the knife he held in his other hand if I tried to scream. I remember his distinctly African-American voice mouthing obscenities, calling me a privileged white bitch, spewing at me with his alcohol breath.

He forced me into the cover of bushes and then pushed me to the ground. He told me that I would enjoy it, what he was about to do to me. That some white-bred frat boy would never satisfy me after he was through. After yanking up my skirt he slid the cold, flat side of the knife slowly up my inner thigh. My heart stopped. And then the black man violated me while I kept silent."

I looked up from the letter and gasped as my heart did a free-fall and the tears pooled in my eyes. I heard myself begin to whimper as I slumped to the floor, feeling nothing but pity for Mother. Then I was struck with a sickening sensation of shame. Guilt. I should have forced my mother to talk about her mental state long before she became ill. I was just as evil as her attacker for not recognizing her pain, inquiring about it. But it never occurred to me that she was anything other than irrational and cold. Bigoted. After wallowing in defeat for quite a while, I resumed with her letter.

"Humiliated, frightened, and ashamed, I never told anyone. Not the police, not even your grandparents. Instead, I brewed a deep and consuming resentment.

In the dim moonlight I couldn't clearly see his face, so I lived in fear, suspecting every black man I saw or met. I found myself fearful of the entire African-American race. I was powerless to control my own thoughts, no matter how irrational they were.

When I discovered that I was pregnant with my rapist's child, I quickly aborted the fetus. After that, I know I should have sought professional help for my mental state, but I was still too ashamed, too frightened.

What that vicious man took away from me was not only my honor, but my ability to trust anyone. It was not until I met your daddy that I slowly began to accept love. But even he knows nothing of my rape, nothing of my abortion. When I disapprove of your involvement with Anthony, he simply thinks that I am an old-fashioned, dyed-in-the-wool Confederate who just won't tolerate interracial relationships.

Now as I lay dying Olivia, I regret not being able to speak with you and admit my mistakes. I regret the fact that you will not return my calls and I will likely not see you before I pass from this world.

Olivia, since you are reading this letter, I will assume that I am gone. Now that you know the truth, can you understand my misgivings about Anthony? Please see this from my perspective as a victim haunted by a tragic memory I could not share with anyone. Can you ever forgive me, my daughter?

I know that this is all too late, but please accept my love again. Even in my absence. I love you, Olivia.

Mother"

Oh, God how I longed to hear those words. I held the letter to my chest as I cried for what might have been an hour. Finally I began to read my ancestor's journal, which was once so important to Mama...

Chapter 1: Marianne's Journal, April 1846

"Such beautiful leather on the cover, with so many blank pages inside. Just waiting to be filled with my thoughts, dreams, and ideas. A wonderful gift, although I suspect that Mother presented it to me because "a woman's place is to be silent and respectful." If I keep my thoughts on paper, I might be prevented from voicing them.

Oh, but I am far from being a woman, not quite fourteen. Many girls my age are speaking of the type of man they wish to marry and the number of children they shall have. It is appalling! Being a grown woman is not my desire now and maybe never shall be. I relish my days ahead as a girl, without the responsibilities of womanhood. I have no desire to run a household, command a staff of Negros, and subject myself to the demands of a husband. Willa and I secretly laugh at the notion of having husbands and birthing babies. We think men are vermin, except for Seth, my younger brother. I also think Father and Foster are keen, but Willa does not know them well. My older brother Foster is not fond of slaves and will have nothing to do with her. Father is similarly minded. He owns Willa. It seems strange that she has a master and even stranger that her master is Father.

Willa came to us with her mother Heddie when she was eight years old. Before my twin brothers Gabriel and Garrett were born, Mother had her first bad spell. In that state, she would be no more prepared to take care of babies than my father. I remember it well...Mother wailing, weeping, hysterical.

Most fortunate for us, Uncle Charles owned Heddie who had recently gave birth to twin babies. Under tragic circumstances, the babies died within weeks. Then, when my Aunt Charlotte learned of Mother's ill condition she urged Uncle to send Heddie to us as a wet nurse. In exchange for Mammy Heddie and Willa, Father traded a few work horses with Uncle. Imagine that! Willa and her mother in exchange for some horses.

Heddie's dead twins were not the only ones they left on Uncle's plantation. Willa has a father and two older brothers. Most likely she will never again lay eyes upon them; for that is the way slavery works here in South Carolina.

My twin brothers loved Mammy Heddie right away it seemed, taking well to her nourishing milk. Sometimes when she would give them over to my mother they cried and cried. Mother's eyes would look vacant and steely, as if no love existed for her own flesh and blood. Then when she would hand them back over to Heddie, the warmth would return to her eyes. She would just go on as if all was well. But things are far from well. Since the birth of the twins, Mother teeters between reasonable and absurd. Up and down, never the same person for long.

It pains my soul the way Willa is treated like property at times. Mother is often heartless, and I am most ashamed of her behavior, although many of her shortcomings are due to her unstable mind. Even so, Willa and her mother live as servants of this house, which I think should exclude them from the wrath our society bears against other Negros. It still does seem so silly to refer to my best friend as a servant. How that stings of hypocrisy!

I recall to this day how Willa first appeared to me when she came to our plantation house. Before she arrived, I had not experienced any contact with a Negro child close to my age. Of course, we have always had servants in our home. There was Old Ned the butler, Joelle the cook, our nursemaid Sissy, old Juniper, and Polly, the young maid who left suddenly after her baby was born. I just never knew someone near my age with dark skin. I remember how startling it was for me..."

Chapter 2: March, 1842

When Josiah Witherell heard the carryall pull up to the side porch, he came around the house to inspect the goods obtained by trade with his brother in-law Charles. The coachman dismounted, bowing his head to Master Witherell, awaiting command to assist two females in exiting the well-worn utility carriage. Josiah disregarded the dutiful coachman and stepped up to withdraw his new slaves. The first to alight the carriage was a child, followed by a woman. They both wore the burden of what must have been a tumultuous and hasty departure. The woman appeared ghostly in spite of her dark skin, with haunted-looking eyes and a thin, bony body. The child was no different, except she was weeping. Tiny tears trickled down, leaving clear tracks on her small, dirt-stained face. This was of no consequence to Josiah, who looked them over with eyes of disdain.

"My God, you are filthy!" He declared in a haughty tone, looking directly at the scrawny child. "The horses I traded had a more pleasing aroma." He shook his head, wondering if he had executed a poor trade with Charles and would at best gain a field slave with a young mouth to feed.

"Juniper! Juniper! Get your black hide out here!" Josiah called out to one of the house slaves. "That Charles! I'll fix his flint," he muttered, then looked directly at the weather-worn woman. "What am I to do with the likes of you?"

At the side door appeared Juniper, a twitchy, tall slave woman who flitted over to the carriage, almost tripping over her own feet. Nervously she answered to Josiah, "Yes, Marster! You call me? Yessir!"

"Do something with these two sad looking creatures!" Josiah barked, gesturing to the two in front of the carriage. "Boil some water, clean them up. Do not bring them into the house before the mistress until they are clean. Mrs. Witherell will have a spell if she sees them like this. Go!"

With that command, he was gone, back up the porch and through the door before Juniper could respond. "Yes, Marster..." she replied to his former visage, and then turned her attention to the coachman.

"How're you, Daniel?"

"I be fine, Juniper. You best be doin' what the Marster say now. Let me clear out this car and get it back to the shed." Daniel, the tall and sturdy coachman with sparkling black eyes, nodded kindly at the mother and daughter, and then reached inside the carriage to retrieve the small parcel they brought with them. He gently placed it in the mother's hands.

"Here you be ma'am. You take care of yo'self and that little one now," he tenderly said and then climbed back into his seat. "Bye now Juniper." In an instant, he took the leather reigns in his hands, shouted to the horses, and left as the two Negro women and the child stood looking at one another.

"Let's get you scrubbed up, then. Best get done 'for the Missus come callin' for ya. She knew you'd be here today. My name's Juniper, by the way. What's yours?"

The woman spoke softly, quietly, "Heddie, my name be Heddie and this here's Willa, my baby girl."

"Well welcome to Heavenly Miz Heddie and Miz Willa. You here to take care of Missus' baby boys, I know. Them's some babies. Cryin' all the time. Missus never know what's wrong. I'll tell you all about the Missus. She's a strange one, she is! Here, let's get on down to the wash house and be quick. Ain't goin' get nowhere at this rate."

Juniper urged them on down a path about sixty yards away from the main plantation house, skipping along in her usual jittery manner. The laundry house was no more than a large shed containing several iron basins of various sizes. In the massive fireplace hung black kettles filled with bubbling liquid.

Juniper ordered one of the older Negro women in the shed to draw off some of the boiling water. Then she instructed her to pour it into one of the basins while another woman fetched clean cotton gowns. Next she directed Heddie and Willa to strip off their garments. Never afforded the luxury of modesty, both complied and were soon standing naked. Juniper scooped up their filthy clothes and threw them into the pot of scalding water.

Juniper had the matronly Negro woman fill another wash basin with a mixture of boiling and cool water to make a tolerable bath. She handed Heddie a bar of Castile soap and a frayed cotton cloth. Dipping into the tepid water, Heddie moistened the soap and formed a rich lather. After cleaning, rinsing, and drying Willa, she began working on her own sun-toughened skin. At once she recalled how her beloved husband Alfred would kiss the nape of her neck. It was always his distinctive way to soften her demeanor after a long day of field work.

She moaned, making a heavy, sorrowful sound that soon escalated to an all-encompassing wail. Falling to her knees, she huddled down on the dirt floor and cried in spasms of grief for Alfred and the sons she left. She cried for the twin babies they just buried back at Southwind.

Eight year old Willa was overcome with confusion, throwing her arms around her mother. "Mama, oh, Mama! When will papa and the boys be comin'?"

Juniper, who was busy stirring the pot containing their clothing, looked up from her chore. What a sight it was to see mother and child naked and in a fitful heap on the floor. Her heart filled with pity as she dropped the stirring stick and cried out, "Dear sweet Jesus. You po', po' child. Oh Holy Lord Jesus! Child you ain't never goin' see your papa again. That's the way it is. Po', pitiful child!"

Chapter 3

The living quarters for the house slaves were situated just behind one of the cutting gardens on the plantation. As one born in bondage, Heddie knew at first glance that her accommodations at Heavenly were going to be far superior to those at Southwind Plantation. From the outside, she admired the clean and orderly appearance of the white-washed dwelling where female house slaves lodged, according to Juniper. Inside, she found that its small rooms afforded some privacy, something foreign to her experience at the other plantation. Each small sleeping room consisted of four beds and a set of shelves for storage of clothing and personal items.

"Oh, Mama! Look!" The mournful scene from the wash house faded with Willa's excitement for her new living quarters.

Heddie's own face brightened when she saw the frames fitted with what looked like fluffy, clean mattresses. She guessed that they were filled with soft cotton. Folded upon each bed was a quilted coverlet and pillow, items she never dreamed she would possess. Immediately she thought of Alfred back at Southwind, destined to sleep on the often-damp dirt floor of their cabin. There, they had no luxuries like mattresses and pillows. The thin wool blankets they owned barely kept them and their children covered from the evening chill.

"Heddie, you be sleepin' in the Big House near them babies. Marster put me in charge of keepin' an eye on you' bitty one 'til she a mite older. But you can see her anytime you want," Juniper explained. When she noticed Heddie's tears, she continued, "What's a matter, sweetie? Your bitty one be quite happy here. She be here with me and I watch over her like she my own."

The thought of being separated from Willa only increased fragile Heddie's crying, which started her daughter on the same path of woe. The two wailed in unison, leaving Juniper bewildered and twitching, not sure what else to do.

"Oh, missy…how can I help you and the little one? You cry like Marster and Missus's baby boys! Now what ever will I do with you?"

"So sorry, Juniper. I done lost my sweet little babies to death…then I get pulled away from my darlin' Alfred…my boys. Now I lose my little Willa. She be with you…and I got nothin' now. It be all gone," Heddie whispered in a thready voice.

Completely broken, Heddie wanted no more than to collapse on one of the downy beds and continue to let the misery run its course through her bones. Death would surely be a welcome friend and comfort to her. If not for Willa, she would have prayed that the Lord take her to end the wretchedness of her new life.

As if reading her thoughts, Juniper stumbled over to Heddie and the child, embracing them both in her long, gangly arms. Then she pulled Willa to one of the beds and tugged Heddie to the other. She unfolded the coverlets and gently placed one on each, tucking them in as gracefully as she could manage.

"Oh, now I know you had a long journey and a tough enough day. I know ya can't be feelin' too good after that trip and I'm goin' to tell Missus that you come down ill and can't take care of them babies tonight. She just have to put up with 'em one more night."

With conviction, Juniper's long legs carried her out a creaky front door and she was off to the "Big House" with her declaration to the mistress. Heddie and Willa looked at each other in confusion. Wiping her wet eyes and nose on the sleeve of her cotton gown, Willa's innocent face was full of questions for which Heddie held no answers. There was nothing to say that would calm her daughter. Nothing to dismiss the fear of uncertainty that hung over both of them like a rain cloud, ready to burst and drown them. Heddie felt most unequipped as a mother, unable to rescue her own child from this situation. How could she make the separation from Southwind seem bearable to Willa, when she could not do the same for herself?

Suddenly the reason behind their exile from Southwind made itself known when Heddie's swollen breasts began to leak. Up to that moment, since leaving Southwind she felt nothing but pain in her breasts and her heart.

"Oh, Lord a'mighty!" She wailed, pulling up the coverlet and folding her arms around it and her chest, hoping to stop the milk flow. It was no use. Within minutes she soaked through her thin cotton dress and the coverlet. "Oh, sweet Jesus! They ain't no peace in this life for Mammy Heddie!"

"Mama!" Willa scampered out of bed. At Heddie's side she wrapped her thin arms around her until she felt the sticky wetness between them. "Mama, what's a matter?"

"The Lord playin' a hoax on mama, Willa, that's all they is to it. The Lord sayin' Heddie need no rest, Heddie the slave best be goin' off to work for the new Marster! Now where that Juniper off to, tellin' lies 'bout me, get me in trouble 'fore I even meet the Missus!"

"I hear my name?" Juniper asked as she returned from the plantation house. "Best not be bad mouthin' old Juniper who got you the night free from duty. I tell the Missus that you took ill all suddenly and best not be near them babies or they catch it too. She says you best be well in the mornin', but you stay away from her tonight. So you and Willa just stay in here, let Juniper take care of ya. How 'bout that?"

Heddie took a few minutes to absorb what she heard. The mistress of the house giving a slave pardon from duty was unthinkable. As a field slave, she worked from sun up until sun down regardless of her health or emotional state. She worked up until her children were born, practically gave birth to Willa between rows of cotton. Could this new Missus be humane? Or was this a trick destined to put her in jeopardy with the new owner?

While Heddie was thinking, Juniper noticed her milk-stained gown. "Oh, dear Lord! You soakin' wet! Let me get somethin' to help sop you up." She popped up, flew out of the room and then returned with plenty of cotton cloths and another gown, offering to help her change. Heddie obliged and silently thanked God for the likes of Juniper, the kindly nervous slave who was surely sent from Above to help her and Willa on their first night at Heavenly Plantation.

Chapter 4

Heavenly's gardens were a source of considerable amusement to Juniper. How ironic that she encountered a tremendous sense of freedom while watching the hummingbirds, bees, and flowers. Yet, she was bound in slavery. True, house slaves fared better than those working the rice fields, but captivity was still captivity no matter how experienced.

Juniper never ventured away from Heavenly Plantation, but was sure that no other place on Earth equaled its perfection. Her imagination would never go past the magnificence of the South Carolina soil beneath her bare feet, the beauty of the old oak trees curtained with wispy Spanish moss. The very fragrance of the air, infused with the scent of hundreds of sweet flowers and herbs from the gardens intoxicated her, made her giddy with delight.

Daughter of Heavenly's trusted and cherished cook Augustine, Juniper's much lighter complexion identified her as a mulatto, the product of an affair between her mother and some visiting Witherell relative. Whether the affair was one of consent remained in question, but that was a subject Augustine never addressed with her. The possibility of uncovering her paternity was simply of no concern to Juniper.

During her adolescence, when Josiah Witherell was just a boy himself, Juniper's behavior was markedly different from her peers, both black and white. She was highly excitable and easily agitated. Nicknamed "Twitchy" by Josiah, who was ten years her junior, she was thought to be useless to the household and destined for manual slave labor in the fields. Josiah's insults never fazed her though. She seemed impervious to remarks made about her apparent afflictions and vowed to work harder to prove her worth to the family in the Big House, as they commonly referred to the plantation mansion.

Learning to ride a horse was the key to her preservation, along with the pleadings of her mother. Augustine feared that Juniper would not last long toiling among the swampy acres of rice and suggested that the Witherells harness her energy by taking advantage of her riding abilities. Soon Juniper became invaluable as a courier who would ride out over the massive plantation delivering messages to the overseers. She coursed the multiple acres with precision, possessing innate navigational abilities and riding prowess. Soon the little mulatto girl earned the respect of the household, including Josiah, who ceased calling her Twitchy.

As she grew into womanhood, she continued to ride but was also given responsibilities within the house that required less concentration and fine motor skill. Although she could not cook a thing, she was charged with supervising the kitchen slaves after Augustine passed away. She was well-regarded by the slaves and efficient in her position. Her duties were expanded so that now she supervised the work of most of the house slaves.

She breathed deeply of the familiar wisteria, camellia, and azalea, the scents of which she never grew tired. Deeply appreciative, she silently thanked God for Heavenly Plantation, the Witherell family, and her position as a favored house slave. Although she did not understand why slavery existed, she counted her particular situation a blessing, having heard stories of torture and deprivation at the hands of malicious masters from slaves raised elsewhere. She also knew firsthand that some of the overseers on her own plantation were not models of justice. Although Josiah Witherell did not condone cruelty and violence toward slaves, the actions of his overseers in the fields were seldom curtailed. It was his position that they rule their slaves as they saw fit, with as little interference as possible.

After checking on the kitchen and housekeeping staff, Juniper dreaded what was next on her morning agenda. Although Margaret Witherell had her own attendant assuring her comfort, Juniper insisted on personally tending to the mistress several times daily. The morning visits were often the most unpredictable, so she came to fear them. Still, she felt it was her duty to make sure her mistress was well served.

The early morning Margaret was either despondent or volatile, never on even keel. Some days she would barely notice Juniper's entrance into her chambers; other times she would immediately begin with her demands. She started sleeping in separate quarters away from Josiah several months before the birth of their new twins, an arrangement that was both convenient and mandatory.

The babies were restless, constantly wanting fed. They cried more than seemed healthy for newborns and this disturbed Josiah, who feared for their mortality. Juniper recalled the joyful mood of celebration surrounding the birth of each of the other Witherell children. She remembered that happiness filled Margaret to the brim and spilled over to the entire household staff. It was always precious to see her with her sweet-smelling new babies; she literally blushed with pride, excessively doting over them. Not a soul could deny that Margaret was a mother in love with her creations.

These twins were an exception. She seemed not to want them at all. Some said that the complicated pregnancy and long, torturous labor ruined her joy. That theory didn't sit well with Juniper, who never thought she would see the day when Margaret would not bask in the glow of newborn babies. Something else was at play, something that required more explanation than a trying pregnancy.

"What mood she in today, Chloe?" she asked of Margaret's personal attendant as she met her on the stairway up to the bedroom of the mistress.

Chloe held the tiny, writhing Witherells in her arms, responding to Juniper in a low, calm voice, "Oh, she pretty feisty, Miz Juniper. You watch yo'self in there. She not too happy 'bout that new nurse. Mad as hell's the truth! Bes' get her in here now. Make the Missus stop the yellin'. I had to take the babes away from her before she kill 'em."

"Heddie needed the night to herself, for God's sake Chloe! She could do nothin' for the Missus last night!" Juniper's voice matched the volume of Chloe's but carried authority, "I bring her up in a bit after I check on the Missus myself."

"Take my word for it, she a mess this mornin' she is. I'd get myself out to the slave house and get that new woman up here now if I was you. Better do it right away!"

"You tellin' me how to do my work, Chloe?" Juniper twitched more than usual, feeling like she could jump out of her own skin. Chloe's demanding attitude and the anticipation of Margaret's wrath was too much for her at the moment.

"Why no, ma'am!" Regardless of their common status as slave women, Chloe knew her place was one of inferiority to Juniper. She instantly regretted the strong tone in which she spoke to her, but the mistress' morning behavior had her rattled. Margaret's mood shifts were getting more erratic and unpredictable.

"Of course not. Go on now, get them babes outta here. You take care of 'em 'til I get Heddie settled in over here. You understand this?"

"Yes ma'am." Chloe hurried on her way, bouncing the twins about to placate their need for constant stimulation while Juniper took a deep, cleansing breath and bounded clumsily up the stairs toward her daily fate.

***

Margaret Witherell sat up splendidly among the expensive linens on her bed. A strikingly attractive woman, she maintained a youthful appearance even after birthing five children and doting over a household and a staff of slaves. Her creamy complexion betrayed not a crease and she possessed a mane of hair that was the envy of all the women in the county. On this morning she wore it casually pinned up in a loose knot with a mass of golden curls escaping to spill down her shoulders.

When she addressed Juniper however, the beauty seemed to recede as anger took over. "Where is she, Juniper? Where is my new nurse? You know I did not sleep a wink last night? Those babies kept me up all night! I cannot take it anymore, Juniper! How could you do this to me, you wretch? Why do you make me suffer? I shall tell Josiah and he will beat the livin' daylights out of you, woman! Strip you down and beat the black flesh off your back..."

"Now Missus, you jus' calm down. You'll do no such to old Juniper, you won't. You know you love me, you do. Ain't goin' do no such! You just upset havin' no sleep, that's all," she continued in a low, soothing voice while fussing with Margaret's pillows and smoothing her blankets. Whatever insults the mistress spewed, she vowed to stay calm and remember that Margaret was not of sound mind these days.

Suddenly Margaret broke down, apologizing to her most trusted and beloved slave, "Oh Juniper! I don't mean to be so cruel, not to you. You know I do love you, my faithful Juniper. What am I going to do with those children? I need to sleep and they are always so hungry, Juniper. I hate the little demons sometimes! I hate them!"

"Oh Missy! Never say that!" The words spoken by her mistress made her shudder all the more. It could never be true. No matter how strange Margaret's behavior, no matter how bizarre her turn in mood, she could never hate the babies.

"But I do. I do. I do..." Her voice trailed off, replaced by sobs. As she wept, tears trailed down her lovely face and increased in proportion to the dramatic heaving of her chest. Soon she was wailing loudly, as if mourning the dead.

"Now, now...take a deep breath Missus before you cry half to death. Deep breath," Juniper urged, putting her long arms around Margaret's shoulders and attempting to draw them back and force her to breathe. The Mistress responded in a rage, grabbing at Juniper's arms, smacking them away and lunging at her in one smooth and impulsive motion, knocking her to the floor with a distinct thud.

Juniper lay sprawled on the hard floor, rangy limbs in all directions, reeling not from pain but from astonishment. "What was that, Missus?" she breathlessly asked, not expecting an answer.

The door to the bedroom swung open and Josiah Witherell burst inside to investigate the source of the loud thump. He imagined his capricious wife falling from her bed and it almost made him smile until he visualized the twins taking the tumble as well. Finally seeing Juniper on the floor he was not sure whether to sigh in relief or laugh at her, given her clumsiness.

"What the devil is going on?"

"Get out! Get out!" Margaret managed to pick up a bedside book and hurl it through the air, aiming for her husband's balding head. She missed her mark and the volume landed with another pronounced thump.

"Another bad morning, Maggie?" Josiah sighed, realizing that his wife would be useless yet another day. "Maggie, did you not sleep well last night?" He taunted her by purposely using a nickname that she loathed. No one ever called her Maggie but her long-dead mother, a woman so cruel she made even the meanest of plantation overseers seem gentle as kitten.

"Get out of here Josiah, you heartless bastard! Next time I throw at you, I will not miss. I will knock the life out of that thick head of yours!"

"Maggie! Why are you so contemptuous to me? Have I not given you everything you ever wanted in life? What about the new nurse? Did I not find you a suitable nurse? You know she cost me a few good horses and the loss of Daniel for a few days in the journey to fetch her. Maggie, Maggie, what else can I do?"

"Just stop it Josiah! Just stop!"

Juniper did not understand why Josiah insisted upon calling Margaret by the hated nickname. It was simply malicious to goad her when she was so fragile. How was it possible for him to have this demeanor toward her when he seemed so affectionate with his children and even some his slaves? *Intolerable Josiah, just intolerable,* she mused, even as he helped her off the floor.

"I'm sorry, sir. That new nurse was mighty sick feelin' last night so I let her sleep. But she be right over shortly, yes she will. Juniper see to it. Then Missus Margaret get some sleep in peace. Mammy Heddie take care of the new babies, yes she will."

"Thank you Juniper, please see to it at once. Mrs. Witherell does need some agreeable sleep, I have to say. She is a tad hateful this morning," Josiah announced stridently for the benefit of his wife. Lowering his voice to Juniper alone, he added, "Did she push you down? Did she hurt you?"

"Yes, she did. But I be fine, no ill feelin', sir. The Missus not well, I understands that, Marster, she not well."

"That will be all, Juniper. Please get the nurse."

"Yes, sir." Juniper obeyed and headed for the back staircase, leaving Josiah alone with his distraught wife. She would rather have stayed nearby, crouching somewhere safe to listen to whatever conversation transpired between man and wife upon her exit. However, once detected, the action of spying would surely result in a thorough flogging, so she carried on about her business.

Chapter 5

Heddie was up before dawn, surprised that there was so little activity within the slave quarters at that hour. Where she came from, the cabins of the field slaves would be buzzing by now as they took in whatever breakfast they could and prepared to head out for a long day of work, rain or shine. Her morning routine never varied. Monday through Saturday—breakfast chores, rouse and feed the children, say goodbye to the littlest two, join the others for the long trip out into the cotton fields.

Alfred. Sampson. Flash. Was her husband thinking of her this very moment? Were the boys missing their mama yet? Wiping away an involuntary tear, she wondered. Alfred would have to see to it that the boys were fed. Make sure that Flash was headed over to Nana Berthie's cabin where he would help out with what his papa called "woman work" in the slave village. Berthie appeared to be one hundred, but was most likely in her sixties. She had more energy than most of the older slave women though, which made her seem younger in spite of her leathery face and the bony structure over which it was draped. All the ancient Negros deemed too old and slow to produce in the fields were charged with the everyday care of the cabins, the cooking, and the young children of the village.

Flash—Edgar—was only ten. Two years older than Willa, but much less mature. Heddie remembered for a bittersweet moment the time she and Alfred nicknamed him. Bashful, often withdrawn, brooding. That was Edgar. But he had a way of aiming a sly smile at you, bursting through the cloud of shyness. Just a flash of light, a forceful ray of sunshine that lingered only seconds, letting you know that he liked you, that he trusted you with the secret that he liked you. That was a treasure for most people. Yes, all he had to do was flash that quick smile and he had a friend. Heddie and Alfred always imagined that one day his magnetic smile would earn him the attention of many young ladies.

Sampson was a strong, tree-like young man of fourteen who was never afraid to speak his mind or raise questions. His parents feared that he would turn out to be too bold for his own good. Headstrong personalities did not mix well with slavery. They witnessed the fate of bold slaves much too often. Whippings, lynching, torture at the hands of white men who were not to be made fools by the bravery of darkies. Heddie shuddered at the memories and the possibility that her eldest could be the subject of someone else's morose recollection.

The possibility of seeing either child was a remote one. Flash's precious smile would only be a product of her memory now and she would not witness Sampson's complete passage into adulthood. She would not have the privilege of visiting the graves of the dead twins or the babies she failed to bring to term. There had been three or four others, she'd lost count. It would be up to Alfred to honor them and mourn for them alone, something she knew would be difficult for him to do.

But still she was grateful. Heddie was blessed to have had so many years of family life with Alfred and the children. In their world they saw families split up and sold off to different plantations hundreds of miles apart. Time after time. They knew their turn would surely come. Why would it be any other way? She still grieved over her dead twins, the loss of Alfred and the boys, but she knew she was blessed. She was allowed to bring Willa with her. She would still be a mother to Willa, watch her grow.

"Miz Heddie!" Juniper interrupted her thoughts. "I hope you is better this mornin'. The Missus be askin''bout you. Had a bad night with them babies. You best be gettin' over to the house just as soon as you get a little bite to eat."

"Oh, yes ma'am. I be hurryin' right away. I so sorry 'bout last night, I truly is. Much better today, ma'am, much better!"

"Why don't you bring Willa with you this mornin', too. I bet Miz Marianne like to meet her. Don't recollect that she ever have any dark child to play with before. Might get her attention 'way from her foolish mama for a while anyways…"

"The Missus be foolish? What are you sayin' Juniper?"

"Oh now never mind, ole Juniper is talkin' out o'turn. The Missus has her bad days and she has her good 'uns, that's all there is to it. Never mind. You find out sure enough. You be fine with her though. She really needs you, she does. You'll be fine, Miz Heddie. Little Willa be fine too. She can run and play with them Witherell children all she want. The Mistress won't bark too much at the children."

During the short stroll to the plantation house, Heddie and Willa were fascinated by their first full view of Heavenly. The grounds buildings were arranged in a similar configuration to those left behind at Southwind Plantation. The major difference here was in the variety of colors represented by the flowers contained in elaborate gardens around the main house. Neither slave had witnessed such a vivid display, as the life of a field slave was generally not very colorful. Drab clothing, the white of cotton fields, colorless grub to eat with only the occasional green, yellow, or red vegetable.

The Big House was indeed large. Two stories constructed of red brick, featuring an extensive front veranda with a covered entrance supported by massive classical columns. Several wide steps lead up to the oversized oak door designed to both impress and intimidate its visitors. Along the front side were windows framed by shutters—black ones for the second story and white for the first. Some type of green ivy climbed up the brick exterior facade, but only to the top of the first floor windows where it must have been trimmed back by the slaves who tended meticulously to the colorful surrounding gardens. Seven chimneys erupted from the roof and towered high over the house, casting long shadows across the lawn.

***

Soon enough, Heddie was introduced to Margaret Witherell. "Thank you, Lord God Almighty! These babies of mine are just too much to bear. I am much too fair to take on two little bitty ones at once. They cry all night long and I am just not up for that nonsense. Tell me you can handle this, Heddie Grigsby, tell me you will keep them happy and out of my hair!"

"Yes, ma'am. Uhh, Missus Witherell, yes Missus. I take good care o' your babes, I will. It be my honor. Miz Heddie treat 'em as her own. I just' lost two bitty ones o' my own, I did, I…"

"I know that and I am truly sorry, I am. Let's not think about that now Mammy Heddie. Let's get fixed on my babies."

"Yes, ma'am."

Margaret threw a glance at little Willa who stood obediently beside Heddie. "You go on now, child. My other children are around this old house somewhere. Why don't you go about and see if you can find them? Go on now." She shooed Willa away with a brush of her hands.

Like her mother, Willa responded in the polite way of a dutiful slave. "Yes, ma'am."

Minutes later it was Marianne Witherell who found Willa near the grand staircase, looking down into the expansive entrance hall below. Not noticing Marianne, Willa was lost in thoughts about what wondrous things might be found in such an enormous house.

Marianne used the opportunity to fully take in the slave girl's appearance. She stared at her curiously. Her first close-up view of a black child. Only grown adults worked inside the Big House and none had their children there with them. Until now. Willa struck her as particularly strange because of the rich darkness of her skin tone, such a contrast to the typical house slaves who were lighter-skinned, some barely perceptible as black.

"Good day, there. You must be the new nurse's little girl. My, you are a tiny speck of a thing, aren't you? My name is Marianne Daphne Witherell. What is your name, little one?"

"My name is Willa, Willa Grigsby. I ain't little, neither, Miz Marianne! I tell you that!" A strong hint of defiance replaced the helplessness of the fragile girl she was only the day before.

"Oh, feisty, too. And mighty dark! I've never seen such a color in my whole life. Why I've never seen a small darky, to tell you the God's honest truth. How old are you Willa Grigsby?"

"Eight, that's what my mama say. 'Course I dark, I's a nigga!'"

"Oh! My mother says that is not a polite word to say! Hmmm...but I've heard her say it many times when she's in one of her awful, troublesome moods. Does your mother get angry much, Willa Grigsby?"

"My mama just sad 'cause she miss my papa. Marster sell us away and leave Papa back at Southwind. I's sad, too. But I'm a lot tougher than my mama, I am!" Willa obstinately held her head just a little higher and stuck out her chest to demonstrate bravery.

"I'd say you are! Can I touch your dark skin, Willa Grigsby?"

"It's Willa, jus' Willa. Here." She moved closer to Marianne and offered a bony arm for inspection. Marianne reached for her, swiping over her skin gingerly at first and then polishing it with more vigor.

"Oh, my! Your skin is soft, Willa. You are just like me. The color doesn't even wipe off!"

"You sure be silly, Miz Marianne! It just skin, not soot. 'Course I don't rub off!" The notion of her black skin rubbing off on someone else made Willa giggle with delight.

"It's just Marianne to you too, Willa." Then Marianne was compelled to conduct more tactile investigation, putting her fingers into Willa's closely braided hair.

"And your hair! It feels...feels like twine! I've always wanted to know, but I never did find out. I mean I've never asked to touch a slave before. Mother would think it impolite to ask. But you are a child and you don't seem to mind."

Now it was Willa's turn to investigate. She reached out to gently grasp a handful of Marianne's pale blonde hair in one of her miniature hands. "Yours a might bit slippery. Feels like corn silks. Nobody has hairs like that. You a spirit from the wood? A ghost?" she teasingly questioned.

"What?" The mention of "spirit" put a sudden sense of fear into Marianne's voice, having overheard the kitchen slaves speak often of ghosts and other frightful beings. Her mother told her that the Negros believed in all sorts of ghastly creatures of the night, strange beliefs and superstitions that went against Marianne's religious upbringing.

"You know, the spirits. Them that come in the night and scare the wits outta the darkies. They say the Marster send 'em."

"Willa, that is not true! My father would never send such things. Such things just do not exist. The Good Book would tell you so. Do you not go to church to pray to the Lord, girl?"

"Heavens no! The church for the white folk! Marster Charles won't allow. The darkies hafta go out yonder to the wood and sing the praises to the Lord. Marster Charles catch us and then the overseer Dobbs beat the daylights outta us!" Willa's eyes widened in fear of recalling the times her relatives and adult friends were severely punished for worshipping amongst themselves. Religious pursuit for slaves was forbidden at the Southwinds Plantation as if to do so would stir rebellion.

"I don't understand, Willa. Our Negros hold church right after us and our own Reverend Wells says the service. How could Uncle Charles be so cruel at his plantation? I just don't know why he would not let you worship!" Shaking her head in a mixture of disbelief and shock, this insight caused Marianne for the first time in her life to wonder what other differences existed between life on their plantation and others.

Marianne instantly recalled the times when she wandered into the kitchen and heard slaves talk about other plantations they had inhabited before Heavenly. She heard them speak of horrible beatings and even deaths at the hands of monstrous overseers and plantation owners. But never had she considered this talk as truth. Margaret always became agitated with her when she repeated the stories and told her that slaves heartily enjoyed spinning incredible yarns. Then she was chastised for listening in on conversations to which she was not invited and warned to stay clear of the kitchen "...lest your little mind be poisoned by the darkies with nothing better to do than gossip."

"Marianne? You see a spirit? You looks mighty pale, even for a white folk! What's a matter?"

"Willa, promise me that you'll tell me everything about Uncle Charles's plantation. Tell me all about your life there. I've only visited once, but some of our slaves come from there and I hear bad things. I cannot believe Uncle is a terrible person. He is my mother's brother and Mother is not always bad..." Marianne's voice trailed off and Willa noticed that she suddenly seemed distressed.

Chapter 6

"She's as dark as the night, Foster. I didn't know that slaves came in that color. You just wait and see for yourself."

"Oh, my sweet little sister. Marianne, of course they come in that color. Darkies come in all sorts of blacks and browns and everything in between. You've never been too far away from this house, my dear sister. I've been all over Heavenly and Charleston too. I know what is out there." Foster gently kissed the top of his sister's head in a patronizing, but brotherly way.

Marianne couldn't help thinking that Foster knew everything, as usual. "Well I have never seen such a dark one. Matter of fact, I've never seen a darky child, not up close. I touched her skin, Foster. The dark just stays on. And she's so skinny. Looks like she hasn't eaten much in her life. I thought she was not much older than Cousin Eliza who's only five. But she's eight. That's just a year younger than our Seth."

"I suppose you will make friends with the little girl, won't you Marianne? Those darkies are different. They're not like us, sister. You be careful or she'll put some kind of spell on you, conjure up their ghouls and chase you into the woods!" Raising his arms over head, he dangled them over her, crossing his eyes and sticking out his tongue. Foster aimed to make Marianne laugh the way he always did, but the gestures only served to irritate her.

"Foster, you stop that. There are no such things as ghouls. Mother said not to listen to the tales about ghosts and ugly creatures! The slaves have it all wrong. The Lord would not let ghouls harm a soul. Stop talking like that or I'll never have anything to do with you as long as I live!"

"You promise that? My life would be so much easier, little one. I'd never have to play silly hopscotch with you again. Seth and I could play Nine Men Morris without your pestering. Oh, I can just think of it..."

"Foster, I hate you! You are a mean, awful boy!" Marianne crossed her arms and tried to look dreadfully upset while trying not to giggle.

"Are you terribly mad at me, dear little sister? I know how to fix that!" He threw his arms around her and hugged as tight as he could. "Say uncle and I'll let you go!"

"No, never!" She refused to play at his game, all the while stifling laughter. She understood that her older brother loved her deeply and would never let her down. Never hurt her intentionally, never abuse the trust they held between them.

"Foster! Quit bullying my big sister!" Seth commanded the acknowledgment of neither sibling. "Foster! Stop it…at least until I can help you." He joined the pair, wrestling to get between them, grabbing at Marianne's armpits to tickle her mercilessly. Soon all three were falling down, cackling with delight. Child's play.

"Get off the ground immediately! What kind of behavior is this? Not becoming for a Witherell in front of God and the entire world!"

It was Mother. Old Ned the butler, half afraid the Mistress would charge right through the massive door, had less than a second to open it. He stood there, looking astonished as Margaret bolted down the front steps of the mansion toward her children out on the precisely manicured front lawn. Not since the birth of her bothersome twins had Margaret Witherell ventured out of the plantation house.

The shenanigans abruptly ended. Each young Witherell's face told a story of surprise, followed by terror. Fear of their mother. *What mood now?*

"We were just playing, Mother", Seth dared to speak first. "We were not fighting."

With reproach in her voice, Margaret continued, "That did not look like play! Savages. Wild animals. Not my children! Not in front of everyone!" She cast her eyes over the expanse of Heavenly, to an audience imperceptible to the world.

"Mother, there is no one watching." Seth knew with the last syllable that he was treading dangerous ground with this woman, his beloved mother of nine years.

"GOD is watching, my children! I shall not have you scrapping on the lawn. You behave like common slaves, as if your actions matter not! Get in this house and you shall take your punishment like good, obedient children!" She once more surveyed the landscape to see if there were witnesses to her children's ill behavior. Finding none, she quickly followed her offspring up the steps, slamming the huge oak door behind, closing out the world.

She cast a hateful look at Old Ned who took his cue to carry on about his business and not concern himself in Witherell family matters. He retired to the kitchen where he would report to Joelle yet another episode where "The Missus done lost herself to the demons." It seemed that Margaret's erratic behavior was daily supplying new fuel for the fires of gossip among the house slaves.

For the unfortunate Witherell children, this unreasonable woman was growing more familiar. Yet, half an hour later, she would be wonderful again, spoiling her children with praise, lavishing kisses upon their cheeks. *Speak to her softly, treat her with reverence and walk on eggshells in her presence. Never upset her in the least.* The memory of a stable mother stood in the way of comprehending that the terrible changes in her might be permanent. Perhaps tomorrow they would all awaken to the sweet, gentle mother whose mood never strayed from the loving, mild-mannered Southern belle she was. Or maybe the next day, next week.

"Go upstairs, all of you! Wait in your rooms for your father."

Pausing briefly at the top of the grand stairway, Seth looked down into the hall below and caught a glimpse of his mother. Such a sharp contrast to her beautiful portrait that graced the wall directly behind her. The two were dissimilar in every way—his mother's face presently cold, lined with pain; the face in the painting soft, kind, free of hurt.

Margaret hurried on to find her husband. As usual, she would complain about the children and demand punishment. Josiah would listen intently, knowing well that he hadn't the heart to mete out some of the horrendous reprimands his wife ordained. Swiftly he would visit each child, tell them that Mother was not well and ask them never to admit to her that the punishment was not given.

Margaret's ideas of retribution swept a wide range. She might have the children acknowledge their wrongs in writing and vow never to commit the offense again. Or she might prescribe lashes on the behind with a scaled-down version of the whip used by the plantation overseer to correct the slaves. Upon prescription of the latter, the Witherell child would wail in pain and submission as Josiah firmly whipped the bed mattress. Margaret was never witness to the administration of punishment; she was simply the prescriber. In that way, her hands were clean when she came to her senses and her conscience told her that it was irrational to expect perfect children.

This was life in the Heavenly Plantation house, this pristine slice of life in coastal South Carolina. It was no wonder that Josiah found it more attractive to take business trips lately and escape his wife's tantrums. Since Margaret herself would not administer punishment, she was forced to wait until Josiah returned to dole it out to the children. More often now, by the time he did return, the memory of their accused "crimes" slipped away from her. Josiah therefore rationalized that his frequent trips were an obligation to his offspring. It was his way to make their lives better, a sacrifice made for their psychological well-being. If the trip was advantageous from a business stance, that was a blessed side bonus.

The existence of this new volatile Margaret stabbed at Josiah's heart. The Witherell children first noticed the change in their mother after the twins were born. It appeared that the babies urged the demon out into the open, so it was natural for them to assume they were the cause of their mother's instability. Two babies at once, too much for a delicate flower like their mother.

But Josiah saw the new Margaret earlier. And he would never tell his children that he was the true cause of her misery and aberrant behavior. The innocent babies were simply perfect scapegoats. Josiah knew somehow that the older children would never dare blame them directly though. They would grow to love them as they should.

"Father, are the babies evil?" little Marianne would ask.

"No, darling, they are not evil. They are just demanding infants. Your mother is not well," Josiah would answer. He would never admit the truth, that he had been the evil one. Never.

"Father, why is Mother so angry with you? Doesn't she love you as always, Father? Why does she shout at you? Why does she not want the babies, Father?"

The questions were always asked and Josiah forever answered, "Your mother is not well, but we will help her get better. Just be good and do as she says. Always love her and know she loves you. She cannot help the things she says. Just love her; she is not well."

Chapter 7

The first night without her mama was agonizing for Willa who reverted back to the defenseless waif who stepped on the grounds of Heavenly just days before. All the courage summoned to explore the Big House and face Miss Marianne vaporized as reality settled into her head. Mama would stay near the babies, answering to their needs every hour of the day. Willa was not part of that picture; she was now in the care of Juniper, the slave woman who seemed to know everyone and everything about Heavenly.

"It be alright, Willa. You in good hands with me, I promise. You still see your mama, right in the mornin'. You can keep her company while she tends to the babies. All the day you can do that, ev'ry day. The nights you be with me, that's all. We be good company for each other, we will."

"But I want my mama. Never been away from her before. Juniper, why can't I sleep in the Big House with her? I can help with them babes, jus' like I did at home. Before the twins passed."

Eventually the pleading and questioning stopped and Willa fell into a deep sleep that lasted much longer than appropriate for a slave, even a young one. She too would be expected to handle chores around the quarters and gradually inside the plantation house. Her time would soon come. Juniper let her slumber on past eight o'clock. In just a few short years she would be waiting in the service of Marianne Witherell, only three years her senior, as the plantation daughter's personal slave.

Such a pity, thought Juniper. Had the girls shared the same color skin they might grow up the best of friends. As it was, they would likely be playmates only until Willa filled the role of servant. Then she'd be nothing more than another slave, although a trusted one. *She'll soon find out.*

"Juniper?"

"Yes child? The little one finally wake herself up? You sleep well, honey? Miz Juniper know you sure did!"

"Yes ma'am. When can I see mama?"

"Child we have plenty o' time. Plenty o' time. You needs some breakfast first, but you're way too late to eat with the rest o' the house. Juniper save you a bite though. Let's go on and get it."

In one swift, but jerky motion, Juniper scooped up the tiny girl, moved her toward the slave kitchen, and planted her on a bench at a long table. She retrieved a biscuit smeared with fruit preserves and a small piece of ham. She set it in front of the little girl. Although the portion was likely a leftover from a plantation house meal, Willa was unaccustomed to such lavish breakfast treats. Her eyes grew large as she swiped at the preserves with the tip of her index finger, touching it to her waiting tongue. Never had such a delicacy met with her taste buds before now.

"Oh, Miz Juniper! What a'mighty is this?"

"Berry preserves, child. Good ain't it? Don't tell me you never had that 'fore now!"

"Never on my life!"

"Well I'll be! Now you best be hurryin' up with that. Old Juniper promised to take you up to the Big House this mornin' while it still be mornin'."

"When can I see mama?"

"Real soon. I 'spect now she be catchin' a nap after bein' up with the babes all night long. At least I hope she is, the pitiful thing!"

"Why does she take care of them babies? They ain't ours. Ours dead."

"That be yo' mama's new job, child. She the nurse for the babies, you know that."

"Why don't the Missus take care o' her own babies?"

"Oh, sweet child. The Missus be very sick. She not well."

"She look fine to me, she did."

"No, she's not. She's not right a'tall. It's her head. Now don't you never say a word o' this to her or any o' her chillun, you hear? She be real upset."

"Yes, Juniper." Willa finished her little breakfast quietly, mulling over Juniper's words about the mistress and her ailment, not quite sure what to think. Usually sick people at Southwind were vomiting, bleeding, or wailing in pain. Some of them died. Like her twin brothers. They suffered for days, unable to feed at Heddie's breast, crying inconsolably. She was unable to identify the source of their discomfort. Then they just died. Willa didn't think the mistress looked like she was in any pain at all.

***

Willa found Heddie at her new post in the nursery room adjoining Margaret's beautiful bedroom. The nursery was also well-appointed with fine furnishings and luscious fabrics imported from places in Europe even the wealthiest Southerners could never afford to visit. Heddie's sleeping accommodations--much less grand--consisted of a thin ticking-covered feather mattress on the bare floor. Still, far superior to the damp, dirty floor of the cabin at Southwind.

The carved oak rocking chair was her favorite piece of furniture. In it, she spent most of the night rocking the babies alternately and then together as they defied sleep. When she finally lulled them both into slumber, she was afraid to move and break the familiar back and forth cadence in the chair. She did not mind. At Southwind she never had the luxury of a rocking chair with her children. It was comforting to feel the warm twins on her chest, smell their sweet aroma, hear the rhythmic whirr of their innocent breathing.

During the dark and still hours of the night the babies shielded her from the full impact of the loneliness that was hers. It was indeed lonely missing Alfred and the boys, and being temporarily separated from Willa. Finally she had to place the children in their cradle so she wouldn't fall asleep and drop them to the floor.

This morning Willa found Heddie in the chair, rocking herself while the twins slept in their cradles. Willa wanted to run to her, throw both arms around her neck, plant kisses on her. But Willa was a smart child and understood that the babies came first. *If the babies cried, Mama would be in trouble with the Missus and who knows what would happen then. What do sick people do when they get angry?* Willa wished not to find out.

"Come on over here, child. What's wrong with you?" Heddie read uncertainty on Willa's face, but had no idea what was going through her daughter's mind.

"Oh, mama I sure missed you."

"I missed you, too, now come kiss your mama, baby girl."

Willa provided a gentle, reluctant kiss to her mama's nearest cheek, but it wasn't enough to satisfy Heddie. "What you call that, Willa child? No way to love yo' mama. What's got you, girl? Don't you be scared o' them babies. I got 'em both asleep now. They be out for a bit while I get some rest myself. You can kiss me without makin' much noise now surely!"

With that invitation Willa could no longer resist the urge to grasp her mama with great, but quiet delight. They embraced as if they'd been separated for weeks when it had only been overnight. Heddie wondered how she would get through her new servitude while worrying about her precious remaining child. The tears that were a constant since leaving Southwind Plantation returned, sliding down her face. She tried to turn her head from Willa, but it was no use.

"Mama don't cry. Miz Juniper is good to me. She keep me safe and she let me sleep over near her. She fed me this mornin' and she showed me the way over here to you."

Heddie could not help but think, *how has my little one grown up enough to read my mind?* Willa was only eight and back at Southwind she was among the slave children cared for by the elders as she, Alfred, and Sampson toiled in the cotton fields. Back there Heddie was happy keep her as innocent and childlike as possible. Her day for chores and hard labor was just waiting there on the horizon, a hungry wolf watching its prey. She often babied the girl, doting over her, allowing her to sleep next to her and Alfred whenever she became frightened in the night.

"Oh Willa Rose, my baby girl. I miss you somethin' bad. I think 'bout you all night over there alone without me and Papa and the boys. I think 'bout you cryin' out and nobody bein' there for you. But there ain't nothin' I can…"

"Mama, there's Juniper. She take care o' me just fine. Not like you and Papa, but jus' fine. No mo' worries, Mama. Please, no worries…"

The pair held on tighter until the grief seemed to pass. Willa looked at her mama closely, noticing the dark circles under her eyes and the untidy condition of her hair which was usually plaited neatly to her head. She took in the awful smell of the gown she wore. Declaring the verdict of her scrutiny, she said, "Mama, you just be a mess! You look like you never got no sleep and you smell…you smell awful rotten."

"Why child, so nice o' you to tell me that."

Immediately Willa wished she could take back the words. She was accustomed to seeing her mother disheveled by working the cotton fields all day, but now she was suddenly aware that she was embarrassed for her. In this setting—the plantation house, the Big House. Those white folk had no right to make her take care of babies that weren't hers, for whom she held no love. No right to reduce her to this foul-smelling, wrung out woman in such a fine, expensive room.

But Heddie was not angered by her child's comments. "Willa, I know I be an old mess. That's just what happens when babies cry most o' the night and spit my milk all over me! Po' little things. They just miss they own mama. Bless these little hearts…" Heddie's voice trailed off as her mind journeyed to her own babies, now so very cold in the single grave they shared back in Georgia. The grave dug by their pappy and marked with a cross made by their mammy from two sticks fastened together.

"Oh, Jesus Lord God, my God," she whispered, neither condemning nor questioning the Creator, "my babies be in the grave. What I would give to have another day with 'em, Lord."

The pain was back, as raw as the moment she felt life slip away from her infants within minutes of each other. The days that followed the twins' deaths were horrendous. It was a frightening thing for anyone to witness, anyone who knew the always hopeful Heddie. The weeping was non-stop, as if the Earth had opened up to consume not only the Grigsby's, but the entire plantation. Heddie talked out of her head and swore she saw the viperous teeth of snake Satan take hold of her and shake the babies out of her grasp.

At night in her dreams she relived every past beating. The sensation of each invisible whip crack would cause her to flinch in her sleep. She dreamed of rivers full of fresh slave blood and saw vividly the suffering of her ancestors crowded below deck on filthy slave ships crossing from Africa. She woke in violent fits of rage against God, disturbing Alfred and her children.

Although Heddie had cried her share of tears when she arrived at Heavenly, nothing compared to the ones she shed back in Georgia. Her hasty departure from Southwind —from Alfred and the boys, from the only life she'd known— was dramatic enough to suspend her deepest emotions.

But now it was time for those emotions to thaw. She began to sob quietly, still mindful of the slumbering twins. Her chest rose and fell in heavy waves. No soul in the world seemed as tortured as she, even though family separations and deaths were a routine part of slave life in the South.

Standing motionless, stunted by the fear that her mama would crumble before her eyes, Willa could say nothing. There was simply no way to comfort the only person she had left in her life, no way an eight year old could make all the terrible pain go away.

Juniper opened the door to the room with all the care she could muster to avoid disturbing the babies inside. The sight of Heddie's grief stirred her as she realized what the woman must surely feel. So soon after putting her own babies to rest, having to nurture the difficult infants of her master suddenly seemed far worse than the tortures revealed by slaves imported from other plantations.

"Oh my, child." With long arms she pulled Heddie out of the chair to hold her tightly. She noticed the strong putrid smell of baby vomit, but paid no mind. "Po', po' dear, you is. You jus' cry and let it all out now. You go right on, child."

At that moment, Willa knew that she and her mama had a true friend in the twitchy old Juniper. The slave woman was a gift from God Himself, someone to watch over them since Papa and the boys were so far away. Quietly she watched her mama relieved of as much burden as the moment would allow and knew a small sense of comfort herself.

"You feelin' a little better, child?"

"As much as I can, Juniper. God bless you for your concern." Heddie breathed in deeply and then exhaled slowly as if the agony in her life could be cleansed.

"Let's get you out of that smelly old gown. Them babes sure do a batch o' spittin' up on you! The Missus would be mighty angry if she smells you that way in her nice house."

Just for the privilege of holding them close, Heddie had no qualms. Vomit was a small price to pay to feel them suckling and taking nourishment from her body, to feel their soft skin, hear their coos. "Course you right, Juniper. Must be fit to be seen by the mistress, I s'pose."

Juniper reached into the depths of a cavernous armoire and withdrew a sack tied up with a red ribbon. "The Missus give you a few dresses, she did." Undoing the ribbon, she pulled out the treasures. Margaret did indeed provide three gowns that, although well-worn, were finer than anything Heddie and Willa had ever seen. Proudly Juniper chose a pretty blue frock that greatly contrasted the shabby gray one Heddie wore. The Mistress Witherell seemed to dote on the appearance and cleanliness of her slaves, unlike many a Southern planter's wife who demanded a clean household, yet allowed filthy, vermin-ridden slaves to labor there among their finery.

"Let me help you with this, child."

"I'll be fine, Juniper. I 'spect you have chores to tend to. Thanks kindly."

"Yes I do have a slew of chores to do. I best be goin' on then. You let Juniper know if you need anythin' else, you hear?"

"Yes ma'am."

"I see you later then, Miz Willa." She winked at the child in a motherly, reassuring way.

"Yes ma'am." Willa gave Juniper a look that was full of respect and love, confirming the bond she was forming with her.

"Here, mama," Willa offered, unfastening the buttons on the back of Heddie's gown. As she helped her slip out of the smelly cotton dress, she caught sight of the hideous scars on her mama's back- scars that never failed to make her flinch. She hesitated, staring for a moment. Heddie knew what she was doing.

"Darlin', you alright? I hate it that you have to see them scars."

"Mama, I love you."

"I love you, darlin." They embraced, leaving Heddie's back exposed. Mother and child, clinging to each other in quiet, reflecting on the miseries of the past. Willa lightly stroked the repulsive mass of lumpy scars as if able to smooth them away with her innocent touch.

The door behind them suddenly opened. "Willa, are you in here? I have been lookin'..." The sweet voice of Marianne Witherell stopped abruptly as she took in the sight before her. She gasped as did her companion, younger brother Seth.

Heddie scrambled to cover herself.

"I am sorry, Mammy Heddie. I...I...I... didn't mean to barge in on you like this. I did not know you were dressing. I was looking for Willa so she can meet Seth...my brother Seth."

Marianne noticed that Seth was as pale as the ghosts of which Willa previously spoke. Attempting to cover her own shock, she quickly added, "Oh Mammy Heddie, what happened to your back? You poor dear!" She reached out to the disfigured woman gently, as if Heddie were one of her fine porcelain dolls.

"Miz Marianne, no need for you to worry. These are old, old scars, they is." More concerned for the innocence of the master's children than embarrassed for herself, she did her best to minimize reality. They were old scars indeed, but the infliction of the wounds that caused them was as new to her as the morning sun. The passing years would never erase that history. The beatings she received as a younger woman were inflicted by savage overseers employed by the man who ripped her away from her precious husband and sons. That man was the very uncle of the Witherell children, but she was Christian enough not to pass judgment on them for the sins of their mother's brother.

Willa was at a much different place than Heddie and she spoke boldly, "Them scars from the whip! My mama was whipped by them bad men. They liked to've killed her, they did! My mama do nothin' to them but they whipped her and tore her up to bleed. I saw it myself when I was a little one, I did! I cried and mama cried and papa yelled!"

"Willa! Enough child! Keep quiet for them babies!"

"Mama it's true. All the blackys get beatin's now and then. It's true."

Seth spoke for the first time, "Why would they beat you? What did you do? Must've been awfully bad!" Clearly he knew nothing of the often-barbaric practices of slavery.

"I tell ya, she did nothin' to get them beatin's! That's what happen to slaves. The overseer beat ya for nothin'. Make no difference if you did or didn't do somethin'. They just whip and whip and whip. My papa and my mama, but mostly my papa. He would bleed and bleed..." She vividly recalled the horrors of life at Southwind. At eight years old, she had seen enough misery to fill the heads of the Witherell pair with enough fodder to feed a lifetime of nightmares.

"Why I've never seen a slave beaten like that around here. Our father would not allow it; he is a good man. Even the field slaves love him and they are happy here." Seth was faithful to his father without question.

To their good fortune the Witherell children were never exposed to the truth about slavery. True, slave life at Southwind was far crueler, especially for bondsmen and women in the fields. But even on Heavenly, slave life could be brutal at the hands of an angry overseer or slave driver. They were never privy to that, spared from all but the rosy picture of Southern life painted by their parents. Slaves were simply staff members in their house, workers in their vast rice fields, content participants in the business of producing a fine crop and preparing it for export.

From the perspective of the Witherell offspring, slaves were a blissful lot, often engaged in spirited song as they toiled. The house slaves were forever praising "Marster and Missus" and extolling their virtues as kind and provident caretakers. They constantly reminded the children how "blessed you is for' havin' a mammy and pappy so wise and generous." Their parents did, after all, provide their slaves with clean clothes, sleeping quarters, food (albeit the family's leftovers), and presents at Christmas holiday. They had no idea what went on out in the other parts of the plantation, assuming that even the slaves in the rice fields were treated the same way.

"I bet your drivers beat the darkies in the field, too. I bet they starve 'em and beat 'em, jus' like they do all over. Miz Marianne, Marster Seth, you never been to the field?" Willa had far more intelligence on the subject of slavery and suspected correctly that the two plantation children were simply naïve.

"Why no, Father would not allow," Marianne answered for the pair, "and Mother would be terribly sore if we did. She says that some of your kind are brutes who might harm us if we were disrespectful."

"Foster goes to the fields when Father is away. He tells me so."

"Quiet, Seth. Foster would not disobey Father. I know that. He tells you stories, that is all. You're just jealous of him!"

"Am not! Don't you tell me what I am! Silly girl!"

"Hush you two. Them babies will be bawlin' soon enough. Why don't you leave my mama 'lone now? Go on out!" Willa was stern enough to displease Heddie.

"Willa!" she whispered strongly. "Never speak to the Witherells with that tone, girl." Addressing Marianne and Seth, "Forgive my child, Marster and Missy. But you best be gettin' on before your mama comes lookin' for ya."

"Yes, ma'am."

"Willa, you go on. Maybe you can tag along with 'em too."

"Mama, you need me here. I'll stay right here and help you when the babes wake."

"Don't you back talk me girl. Go on." She winked at her daughter and kissed her little hand. Secretly she wanted Willa and Marianne to strike a kinship that would last many years. Perhaps such friendship would help to secure a place for Willa as Marianne's personal slave, sparing her from backbreaking, difficult work in the rice fields.

Chapter 8

Three small figures headed down the grand staircase, Seth in the lead followed by sister Marianne and then dark little Willa. The day was still early and full of possibilities. For Seth, it was an awakening of sorts. Was it possible that the scars on Mammy Heddie's back were the product of an overseer's beating? Heavenly's own overseer was a family friend named Duke Henry. Seth had a difficult time imagining Mr. Henry behaving savagely toward any slave or condoning it by his drivers out in the fields. Whatever might have happened at Southwind probably had no bearing at Heavenly. Or did it?

"Marianne, what do you say we follow Foster out into the fields today? We shall just see if any of the Negroes get a beating."

"You callin' me a liar? I know what I saw with my mama and my papa. They got beatin's all the time. My mama say I hafta be polite to you white folks or I get the lash too. But never you goin' call Willa a liar!"

"No, Willa, Seth does not mean to call you a liar! We just know our father would never allow such horrible things and we know nothing about what happens at Uncle Charles's Southwind. We are so sorry for your mama. Please don't hate us Willa. We want to be your friend." Marianne spoke up, always the peacemaker, hoping to win the affection of the slave and satisfy some of her curiosities about an entire race of people. Never had she known anyone she could question in detail, having been forbidden to bother the grown up slaves in the household.

"Speak for yourself, Marianne," snorted Seth, always the wild-eyed mischievous boy looking for adventure. Up to now, all girls were a bother and none other than his big sister would be his friend, not even the novel black one.

His mind was suddenly fixed on disproving that any dark deeds were taking place away from the plantation house. His parents' strict mandate was to stay clear of the slave village and fields, but that mandate was beginning to sound like a challenge to him. With or without Marianne, he would follow Foster into the unknown and prove Willa wrong about his family's plantation.

"Are you with me or not, Marianne?"

"Seth you know we are not allowed to go out into the fields. Father will be so upset with you!"

"Then you just keep your mouth closed about where I am going. Mother asks, you tell her I ran over to the James place. I mean it. Don't you go telling her where I've gone, Marianne. If you want me to be your brother, you swear to it. Right now."

"Seth, don't you be so silly. Of course, you'll always be my brother, you cannot change that. I won't lie for you, but I will do my best to avoid Mother and then she won't ask a thing of me. Fair enough?"

"Girls! You go play with your new little friend and the two of you steer clear of the house. Maybe you can find something useful to teach the little darky. Like how to play with dolls or something. "

"I don't play with no dolls!" Willa grunted indignantly. It was true, she had never owned a doll so the thought of playing with one made her feel ashamed, angry, and defensive. "Dolls for babies, not for me! Little crybabies play with 'em!"

"That's okay Willa; I don't really like dolls either. Seth knows that and he is just teasing. Don't pay attention to him. Let's go find something to do while he tries to get himself into big trouble with our father." She motioned for Willa to follow her toward one of the plantation's numerous flower gardens. "We will look at butterflies."

Willa glared disapprovingly at Seth for a moment before she turned away to follow Marianne. Maybe the white girl wasn't so bad, but the boy was certainly not someone she could ever see herself coming to like.

"We'll go to my favorite garden of all, right over here. There are statues that my mother brought over all the way from Paris. That's in France, very far away. The butterflies like to land on the statues after they've had their fill of nectar from the flowers. I hope you like butterflies Willa."

"I s'pose I do. Never thought too much 'bout them."

"You cannot be serious! Who doesn't think about butterflies? How can such things of beauty not occupy the thoughts of a child your age?"

Willa felt defensive again, lashing out at Marianne. "Butterflies! You think that's all I got to worry 'bout? Nothin' good about them butterflies, far as I know. Jus' bugs, that's all they are!" It wasn't her fault, but Marianne could not comprehend the thoughts running through the mind of a slave child. Thoughts about having food to eat, having your family stay together. Hoping and praying that you won't have to hear your mama cry in pain and your papa beg for mercy at the hands of someone with a dangerous whip. Noticing butterflies was a luxury for white folks.

"I'm sorry Willa. Will I ever say the right thing? I keep making you upset. But what is it about butterflies? I don't understand."

How could an eight year old explain that until now there was no reason to look at butterflies? No hope to ever play with a doll? How could an eight year old reveal the horrors she'd witnessed since the day her memories started? How much pain was wound up tightly within her and would probably never be released? Willa did the only thing she could and surrendered to the tears welling up behind her dark eyes.

Marianne reacted quickly, taking the miniature girl in her arms and wrapping her up in a sisterly embrace. "It's okay to cry. You go on and let it all out. I know it must be strange having to move all the way here to Heavenly. You must miss your kin back at Southwind. You just cry. I am your friend, Willa."

"Who is the bawling little baby? Is that the new pickaninny? What's her problem?"

Marianne looked up to see her older brother Foster towering over them upon Heaven's Prince, his beautiful thoroughbred horse. Ordinarily she would be pleased to see him, her ever-perfect big brother. She was the apple of his eye. Still, he was a boy, insensitive as any.

"Foster!" she scolded him. "Do you mind? Where are your manners?"

Willa broke free from Marianne's kind embrace, wiped her wet nose with her sleeve and her tears with the back of her hands. Her eyes became cold and fixed upon Foster. Something about his demeanor told her not to speak to him, not to comment or show boldness. Unlike Seth, who was near her age, Foster carried himself like a man. He looked like the sort of boy who would enjoy being provoked just so he could react. If she talked to him the way she had talked to Seth, he would have her whipped or more likely perform the deed himself with complete satisfaction.

Dismounting his blood-bay steed, Foster continued, "Well hello there. Aren't you an odd-looking little thing? I've only seen skin that dark way out in the rice field. Are you lost, girl? Want me to take you back out where you belong?"

"Foster! Stop it! This is Willa and her mama is the new nurse for the babies. She belongs right here!"

"For now. We'll see how long she's around here. Soon as she can work out there," Foster pointed out, far beyond the plantation lawn, toward the rice fields, "she'll be gone from here. We never keep the dark ones around, you know that sister. The dark ones can't be trusted…"

"Foster! Stop that talk. Stop it this minute! You are upsetting Willa."

Willa remained silent, trying hard to suppress the agitation she felt, clenching her teeth and forcing back tears.

"So I am. Have you seen Seth?"

"Yes. He is the one you need to be concerned about, Foster. He wants to follow you into the fields this morning. You need to stop him before Father catches him."

"Why would he do that? He has no business in the field. Father only now allows me to go out there. Seth is too young."

"It's a long story, but he wants to find out if Mr. Henry beats the slaves."

"Of course he beats the slaves, Marianne. They are slaves! Why would he not beat them? Keeps them in line. Makes them work harder."

"No, Foster. Say that is not true. Mr. Henry is kind." Marianne's eyes pierced Foster's eyes, pleading with him for confirmation of what she had always known as the truth.

"Of course. Duke is a fine man, generous and good to all who deserve his kindness. He's also an excellent overseer and he minds the business quite well. He also does not hesitate to exact due punishment to slaves who deserve it. That is what an overseer does, my dear sister."

"But…Willa's mother has scars. Deep, hideous scars on her back. From an overseer at Southwind. She did nothing to deserve them, Foster. We don't do that here! Father would never let that happen!"

"You are so naïve my little sister. Please, don't concern yourself over this, it is nothing to you. Best not discuss this anymore, especially not with Mother and Father. I will handle Seth. Just carry on, play with your blacky friend here." Taking Marianne's head in his hands, he pulled her forehead to his lips and kissed it lightly. Back atop the saddle, he kicked the horse into action and headed out in search of Seth.

Marianne was bewildered as her mind conjured up images that threatened to traumatize her. She shivered, trying to physically shake the mental pictures, but they would not leave her. What she saw was Heddie and Duke Henry---Heddie crying out as Mr. Henry lashed her madly with a long, black whip. The whip cut into Heddie's flesh like it was butter. She could hear the crack, smell the searing of tissue and the scent of blood. The look on Mr. Henry's face betrayed all she had ever known about the man. The horrific expression on Heddie's face confirmed the truth, the reality of slavery.

Chapter 9: Marianne's Journal, April 1846 Continued

"I recall so vividly that first encounter with Willa and the notion that cruelty toward human beings existed here at Heavenly. Seth did indeed make it out to the rice fields that day in secret, escaping the attention of both Foster and Father. What he witnessed and later revealed to me was a scene of such revulsion that I cannot bear to detail it here on these pristine pages.

Briefly, Dear Journal, I will just note that a slave was accused of stealing one of our horses and nearly paid the price with his very life. Seth watched him tortured upon the order of a slave driver, a black man himself. The accused pleaded for his life, telling that he borrowed the horse so that he could swiftly get to a nearby farm where his mother lay dying. Upon return to Heavenly, he met with Duke Henry and the driver, who had him tied behind that very horse and dragged until he almost perished.

That day was a turning point in my life, as well as Seth's. When he returned from the field, he was shaken to the core; noticeably terrified. He looked at Willa with apologetic and compassionate eyes, as if he suddenly became aware that she was not just a slave girl, but a human being who needed us to protect her.

Seth never told Mother or Father about his excursion and what he witnessed. He was afraid to tell. He understandably saw the family business in a different light and detested Foster for being party to the unsavory nature of it. Although Foster was not present when the slave was tortured that day, Seth seemed to hold him responsible for the actions of Mr. Henry and the driver. This is something I will never understand.

Seth and Foster have never been close brothers. However, I am fortunate to share a special bond with both of them separately. Foster, who is older and more mature, has a personality that often abrades people if they are not familiar with him. He seems callous and insensitive, but I know better. His terse attitude is just a cover behind which he hides. He is easily hurt; his ego is quickly bruised when Father or Mother criticize him.

As the eldest, he shoulders more responsibility than Seth and me. Our parents expect so much of him and he often delivers just what is required. However, if he fails at any task, no matter how small, Father most certainly points out his faults. Foster in turn becomes sullen and cold, often turning on those in his path. Except for me, of course. I understand his displeasure at having his flaws called out, but not his harsh treatment of others. Still, I love him totally and hope that with more maturity he will handle himself in a more agreeable way in all situations.

To me, Foster is a wonderful brother and friend. In spite of the shortcomings of his personality, he is extremely handsome and most often a gentleman who will make a fine match for a special lady one day. I cannot say the same for Seth, who is still so immature that it makes me wonder if he will ever be a good match for marriage. Foster only tolerates Seth, calling him a fool or some other unkind thing. I know that Seth will outgrow his childish ways at some point, but he will always be adventurous. That is the difference between my dear brothers—one a serious, business-like young man and the other a happy-go-lucky boy!

As for Willa, Foster holds much contempt toward her. I cannot believe it is a personal dislike, for Willa has done nothing to Foster. Nor do I believe is it his general contempt for the African race. Rather, I sense that Foster is tremendously jealous of Willa's claim to my time. Since our first meeting, Willa and I have become inseparable. With Seth, we form a tight threesome. Foster shall never understand that. He seems intent on badgering Willa and constantly derides her by calling her names such as pickaninny and darky, although I plead with him to stop. Nevertheless, I do my best to serve as a buffer, keeping them as far apart as possible.

And so it is. Mammy Heddie continues to care for my brothers Gabriel and Garrett. As four year old darlings, they look to Heddie as if she is their own mother, with love and total devotion in their eyes. No surprise, since our mother is less and less nurturing these days. Mammy Heddie also has duties in the kitchen of our house, helping Joelle, our aging cook. One day I am sure she will take over the cook's position altogether.

Willa is probably the best friend I shall ever have. Contrary to my first impression of her--that she was frail, tiny, and delicate—she is as strong as any soldier I've ever read about in history class. Stubborn, too. She has witnessed unspeakable wrongs in her short life, but she is sturdier for that. She is unafraid now, speaks her mind, and behaves bolder than I. She reminds me of Seth in many ways. How funny it is to recall how he wanted nothing to do with having a slave girl as friend and playmate. They are actually quite inseparable themselves!

Coming to Heavenly, even though she had to leave her father and brothers, has surely been a blessing to her and to Mammy Heddie as well. From what I've discovered, conditions everywhere at Uncle Charles's plantation are far more wretched. Here, at least the house slaves are part of our family. Next to Juniper, Dear Journal, I shall have to confess, Mammy

Heddie is closer to me than even my mother (given her peculiarity in the past several years).

One more confession. If discovered, I could be in serious peril, and thus bring catastrophe upon my entire family. Only Willa and Seth are party to this secret, which I reveal here only to relieve myself of the burden of guilt it brings. I detest being deceitful to my parents, but in this instance it cannot be avoided. Mother is not in a state of mind to understand, and Father is so occupied by the family business that he need not worry on my account. So it is best to keep this between the three of us, tight as we are.

Willa has many advantages as a servant in this house. Yet she is not free, she is still enslaved. In that condition, she is not privy to the most precious gift that can be given to the mind of a young person, the gift of an education. The gift that makes practical the very task I undertake in writing here upon these pages. Giving true life to memories, ideas, and feelings through words. Reading them back to myself. Magical gifts indeed.

I shall be blunt. It is against our laws to teach a Negro to read. Willa is denied the multitude of treasured books we keep in our library. Yet she is trusted to roam freely in this house as my playmate, sleep in my room whenever she pleases, and sup with me as my sister. But fill her head with book knowledge? This is forbidden, so the laws state.

Here I confess my sin. I have taught Willa to read. She is amazingly bright and it took not much effort for her to grasp her letters. She reads as well as me. Quietly and in private she reads the books I present to her. Books by Irving, Dickens, Emerson, Austen, Radcliffe. Magazines smuggled from Mother's collections-*Lady's Book*, *Saturday Evening Post*, and the like. These are new worlds for Willa to discover and even when the reading is more difficult or the words unfamiliar, she never gives in to doubts about her abilities.

We research the American Dictionary of the English Language together to unlock the mysteries of words unknown to us. All of this late in the night, when no one in the house will suspect our adventure. Except for Seth of course, who often scoffs at our fascination with serious novels. We tease that he has never mastered reading anything beyond Aesop.

In telling this deep secret, I feel some burden lifted. I am not proud of deceiving my parents, but I see no other way. Strongly I believe that in this country all people should be entitled to education, no matter their station in life. If I ever approached the subject (of teaching Willa to read) with Mother, or my schoolmaster, they would be angered that I even suggested the notion. Adults are easily upset at any assertion by me that there is something wrong with slavery. To those assertions, they kindly suggest I keep my thoughts to myself and my mother reminds me that without our slaves, we would be ill-equipped to live the life that we enjoy.

So, while I am powerless to alter the realities of slavery, I will do everything in my being to give Willa a better world here at Heavenly. As long as Mother and Father know nothing of my instruction toward her, we shall be safe. Oh, and Foster shall never know. I especially dislike the fact that he would be so disappointed in my deceit. But even he will never need to know, much as I trust him and look up to him in other matters. Simply put, Willa will continue to be my friend and confidante, and we will share this secret (and perhaps a thousand others) as we grow into women. This journal shall be my confidante as well. Surely Mother imagined it a harmless vessel into which I would pen my thoughts, squashing down all my opinions regarding right and wrong, thus silencing my voice. Alas, it has become my chamber of secrets."

Chapter 10

Summers at Pawleys Island away from Heavenly were "pure Heaven", as Willa paradoxically described them. Each year at the end of May, after the rice crop was securely planted and sprouting, the Witherells packed up the household and moved it to Seaside, a vacation home on Pawley's Island. The resort home was a gift from Margaret's family, deeded to her and Josiah on their wedding day. Each and every slave connected with the Big House worked nonstop to facilitate the move, packing up any commodity the Master and Missus felt necessary for their comfort and survival. Much of the Negro house staff accompanied the family to provide services at the summer house, although the structure was considerably smaller than the mansion at Heavenly.

All of the Low Country families of fortune feared the seasonal outbreak of malaria that often ran through communities along the river like a ribbon of death. Somehow the field slaves were able to endure the intensity of the South Carolina summer heat and humidity; they also seemed immune to the evils of malaria. Most of the white folks felt it had something to do with the practice of voodoo or a special mystical gift obtained from their African ancestry.

Pawleys Island afforded the house slaves free time unheard of at Heavenly and they used it to play games, swim in the ocean, and work on handicrafts. The duties of cooking, cleaning, fetching, gardening, and driving family to and fro were lighter and less demanding. Still, Margaret Witherell insisted on bringing most of her house staff because "it simply wouldn't do having them back at the Plantation with the rest of the darkies".

The relationship between Josiah and Margaret was noticeably more agreeable at Seaside, almost as if much of the tension dissolved simply by breathing in the salty scented air. Like the slaves, they took pleasure in a variety of pastimes. They spent time with their island neighbors, taking turns hosting picnics and small dance parties. Foster, Marianne, and Seth seemed pleased with the renewal of their parents' marriage, if only for the summer. It would be a few magical months before spirits would begin to sag in preparation for the return to Heavenly and in essence, reality.

Heddie remained a constant in the lives of twins Gabriel and Garrett. Still charged exclusively with their care, she reluctantly gave up some control during the summer months when Margaret felt well enough to be a mother.

Heddie grew to love the boys, realizing that the bond was largely based on her desperate need to forget the ones she lost.

Life on Pawleys was a liberation compared to the more regulated life at Heavenly. Willa's ties to Marianne and Seth were equally strong, resembling sibling relationships instead of master's children to slave.

Back at Heavenly, the Witherell children had their own private sleeping quarters while Willa continued to live in the house slave quarters. However, sleeping arrangements were often disregarded whenever Marianne and Willa decided to stay up late to read or discuss whatever issues they pleased. At Seaside, Willa was expected to stay in Marianne's room, since she was brought along solely as a companion with few household duties.

At the plantation house, all of Marianne's barely-worn cast-offs went to Willa, resulting in her being better clothed than many of the white visitors from other plantations. The normal dress at the summer place was relaxed and casual for the Witherell children, so none of their more formal attire was carried along for them. Needless to say, Willa's fancy second-hand wardrobe remained at Heavenly while she wore plain cotton dresses on the Island.

Although she was not allowed to join the family at the Heavenly manor dinner table, neither was Willa expected to serve the Witherells their meals. The house slaves ate later in the main plantation kitchen after all the evening chores were completed, dining on the family's leftovers and table scraps. However, Willa's companions always tried to save fresh food for her and Heddie. At Seaside, Marianne, Seth, Gabriel, and Garrett always dined in the separate kitchen while the adults, who now included eighteen year-old Foster, ate leisurely at the family table. Willa was allowed to eat with the Witherell children instead of waiting to eat with other house slaves later in the evening.

Children never attended the Island Society dances or dinner parties to which their parents and older siblings were invited. This summer Foster attended every social function with Josiah and Margaret. There he was expected to woo the young daughters of other wealthy families who attended the soirées with their parents in hopes of finding a beau for courting back home. All efforts were to lead up to socially, financially suitable marriages destined to preserve the prosperity of both the represented families.

As she watched her brother preen before the looking glass prior to the evening's engagement, Marianne couldn't help but marvel at her brother's good looks. His sandy blonde hair owned the slightest hint of copper that contributed a warm glow to his appearance. His facial features included ice-gray eyes, an impeccably sculpted nose, and full lips pulled over perfectly spaced, brilliantly white teeth. Foster's wardrobe was ever flawless as a result of his father's indulgence and good line of credit with every fine clothier in Charleston.

"You will surely make a fine match for any girl, Foster. You're much more handsome than your friends. I'd be surprised if any of them will ever court a lady!"

"Sister, you are such a child. Not every girl is as shallow as you and interested only in a gentleman's looks. But yes, I am by far the better looking in my circle of friends." Foster raised his nose in the air, feigning snobbery and then chuckled. Looking down to his sister and touching his index finger to her nose, he said, "My dear, no man on the Island has a sister as beautiful and wise as you! Just think, one day you'll be old enough to attend the summer parties and all the young gentlemen will want to fill your dance card. But they will have to meet my approval first and I'll be the judge to see who is fit for my sweet Marianne."

"Foster, you spoil me so! I will never find a beau with the charm of my older brother."

"You're right, but I shall do my best to find one similar to my own greatness. That would certainly count out my horrendous group of friends! To those rogues, you will be off limits!"

"Marianne! Marianne! There you are!" Willa entered the room out of breath and was suddenly sorry, finding her best friend with Foster. "Excuse me. Master Foster. I thought you had already gone to the party."

"Oh, just the little slave I'd hoped to see. Marianne was just telling me how dashingly handsome I looked and I'd like to get your opinion. How wonderful do I look, Miss Willa?"

It was increasingly difficult for Willa to disguise her contempt for Foster, but because Marianne practically worshipped him, she conceded to her better judgment. "Why Foster, you do look almighty handsome, you do. The ladies at the party, they'll just be fallin' all over themselves waitin' for a dance with you, they will."

"That's exactly what I think Willa. Oh, to be there and watch my brother make his entrance and see the ladies blush!"

"Yes, that would be somethin' now wouldn't it? Yes, it sure would!" Willa reinforced Marianne's enthusiasm with false enthusiasm of her own, hoping to excuse herself as quickly as possible from the room. "I best be checkin' on Seth to see if he's ready for the stroll we was fixin' to take on the beach. You comin' along Marianne?"

"Why don't you go find Seth, sister? Willa can stay here and help me into my jacket. I haven't had the fortune of speaking with her lately and you know I'm doing my best to get to know her since she's so close to you and Seth. I am just so busy back home, you know. Go ahead, sister. Find Seth."

"Foster, this is sweet of you. I'll be back soon, Willa. Go ahead and help my dashing brother." With that Marianne left Willa alone with the brother she adored, naïvely thinking that they were continuing to forge a bond of friendship.

"Good. I've wanted to be alone with you for the longest time, Willa." Foster stooped down to be level with the fourteen-year old girl's height, and leaning in, he remarked softly, "You are becoming quite a little woman, I see." His eyes trailed down to her breasts, the bumps visible beneath her thin cotton dress.

"Yes, such a woman, I have to say. What with my dutiful sister and my foolish little brother tutoring you to behave like a lady and all." Foster looked directly into Willa's eyes, then to her mouth. Putting a finger up to her lips he began tracing their outline. "Why you've almost entirely lost that nigger way of speaking." He laughed, withdrew his finger and shot his eyes back to hers.

"And don't think I don't know about my sweet, kind-hearted sister teaching you to read. I do. She is such a dear, isn't she? Just doesn't know what kind of predicament she put me in."

He paused for a few seconds, placing his thumb and index finger to his chin as if seriously pondering his next remark. "You see, I am tempted to tell. My parents would understand her sympathetic nature, of course. She has always befriended strays. Animals. Oh… but with you, my little Willa… with you they would not be so understanding."

He continued to look into Willa's face for her reaction, but she gave him none.

"You know Willa, I've yet to be with a woman in the way a man is urged to be. It just wouldn't be right to do that with the pure white society ladies here, just not gentlemanly. But I suspect there's nothing wrong with learning what it is to feel like a man with a dirty little slave girl like you. I'm sure my father would approve, although it would likely upset my dear mother," He snickered as if he'd told a cleaver but inappropriate joke.

Willa could feel his hot, threatening breath on her face as he edged closer, closer, then stuck out his tongue and lightly licked her cheek. Willa, frozen in fear did not respond, although she could feel her stomach knotting up in revulsion. *Be still, be still and he will stop.*

"Mmmm…not what I expected. Not disgusting. Should I taste some more?" His furrowed his brow in contemplation. "No. No. I think I'll wait. Yes…I'll wait a while. Let you grow some more. Like an apple on one of our trees back home. Precisely, like an apple. You're too green now. But when you're ripe…that's when I'll pick you. My own sweet dark apple. Until then I'll just keep my eye on you. And you won't say a word to anyone. Not one word. Not to Marianne, not to Seth. Not even to your ugly, black mother. Do you understand?" He put his fingers around one of her arms and squeezed tight. "Do you understand? Speak to me!"

Willa's throat was parched as if she'd had her mouth open all day in the hot Southern sun. She tried to speak, but the words were stifled somewhere deep down within her. She gasped.

"Answer me, black little wench!" His grip tightened on her arm while his other hand grabbed her jaw forcing open her mouth.

"Yes." The voice she found was strange and not her own. "I won't tell a soul, Foster."

He let go of her arm, but retained the hold on her jaw and pulled her close to his face. He smeared a wet kiss on her lips and then forced his tongue into her unsuspecting mouth. She fought the urge to vomit while breaking free from him.

"I'm not through with you yet, you little black wench!" he called out to her as she ran as swiftly as her small feet would allow.

Out of the house and down the path to the shore, she passed Marianne and Seth who thought she had noticed them and was playing a game of chase. They began to run after her.

"Okay you win, Willa. Slow down!" demanded Marianne, tripping over her skirts, falling into the warm sand, laughing. "I give up!"

Seth ran back toward his sister to make sure she was not injured. Finding her all splayed about, he soon joined in her laughter while Willa continued to run until she could no longer hear her friends behind her. Then she fell onto the beach herself, but was not laughing. She cried as hard as she'd ever cried, making fists that she drove into the innocent sand. In her mind she replayed Foster's words, again felt his clasp on her arm, his oppressive tongue on her, in her mouth. Bending over, she retched until she no longer had substance to spew. Suddenly Pawleys Island had become hell.

Chapter 11

In the early spring of 1850 Willa had her fifteenth birthday and the gift she was given was a position within the Witherell household. Such a position marked the end of her childhood and her passage into servitude.

The carefree days of waiting on her friends to return from school and play games with her were suddenly over. No more long walks, no more horseback riding for fun. No more climbing trees and sitting out under the stars on the lawn. Margaret declared it so.

Margaret wandered into Marianne's room one afternoon for an unprovoked inspection. When she opened the door to her daughter's chifforobe closet, she saw her clothing and shoes in disarray. Quickly she became agitated, activating a shrill vocal alarm.

"Juniper! Marianne! Come here at once!"

Heddie heard her mistress's call and ran out to the detached kitchen behind the house where Juniper and Marianne were assembled making a birthday cake for Willa. They all scurried out the kitchen door, traversed the covered walkway to the house, and bound up the rear staircase. As Margaret continued to beckon, it was clear that her voice came from Marianne's bedroom.

Marianne knew that her room was rarely a point of concern to her mother. Instead, Margaret focused only on the appearance of Heavenly's common areas, those visible to her guests. Immediately she thought about the journal she thought was safely tucked under her mattress. Her mind flew to the many entries she penned admitting to viewpoints she knew differed from her mother's. The confession to teaching Willa to read. *What else, what else?* She silently panicked.

Once inside her room, Marianne's' relaxed when she saw Margaret's attentions fixed upon her messy closet. *Thank you, God,* she quietly prayed.

"What is this?" she gestured to the contents strewn about the chifforobe. "Have you not learned to care for your things better than this, Marianne? Just who is charged with caring for this room, Juniper? What kind of home do you think we keep here at Heavenly?"

"I sorry, Missus. I was about to do the tidying up myself this afternoon. Myra's ailin' today, ma'am. I was goin' to take care up here as soon as we finished out in the kitchen."

"No excuses, Juniper, you old crow! Whatever you are doing in my kitchen can wait. That's what we have Joelle for!"

"Oh Mother, please. We're making a birthday cake for Willa. She's fifteen today! Please let us finish and then I will help Juniper straighten out my closet."

"You absolutely will not help her! Willa's birthday! Apparently you would rather run about with that slave than to see that your room is well kept. You certainly have a lot to learn before you become mistress of your own house one day!"

"I will take care o' this now Missus, I will," Juniper persisted in order to please Margaret and take the attention off of Marianne. "I finish the cake later, Miz Marianne. Don't you worry yo'self."

Then Margaret's eyes lit up. She beamed as if struck with sudden brilliance. "Where *is* Willa? Just how old is she? Go find her! It's high time she started acting like a servant."

Juniper knew what was next. She feared this day, knowing it would appear soon enough. Her nerves were suddenly set afire, tingling and making her feel edgier than usual. Why hadn't she warned Willa that her life would change dramatically one day and that her childhood would come to an end? After all, it was destined to be. *Reckon it best to happen now.*

"Go and find your friend, Marianne. Tell her that this will be a special birthday for her. Bring her here."

Marianne sensed something sinister in her mother's voice. "Mother, what are you going to do?" Margaret glared at her daughter, signaling urgency. *Do it now.* Reluctantly Marianne obliged and left to find Willa while Juniper began to straighten the things in the chifforobe.

"Leave it for the girl, Juniper," Margaret scolded.

Juniper jumped back away from the closet. "Yes, ma'am."

***

Willa was out in the cutting garden where Chloe's sister Myra was tending to the weeds. Myra told her, "If I don't keep the weeds down, the Missus have my hide, she will. She come out and cut late in the day after the sun is low. Or she come first thing in the mornin' and she always 'spectin' the weeds to be gone from her precious flowers. One o' these days I's goin' pluck out a few flowers along with the weeds and I'm goin' take 'em out to the old slave graveyard for my dead husband Charles. You 'member him, Willa? Few years back he died? He was somethin' else, he was. That Charles..."

Willa let Myra ramble on as she tended to do while she breathed in the heady perfume of flowers and surveyed the butterflies she came to love. When she caught sight of Marianne, she called to her, "Look at all these zebra swallow-tails! Have you ever seen so many at once?"

But it was hard for Marianne to be enthusiastic given the uncertainty of her mother's mood. "Willa, my mother wants to see us at once. We need to find out what's on her mind." She was an unwitting party to Margaret's instability, the unwilling messenger of gloom to Willa. Certainly Mother didn't have anything delightful in mind for her friend's birthday.

"Willa, my mother is acting peculiar and I have no idea what is in her mind. She was angry that my closet was in disorder, but I know that has nothing to do with you. I'm sorry that she is in a mood and I hope she is not unpleasant to you on my account."

When the girls arrived, Margaret met them at the door. "Willa, my dear. You know how fond I am of you, don't you?"

"Yes ma'am." Willa looked confused, wondering where the conversation would lead. She wore the same questioning expression as Marianne.

"You know there are many things for a slave to do around Heavenly Plantation. I've let you remain a playmate to my daughter for a long time, now haven't I?"

"Yes Ma'am you have."

"I've been thinking though…you're getting a little old for play and so is Marianne. It's time she had a personal servant to see to her needs. She's seventeen after all, and it's time she started learning what it means to be a plantation woman. She needs to learn how to dress, how to talk, how to carry herself like a respectable Southern belle and not a child."

"Mother, I don't see how this has anything to do with Willa."

"Don't interrupt me daughter! You prove my point, as a true gentlewoman would do well to hold her tongue at times!" She shot Marianne a look that demanded immediate silence and the young woman nodded in resignation.

Margaret exhaled and turned back to Willa, "As I was saying, Marianne's life will require changes over the next few years as she grows into her rightful place in our society. She needs someone to be completely devoted to her. And I believe that person is you, Willa Grigsby. From this day forward, you shall be Marianne's personal slave. You will see to her every need. As such, I won't allow you to sleep in her room anymore. Nor will you wear her clothing; you will dress like her servant. It is time for you to take your place in this household and for Marianne to accept that you are a slave and not her playmate now."

Willa suffered a sting to her heart so sharp that she had to grab on to a bedpost to keep from toppling over. She cast a pitiful look toward Marianne, but her friend turned away in embarrassment.

"Do you understand, Willa? Marianne?"

"Yes ma'am," Willa heard herself sounding out the words.

"Yes Mother." Marianne's mind was racing although she sounded calm and obedient. Over the years she'd become expert at appearing compliant where Margaret was concerned. On the inside though, she had no intention of ever treating Willa like a slave.

"Good girls. Now go have Juniper finish the cake for your servant, Marianne. Have a nice little birthday for her and then she can take over this tidying of your wretched bedroom. I will be meeting with our neighbor Mrs. Adamson in the library shortly, so go on about your day. That is all Willa."

"Yes ma'am. Thank you, ma'am." Willa tried to be sincere and thankful to have a position of subordination to Marianne, knowing that her fate could be much worse.

As soon as Margaret left the room, Willa felt the tears gather in her eyes. What a fool she was thinking a white girl could be her best friend. For so long she felt that she fit in with her and Seth, like they were part of the same family. How wrong she was, and now this was proof of her imprudence. To preserve her dignity, she bolted from the room before Marianne could witness her shameful crying.

"Willa, wait! Willa stop! Willa, please don't go. You are still my best friend!"

Willa didn't stop. She ran as quickly as she could away from the Big House and its surrounding buildings, in the direction of places foreign to her. She didn't stop until she ran out of wind, throwing herself down on the ground in exhaustion. When she regained her breath, she propped up on two elbows to look around. From her vantage point she saw Negro slaves in the distance, toiling away in the rice fields of Heavenly. Instantly reminded of Southwind and the life she left so long ago, the humiliation she felt minutes before was replaced by a hollow sense of sorrow. She wept for a long while before physical and emotional drain forced her eyelids closed. Willa fell into a deep sleep.

Chapter 12

"Get up, nigger!" Willa was awakened by the nudge of a hard-toed boot to the left side of her ribcage. "Get up, I said!" She understood that the form towering over her meant business when he nudged for the second time.

Willa grabbed her painful side and pulled herself up to stand before the man she knew was Duke Henry, the overseer. She wiped the sleep from her eyes and focused on his leathery face. He was a stocky man with dark gray eyes the color of the sky just before a violent storm. Silvery curls poked out beneath a worn out, dirty hat. As he spoke again he displayed teeth that seemed much too large for his mouth.

"What are you doin' out here, girl? Are you tryin' to run away, is that what you're doin?"

"No, sir! No. I belong to the Big House. I…I', Miss Marianne's…uh, Marianne's servant." She started to say "friend", but promptly thought best to state otherwise. The white man would surely scoff at the notion of her friendship with the master's daughter.

"Then what are you doin' out here? You tryin' to get away from the Big House? I bet Miss Marianne be mighty upset to find you out here. I best be takin' you back. Reckon she'll let me give you a good lashin' for this, little darky!" He laughed as if amused at the prospect of whipping her.

Duke Henry mounted his horse. Willa expected him to pull her up behind him on the saddle for the ride back to the Big House. Instead, he made a loop at the end of a rope and in one swift motion he threw it over Willa, tightening the loop around her waist.

He seemed to enjoy the look of confused alarm on her face. "You think I'm goin' let a nigger ride on my horse?" Duke laughed again, shaking his head, "You walked out here, you can sure as hell walk back, girl. Teach you to go out where you don't belong."

With a whistle his horse began to trot back toward the plantation house while Willa struggled to keep pace. Once she stumbled and as she slipped on to the ground the rope tightened ever more, cutting into her waist.

"Stop! Please! Stop!"

Duke jerked the reigns to pause his stallion. "Keep up with me, girl. Get on your feet and keep up. We're almost there. Get up dammit!"

Marianne was the first to see them cross the threshold of the oak-lined driveway leading to the mansion house. Questioning her eyesight she blinked twice to confirm that her beloved friend Willa was tied to a rope held by the overseer. "What are you doing Mr. Henry? What are you doing?"

"This thing belong to you, Miss Marianne? You need to keep a better grip on your slave girl, missy. She tried to run. If you don't mind, I'll give her a beating she won't forget, and then she'll never run again. Be happy to."

"No! My God, Mr. Henry! How could you suggest such a thing?" She ran to Willa, released her from the rope, and held fast to her. "I'm so sorry Willa! So sorry!" She kissed her friend's cheek and continued to hold her close, begging her forgiveness.

Lurking from behind a potted palm, Foster witnessed the scene from the veranda. He fought to contain spasms of laughter. It pleased him to see Willa in ropes and held captive by Duke Henry. He enjoyed watching her degradation, but soon decided it was time to step up and play hero for his younger sister's benefit.

Stepping down from the porch, he made haste over to the three in the driveway. "Duke Henry, what are you thinking? My good man, you have offended my sister and her servant. I trust you will never let this happen again!"

"Master Foster, of course not. How was I to know that this was your fair sister's? I intended no harm, just tryin' to help the family, as always. I thought she was a runaway, you understand."

"That will be all Duke, you may leave."

"Yes sir. Give my best to your parents, will you young man?" With a tip of his tattered hat the man rode away.

"Marianne, why don't you go up to the house and ask Juniper to bring us sweet tea? We can take it on the veranda, the three of us. Willa seems quite upset and that'll be just the thing to calm her down. Go on, sister."

"You are right, Foster. I'll go do just that."

Marianne set off for the house and as soon as she was out of ear shot, Foster turned to Willa, "That was Duke Henry. I'm sure he'd have liked to use his whip on your sweet tender flesh! Good thing I came to your rescue, little slave girl. Now I'd say you owe me something for my trouble. What do you think?"

Unable to reveal what she really thought of him and his so-called rescue, Willa simply replied, "Thank you Foster." She forced a smile and turned to walk away.

"No, no. Don't you go anywhere. I am speaking to you. It's just the two of us for a minute, Willa."

"What do you want from me, Foster?"

"Oh I think you know what I want, what I will eventually get. So, I understand it's your birthday today. Do you want your gift from me now or later? I can take you off to a place where no one will see us, no one will hear us. You're old enough now, you know that. Just say yes and I'll give you the best present you'll ever get. You know what I want girl, and it's the same thing you want."

The sick feeling she had the night Foster kissed her at Seaside returned, but she had to ignore it and get away from him. *Run,* she told her legs, *run!* But her legs disobeyed, becoming wobbly, giving out beneath her. Her world grew black.

***

This time when she awoke, she was looking into the compassionate face of Seth Witherell. "Willa, are you there? Willa?"

"Hello...Seth?" Her voice was faint, almost a whisper. "What happened to me?"

"You had a spell. Foster carried you in and put you on Marianne's bed. She's downstairs getting you something to eat."

"Foster? Where is Foster?" Alarm strengthened her voice and was impossible to disguise. The thought of him carrying her, touching her body with his hands, going anywhere near a bed with her, sent shivers up her spine.

"I don't know. He just brought you in, told us you fainted, and then he left. No need for panic, I'm sure you can thank him later."

Thanks were not what she had in mind. Not at all. "Were you here when he brought me?"

"Yes, I asked him to bring you up here so you would be comfortable. It's okay. He didn't drop you or anything. He might be a sharp-tongued jokester, but he would never hurt you, Willa. He only talks big, likes to taunt. He does the same things to me, but that's all there is to it, just talk."

If only you knew the truth about his disgusting tongue and the kind of hurt he wants to give me. She kept the bleak thoughts to herself because to reveal them would bring shame upon her and possibly result in expulsion from the Big House. *Keep your mouth shut, Willa. Do not utter a word against Foster Witherell.*

Seth truly was a remarkable boy. He was considerate and always treated Willa like a friend and not a slave, just as Marianne did. As she thought about it, Seth was actually spending more time with her lately, now that Marianne was getting older and beginning to spend time with girls from her school. A sudden tinge of sadness threatened Willa, so she turned away from Seth.

"Thank you," she spoke into the pillow nearest her face, "you are a good friend. I'm afraid that will change. We are getting older Seth. Your mother made me Marianne's servant today. I'm sure she won't allow you and me to be friends either."

"I know about that, Willa. My mother gave me a personal servant, our coachman's son Lazarus. Lazarus is an apprentice with our blacksmith, but Mother said it didn't matter. He's the only young man she trusts to look after me. But I want Lazarus to keep up with learning his trade. That will keep him from ever having to go to the fields. He is my friend after all, just like you Willa. My mother can't take that away. I won't let her." He brushed her face lightly with his hand and then lifted her face up to meet with his eyes. The look he had for her went deeper than friendship.

Willa could not help the smile that broke across her face. She felt a sudden unfamiliar rush of emotion that caused her to giggle as she wondered if it were possible for a Negro to actually blush.

Oblivious to the special moment, Marianne broke the spell when she opened the door to her room. "Willa! I am so happy you've opened your eyes! Look, I brought you something to eat. You must be starved. Then we'll have cake!"

"Miss Marianne, I am supposed to be servin' you, I do believe."

"That is nonsense! When Mother and Father are not around, I will serve you! Willa, you are still my greatest friend no matter what. You shall always be my confidante…"

"You've plenty of friends, Marianne. I'm your servant. I understand that now. I know what I am."

"Oh Willa!" She put her arms around her companion, her new servant. "Just be quiet and eat your supper."

"It's alright, Miss Marianne. And thank you."

"Stop that "Miss Marianne". You're starting to sound like a slave again. Haven't we been working on that all these years? You have education, my friend. Do I need to make you read more of my school books? Must I force stuffy old eighteenth century poetry on you again? Or perhaps William Shakespeare…"

Picking up on Marianne's lead, Seth struck a ridiculously haughty pose and began:

"Cowards die many times before their deaths;
The valiant never taste of death but once.
Of all the wonders that I yet have heard.
It seems to me most strange that men should fear;

Seeing that death, a necessary end,
Will come when it will come."

The three laughed, Willa finding lightness in her friends' repartee. She realized that she *had* lived the life of a white girl for quite a while, after all. Reading books, playing games. Living mostly in separation from the other slaves, taking for granted that she was actually one of them, one of the forced help.

In reality, she knew she had none of the privileges of her white friends, but it never mattered before. She never had any use for freedom and there were no alluring thoughts regarding life away from Heavenly. Maybe there never would be. She believed Marianne, that she would never treat her as a servant, at least not in private.

Chapter 13: Marianne's Journal, June, 1850

"This summer Willa seems to enjoy Seaside less and less. I do not understand. It is as if the magic of the Island has disappeared for her. She used to get excited several months prior to our vacations. But not anymore. This year she seemed to dread it, as if she is expecting something bad to happen.

But enough talk of that. Today is like no other day, Dear Journal. Today I turn eighteen! I am officially a woman in the eyes of society. As a woman, I will be revealed to that society at my debutante ball. Since we are summering at Seaside, this will be the place of my unveiling. How romantic is it that we are here where island breezes stir the air, filling it with the mysterious combination of salt water scents and the perfume of a thousand exotic flowers. Here I will begin my journey into womanhood!

Of course I will also be introduced to the formal society at St. Cecilia's in the winter, but my initial coming out is here, at my treasured Seaside. The house is smaller than ours at Heavenly, but as I write it is being transformed, from the inside foyer to the enormous outside terrace. Baskets of lovely Crinum and Formosa lilies, along with Lantana and white Gloxinia were arranged to show their brilliant colors! Glowing candles are set inside sparkling glass chimneys.

The servants are working hard to make this a perfect evening for me. Cook Joelle is out in the kitchen with Mammy Heddie preparing the most delectable foods to tempt all our guests. And Father has procured the best champagne of which I will imbibe for the first time in my life.

Mother is on her best behavior today, as she is nearly all the time at Seaside. She ordered the most exquisite gown for me from faraway Paris, made of satin and overlaid in gossamer fabrics, all the palest shades of pink. For my hair, Chloe and her sister Myra have prepared the prettiest ring of flower blossoms to match, with thin silk ribbons fashioned to trail down my back.

My only qualm about today is that Willa will not share in my joy as much as I would like. She is trying very hard to put on a smile and pretend happiness for me. I know it is difficult for her because she is not allowed to attend the ball. First of all she's not old enough. Second, she is a slave and it is simply not allowed. But I know she understands this. If I could influence society, I would make it possible for her to do everything I do. I love her so dearly and it hurts that she must be excluded from the happiest day of my life.

Willa will turn sixteen in the spring of next year and I intend to have a magnificent party just for her. Mother and Father will simply have to consent. She is my friend first, my servant second. I will invite all the house slaves, along with Seth, Foster, and the twins. We shall celebrate our beautiful Willa! Seth adores her as much as I and Foster is quite civil to her since he vowed to befriend rather than antagonize her. However, I sense that she does not trust his intentions, as she seems more inclined to go out of her way to avoid him. Secretly I fear she is infatuated with him and it must torture her so when he brings around the girls he is courting. Poor Willa! I would never mention it to her because I know she would blush. I'd rather spare her from embarrassment, as deep secret crushes are not always comfortable for even best friends to discuss, especially in the case here.

On the other hand, I know someone who is quite taken with her. That would be Lazarus; he is simply smitten with her. It is apparent every time he is near her. He hangs on her every word as if everything flowing from her mouth is poetic. He watches her with love in his brown eyes. And he is a handsome Negro who would make a good match with her.

Of course she is oblivious to his affections and when I mention this to her, she says she's much too young to think about a beau. As her best friend I often forget that she is two years my junior! But next year she will be sixteen and that seems old enough to begin thinking about a beau. She told me that her own mama and papa married at just seventeen! I am aware that most Negros marry younger than people in our white society. They don't have to endure the formality of debutante introduction balls, cotillions, and dance cards. All the pretenses. Sometimes I think I would gladly trade for simplicity.

It is inevitable that I shall marry someday. Since Mother and Father are so strict with me, I am sure it will be a long, complicated journey to find the right man who meets with their approval. I dream of suddenly meeting the prince of my dreams, like in fairytales, and falling in love. He will dote on me and love me so completely that time will stand still for us. My life shall be magical and fantastic! But alas, he will ask for my hand and my parents will decline. And I shall end up marrying some toad who comes from an outstanding family, but lacks every quality I find important in my prince. What then?

Oh, I must stop thinking the worst. I am spoiling my joy for this evening. I must focus on my initial dream of meeting my prince, perhaps tonight. Perhaps he will be my first dance partner. He will sweep me over the floor, outside on the terrace and we will dance under the stars. Then he will ask for my hand, my parents will agree, and we will marry in the winter to be introduced as newlyweds at the St. Cecilia ball in January!

Oh, and what will happen to my friend Willa? What I plan is that she stays on with me as my servant in the eyes of society. As is true now, I can no more order her around as a slave than I can any other friend I have. We continue to be close and I expect that shall go on forever. She will certainly marry Lazarus one summer, right here at Seaside. And we shall have a barbecue on the beach. We will both be wives, happily waiting for the day when we become mothers at the same time!

With all my daydreaming I've lost track of the time, Dear Journal. I must ready for the best night of my life! Adieu!"

Chapter 14

Willa carefully removed the delicate ball gown from the armoire in Marianne's Seaside bedroom. Besides being the dutiful servant, she was also a dutiful friend. She wanted Marianne to look her best as she began smoothing out the gown pink layer by pink layer. Marianne's night would be perfect and later on, she would reveal to Willa all the details of the night. She would talk about the party guests and tell her how champagne tastes. She would describe the young men who filled her dance card, and explain what it was like to have a gentleman's kind attention. She would reveal how it felt to dance while everyone watched as she swirled and twirled on the floor; how it was to feel exquisite and special.

Of course none of it would ever happen for Willa. Over the last few years she began to accept her lot as a slave, although her life was an easy one compared to what her own mother had back at Southwind. Together she and Heddie had a good life at Heavenly. It was just the reality of the situation that tugged at Willa's heart. The reality that the possibilities for her life were severely limited.

She was covertly envious of Marianne and the brilliant future for which she was destined. She was starting to sense that their relationship was shifting from that of two best friends to one of trusted servant and mistress. Willa knew that when Marianne eventually married, she would never serve as her bridesmaid. Instead she would be in attendance serving her in some domestic capacity. Not even an invited wedding guest. Josiah and Margaret Witherell would see to that.

She didn't begrudge Marianne though; she truly wanted her to be happy and live the life to which she was entitled. Loving her as a sister, Willa would always put Marianne's happiness over all else. She was no longer feeling shameful of her station in life, at least not in front of any of the Witherells. She would never admit shame to Marianne, would always put on a carefree, happy face for her.

Willa's thoughts were broken by her best friend who appeared in the doorway. Marianne was beautiful, a true Southern belle. Her already slight waist was constantly cinched in further with a corset to yield a midsection the diameter of a tree sapling. Her breasts expanded gracefully to fill the bodice of her lovely gowns and balance the puffs of fabric filling out the skirts below that tiny waistline. Soft champagne-colored curls were usually trussed atop her head, showing off creamy white shoulders that were no longer allowed to see the sun for fear of damage. Marianne's face was a portrait of delicate features. Bright blue eyes that mirrored a cloudless sky, a small porcelain nose, impossibly high cheekbones, and lips naturally crimson like winterberries.

"Willa, isn't it grand? It is so perfect, so perfect!" Marianne gushed about the gown that was fit for a woman of nobility, of fairy tales.

"It sure is lovely, Marianne! It's almost ready for you, just let me finish fluffin' it all out."

"Oh Willa, I know this is a difficult day for you. You deserve a beautiful gown like this." Then after a few seconds of consideration, Marianne added, "Oh, my goodness! Why don't you try it on first? Please? I want you to. Please? For me? Let's see how beautiful *you* are in it!"

"You're not serious. I couldn't, Marianne. What if your mother comes in? She'll have me whipped for sure."

"No, we'll latch the door! Wait a minute. Let me get your mama. She should see. No. Let's just surprise her. And Seth, Lazarus. Here, I'll help you into it."

She was absolutely serious and proceeded to latch the door and then unbutton the back of the gown. Even without a corset Marianne had no doubt that the gown would fit her best friend's still waif-like frame. She held it up as Willa stepped into it tentatively, as if it was a glass shell. It fit perfectly, as she expected. Carefully she buttoned it up the back and asked Willa to whirl around. She complied, spinning in a circle so that the gown unfurled in a delicious puff.

"Oh, Willa. You look so elegant! I have to say that you look like an angel. An absolute angel! Go see yourself in the looking glass! You will be delighted!"

Willa sauntered slowly over to the mirror, half afraid that she would accidentally tear the gown, half afraid of what she would see looking back at her. There she was, resembling a society girl. She curtsied and the two giggled at the gesture. Then Willa beckoned Marianne to come waltz with her, as they'd done several times while Marianne was learning the steps to the popular dance. They glided about for a few minutes, laughing like the silly children they once were.

"You look so exquisite, Willa! I'm going to get Mammy Heddie…and Juniper, and the boys. Don't you move!"

Marianne rushed out of the room, but shut the door behind her, leaving Willa alone with the vision in the mirror. Where there was once a skinny, unremarkable black girl stood a prettier, shapelier young woman. She reached up to pull her multiple braids together and held them in place on top of her head. She sucked in her breath, stuck out her chest, held up her chin and attempted to look haughty, imagining herself as a debutante.

Then, snapping out of the spell cast by the gown she quickly moved to the door to latch it, fearing discovery of her indulgence. Getting back in front of the mirror, now all she saw was a slave girl with the blackest skin, a dramatic contrast to the delicate pink of the rosy ball gown. The disparity between the fine fabrics of the gown and her coarse African hair was apparent. Her deep brown eyes fixed upon her coffee-colored complexion, her wide, flat nose, and the expansive pink lips that stared back at her. What she saw was plain.

Before Willa had more time to consider other realities about her appearance, Marianne was knocking at the door, calling out her name so she would know it was not Margaret. She undid the latch and Marianne quickly ushered in Heddie, Juniper, Seth, and Lazarus.

Heddie's hand instantly went up to her mouth in awe of the vision before her eyes. Tears rolled down her cheeks. "Willa, my li'l girl. You look so pretty, just like a princess my darlin'!"

"Oh mama, it's just a dress. I'm not pretty."

"No, you aren't just pretty, you're beautiful! You're a woman. You are just…" Seth caught himself revealing his secret thoughts out loud. In front of him was no longer his childhood playmate, but a desirable woman with skin the color of fine ebony. He felt like a man, not a boy at that moment. It was difficult to move, to breathe, to complete his own thoughts. His eyes were fastened on Willa.

"Seth, you are such a funny boy. It's our little Willa, remember?" Marianne returned him back to reality with an inaudible thump where he stood looking like a fool in front of Willa.

As expected, Lazarus was also mesmerized by the girl he thought about day and night. Now she was a goddess, something out of his reach. No longer another slave, but something ethereal. His heart beat fast, as if it would rupture. He responded by taking flight, running out of the room, slamming the door behind. Everyone's eyes trailed to the door, silently questioning, but not verbalizing anything about Lazarus' reaction.

Juniper's eyes filled with pride as she remembered the skinny, sorrowful little girl she first met. "Marster Seth speaks the truth, he does! You look like a dream, missy Willa."

"Now Willa," Heddie insisted, "you best be gettin' out of that dress and gettin' Marianne into it! The Missus be comin' 'round here soon enough."

"Mammy Heddie, I suppose you are right. I just had to have her see how wonderful she would look. The dress is twice as exquisite with her in it, don't you think? She is a natural beauty! Why if she walked into my party like that, she'd be the one getting all the attention, I'm just certain." Marianne spoke sincerely, but immediately regretted stating the obvious fact that Willa would not be in attendance.

Willa sent a look of understanding toward Marianne, forgiving her at once and setting her at ease. "Mama, Juniper, Seth. Go ahead now so I can help Marianne into this frock before I'm tempted to run off in it", she teased.

Heddie and Juniper complied, followed out of the room by Seth who failed to completely close the door. Moments later when Foster happened to walk by he caught a passing glance of Willa still in the dress. He doubled back to take a second look.

"So what do we have here? Is that our little Willa? My, don't you look swell in my sister's gown! Or are you going to the ball in her stead?"

"Foster! Please don't tell Mother. This was my idea. I wanted her to try it on. She's going to dress me now, so go!"

"You know Mother would be upset at the thought of her black skin on your dainty pink dress, don't you?"

"Stop it Foster, just go."

"As you wish my dear. But the next time I see that dress, it had better be on you, sister. I hope her color did not ruin it. See you at the party."

Shutting and latching the door, Marianne regretted her brother's remarks. "I am sorry you had to hear that, Willa. He thinks he is being funny, that's all. But he doesn't mean to be hurtful. Really. I thought he was trying to be more mature, but he's still a boy sometimes."

Willa knew better, but forged a smile as she began to undress. With the gown off and her plain cotton dress on, she was back to being a simple servant as she helped Marianne get ready for the biggest night of her life. She was excited for her friend, but still pained that this was an evening she could not share with her.

Outside the door, Foster contemplated for a few seconds whether or not to report to Margaret about the audacity of the slave wearing his sister's fine dress. He decided that would serve no purpose other than upset both his Mother and Marianne. Instead he savored the latest vision of Willa, her soft curves under the pink gown, the contrast of her rich, dark skin. The skin like fine European chocolate. She was getting more womanly every day.

He felt himself becoming excited by the thought of grabbing hold of Willa, but knew he had to wait. Tonight he'd attend the ball, make small talk with the attractive girls, whisper tantalizing lies into their ears. Later he would slip into town, drink gin with his friends, and then fully enjoy the promiscuous women who frequented the saloon.

Chapter 15

Foster's first fascination with society's lower class women began when he was eighteen, shortly after his little incident with Willa at Seaside when she was fourteen. He was invited to accompany his father into Charleston one weekend where he expected to begin his initiation to the family business, meeting with the rice factors and learning to negotiate prices for the crop. Along with the business education, Josiah had a different type of initiation in mind for him.

On Saturday night, after dinner with some of the most prominent men in the city, the older gentlemen were ready to retire from the dining room to have drinks and smokes. Instead of encouraging Foster to retire with the men, Josiah slipped his son an envelope. It contained paper currency and a slip of paper scribed with an address and the word "Lilith". The question on his face revealed his naivety.

Josiah leaned forward and addressed the question, "Son it is time you learned what women can really do. One day when you marry, you will thank me that you have acquired the skills to make your puritan bride a happy woman. Give the address to Mr. Bartholomew's coachman and he will transport you to the address, it is a place called Chateau Dupree. The money is for Lilith. Give it to her when you are finished."

"Father? Who is Lilith?

"Oh, Foster, do not tell me you've never heard of a prostitute? I imagine you are a virgin, but are you also so innocent that you've never hear of a brothel, my son?"

"Of course I have. But how do you know Lilith? Who is she to you?"

"Honestly, what do you think, Foster? Do you think your mother keeps me satisfied with her ungodly moods and hatefulness? Don't worry, I've not had Lilith, she is yours. She comes with good recommendation among my friends. Go on, before she gives up on you and takes another client. Get out of here!"

With that, Foster found his way outside to the carriage belonging to Walter Bartholomew, their host for the weekend. He handed an old Negro coachman the address and took note of the kindly, knowing smile the man produced. He was on his way to becoming a man, something that he thought he would share with Willa, the object of both his disdain and his fascination.

Chateau Dupree was situated in Mulatto Alley, Charleston's bordello district. As the location implied, many of the ladies who worked the district were mulattos, women who were of mixed race, Negro and white. The offspring of rich planters and the slave women with whom they took liberties. Their lighter, creamier skin color made them desirable to the men of Charleston and its surrounding areas. Not the snow white wives they had at home, but neither their blackened slaves.

The women of Chateau Dupree were safe game for the wealthy planters, even if they did fetch a steep price. No matter to the rich men, the money they threw down here was more affordable than upsetting the plantation household and the Missus by carrying on with slave women at home.

Foster bid the coachman farewell with the tip of his hat, then walked through a trellis overarched with wisteria vines and up the narrow sidewalk to the building's ornate wooden door. He looked around and noticed soft candlelight filtering through curtains in the windows of floors above. Picking up the heavy brass door knocker he rapped it three times. An exotic-looking mulatto woman answered, introduced herself as Lady Victoria, and beckoned him inside to a gaudy, colorful parlor.

Lady Victoria was dressed in a white satin sheath, unlike any piece of clothing Foster had ever seen worn by a woman. He was sure it was an undergarment and not a dress. Her voluminous breasts spilled out above the bodice of the garment, forcing him to swallow hard. It was impossible for him to remove his eyes from her body. He studied her, following her curves. Soon he became aware that his mouth was wide open, gaping at her like a schoolboy.

The woman sat him in a soft, shapeless chair and he sunk down deep into the cushion. Towering over him, he could not respond when asked his name. Lady Victoria reached down to touch his face with her warm, supple palm and he could smell her perfume. Foster felt drunk although he'd only been in that state a few times since he turned eighteen. She bent over, lowered her face to his and kissed him on the mouth. Not in a sensuous way, but in a sweet, almost endearing fashion.

"I know who you is, honey. I'm a friend of your daddy and you look jus' like him. Such a beautiful boy. Tonight you be a man. So you just sit right here young one and I get you the woman you need. You'll like her, she be real gentle." She disappeared up a wide, red-carpeted staircase.

Soon Lilith sauntered down the stairs alone. She was much younger and unquestionably white. No other color mixed with her blood. Although Foster expected her to look hard and garish, she looked soft and pretty.

Secretly he wished she'd be black so he could relieve himself his fantasy of being with Willa. Then he might be able to leave his sister's friend alone and not want her so badly.

"So. You are Foster. You're only a few years younger than me, so we will be good for each other, darlin'. Wouldn't want an old, used up woman to entertain you, now would we?" She laughed in an almost shy manner. "I am so lucky to get to teach a young one for a change. The old men are so disgustin'," she admitted, "but money is money. A girl has to make a livin'."

"My room is upstairs at the back of the house, I'll take you up." She glanced towards the staircase and back to Foster, noting the look of apprehension on his face.

"Don't worry honey, I won't hurt you."

Mindlessly following her up the stairs, he spoke not a word. Lilith could pass for one of Marianne's friends if he saw her on the street. She was dressed in a gown much like the ones he'd seen his sister wear, unlike Lady Victoria in her scant undergarment.

Foster realized that his toying with Willa, forcing his kiss on her, threatening to have his way with her, was just child's play. This was serious. This was as grown up as it would get. He would enter manhood here at Chateau Dupree and never return to the boy he was. *Next time I toy with Willa, I will mean it. I'll have her in due time.*

Lilith paused in front of her bedroom door and turned around to see that the color had returned to her client's sallow complexion. She could sense his inexperience with women. "It's truly fine, Foster. You will live to tell your young friends, I promise." She chuckled, but not in a condescending way, as she pushed open her door.

What happened next would remain with Foster for his lifetime. Although Lilith was gentle with him, he knew it was an act. She was a woman of the world and the tenderness she displayed was part of the plan to introduce him to adulthood and demonstrate the graciousness of lovemaking. Then one day when within the sanctity of marriage he would prove his virility to his wife. But he discovered that he wanted Lilith in a way that differed from what his father intended.

He planned to own Lilith, use her for practice as often as he wanted. Get her to desire him over all the men who benefitted from her services. Then he could do anything he wanted with the prostitute. She would not even know she was being possessed by him. This night his lust had become one for power, something that would never be satiated physically. He now understood his interest in Willa; it was awareness that he could dominate the slave girl and make her do anything he wanted.

All he had to do was bide his time until he felt Willa was most vulnerable. No one would suspect and she would not utter a word to his sister, or his brother. His night of awakening with Lilith was that indeed.

Chapter 16

"Willa, he is simply wonderful," Marianne gushed after her first chaperoned walk with Gerald Richland, her new beau who was patiently waiting for her downstairs.

"He's not like any of the boys around here. He is handsome, and so very intelligent. Why, he already has his own business. How many boys near my age can say that? Well, I guess I should stop calling him a boy. He's 20 years old, the same as Foster!"

The sound of Foster's name always chilled Willa. Much to her delight, it seemed like he was avoiding her lately. "I'm happy if you are happy, Marianne. That's all there is to it. You be happy."

"Willa, I still say that you should spend more time with Lazarus. Do you not see the way he looks at you? You can be happy too."

"I am happy. Didn't you give me the best sixteenth birthday a girl could ever want? I didn't even feel like a slave, Marianne! That was surely special. I am happy. I got you and I have work to do to keep me busy while you're off with your beau and your friends. I have my mama here and Juniper. And I have my other friends, your brother Seth, and Lazarus. Yes, my *friend* Lazarus. That's all."

"Are you sure you're not just saying that to make me feel better, Willa?"

"No, I ain't. I'm learning to sew, Marianne. I'm useful for once. Not just your maid, but learnin' a trade. One day when I get married I can make my children some clothes; I can make some for yours too. And I can read, thanks to you. And your mama doesn't even mind that now. So I don't have to creep around to do it."

It was true. Margaret had found out that Marianne taught Willa to read, but she seemed pleased. She said it would do well for Willa to fill her mind with reading and books. "It will keep her from thinking about dangerous things, like men", she had said. As long as Willa's selection of books was approved by Margaret, she was more than eager to let her continue.

"It would kill me dead if I thought you were unhappy with me going about without you, Willa. You know that don't you?"

"Of course I do. You go on now and have a fine time with Gerald."

"I can promise you that!" She kissed one of Willa's brown cheeks and hurried down the stairs to her beau.

Willa headed into her servant's quarter, a small room adjoining Marianne's. Its proximity suited both after years living like sisters forced to a nightly separation. Although Marianne often defied her parents and allowed Willa to sleep in her room, it was something forbidden by Margaret and Josiah. But when Willa became their daughter's personal servant, the rules suddenly changed, giving Willa her present space so she could be available immediately for her mistress.

In the Big House, she was closer to her mama who continued to occupy the nursery when the twins moved into larger rooms. Willa recalled the first night in the slave house away from her mama when she was only eight. It was a blessing to be so near Heddie now. Her mother was aging, although not as quickly as she would if she were still a field slave at Southwind. Still, time was passing.

Willa had a bed, a tiny closet for her things, and a table and chair by the window. Here she had just enough light to work on her sewing without the aid of an oil lamp on brighter days. Although minimal, it was by far more than anything she would have had at Southwind. It was cozy. Sometimes her mind wandered there to her papa and brothers. She imagined how things might have been if she and Heddie were not taken away to Heavenly. She would be a field slave by now, unable to read or write. But she'd have her papa, Sampson, and Flash. Her memory of them faded over time, but she still recalled their faces.

"Willa, are you in there?" It was Seth outside her door, his voice pulling her back into the present.

"I am, Seth. Come in."

Ever since Seth saw her in Marianne's cotillion gown, he seemed to look at her with different eyes. Willa could sense this and it worried her. She was afraid that their friendship was jeopardized in a way she could not explain. He no longer acted like a silly boy around her, as if it no longer felt appropriate.

"Willa, you want to walk down to Sullivan's pond with me and cool off your feet?"

"Well, I suppose I could. It's a bit stuffy in here, Seth. Thanks. That would be fine."

Minutes later, as they walked along the path, they chatted about superficial things. When they reached their destination, they noticed a fallen tree trunk stretched across a narrowed portion of the pond. It formed a bridge, the perfect place to sit and dangle their feet. Seth wanted to step out first to make sure it was sturdy enough, so he kicked off his shoes and carefully stepped onto the log. He scaled it with precision, one foot forward, then the other, arms spread wide for balance. His face was serious, all business. Willa picked up a pebble and tossed it at him to break his concentration, but he ignored her. Suddenly one of his feet slipped and he struggled for a few seconds to regain balance. Willa giggled. He looked over to her with an expression that said he was not amused. After all, he was being chivalrous, pioneering across the trunk first for her benefit.

Willa, I would do this and anything for you. Can't you see that? Don't you feel it? He pleaded silently, wishing that she could somehow read his thoughts. Lately he viewed her as more than a childhood playmate. He cared for her in a way he could not verbalize. His forbidden emotions surprised him, but he was powerless to change or alter their course.

Then both of Seth's feet slid on a mossy patch and before he could adjust, he was over his head in ice cold water! Willa reacted without thinking. She climbed on the tree trunk and began to edge her way across with the intention of helping him back onto it. Instead, she also lost her balance, plunging in head first. She panicked, kicking and flailing her arms in a wild fashion, unable to stay afloat. She went under the water, then bobbed back up, gasping and spitting.

Seth's arms were at once around her, circling her waist, forcing her head up above the surface as she choked and coughed, trying to catch her breath. Her small body was even lighter in the water and he had no trouble at all tugging her along as he swam to the shore. Reaching the bank, he pulled her safely to dry land where they both breathed hard and fast.

When Willa recovered, she looked over to Seth, her new hero and savior. She was at once amazed at how quickly he rescued her and upset at herself for thinking she would be able to pull him up on the log in the first place. She started to laugh.

"What on earth is so funny? You could have drowned, Willa. Why did you do that? You know you can't swim, you mad girl!"

"Don't be angry with me Seth," she said when stopped cackling, "I was going to save you. But you ended up saving me! Ain't that hysterical?"

"No, Willa. You could have drowned," he repeated. "What would I do if that happened? Can you imagine me going back home and having to tell Mammy Heddie that you drowned? It's not funny Willa. Not at all!"

Willa saw tears forming in his lovely blue eyes, but when she crawled over to him, he turned his head from her.

"Willa," he was finally ready to admit something that would either please Willa or make her angry as hell, "do you have any idea what you mean to me? What you've come to mean to me?"

"Of course I do, Seth. We are good friends, we grew up together. You and Marianne taught me to be a white girl!" She laughed again, but knew he was serious.

"Okay, you are my second best friend, next to your sister. But then there's my mama and she's my second best friend, so that makes you third best. Oh wait…there's Juniper and she's right up there too. She's number three and that makes you number four…but then there's that dog that comes up from the village and he's pretty special too…"

Now Seth turned abruptly to face her. "Willa! Stop torturing me. I'm trying to tell you something important. It's important! You will probably hate me for this, but remember that day at Seaside when you had on Marianne's gown. That day I first noticed that you are a girl."

"Seth, now who is bein' silly? I've always been a girl! It took you that long to figure it out? I sure do hope you're not plannin' on bein' a professor when you grow up!"

"Willa! You are a girl, not a child anymore. A woman! Don't you know how that makes me feel? You drive Lazarus wild with your beauty. I see him watching you. All of the time. He's in love with you and he can feel that way. But I'm not supposed to feel that way. But I do. Willa Grigsby, I've kept it in long enough. I love you! Not like a sister! Not like a friend!"

She might as well have been back in the pond struggling against the water, thrashing about for air. Once more, her breath was taken, but instead of choking she felt an urgent need to sprint away. Not like the times when Foster disgusted her with his kiss, or his touch. Not like that.

She needed to escape the possibility that she might return Seth's feelings. It was simply not permissible. She loved him as a friend, but never let herself feel more. It would bring only heartache. And besides, she figured that he would never, ever be able to feel the same way. If he ever did, she was sure he would never admit to it. Never. She could not fathom letting her emotions go so far. All the recent times she spent with Seth while Marianne grew into her life as a debutant could never lead to this admission.

But here it was.

Willa began to cry. She rolled over, put her face into her hands and sobbed. "No Seth", she wailed, "No, no, no! How can you be sayin' th me? How? You can't be doin' this. You can't feel that way 'bout slave, Seth! A slave!"

She rolled over again, picked herself off the grass and stood up, towering over Seth. He sat up. Her hands formed small fists that connected to his shoulders and arms. Willa was almost hysterical, wildly swinging at him. Since it did not hurt, he let her keep punching until she was too weak to continue and crumpled down before him.

He put his hands on both sides of her face and pulled her head against his shoulder. "I am so sorry, Willa. I should never have upset you." He put his arms around her, hoping to console her and not elicit more anger. She allowed him to embrace her for several minutes while she listened to his heartbeat.

"I've always loved you Seth. Since we were small children. I fight myself every day I live, I do. You're the Master's son. If I ever told anyone, I'd be sent away. Duke Henry would get his chance to beat me. You ain't supposed to love a slave girl, Seth. You can't."

Tenderly Seth touched his lips to her face and kissed away the tears that streamed down her confused face. Then he found her lips and she let him do what he had wanted to do since Seaside. He kissed her for a long time while drops of rain began to trickle from clouds that seemed as uncertain as the pair. Seth took Willa's hand in his. Looking down, the contrast was striking. White hand, black hand. But for the moment, it was perfect and right.

Chapter 17

After another drunken night in Charleston with his friends, Foster found himself back in the arms of Lilith at Chateau Dupree. His fondness for both Monongahela whiskey and gambling drew him into the city like a moth to flame, but it was this woman who kept him a fixture at Chateau Dupree. Of all the sporting houses in town, this one received his business because of her alone. Sure, he had his fun with all of the ladies there, but after two years as a client, she was the one he always sought when he felt the need to pour out his heart.

Foster came to Charleston frequently with his father as he began to learn the family business, which included many financial interests outside the plantation. He learned that Josiah's sterling reputation as an intelligent and shrewd, but honest and level-headed businessman was earned through hard work and an impenetrable sense of survival. His own father was near bankrupt at one point and it was a younger Josiah who turned the tide for the family, increasing its fortune by making gutsy decisions that paid well.

Foster longed to inherit Josiah's business genius, rather than his mother's instability. His imagination wouldn't allow him to understand why his father ever became involved with such an emotional woman. Although he could remember a time when Margaret was not so erratic, he wondered if the entire female gender was just a bit defective.

Then again, there was Lilith. A prostitute, and a damn good one at that, but a woman who seemed more solid than possible. So matter-of-fact; such a rock for him when he needed to talk, sort through his life's concerns. He found himself wanting more of her, more than just her scorching body. She was a fine musical instrument that he planned to play for a long, long time. He would play this instrument when he wanted, on his terms and she would obey. She would listen when he needed her to listen, love when he wanted her to love. The music they made would be of his choosing.

He knew from the start that he would eventually possess her. It was a longing far apart from his desire for Willa. Willa. His thoughts always came back to her, as if she was an attractive but forbidden toy. A toy he would play with just once and then forget, something to satisfy a frustrated juvenile need.

But Foster finally decided he'd experienced enough of Lilith's hospitality for hire. He desired something else—a more permanent arrangement, if for no other reason than his own selfishness. Having his woman available to any paying man in Charleston was an embarrassment. The sharing was intolerable and his need for her soon took the shape of an obsession.

"Lilith, I have a proposition for you," he said.

"You always proposition me, sugar."

"No, you don't understand. Lilith, I am a man of standing in Charleston and the state of South Carolina, mind you. I'm mad about you, Lilith and I'd like you to become my…"

"Slave, Foster? Is that what you mean? You want me to be your slave?"

"My mistress. Anything you want is yours. I'll make an honest woman of you, Lil. A house, wardrobe, you name it, it's yours."

"Foster, I am honest enough. This is my life. You take it sugar, or you leave it." She sensed it coming on for weeks, his increasing need for soul-bearing conversation with her. His drunken state transformed into serious moods, sudden sobriety.

"No other man in Charleston will care for you the way I do, Lilith. There is no reason for you to be a whore any longer. This can end now if you'll just say yes…"

Not letting him finish, she blurted her first impulse, "You are incredible, you fool! Why would I give up my freedom for you?" She slapped Foster across the cheek in what she considered a playful gesture. The look on his face revealed that he understood it otherwise.

Lilith's lover felt a flash of hot lightning surge through his veins and he laced together his fingers to resist the urge to pummel her beautiful face. His mind flooded with feelings of rejection, humiliation.

"How dare you, woman! Who are you to call me a fool! I am Foster Witherell and I am the best you will ever do, you common whore!" Unfastening his fingers, he seized her shoulders and pushed her down to the bed. He pinned her, applying more pressure as he dug into her flesh and stared at her with black, furious eyes. His usual touch--soft, gentle, sensual— now terrified Lilith as she felt savage force in his hands. For a split second it was just a nightmare until she registered the pain.

He continued his verbal tirade. "You miserable strumpet! You are nothing…women like you are not worthy of me! You're no better than a damn slave…I should drag you back to my plantation and have you whipped like a nigger and watch you beg for mercy!" He spit in her face with every molten syllable. The image of a rabid animal passed through Lilith's mind and she wondered if he would tear her apart. Her terror liquefied, spilling from her eyes in a plea for release.

As if watching from across the room, Foster looked down and saw his fingers digging deep into his courtesan's milky-white shoulders, the shoulders he loved kissing, caressing. His eyes followed to her wet, swollen eyes. *My God! What have I done?*

"Lilith! I...I don't know what to say! Are you hurt?"

Attempting a quick recovery, it was best to feign ignorance to the severity of his violent outburst. She treated him like a terribly frustrated, spoiled boy and summoned her best calm persona. "I've had it worse. Foster darlin', don't you worry a bit now. Tell Lilly all about it. Just what makes you such an angry boy tonight?"

As alarmed as he was about his impulsive violent behavior, Foster was more stunned at Lilith's ability to forgive him so quickly to resume her role as lover and counselor. *Is she this way with all her clients or just with me. How many men pay her asking price, use her body, and then tell her all their deep secrets?*

Lilith knew all about Foster and his burning desire to please his father Josiah, his consistent fear of failing to please him. She learned of his deep-seated disappoint in the woman in his life, the mother who was too delicate to nurture him into manhood as she should have. The woman who should have told him about the value of companionship with virtuous women and avoidance of whores like her. She knew about the sister he adored and the younger brother he despised for unspoken reasons. Foster once spoke of twin brothers as if they were of no consequence in his life.

Lilith also knew that Foster liked to gamble with his Charleston friends, the likes of whom his father would strongly disapprove. His drink of choice was clearly hard-wearing whiskey, the scent with which she was intimately familiar. The bulk of Chateau Dupree gentlemen shared the same proclivity. Secretly she feared that drink would be Foster's undoing one day. She just didn't want his finale to occur during her watch at the sporting house.

"Maybe I should just go."

"And where will you stay, Foster? You always stay here with me."

"It's alright, Lil. You know I am still good for the money. Tonight you'll get yours, don't fuss. You'll just get a good night's rest and be rid of me to boot. Just promise that you won't take on someone else tonight, that's all. Give me my money's worth in that regard, Lil."

"Foster, you're talkin' nonsense, sugar. I don't know what's got you, but you just sleep here if that's all you want. I won't have you out wanderin' the streets of Charleston. I've always looked out for you in this city, you know and if you take to any trouble out there, it'll just kill me. You're special to me, you know that." *Special as in, broke you in first, promised your father I'd watch out for you and not let any of the other girls corrupt you too much, care for you like a best friend I've never had kind of special, she would have liked to say.*

"No, Lilith. I need to go. I'll sleep at my father's office in town. I just need to clear my head, that's all. No need to worry. Just promise you'll be alone tonight, Lil."

"You are somethin' else, Foster Witherell, somethin' else. I just ain't figured out what yet. You win. You pay me for the entire night and I'll put on my ugliest gown and I'll tuck myself in that bed, just like an old school marm."

"Thank you, Lil." He kissed her gently on the cheek as if that would make things right again. Reaching into his trouser pocket, he retrieved the customary fee and placed it on her bureau on his way out the door.

An instant later she picked up his envelope and put it into her secret hiding place. There was never a need to count Foster's money. He was honest and always good for it. She pulled a smile in spite of the lingering pain she felt, reached for her best perfume, and prepared for her next client.

***

On the walk to Josiah's office, Foster replayed in his mind the scene with Lilith. He shuddered, not recognizing the man in his head grappling with the woman back at Chateau Dupree. There was simply no possibility that he was that man. He could be cruel and heartless to people at times, but never to Lilith. His intention was only to possess her, never to inflict physical harm.

Then his mind reeled back to a scene with Willa. He forced his tongue into her mouth, held her body tightly and arrogantly. There was no fright, no loathsome self-revelation. Just lust and desire. Why? He could easily have his satisfaction with any slave girl. Any slave girl should be willing, as by right of family business, he owned them. They owed him that much. So what was his specific reason for wanting to have Willa? She was just another slave, and in his eyes, not that attractive.

But she was important in the eyes of his beloved Marianne and his immature brother Seth. In fact, Seth always seemed to be looking at Willa with more than just friendship in his eyes. The thought angered Foster.

The black wench does not deserve to be in my house with my family! Of this I am sure! One day I'll see to it that she leaves in disgrace.

Chapter 18

The Witherell twins, Garrett and Gabriel, were lovely boys with ringlets of golden hair forming halos on their heads. One look at them and anyone could be convinced to believe in angels and innocence. Mature for their age, it was easy to forget they were only eight. They didn't partake in much of the silliness of boys the same age, preferring to read and engage household adults and siblings in conversation. They adored both Marianne and Seth, but left little affection for Foster, the sibling who regarded them with alternating disdain and indifference. Josiah Witherell also failed to dote upon them, choosing instead to shower Foster with attention. After all, he was the eldest and now an active participant in the affairs of family business.

Gabriel was the mildest twin, soft-spoken and demure. Garrett was outgoing and expressive. However, as is customary with twins, they shared a special kinship, an unspoken oneness that allowed them to know each other's thoughts. Since they had to work diligently to earn their mother's affections, they often resorted to twin intuition to earn her attention. They were like pillars, symmetrically holding up the delicate structure that was Margaret Witherell. If she was upset, one boy would swoop in to comfort her, followed shortly by the other to completely counteract any offense committed toward her. In that manner, they kept Mother at bay, managing her temperament and keeping her erratic mood swings in check.

They were only eight years old, but possessed an intimate wisdom regarding the inner psyche of their irrational mother, certainly a maturity borne out of necessity. Somehow they sensed that Margaret loathed them as infants and they wisely made it their mission to turn the tide. Pleasing her was their forte, but since boys would be boys, it took double effort to sustain her love.

One particular day, Margaret was in fine form after a verbal scuffle with Josiah regarding some unfavorable gossip concerning Foster. One of her society friends spoke of an overseer's involvement with a particular illicit woman in Charleston and suggested that Foster was also subject to the woman's charms. This suggestion came as a shock and an insult to Margaret. *How dare they imply that my perfectly bred son succumb to such activity!*

She confronted Josiah with the notion and he upbraided her for both her naïvety and her intolerance regarding a young man's needs. All the household heard was Margaret screeching, "Josiah you are an indecent, selfish, unrighteous beast of a man who is teaching your own son to become just like you! Damn you, Josiah! Damn you and this Lilith whore, damn you!"

Then they heard an assortment of noises indicating breakage and ruin, followed by the slam of the front door and Margaret wailing.

From their vantage point at the top of the grand staircase, the twins heard scant details concerning their parents' latest skirmish. But judging by the volume of household objects flung about, they correctly guessed that it was a major disagreement. Now was the time to side with Mother and take reign of the situation to their best advantage. The bolder Witherell twin would strike first once Josiah left the mansion in a flurry.

"Mother! Has Father gone mad to walk out on you like that! Whatever is his problem? Please don't cry, Mother!" Garrett feigned great concern, motioning for Gabriel to go fetch the usual handkerchief and carafe of cool water. He flew down the massive staircase toward his sobbing mother, reaching up to dry her tears with a soft, child's hand. "Oh, Mother! Why does Father torment you? "

Garrett's words were a soothing balm to Margaret as she looked down to her small boy's face. Her twins loved her in a way that none of her other children did. It was wholehearted and totally desperate. She sensed that their happiness depended on her approval as she stooped down to kiss the top of Garrett's flaxen head.

"Oh my sweet boy. How is it that you can take away my hurt so easily?" She was genuinely convinced by the comfort offered to her.

Gabriel entered the foyer where they stood, carrying a gleaming silver tray containing a delicate embroidered handkerchief and an exquisite cut crystal carafe with a single goblet. He sat down the tray, proffering the handkerchief to Margaret, "Please, take this Mother and let me pour you a glass of water."

"Thank you, my dear." She gladly accepted and dabbed at her eyes. "What would I do without my little boys?"

Then Margaret managed to scoop them both into her outstretched arms to hold them close for a few minutes. Such rare embraces were treasured, no matter how brief. Each boy would hoard these instances of maternal love like mice storing morsels of food, replaying them during the times of her cruelty. It would remind the twins that she truly did love them; it was only her condition of instability that often forced her do and say malicious things.

When she let go, Gabriel dutifully poured her water and watched her drink it slowly with her eyes closed as she savored every drop of the liquid.

He poured Margaret another goblet full, emptying the carafe. Again she leisurely drank it all.

Then rapidly her eyes opened and she spoke in a stern, commanding voice. "Now boys, I want you to promise me that you will always be good boys. I want you to swear that you will never aspire to be a man like your father or like any other man for that matter! Men are such wretches!"

"Yes Mother, we will never be men," complied Gabriel as dutifully as expected while looking down at his own feet.

"But Mother, we will be men someday. We cannot help but grow up. What shall we become?" Garrett innocently asked, then added, "Who is Lilith Whore, Mother?"

Margaret Witherell's blue eyes sparked like someone rubbed flint to steel. The motherly Margaret made a swift exit, ushering in something resembling more wildfire than woman. Her voice rose. "Exactly what did you hear?"

Several uncomfortable seconds ticked off the grandfather clock in the nearby parlor. "Answer me!" Margaret's delicate and bony fingers made contact with the top of Garrett's left ear and pinched tightly.

"Nothing, Mother!" blurted Gabriel. "We heard nothing at all!"

"I believe I am addressing your brother," Margaret continued, "What do you have to say, Garrett? Just how did you come about that name, Lilith? Answer me!"

"I…I heard you say it, Mother. Lilith Whore, that's what you said to Father. I don't mean anything by it, Mother. I just wondered who she is and why she caused such a fight with Father, that's all."

"You do, do you? Never repeat that name in this house! The name is Lilith and her occupation is whore. Do you know what a whore is, Garrett?" Her eyes pierced through the twin, but feeling their hot glow did not deliver a warm sensation. It was cold. Cold and heartless.

"What about you, Gabriel? " She shifted her attention to the other boy and then spoke to neither in particular. "You will know the meaning of whore if your father has his way with your upbringing. Men just cannot be men without defiling themselves with women like that and then thinking they can fool their wives by covering up their sins! I will have no more of this in my household! No more of it!"

Emboldened by her declaration, Margaret pulled the silver tray that held the empty carafe and goblet, sending the expensive crystal objects crashing to the floor. Both boys flinched, but dared not move too far out of position. With all the strength in her right arm she swung the tray back to increase its momentum while simultaneously grabbing Garrett's left arm and spinning him around to face his backside. She then released the force of the tray connecting it with the twin's buttocks creating a loud thwack! Garrett's knees buckled and he fell on the floor only to be beaten even harder with the silver paddle.

"No Mother, he didn't do anything! Don't hurt my brother! Don't..." Gabriel's cry in defense of his sibling resulted in bringing identical wrath upon himself. Margaret alternated between the twins, no longer discriminating buttocks from other parts of the bodies as she wielded the tray again and again, bloodying noses and bruising flesh.

"No, Mother, no! Please! It hurts!" Both pleaded with her, but she seemed deaf to their sufferings.

"It won't happen again! Not in my house..."

"Missus! What in the name of God is you doin' to them boys?" Juniper ran in to aid the innocents she once helped birth. "Lord have mercy on you, Missus! What is the matter with you?" She rushed at Margaret with all the might she had, knocking her over, releasing the tray from her deadly grasp, sending it sailing through the air with force. It collided with a marble bust of Horace Witherell, bumping it off its pedestal. The statue made an ear-splitting thud as it hit the floor, splintering in half. Then the free-falling tray clanged as it struck one of the marble pieces, as if signaling the end of a boxing match.

Margaret and Juniper lay sprawled amongst the handsome planks of the grand hallway with two battered children looking on in confusion, afraid to move or even cry. Time suspended itself, awaiting the command to resume.

When her attentions finally broke free, Margaret realized that she did something terrible to her youngest children. Yet, as she shoved Juniper's spindly body off hers and managed to stand, she seemed more preoccupied with straightening her tousled skirts than seeing to her twins.

Juniper lifted herself off the floor next. Grimacing, she feared a broken a bone as she stood. However, she was more troubled by Garrett and Gabriel's condition.

"Boys, come on over to me. Let old Juniper have a look at ya. Come on. It all be fine. Your mama ain't meanin' no more harm to ya. I know she sorry, sure enough. Right, Ma'am?" She threw an insecure look to Margaret, hoping the woman would come to her senses and apologize to her own children.

"How dare you! I am the mistress of this house! How dare you be so insolent, you black-ass wench!" The look on Margaret's face was the most frightening vision Juniper would ever witness. Margaret lunged at her, groping for her throat, long fingers with sharp nails digging into black flesh. Suddenly two injured boys animated. Each snatched hold of their mother's fine linen skirts, pulling her backwards to allow Juniper to break free.

"Run, Juniper, run!" Gabriel commanded, holding on to Margaret's dress and turning to wipe a bloody nose on his shirt. "She'll beat you good! Run!"

Margaret turned on the boys, batting and slapping at them both while Juniper managed only to back a few feet away from the trio rather than flee for her life. "Missus, leave them boys alone! They's hurt real bad already, missus! They's bleedin' all over the floor! Let me help 'em, please! Oh God, oh God a-mighty! We gots to do somethin! Somebody help me; get the missus off the children! Oh God, oh Lord!" Her voice grew in volume and proportion to her desperation as she struggled to pull Margaret away from the children.

"Missus! You is hurtin' these babies! Josiah! Chloe! Somebody help me!" She had no choice but to wrap her arms around the strong Southern belle to subdue her and hold on until she settled, giving the boys a chance to escape. They limped away as quickly as their injuries would allow while Juniper continued to grapple with Margaret.

"Let go of me! I will have you flogged for this"

"No, missus! Not 'til you settle down and quit fussin'. Them boys are all banged up. Ain't nothin' they do worth beatin' 'em hafta death. "

"It is none of your concern, slave! None of your concern. Josiah! Josiah! Get her off of me! Josiah!"

Josiah Witherell was nowhere near the house, no place within earshot. Neither were any of the other Witherell children except the twins who were well on their way out of the house in search of someone, anyone to quell their angry mother. On such a beautiful, clear day the other house slaves including Heddie were engaged in garden work or other outdoor maintenance. The call for help was loud, resonating along the gentle breeze.

"Help us! Help Juniper! It's Mother! She's gone mad!" one of the pair screeched to the first responder. It was the overseer Duke Henry, who happened to be riding up to the house in search of Josiah.

"What on earth? Boys! What are you hollerin' about?"

"It's Mother," called Garrett, "and she's angry as a hornet! We can't stop her!"

As Duke drew near, he saw the collateral damage of Margaret's madness. "My God, just look at you two. What the devil happened?" He ignored the boy's words, focusing on the bloody noses and battered appearance of the twins.

"I told you, it's Mother! She beat us for nothing! A silver tray! Mr. Henry, you have to help right away!" Gabriel responded, in a state of panic.

Duke dismounted from his steed, finally in a hurry to aid the boys. "Lead the way!"

The two spun around and headed back into the house, Duke at their heels. When they reached the foyer, Margaret was spewing obscenities as Juniper continued to pin her to the floor. "Get your black hide offa the Missus or I'll horse whip you, nigger!" he raged. Juniper looked up from her place on the hardwood and saw who it was. Immediately she let loose of Margaret's bony wrists and rolled off of her, springing up with surprising agility considering her age and lack of gracefulness.

"Master Henry! I sorry, I sorry! The missus outta control today, that's all. She beat on the boys! Look!" She pointed to the boys in their obvious pummeled condition.

"Don't you ever touch the Missus, you fool! Ever! This will never happen again! I'll see to it!" In one quick motion, he managed to produce a thick, dangerous black leather whip, the likes of which had seen plenty of action. He lashed it at Juniper just once and its force threw her to the floor. The twins reacted in horror, as did Margaret, gasping and shouting in unison. "No!"

"Put down that damn whip," Margaret added. "Boys, go upstairs! Now!"

But the twins ignored her command, transfixed on the scene before them as Duke Henry's vicious leather swung again, trained on Juniper.

"What the hell are you doing? I command you to stop, Mr. Henry! Now! Josiah will not stand for this!" Margaret easily pulled herself up and lunged for the overseer. He dodged her attempted tackle and she fell again to the floor, cushioned by her voluminous skirts.

"Missus, I'm doin' my job, the job Josiah Witherell gave to me. Please don't you interfere with my work," Duke feigned politeness and then proceeded on his mission to make poor old Juniper pay for her infraction.

"Please, Mr. Henry! I mean no harm to the Missus. It was the boys I was tryin' to help. She was beatin' the daylights outta them!" Juniper pleaded.

But Duke persisted in his objective, wielding the whip with even more fury across Juniper until the fabric of her garment was sliced along with her skin. Deep red blood saturated the thin cloth. Then he turned his attentions to her face, applying a lighter, more precise sting that left bloody ribbons across its surface as well.

The eight year olds and their mother watched motionless, defenseless against the cruel man. Unwilling participants they were in a surreal, unstoppable scene.

Juniper's cries for mercy soon turned to a quiet whimper as Duke appeared to finish his all-important job, replacing the whip to its holder on his belt.

"I'll get someone in here to clean up this wretched mess and carry off the slave," he stated coldly as if he just knocked over a potted plant dumping soil on the floor.

After he left the house, both the boys and Margaret finally moved, rushing to Juniper's side. "Oh God! Juniper, Juniper! Oh my God!" Margaret cried as she cradled the brutalized woman's bloody head in her hands. Glaring upward, she appealed to the Heavens with a look so pained that God Himself must have felt pity for her.

Chapter 19

During the walk home from Sullivan's Pond, both Seth and Willa feigned fascination with the beauty of nature that enveloped them, surpassing the need for true conversation. The wildflowers along the path were suddenly diminutive portraits come alive with vibrant color after the rainfall. Their fragrance was potent, intoxicating. Trees provided haven for songbirds whose harmonies rivaled an angel chorus. God created a canvas that was perfect and untouchable. Unlike their newly admitted, controversial love.

Reaching the plantation house, they exchanged a look of agreement. They would go their separate ways once inside the doors, pretending nothing magical existed between them. Time and space would aid the processing of these feelings. Too much was at stake to simply forge ahead and let Nature take her course.

While the kiss was unexpected for Willa, it was the fulfillment of a desire Seth carried in his heart for a long time. Visions of bliss intermingled with those of grief and misery. He entertained the possibility of experiencing true love at the risk of jeopardizing a true friendship. As if that was not enough to force a clear head, there was the reality of Willa's heritage as a black slave in service to his own family. He'd heard plenty of stories among his male friends of older brothers who had sexual relationships with slave girls in secret. To Seth, that sounded unscrupulous, immoral, not at all what he wanted with Willa.

Part of him reasoned that if he kissed her once, his pent-up tension would release, quieting the affection he felt toward her. He'd see how absurd it was to kiss his friend. He envisioned them both laughing, feeling silly, and vowing to never let something as ridiculous and trifle as a kiss come between them and their childhood alliance.

But he was wrong. Yes, the kiss released tension but in doing so, took it a new direction that made him want more. They entered uncharted territory on the pond that had nothing to do with the water's current. Now they could never go back. Friendship had been so easy, so carefree. Now what?

There would be no one to confide in about the kiss. Marianne would be upset and Foster would likely rebuke him for doing something so wrong with a slave. Gabriel and Garrett were far too young to understand and would run to Mother and Father with the secret. And that would be the end.

Willa would be cast from Heavenly, as if she had committed a crime. He would never see her again. The idea of losing her made him feel sick inside.

It was with a sense of dread that Seth approached the massive front door of the mansion, while Willa remained a fixture on the stairs below. With a pull of the handle, all thoughts faded from his mind. Immediately he heard the shrieks of terror inside. On the floor of the elegant entryway, he saw the body of a black woman, blood-soaked and whimpering in obvious pain. Her clothing was shredded and her face unrecognizable from lacerations slashed into its surface. Heddie was attempting to wrap the woman's wounds with white cotton while trembling and sobbing, pulling the wraps tourniquet-style to stop the flow of the blood. There was so much blood.

Seth became aware of Willa standing directly behind him, her warm breath on his neck, gasping in horror. Her arms circled around his shoulders in a frenetic attempt to counter the sudden weakness in her knees and keep herself upright. Time froze momentarily as they processed the gory vision before them.

Then Margaret Witherell called out. "Seth, get on a horse and ride out to Doc Capshaw's. We need him here NOW!"

"Mother, what happened here?"

"Now, Seth. Can't you see she's bleeding to death? Juniper is bleeding to death, son. Go NOW!"

"Juniper? Oh my God! Juniper!" Willa slid past Seth, just as Chloe appeared with a heaping tray of warm, freshly steamed towels. Willa seized several of the cloths and knelt to Juniper, gently applying them to her face where the wounds gaped. Juniper winced in reaction.

"It's goin' to be okay, Juniper. Let me help clean you up. I know it hurts, honey. Just let me get you cleaned up and it'll all feel better," Willa said reassuringly while glancing at Heddie with a look of question on her young face.

***

Seth was already out the front door, down the steps, and headed to the stable. Bolting through the unlatched door, he disregarded Lazarus and began to saddle up Smokestack, the swiftest horse on the plantation next to Duke Henry's, which was nowhere in the stable.

"What is it with all o' you today?" questioned Lazarus. "Everybody in a big hurry. Duke Henry took off like a shot jus' a while ago, too. What's goin' on, Master Seth?"

"It's Juniper, Laz. She's in a really bad way and I'm goin' to fetch Doc Capshaw. I don't know what happened to her, but she's been beaten. Really, really bad. My God, she could die! Where in the hell is Duke? I could be using his horse!" Seth continued to ready the steed, not waiting for a response.

"Dunno. Just left a while ago like his head was on fire. Never know 'bout that man. Can I help you with this?"

"No thanks. I'm fine. Go in the house and see if you can help the women, Laz. I'll be back as soon as I can with the Doc." With that, Seth led Smokestack out of the stall, promptly mounted, and seated himself for a fast ride. Then he expertly signaled the animal to get moving.

As he rode, Seth's mind raced to match the speed of the horse, replaying his feelings for Willa, the kiss at the pond, the scene back in the foyer at Heavenly. Was it guilt he felt? What had happened to Juniper and could he have somehow prevented it by not choosing to spend the day with Willa away from the plantation house? Was Willa feeling the same guilt? Was this happening as punishment for his feelings for Willa?

Finally arriving in town, Smokestack flared and snorted as he was pulled to a stop and tied up outside the Capshaw residence. Seth dismounted and ran up the pathway to the door, rapping frantically on the brass knocker.

"Doctor Capshaw! It's Seth Witherell! It's urgent!"

Heavy footsteps preceded the opening of the door to the Capshaw home as a large, round-faced man stood before Seth. "What in the world is going on, young man? You are perspiring like you have the pox." He took a step backwards, narrowing his eyelids. "You don't have the pox at your house, do you, son?"

"No, no, Doctor. Nothing of the sort. It's Juniper, Doc. She's been hurt and she's bleeding. She needs your help. Quickly!"

"You come here all excited over a slave, my boy. That is rubbish. I am ready to sit down to dinner with the missus, now. I'll come out later and check on her. Go home, Seth. She'll be fine, I'm sure. Your other slaves will tend to her just fine."

"No, Doc. My mother asked for you. My mother!"

"Well why didn't you say that, son? I'll get my bag and have my carriage made ready. Come on in and sit with Mrs. Capshaw for a spell."

"There's no time! My horse is ready. We'll ride together."

"Oh, rubbish! I am a big man, Seth. Your horse hasn't the strength. We can hitch him to my carriage, if you'd like, along with my steed. Won't take but a minute, son. Come on now."

The doctor led Seth to the dining room where dinner was indeed on the table. The difficult ride made Seth hungry and the smell of the roasted fowl and glazed vegetables was almost unbearable, but he steeled himself to finish his mission.

"You remember the young Witherell boy, don't you Annabelle? This is Seth. His mother Margaret has requested my assistance at Heavenly, my dear. I'm on my way out to have old John hitch up the carriage. I'm afraid you'll have to dine alone."

"Yes, I remember Seth", Mrs. Capshaw recalled and with kindness in her eyes turned her attention to the boy. "I hope your mother has not fallen ill, Seth."

"No, ma'am, not my mother. It's our..." he fumbled for the right word, not wanting to call Juniper a slave, "my mother's best servant, Juniper. She's been badly injured, I'm afraid. I have no idea what has happened, but she is bleeding badly..."

Seth caught the lady's disgust at the mention of blood. "Beg your pardon, ma'am".

"Oh, dear. You must see some unbearable things on that plantation, with all those slaves, I mean."

"Forgive me for taking your husband away from his dinner, Mrs. Capshaw."

"Won't you let me get you something to take back with you, Seth? You look absolutely famished, my child. Jenny! Jenny!" Annabelle Capshaw called out for her black servant, who appeared at once.

"Fix up a traveling basket for Seth and the Doctor. At once, Jenny!"

"Yes, ma'am," Jenny the servant replied, blinking at Seth as she immediately went to work assembling the food basket, sparing nothing in acknowledgement of the doctor's tremendous appetite.

Chapter 20

Doc Capshaw offered to drive so that Seth could satisfy his hunger first, but the young man resisted. He preferred to be the one in the driver's seat, knowing that his appetite could wait. Better the doctor take his meal now so he could focus on saving Juniper's life once they arrived at Heavenly.

The return trip was slower using the heavier carriage. Seth commanded the reins, driving the horses as fast as he could manage. He skillfully balanced speed with caution to avoid the possibility of Doctor Capshaw choking while he feasted on the contents of the picnic basket.

When he finally saw the palmettos and live oaks lining the entrance to Heavenly, Seth breathed a sigh of incredible relief. He pulled the horse team right up to the front staircase, climbed out of the carriage seat and dutifully helped the doctor down with his medical bag.

The massive door to the mansion opened and Willa poured out, blood on her simple dress, red smears on her hands. She wore a pensive, but strained look on her face as if she was lost. Seth's pace quickened as he met her at the top of the steps while Doctor Capshaw proceeded into the house.

"She's gone."

"What? Willa? What do you mean?"

"Gone. She's dead Seth. Juniper is dead." As soon as the last words escaped her mouth, Willa crumpled to the porch and cried. Seth knelt down to hold her limp body in his arms.

Inside, the doctor saw that his services would not be needed by Juniper after all. Instead, his attention focused on Margaret Witherell whose behavior was even more absurd than the last time he tended to her.

"It's all Josiah's fault, Benjamin. It's his fault. He caused this. Go look at my twins, Doc. Go look at my little Garrett and Gabriel. It's that husband of mine. He makes bad, bad things happen around Heavenly. Go find my little boys!"

"What are you talking about Margaret? I don't know what happened here with this slave, but Josiah cannot be blamed, surely. He directed his eyes to Heddie, "You! Where are those twins? Go get those boys. Now!"

"Y-y-yes-ss, s-sir." Heddie reluctantly moved from her place on the floor next to Juniper. She too was covered with blood. Covered with Juniper's blood. As she stood and backed away from Juniper's body, she blinked hard to test whether the sight she saw was real or imagined.

Finally she ascended the great staircase to find her two young charges, wondering what they had witnessed. She checked their sleeping quarters first, but found neither child. She looked in her own room and saw no one. As she turned to walk away however, she heard a peep from under her bed. Quietly she tiptoed back in and bent down to see two frightened children huddled together underneath the mattress.

"Boys," she whispered. "You need to come on down stairs with me now. I ain't goin' let nobody hurt you. You know Heddie loves you like you's my own. We got to let the doctor take a look at ya. Come on now."

With gentle coaxing, Gabriel and Garrett followed her like little sheep down the back stairway out to the kitchen where Willa told them to wait. Heddie intentionally avoided the front entrance and the dead body of Juniper.

"Doctor, the boys be out back in the kitchen. No sense in them seein' this mess. 'Course I don't know what they did see. God have mercy! Maybe they saw everything! Doctor, is the Missus goin' to be alright? She's talkin' outta her head. Josiah nowhere to be found, as far as I know. I jus' got back here and it was the Missus holdin' Juniper and nobody else. Do you s'pose the Missus did that to her?"

"Woman, there is no way for me to know what went on here! For God's sake! Mrs. Witherell needs to rest. You need to look after her. Go on, now. Help her up to her quarters. I have some elixir for her to take. Can you handle that?"

"Of course I can," Heddie asserted as she took the bottle from the man and headed back to the hallway to follow his instructions regarding Margaret.

"Come now, Missus, you done been through a mess. You need to be put down to bed. Don't you worry, the rest of the servants be home soon and we'll take care of Miz Juniper, mighty God rest her soul."

"Will you take care of her Heddie? Please? Please get her cleaned up and dress her in something pretty. Josiah should not have done this. Juniper didn't need to go this way. It's his fault, isn't it Heddie? He let all of this happen. Didn't he, Mammy Heddie?"

"I don't know ma'am. Let's jus' get you upstairs. We'll sort it all later, we will." Slowly Heddie helped the Mistress of the House up the staircase and into her room, out of her stained skirts, and into a sleeping gown. Margaret did not fuss, but compliantly drank down the medicine she was offered. After her mistress was settled, with a heavy heart Heddie made her way back downstairs to begin cleaning her best friend Juniper's lifeless body.

***

Inside the kitchen, the doctor was surprised to see the twins in such disarray. He began his examination by noting the bruises, the dried blood, and the abrasions about their bodies. He kept his initial thoughts to himself. *What the hell have you done, Josiah? Margaret? What by God has happened in this house?*

Then he tended to the boys immediate wounds with care, ordering an incoming slave to the icehouse so he could make cold compresses for their swollen, possibly broken noses. After he treated their physical injuries, he began a line of questioning, anxious to uncover the cause of their fragile condition. Although he was concerned as a physician and family friend, his main objective was to satisfy his own curiosity. Wherever Margaret was concerned, the Witherells were an odd lot.

"Boys, you can tell me what happened. You can trust me; I am your family doctor. Was your father home when this occurred?"

Gabriel spoke first. "Father is not here, he had an argument with Mother and he left. Mother became angry at us and she...she..."

A fresh round of tears began to well up in his eyes and his brother Garrett instinctively took over the telling.

"She hit us with a silver tray and she would not stop. She kept hitting and hitting and hitting. We were crying and asking her to stop, but she was so angry. She's angry at Father! She didn't mean to hurt us, Doctor! Our mother didn't mean it! Don't tell her we told you!"

"There, there, boys. Now calm down, both of you. It's over. Nothing can hurt you now," he tried to reassure them. "What about Juniper? Did you see what happened to Juniper?"

Garrett resumed, "Juniper tried to help us, tried to get Mother to stop. She tried to help us, but it infuriated Mother. Mother started hitting Juniper!"

"Margaret? She beat Juniper to death? Oh my God, my God..."

"Duke Henry came in and he began beating Juniper with a big, black whip! He wouldn't stop! He just kept whipping her over and over and over! We ran away! We ran and hid in Mammy Heddie's room so he wouldn't find us and thrash us too!"

"Is Juniper dead? Did he kill Juniper?" Gabriel, the most tender of the pair was shaking now.

"Yes, my child, I'm afraid she is dead. So, you didn't see Mr. Henry leave the house?

"No. I told you we ran upstairs. We were afraid to come out." Garrett began to cry and with Gabriel's sobs the sound was unbearable to the doctor, who had little tolerance for children.

"Your wounds will heal fine," he tried with little effort to sooth them and then spoke directly to Fairy Mae, the slave who fetched the ice, "Take these young men up to their quarters and see to it that they keep the compresses applied until the swelling retreats. Do you understand?"

"Yessir."

Chapter 21

After Seth and Lazarus carried Juniper into the kitchen, Heddie and Willa managed to remove her obliterated garments. There on the same table where she often helped with food preparations, Juniper's motionless body was thoroughly, lovingly cleaned and dressed in a snowy white cotton gown. The women worked in silent tandem, occasional tears slipping free to spill down solemn faces, soft sniffles escaping to break the hush now and again.

Heddie sighed, suddenly feeling the weight of the task, reliving the heartbreaking moments after her babies had died so many years ago, reflecting what Jesus' mother Mary must have felt when commissioned with preparing her own son's body for burial.

"Oh Willa…will this pain never end? Will happiness never find us and bless our souls?" She reached out to pull her daughter close and both sobbed together over the body of their beloved Juniper, hearts heavy with grief, minds full of question and disbelief.

Slowly the rest of the house slaves began returning from their Sunday pleasures away from the plantation, only to hear the news of Juniper's passing. The House and the slave quarters became places of great wailing and despair, the loss evident as a dark pall settled over every inch of the manor. Only Margaret could escape from such dimness, peaceful in her medication-induced slumber.

Marianne returned from her day with Gerald's family, escorted by her beau and his father. "Thank you so kindly for such a delightful day, Mr. Richland," she offered to her host. "I do hope you'll allow my family to return the hospitality to Gerald very soon, sir."

"Of course, my dear, I am sure Gerald would enjoy spending time with your family as well," replied Mr. Richland as he held Marianne's arm to lead her up the stairs to the front door. "Perhaps we can discuss that with them now."

Marianne rapped at the door and waited for their butler to formally welcome her guests into Heavenly. After several minutes with no response, she rapped again to no avail. With a slightly concerned look, she turned to the Richland's, "I cannot imagine why our butler Ned is not answering. My apologies to you both." She allowed Gerald to open the door and then beckoned both into the great entrance. Unknown to her, Chloe and Fairy

Mae just finished scrubbing blood off the polished wooden floor and straightening anything otherwise askew.

"Welcome to Heavenly Plantation house, Mr. Richland. If you will follow me into the parlor you can be seated while I find my parents and someone to offer you refreshments. Again, I must apologize."

The two gentlemen followed her into the parlor and stood until she tugged the bell pull and seated herself on a comfortable chair across from the Richland men. When Ned appeared, they looked at him with the distain customarily shown an insubordinate servant. Marianne's eyes did not expose the same emotion; rather she looked at Ned with question when his face seemed mysteriously bleak.

"Miz Marianne," he nearly whispered, "somethin' very bad happen here today. You best stay seated and let old Ned tell it."

"Go ahead, Ned. What is the matter?"

Ned looked at both the gentlemen and then lowered his eyes to the floor, "Miz Marianne, Juniper be dead. She got killed by Duke Henry, so far as we can tell. I so sorry, Miz, I sorry I had to be the one to tell ya."

"Oh, no. No. No." Marianne felt a hot pain tear through her body like a lightning strike. Her breathing stopped and she felt the room grow small until it was totally black. Gerald lunged forward to catch her as she slumped toward the floor unconscious.

He picked her up into his arms and carried her to a sofa, laying her down gently on the cushions. He patted her face and called her name repeatedly while his father commanded that Ned bring water to revive her. But Ned was already gone and back with a pitcher, drinking goblet, and a towel. He poured some of the cool water on the cloth and placed it on Marianne's forehead, causing her immediately to regain awareness. She sat straight up and drew a deep breath as Gerald filled the goblet and had her take a drink.

"Ned, tell me what happened! Where is my mother? My father? Seth? Willa? Where is Willa?"

"Calm down, my dear," Mr. Richland began, "or you will faint again. You must calm yourself."

Gerald agreed with his father, "Please take a deep breath, my sweet. You turned a dreadful color and I fear for you."

"But...Juniper! She's like a mother to me, she truly is! She cannot be dead! She cannot be! Ned, what has happened? Tell me! Tell me!" Her voice was loud and urgent.

Josiah and Foster arrived home at the same time, both oblivious to the dire events of the afternoon at Heavenly. They were immediately drawn to Marianne's tone echoing from the parlor.

"Marianne! What is going on, my love?" Foster assumed that perhaps his emotional sister spilled tea on one of her fancy dresses.

She ran to her brother, throwing her arms around his neck with such force she nearly knocked him over.

"Easy there sister!"

"Oh Foster, Juniper is dead! Duke Henry! He's killed her..."

"What the devil? You must be mistaken, my child! Why would he do such a horrendous thing?" Josiah interrupted his daughter, shocked at the accusation. "Duke would not do such a thing! He knows how we feel about Juniper!"

Old Ned interjected himself into the conversation. "Marster, it be true. He beat her, he did. The boys saw him do it and so did the Missus."

"Ned, you can go now. Stay out of this, do you hear me? Do you hear me?"

"Yes, Marster." The elder servant lowered his eyes to the floor and retreated to the hallway, leaving the shock and disbelief behind in the parlor.

Marianne cried into Foster's shoulder, heaving in spasms of anguish as he patted her on the back, all the while glaring at the Richland's with cold and skeptical eyes. Gerald felt the icy stare and ignored it, addressing Josiah instead.

"Mister Witherell, I believe you've met my father Thomas Richland. We were just bringing Marianne home when she received this terrible news. Now that you and her brother are here for her, we should be going on our way."

Josiah nodded to acknowledge the senior Richland. "Yes, thank you gentlemen. Thank you for being here with my daughter. I will see you out."

Gerald moved over to Marianne and Foster. Not wanting to intrude on her grief, he lingered briefly to offer his condolences to both and then followed his father and Josiah to the door.

Marianne struggled to speak. "Oh... Foster, how...how can this be...possible?"

"We will get to the bottom of this sister, I promise. Duke Henry will not get away with this malfeasance. I promise you." Yet with Marianne's face buried in his shoulder, his face told another story. He looked satisfied.

Chapter 22

Josiah Witherell soon learned the truth about what transpired the day Juniper was brutalized and killed. What he did not understand was how Margaret could blame *him* for driving her to injure the twins. When Juniper tried to protect the children, Margaret should have recognized that. Duke was defending Margaret, did not know the circumstances, and did not know that Juniper was only trying to release the boys from Margaret's fiery, unexplainable wrath. It was all a horrific misunderstanding.

Josiah loved Juniper like a dark sister. The beating was severe and she certainly didn't deserve to perish in such a senseless, bloody manner. But Josiah could not afford to lose Duke Henry and chance another overseer who might take advantage of him. He was certain that Duke was totally, unquestionably loyal to him and only to him.

Now Margaret was upset. The children-except for Foster-were upset. They wanted Duke gone from Heavenly, but it was no solution to dismiss him. It would be impossible to replace a man who could wield authority the way Duke Henry did. He made obedience happen at Heavenly, out in the rice fields. He would stay in the fields from now on, never wander up to the Big House. If he'd stay away, the family would soon forgive Josiah for not taking immediate action and commanding his dismissal.

Juniper was memorialized with a burial at the back edge of the Witherell family cemetery. Such an accommodation was unheard of in the South. This was a generosity never afforded a slave. The neighboring slaveholders would be appalled, but Josiah had no qualms about giving Juniper a place in his family's hallowed ground, although her grave was marked with a simple stone bearing only her first name and date of death.

The Witherell slaves wore a badge of woe for days on end, from house slaves to field slaves who remembered her from her days as a girl riding out on a horse to alert them to mealtime. She would be well recollected for generations at Heavenly.

Her death left a deep scar in the lives of Seth, Marianne, Heddie, and especially Willa who sought comfort in the arms of Seth as often as possible in secret. He seemed to understand her pain even more than Heddie and his touch consoled her in unexplainable ways. Their kisses grew more frequent, more passionate. There was a constant current of emotion swirling between them when they were together. When they were apart, the longing was intense.

It was love. It was the kind of love Willa had witnessed between her own mama and papa. The type of abiding love that existed amongst the "married" slave couples she knew, who were never married in the eyes of the law, but rather in their hearts and with the intimate consent of God. Could she and Seth experience the same sort of marriage one day?

The answer was "no"; it would always be "no". She was black; he was white. Unless a miracle turned the South into Heaven overnight, there would be no way for the two of them to be together. The cruel irony of living in a place called "Heavenly" made Willa cringe. This was not the Heaven where God saw all his children as the same, like the Bible said. Sometimes she regretted having been taught to read that book because it always gave her a sense of hope. Until she looked around and knew that she was just a slave and the world would always see her that way.

Their love continued to flourish into the summer, bringing freshness to the vacation months at Pawleys Island. Willa was able to finally disregard the shadows cast by the summer when Foster forced his lips upon hers. Her lips were now the possession of Seth's and their rendezvous were nightly while Marianne was distracted with her beau and Heddie was distracted by the twins who clamored for her constant attention.

***

The return to Heavenly Plantation in late summer brought no change in their hidden relationship. Finally, one perfect day beside the pond where their true feelings took root and started to flower, something happened. The solution to their forbidden love became unmistakably obvious. Their great obstacles were too monumental to overcome by any other means than escape.

Seth was the first to verbalize the drastic notion. As they sat holding each other on a sun-drenched boulder near the water's edge, he suddenly pulled out of their embrace. "Willa," he began, startling her with wild, feral eyes, "there is only one way we can be together! You know as well as I what that means! There is only one way Willa!"

Partially alarmed, but mostly excited by his unexpected outburst, she waited for what her instincts predicted he would say next. She felt her heart beating madly in her chest, felt a slight dizziness, breathlessness.

"We have to run, Willa! We have to go North! We have to go as far away from slavery as we can and we have to do it very soon!"

Willa was silent as he continued, holding her breath, paralyzed by both fear and a strange sense of optimism.

"I love you, Willa! With all my heart, I love you and we were meant to be together. Damn slavery! God knows that we should be one! Willa? Willa?"

With a slight gasp as her body forced her to resume breathing, she fell backwards, off the boulder and into the soft, lush grass.

"Willa! My God, Willa!" Seth leaned over her, thinking she had suffered an attack. He patted her face urgently, but gently and instead of seeing that she was staring up at him, he shot over to the edge of the pond. In one continuous motion he scooped water into his cupped hands and sailed back over to Willa, splashing her with the cold liquid.

Her eyes opened wider in reply to the chill. "What are you doin', Seth?"

"You frightened me. I thought you... I thought I...hurt you. I thought I hurt you. Tell me you are fine, Willa. Take a deep breath, now..."

"I am fine. How could you ever hurt me, Seth? I am just fine," she answered him as she began to sit up.

"No, you stay there, Willa. Just stay there for a moment and rest."

"No, Seth, I am fine. I'm just so surprised by what you said. You didn't hurt me, Seth." She persisted in moving as Seth gave in and helped her to her feet. "I think I was holding my breath and then I lost my balance and fell over. Seth. Running away. Leavin' Heavenly. I've often thought about it, you know. I just had no idea that you did, too."

"Then you agree? That we need to leave? I know it sounds impossible Willa, but I've heard of others escaping to the North. It happens. There are people who can help us."

"Oh, Seth. I have heard of those kinds of people who help slaves go north. Slaves. But you're not a slave."

"Then that makes it easier for me to go away, doesn't it? And I can help you. We do it together. We make a plan, Willa. We do it together."

Willa let her trepidations begin to cloud the fleeting sense of hope. "And then what do we do when we get to the North? You think white folks up there'll take kindly to a nigga and a white together? You think they won't kill us both? They'll kill us both, or send you back to South Carolina while they beat me and drag me to some other plantation. Far away from you! We will never be together, either way! We will be apart either way, Seth!"

"Willa! You have to settle down so we can think about this. I refuse to believe that there's no place we can go to be together. I love you! We'll be married and have our family, Willa! Don't you see that this is possible? It has to be possible! Staying here, we never have a chance. We have to try, Willa! We have to think of a plan."

Tears formed quickly in her eyes and their weight sent Willa to the ground once more. She sobbed into her hands, feeling the familiar hopelessness that only her time alone with Seth was able to lessen. Being so deeply in love was taking its toll on her emotions.

"Just stop it, Willa," Seth commanded with some gravity to his voice. "We have to think and you must be strong. We both must be strong or we shall never find a way to be together. Can you be strong for us, Willa? Can you?"

Willa found a way to pull herself together as she fought bravely to overwhelm the sense of despair that continued to mount up inside of her. She breathed deeply to regain composure and reached up to let Seth once more help her to stand. She wiped her eyes with a handkerchief he offered and then stared intently into his eyes. Gone was the wildness, replaced by a sensibility that comforted her. He was serious. He was sure.

"Alright then. Where do we start, Seth? You know I want to be with you more than anything in this life. I can't bear the thought of being separated from you and that is why I'm so afraid."

"I understand. I feel the same. I have to force myself to have courage, but I will do that. For you. For us both. We have to try something, Willa. We cannot continue to scurry off and meet like this and not expect to get caught. Duke Henry might be the one to find us and then what he did to poor, dear old Juniper will look like child's play, I fear."

The mention of Juniper's fate send an icy shiver down Willa's spine as she recalled the scene in the entrance hall the day of the attack. Seth saw her reaction and put his arms around her. He kissed her forehead and then her lips. "I am sorry, my love. I don't want you to think about that. But we have to focus on what is true. My soul aches for you, Willa. I cannot bear to think about what our lives will become if we stay here. Think about that. Marianne will marry Gerald, no doubt. His family owns plantations in Mississippi, you know. They'll most likely settle there and you will be sent to live with them. I will soon be sent away to college in Columbia since Foster did not go. We'll be torn apart; there is no question."

"Then we have to tell Marianne that we are in love, Seth! She and Gerald can help us. Don't you think? They can insist you attend university in Mississippi! Then we can still see each other and…"

"Willa! This is not what I want, not what you want! You know that! I want you as my wife! I don't want a slave mistress! I will not be like my father, pretending to love my mother and then bedding down with a slave while she looks the other way!"

"What are you talkin' about, Seth?"

"It's true. My father had relations with one of our female slaves!"

"How do you know this? What does this have to do with us, Seth? You're not a married man having an affair with a slave! It's just not the same!"

"Foster told me everything about Father. He and Father are close and he wanted Foster to understand why Mother is always so angry. Foster was supposed to keep his secret, but he told me. He told me not because he wanted to share a brotherly bond of secrecy. No, he did it make me hate my father for hurting Mother. But I don't hate him. I understand him and the fact that attraction can happen between anyone regardless of color."

The tears in Seth's eyes told Willa that a raw nerve was exposed. She felt his love, his desire, his passion. She too ached for him. His heart, her heart, both in danger of bleeding beyond repair. She touched a finger to a tear and traced it down his face, then put her lips to his and kissed, tenderly. His response was equally gentle, but while they kissed they both felt a fire. His hands suddenly wanted to explore where they never dared and as if foreign and not under his control, they moved down her body, feeling the outline of her curves. She consented by remaining still, letting his hands roam the landscape, feeling the pleasure of his light touch.

His hands became more urgent as they found their way to her bosom. Their kisses became more fervent, wetter with desire. They were journeying to a place neither had dreamed of finding together. Not yet. Understanding, yet not speaking, they both moved to the sweet-smelling grass where Seth gradually eased himself on top of Willa but not bearing his entire weight as he imagined her as fine china that might easily break. They continued to kiss and feel the burn between them intensify until Seth began to undo the front of Willa's cotton dress.

Suddenly she felt naked although he had not removed anything yet to reveal her flesh. "We can't do this, Seth! I'm sorry, but it's just not right!"

As quickly as they had landed on the grass in passion, they were both up on their feet and looking like bad children caught in the act of stealing sweets from the kitchen.

"Willa, I'm so sorry! I didn't mean to upset you. I love you."

"I know that, Seth. I love you, too. That is why we cannot do what we were about to do. It's wrong in the eyes of God. We have to control ourselves, save ourselves. We have to stay clear so we can plan." She had just pledged to run away with him, far away from Heavenly.

Chapter 23

"And where have you been all day, little brother?" Foster looked less concerned and more annoyed with his sibling as he watched him stroll up the lane leading to the plantation house from his vantage point on the wide veranda.

Seth paused, considering his answer for a moment, then responded defiantly, "No place that should concern you, older brother!" Confidently, he proceeded up the stair steps and on to the grand veranda, heading toward the front door.

Foster's eyes followed him. "Just stop there, boy! I've been looking for you. Get over here."

Seth spun around to face his nemesis, marching over to look him straight in the eye with continued self-assurance, angry to be called "boy". "I don't answer to you, Foster! My whereabouts are of no concern to you. Mind yourself and don't worry about where I go and what I do! Don't you think I grow weary of you and your taunting, Foster?"

"Hah! I should slap you for such an insubordinate attitude toward your older, more intelligent brother. Better yet, I should drag you out to Duke and let him deal with you." He laughed out loud, throwing back his head to howl, amused by his clever retort.

Seth understood the reference to Juniper's death at the hands of the overseer and the mockery enraged him further. "How dare you? You bastard! You heartless, callous bastard!" Instinctively he drew back a fist and delivered a powerful punch to Foster's gut. It was a good, strong effort, fueled by anger, emboldened by a duty to defend the memory of beloved Juniper.

But Foster was stronger and even swifter with his response. Instead of doubling over in pain as expected, he seized Seth by the shoulders and spun him about in an uninterrupted, violent motion. The crook of his elbow folded around Seth's neck and he applied enough pressure to cause him to gasp for air. Seth clutched and tugged at Foster's arm for release, but was clearly no match for the elder sibling, who was taking extreme delight in his dominance.

"Now who has to answer to whom, little brother? How does it feel to be at my mercy? What's the matter? Can't breathe?" The evil in Foster's voice, coupled with his brute strength was overwhelming, until he loosened his grip and began to laugh again. Almost like two boys playing in the schoolyard. Except one had such malice toward the other that it was apparent in his darkened eyes and his cold, mocking laugh.

"You are such a fool, boy! I could have crushed you to death and you could do nothing in defense. See what your illicit thoughts are doing to your manhood? Time to get yourself a real woman and grow some ballocks, boy!"

Seth coughed and struggled for breath. "What...what in the hell...are you speaking of...Foster?"

"I have seen you and that nigger, little brother. Sneaking around like thieves, holdin' hands. Touching. Disgusting!"

Seth could not believe his ears! Foster's words conveyed more intimidation than the physical punishment he'd just dispensed. He and Willa had been so careful and Foster was hardly around the plantation house anymore. How could he have known? He was exposed, privacy stripped away like bark from an ancient, dying tree. His body tensed, froze in fear as Foster continued.

"What else do you do, Seth? Had any of that black honey, yet? Is that what you do with her? Maybe that little dark whore is making you her slave boy? Is that it?" Foster's eyes bore into Seth's, expecting an admission of the truth, hoping to confirm why Willa was not receptive to his own advances.

"Well, what do you have to say for yourself? Speak to me, boy!"

"She is not a whore! Who are you to call her such? You are nothing but a whoremonger yourself with the women in town! She is nothing like your women, Foster! Nothing like them! I am in love with Willa! I love her and no one will stand in my way of loving her. Not you! Not Father or Mother! No one!"

It was out now. His love was no longer a secret. Confessed to the person whom he despised most besides the murderous Duke Henry. In Seth's mind there was actually little distinction between the two men now. One a killer, the other a vicious snake.

"What did you say? Love? Love?" Foster roiled with condescending laughter, robust and without soul. "What the hell do you know about love, boy? Lust maybe, but love? A Nancy-boy like you? You've been too busy following around after Marianne to pull yourself out of boyhood! I would rather think of you sneaking around to bed every schoolgirl in the county. That's forgivable; that's what manhood is all about, Seth! Love? A slave? That's egregious!"

"How would you know anything about manhood? You are a drunken whoremonger! No real woman would ever want you, Foster!"

"Why you…you little fool! Now you've truly incensed me with that!" This time Foster was not feigning schoolboy as he slapped Seth fully across the face, raising an immediate red welt. Before the wallop even registered in Seth's mind, he was struck with a blood-drawing bash in the nose that sent him reeling backward on the floor of the porch.

Foster looked at his brother with contempt, offering no assistance. "Don't worry, Seth. I will keep your little secret. Your silly affair is of no concern to me, you are quite correct about that. Just promise me one thing brother, in exchange for my silence." Without waiting for Seth to answer, he continued, "Promise me you'll not waste your first manly encounter with that black strumpet. She does not deserve such an honor."

Before Seth could retaliate, Foster was gone, off to summon Lazarus to his master's side to take care of his bloody nose and battered ego. He didn't intend to hurt Seth, just to rile him about Willa. But it got out of hand. His obsession with Willa was not explainable. In fact, it was becoming uncontrollable, forcing him to begin following the couple. He often crept around in silence, watching them together as often as he could in between his visits to Chateau Dupree and the family business that took him away from Heavenly.

When he found Lazarus, he wasted no time with his insults. "Nigger, your Massa needs you. Seems he's been in a small accident and he's a bit bloody at the moment. Get your black hide over to the Big House; he's on the veranda for you. Now!"

"Yes, sir! I am goin'!" Lazarus sprang to life with the speed of an agitated bull. Seth was his best friend as well as his master.

***

When Lazarus arrived on the terrace, Seth still lay there stunned and in pain, not certain which was worse—the revelation that Foster knew about him and Willa or the throbbing ache from both traumas to his face.

"Seth! My God, what happen to you? Did Foster do this?"

"Yes. I will live, Laz. Just help me up, that's all. Please? I am just a bit lightheaded."

"Yes, Massa Seth."

"Enough of "Massa". My parents are not here and you don't have to call me that. I always tell you that, Laz. You're my friend, you know that."

"Yeah, yeah I do. Let's get you over to the kitchen. I'll draw up some water and clean you up. You sure be lookin' a mess! What in Sam Hill did you do to make him so mad?"

"Not a thing, Laz. I was in the wrong place, that's all." Seth pretended to shrug off the incident and the conversation leading to it, but in his head he reasoned that a plan to run away with Willa needed to materialize quickly before their love was revealed to anyone else.

Chapter 24: Marianne's Journal, September 1851

"A few days ago, Seth and Foster were witnessed having a scuffle. Chloe and Myra were privy to this, but were not close enough to hear exactly what transpired. They said they suspected it was their usual brotherly tussle, but when they spoke with Lazarus later, he confirmed that it was some sort of argument. Laz himself did not know the exact nature of the ordeal, but said that Foster had bloodied Seth's nose!

My brothers! My family! It seems that life on Heavenly is scarcely the same since Juniper passed on. She was such a vital part of this household. She was the one who could calm Mother, reason with Father, and untangle the boys when they behaved badly like boys often do. Heddie relied upon her for direction. Willa treasured and adored her, as I did. I loved her as I do Mammy Heddie. I could tell Juniper things I would never share with Mother.

Never have I felt such emptiness here in my own home. This great house has been tainted with Juniper's death. A shadow is cast that will never disperse. When I pass through the entry where she was beaten by Duke Henry, I feel sharp pains for her in my heart. I am reminded that she died in such desperation, in such a lawless state that surely her soul will not soon find rest.

This uneasiness causes me to wish for my departure from Heavenly, and I oftentimes long for the day when Gerald asks me to become his wife. Contrary to the girl I was when I began this journal, I have grown fond of the idea of marrying and settling down into the life of wife and mother. Commanding a household is no longer disagreeable to me as I look forward to having a home of my own, gardens to tend. Gerald's family several plantations throughout the South and he is expected to make one of them his own very soon.

The notion of leaving Heavenly Plantation used to frighten me terribly. Since Juniper's death however, I no longer fear it, as if her passing matured me in such a way that no other event could have. I've grown several years in the course of months. Her death was an abomination. Duke Henry had no cause to beat her the way that he did.

Slavery become an actual and loathsome thing to me only after I saw the hideous scars of the whip on Heddie's back (now so long ago, when she and Willa first arrived here). Before that, my eyes were always shielded from its true nature. After I became aware that slaves were sometimes tortured, I hated slavery and made it my personal responsibility to be as loving as I could be to our house staff. After all, they are my family as much as my blood relatives. More so, in many instances. And they are generally treated respectfully by Mother and Father. Oh, not always by Mother when she is in one of her dark spells. During her spells, no one is spared from her disdain. Black or white, all are vexed by her behavior and one fares no better than the other!

I was never naïve, though. I've always understood the necessity of slaves at our plantation. If we did not have the labor to plant and harvest our rice, we would have no livelihood. Gerald's plantations operate in the same manner. I realize that one day I will be the mistress of a plantation. But we shall not tolerate cruelty, especially not the beating of any human being on our plantation!

On a brighter note, Dear Journal, Willa is in love. Although she has not confided in me, I can tell. I know this because I see in myself the same traits she exhibits. I am so thoroughly in love with Gerald that I glow the way Willa does! In spite of all the pain felt here at Heavenly, true love has found a way to prosper for us both. The ever-present sparkle in her eyes tells her secret.

Now I have never seen Willa and Lazarus behave as if they are in love in a public sense. They stubbornly keep quiet about their adoration for each other, I am afraid. But Willa is a new person, a deliriously happy person. Even Pawleys Island captivated her spirit this summer, following several years when she seemed to loathe it. Instead of her familiar restlessness, she was playful again, drinking in the beauty of the island and enjoying every moment.

To my amazement, Willa and Lazarus spend a significant amount of time with Seth and by now my brother has to feel like the fifth wheel on a carriage. I should think he'd wish to leave the couple to themselves. While it is appropriate for a girl to be chaperoned, I question the necessity of his presence with Lazarus and Willa, as theirs is a different culture. Courtship has not the same formality.

Oh dear Lord! Is it horrible of me to think of Willa as a part of a different culture? She is my trusted friend. My true companion since I was ten years old. More sister than servant. Oh, Dear Journal, I am pulled between this life as a Southern gentlewoman and my girlhood as simply Marianne, playmate of Willa. It pains me to view her as a slave, yet my society deems I make the distinction. This is the quandary I face.

If only Willa and Lazarus would soon declare their love! Then I would strongly request that Father and Mother release them from bondage and allow them to marry and establish themselves here on Heavenly. Lazarus would ply his trade as blacksmith and Willa would sew lovely things to sell in the city. Then when Gerald and I surely wed, they would accompany us to whatever plantation his family chooses and resume their crafts. Willa and I will have our children together, as we always planned.

It would be wonderful for Seth to settle close to all of us. He has no fancy to run Heavenly with Foster; I do know that much is true. He'll graduate school at South Carolina College, and then venture south because he cannot bear the thought of being separated from his dear sister Marianne! He will run many successful businesses, find a proper bride, and immediately start a family. His, mine, and Willa's children will form strong and resilient friendships just like we did!

We will all visit Mother, Father, and Heddie at the Christmas holiday and each summer at Seaside. Foster will visit me often, because he loves me so dearly. He will bring gifts and stories from Heavenly and somehow he and Seth will settle their differences. He'll stop taunting Willa because he will finally outgrow his childishness and see that she is a truly wonderful girl.

Oh, Dear Journal, I am daydreaming once more. What lies in store for all of us is not truly known, of course. But I feel it is possible that some truth lives in my imaginings. I sense change entering our lives, and it just has to be agreeable. It has to be."

Chapter 25

Seth found a sanctuary for himself and Willa, safely away from the main house. The rice house was their hiding place until recently, but the hustle and bustle of harvest deemed most of the work barns unsafe, forcing them into a small abandoned storehouse. He was quite thankful for the dilapidated outbuilding that had long ago surpassed its usefulness, too small to be relevant and largely forgotten.

Sneaking out of the plantation house, they ran through a gentle rain to their secret destination. Anxiously pulling open the tattered door, both fell down to a nest of dry straw on a pallet to nestle in each other's arms. They kissed and then held tightly to each other, listening to the patter of rain on the storehouse's tin roof. It was a comfortable fit, as always when they were alone, each time bravely fighting the demon of temptation to take their physical union farther. They found strength in making plans to leave Heavenly.

This was a special night and Seth wondered if Willa could feel his heart pounding faster than usual. He could hardly contain his excitement. "We have to do it soon, Willa! I told Lazarus about us and he knows how to help!"

"What? You told Lazarus? Why, Seth? Why?"

"We can trust him, Willa, we can. Oh you should have seen the look on his face. It was just horrible! Did you know that he is in love with you, too?"

"Oh, Seth. He's my friend and that's all. He's never let on a thing to me about bein' in love. That's just not true."

"But it is. He admitted this to me, Willa. He's adored you as long as I have. When I told him that you love me and that we want to be together, he all but cried. But now he understands why you have never seemed interested in him. He'll help us because he loves you and wants you to be happy. What a dear friend!"

"How can Lazarus help us? He's a slave himself. If he knew a way to run, why is he still here at Heavenly?"

"He will never leave Heavenly. He's learning a trade and he is safe here. He will never be in the fields with Duke Henry, it's a fact. His only worry is that he will never have you. Willa, he knows some people who will hide us and give us safe passage as far north as we care to go. They are white missionaries who come through and visit the slave village."

"Could it be true, Seth? What will happen when your father finds you missing? He will have everyone in the county looking for you. He will have slave patrollers and the dogs looking for me."

"We'll travel fast and besides, no one will question missionaries. We have a chance and we must take it, Willa. It is worth the risk. Do you think I would let patrollers have you? I would rather die first."

"You are so sure, Seth. That's why I love you so. But I'm terrified." Willa buried her face deeply into Seth's chest and whimpered.

"Please don't cry, my love. You have to stay strong. The missionaries leave tomorrow night to begin the journey north under a full moon. We'll depart with them."

A loud thump from outside punctuated Seth's last statement and startled Willa. She gasped, but with one finger to his lips, Seth cautioned her to remain silent. Carefully he lifted himself up off the pallet. He tiptoed across the dirt floor of the dark building, hoping to sneak up on the intruder who was probably lurking just outside. Not just any intruder, he assured himself. The faceless noise was likely Foster, creeping about, spying on them both.

Seth quietly inspected, peering through every crack in the structure, searching the perimeter outside until he was satisfied that whatever or whoever made the sound was gone. Returning to Willa on the pallet, he repositioned himself next to her and held her tight.

"It was nothing, just an animal looking for shelter from the rain," he reassured her, not mentioning his instincts about Foster because she was not aware that they were the product of his scrutiny. To reveal what he knew would only bring more worry.

"It just scared me, Seth. If there was someone out there, they might hear everything we've been talkin' about."

"It will all be fine, Willa." He prayed silently that he was right.

Chapter 26

Fifty yards away, Foster slowed his pace from a sprint to a slow run. He was soaking wet, his knee throbbing from the fall off his perch outside the storehouse. But it was worth it. The pain was minimal compared to the ammunition he had against his younger brother. And Willa. He would celebrate his good fortune with the seediest of friends and copious amounts of his beloved Monongahela whiskey. And then Lilith.

By the time he finally arrived at Chateau Dupree late in the evening, Lilith expected this to be like many nights before when Foster imbibed too much. After a failed attempt to be intimate she would expect him to pass out in her bed and awaken the next morning with a pounding head and no recollection of the hours before.

She expected to nurse him back to health with a little breakfast and plenty of strong black coffee. Then she knew he would slip from the sporting house satisfied, leaving her payment in the customary spot on his way out.

Not this night. She could see lusty determination burning in his eyes and knew she was in for an evening of defending herself from his ridiculous idea of settling her down. "Lillll, mahhh baaaby! I want... you, Lillll ...I love... you... Lillll ..." he slurred, drawing out his words too dramatically, even for a Southern man. He stumbled in the doorway, falling limply into a settee like he had no supporting bones. "Le... me... make you my... mistress, Lil. I'll keep you forever...forever. Even after... I marry some...damn frigid society woman. You know how much I enjoy ya, Lillll...come here en love me, dahlin'! Oh, hell...maybe I'll just marry you, baby." he prattled.

She stood her ground, hands on her shapely hips in defiance. "Not now, Foster, not now. I told you sugar, we won't discuss this. I can't give up my life for you, Foster. I'm not one to keep myself for one man. And you know damn well that I sure ain't the marryin' kind!" Lilith tossed her head back, letting out a good-humored whoop at her lover's expense.

"Your mama would simply die and your daddy...my Lord, why he'd just disown your sorry ass! Then what would you have, Foster? Nothing, that's what. Not a damn thing! And Foster with no money could never support me because you know I like the finer things."

Lilith firmly restated what she had communicated to him for months. Then, believing him too drunk and weakened to react, she added,

"And you know I just can't love you that way, Foster. I won't love you Foster. This is a business arrangement and if you want it to continue as such, you'll stop pesterin' me about settlin' down."

"Don't love me? I give you everything dahlin'...don't love me? Don't LOVE ME?" he continued to repeat himself, getting louder. He rose off the settee. The determination in his eyes transformed from lust to something Lilith could not identify. Although he had attacked her once, he was immediately remorseful so she assumed he was harmless. Now he was laughing at her in such a mocking, demonic way, it revealed that she was never safe.

At once he rushed toward her, drunken clumsiness vanishing, suddenly sure of his actions. He thrust the prostitute to the floor and stood over her in deliberate domination. "You, you insolent, filthy harlot!" Without another word he kicked her firmly in the ribs.

"Oh, God! Foster what are you doin'?" Lilith's shock turned to anguish as he kicked harder and then reached down to pull her off the floor with hands that demanded resolution.

He heaved her violently to the bed, and then looking into the eyes he actually loved, he slapped her across the face repeatedly, following up with fists to her chest.

She tried to scream, but no one would hear her. It was the usual raucous Saturday night in the sporting house. The sounds of slapping, shoving, and shouting were common in this place where fine Southern gentlemen lived their darkest fantasies with the women of Chateau Dupree. They did things to these women that no respectable wife would allow and as long as they paid their price, there were no repercussions. Money spoke in ways that made up for temporary pain. Seldom was it more than that.

But not this night, not for Lilith. Foster continued to flay her with more force than he knew he possessed, delivering blows like a madman. He was uncontrollable, fighting her for every perceived wrong done to him in his life. He saw his father, expecting too much from him; his mother, contorted in one of her irrational moods; Marianne, convinced that he was perfect. Then he saw Seth and Willa lying together on the pallet in the storehouse, imagining the sweet intimacy they must share. His mind flashed to the hateful rejection from Willa when she rebuffed his kisses. Then he beat Lilith until she lay broken, bruised, and bleeding beneath him.

When he came to his senses and grasped the impact of his violent actions, it was too late. She was seriously damaged. He looked at her once-beautiful body, the body that gratified him more times than he could count.

She was barely conscious, opening her eyelids scarcely a slit when he called her name.

"Lil? Lil? I...I..."

He needed more alcohol to make the images in his mind go away. Images of what had just occurred. Fist after fist, slap after slap, the angered kicks. The beating he gave this woman! He found his way over to her makeshift bar on a table near the door, still stumbling and woozy from his earlier binge. He poured a glass of scotch and threw it back, attempting to make it all disappear. Then he poured another, but set it back down on the table. He looked at Lilith again. She was having difficulty breathing; with every rise and fall of her chest she struggled, laboring against cracked ribs.

He took the full glass of scotch over to the bedside and with his free hand he forced open the woman's mouth. He put the glass to her lips and poured in a measure of the alcohol. She choked and sputtered, unable to enjoy the medicinal benefit of the burning liquid. All the while her glassy eyes strained to look up at Foster. He sensed their questions. *Why, Foster? Why did you do this to me?*

It was Willa he wanted to hurt. Willa he wanted to suffer, not Lil. She had to pay for corrupting his brother and making him want to risk himself for her. His stupid, useless brother. Wanting to run off with his little black slave. That black wench who didn't want Foster. She had to pay for her ignorance!

Then he kissed Lilith's forehead and laid her back down in her soft, silky bed. Instead of further tending to her wounds, he freshened himself and dressed in a clean shirt and coat he kept in her wardrobe. He wadded up his bloodied clothes and threw them into the fireplace where he watched them blaze to ashes. Then stopping to leave her fee in the usual place, he swaggered out her bedroom door, down the stairs, and out one of the side doors, leaving Chateau Dupree via the dark alley where his horse was tethered.

Chapter 27

Foster slept off his Saturday night drunk at a cheap hotel in Charleston and woke with a distinct throbbing in his brain. At first he imagined himself in the warm comforts of Lilith's bed. Until a series of intruding visions began to play in his head to remind him what his fists did the night before. What he did to the woman he thought he loved and possessed. He saw images of her face turning pale, her gasping, her clawing to be free of his clutches. He recognized the blood. He looked at his hands as if they were not his, contemplating how he could divorce himself from their actions.

Slowly he rolled his unclothed body off the bed, taking care not to agitate his aching skull too much. He needed more drink. That would bring relief from both the crushing pain and the images. However, as he surveyed his shabby surroundings, he saw nothing resembling a bottle of comfort. He found his trousers on a threadbare rug next to the bed and stepped in to them ungracefully. He stumbled over to the looking glass hanging crooked on the paint-chipped wall directly in front of the bed. Staring back at him was a man he did not recognize, a man who needed a shave and something stronger than whiskey to wash away the appearance of guilt.

And there was something else reflected in the mirror. From the bed it began to move. Foster jerked around to see a naked-chested half-black woman arise from the tangle of bed linens. She was not pretty. Not like the mulattos at Chateau Dupree. She smiled and her head of black, tousled hair bobbed as if her neck was not stable enough to support it.

"Mornin'." She laughed weakly, opening her mouth to expose badly stained teeth. Her bloodshot eyes trained on Foster as she attempted to dislodge from the blankets. She teetered before him, grabbing hold of the pitted brass bed frame for support. Her totally bare body revealed a woman easily twice his age with sagging skin stretched over a thin, gaunt mulatto frame. She had thick, toughened scars running across her abdomen and upper thighs, clearly the artifact of a severe whipping.

The sight sent a shiver down Foster's spine and he suppressed a wild urge to vomit. He doubled over, feeling the room spin and then made his way back to the foot of the bed where he took a seat, facing away from his disfigured guest.

"What's a matter, fancy boy? Ain't you never seen a scarred up old half breed before now? You sure didn't mind me last' night when ya was all over me. Sure didn't mind it then, no sir! All drunked up and callin' me sweet names. I put up with that, but ya better be payin' this old wench a little extra for all the cryin' ya did. Ain't no man worth puttin' up with for that mess!"

"Get out! Get your ugly hide out of here! Now!" Anger from the prior evening returned with a vengeance, turned on the unfortunate soul Foster had no recollection inviting into his bed.

Then the aged prostitute he assumed was still intoxicated became threateningly sober, "Pay me, rich boy! Or I'll tell what I know about the things you done to that girl over at Dupree last night. I'll tell the law that you done beat the daylights outta her, just like you said when you were cryin' like a bitty baby!"

"Find your clothes, old woman and get out!" Foster stood up, reached into a trouser pocket and pulled out several gold dollars, tossing them in her direction.

She gathered up the coins and then quickly donned her clothes, nothing more than a scruffy calico underdress over which she pulled a tattered black satin palatine cape. She hastened to marshal her long black hair into a chignon and secure it with a large pin retrieved from the bedside table. Finally she lifted the hood of the ratty old palatine over her head and scurried out the door like a rat escaping the trap.

Foster shook his head as if to rid himself of the visions of what must have happened between him and the surely woman. He perplexed himself. *What in the name of God was I thinking when I met up with that creature?* He now wanted no more than to thoroughly bathe his tainted body and wash off the offensive scent of the woman. Problem was, he could not return to Chateau Dupree and expect Lilith to take care of him.

After untying his horse from the hitching post outside the dilapidated hotel, he surveyed the landscape. No one was watching as he mounted and commanded Heaven's Prince toward the direction of the plantation.

Chapter 28

Back at Heavenly, Seth assembled Willa and Lazarus to discuss plans for the moonlight escape, meeting down by Sullivan's Pond. Willa felt uneasy there, as if she was sharing a deep secret with Lazarus, a secret that he had no right knowing. She consoled herself by the reminder that he offered to help with the escape, certainly a difficult decision if he truly did have feelings for her. She choked back her emotions and resolved to clear the air between them.

"Lazarus, we sure do appreciate your offer of help. You're Seth's best friend and you're special to me, too. I want you to know that, Laz. You're my friend and if I ever made you believe there was more to it, then I'm sorry. I just…"

"No, Willa…you done nothin' wrong, girl. Nothin' to be sorry for," he interrupted, feeling the heat rise in his cheeks. "I'm the one with the feelin's other than friendship. It's my misunderstandin', not yours. I just want you happy. If you be happy with Seth, then it has to be that way, that's all."

Willa put her arms around Lazarus in a sisterly embrace, making him uncomfortable as he watched Seth for a reaction.

"She is right, Laz. You are my best friend and I will miss you. We both will miss you. And Heavenly." Seth's voice lowered as he looked around, eyes sweeping wide from the plantation house in the distance to the outbuildings and rice fields.

"You're not sorry, are you Seth? For what we're about to do?" Willa had to be sure.

"No. I know you will miss Heddie dearly, as well as Marianne. We'll both miss so many people we love. But we are going to be together. At last."

As she broke her light embrace with Lazarus, Willa formed a new attachment with Seth and held tight in accord with his statement about togetherness. Lazarus looked away, clearing his throat to signal that he preferred to get down to the urgent business at hand.

Seth noted his mild annoyance and broke the embrace, stepping back from Willa. "So, when will the missionaries take their leave tonight, Laz?"

"An hour after dark, Seth. You both get to the old storehouse right after sundown. Don't come together though. If anyone sees you together, they might recollect it after you're found missin' and know somethin' was up between you. Maybe you get out there real early, Seth. Then Willa later."

"That makes good sense. Willa will spend today with Marianne up until she leaves with Gerald for supper. She is going with Gerald tonight, isn't she Willa?"

"Yes. I'll leave after her, after I have a chance to say some things to my mama."

"But you can't let her know, Willa. I know this is going to be hard on you, but you cannot tell her what we're doing. Promise me?"

"Of course, Seth. I wouldn't risk harming you and I couldn't risk it for Lazarus either."

"When it's dark enough, I'll bring the missionaries away from the slave quarters and over to the storehouse. They'll have two wagons. One has a false floor, so there is space to hide you both. But it's small, you'll be mighty close."

Seth and Willa looked at each other, erupting in a giggle, sharing a single thought.

"For a darky, you sure turn blush, Willa girl," Lazarus commented while he felt a pang of jealousy. *Oh, to be that close to Willa*, he ruminated.

"Sounds just too good to be true, Laz. Nobody else in the whole world I want to be that close to." As the words left her lips she immediately regretted letting them slide by, feeling guilty for speaking that way in front of Lazarus.

He disregarded the remark and continued with the plan, "They will keep you hid until they get outta the county. Then they only have to hide you, Willa. They probably dress Seth in some old clothes belongin' to one of theirs and make like he's family. Sorry, Willa, but you'll be in that li'l space by yourself."

Willa's heart temporarily sunk, but she rallied as she considered the entire plan. "It's alright. We'll be up North before we know it, right?"

"I really will miss you two! You've been the best part of livin' at Heavenly and it'll be mighty sorrowful when you're gone."

"How long do you think it'll be 'fore they start looking for us?"

"Willa, we are not going to think about that. The missionaries will put us a full night's journey ahead of anyone looking for us. It will work. It just has to work."

Chapter 29

The evening quickly approached, in spite of Willa's psychological attempt to lengthen the daylight hours. Spending as much time with Heddie as she could, the burden of the information she held in her brain was almost unbearable for the girl. She had to keep reminding herself that freedom would soon be within her grasp. She continued to imagine living a life outside of bondage and fear of the whip. Although she was certain the white folks up North would never welcome her and Seth as a couple, they would be free to live in private as they chose. They would marry in their hearts and make their vows to God alone. They may be forced to live in public secrecy, but whatever they did behind closed doors was their own choosing and no white person could punish them for it.

Thoughts of the future were sketchy for them both as they contemplated their very survival once beyond the Northern border. They would be at the mercy of the missionaries for passage and sustenance, but upon arrival they would depend solely on the meager savings Seth accumulated in his short lifetime. But they were not without intellectual and physical resources. Seth was strong and able to use his body for labor, certain that in no time he'd also use his mind to create some sort of business enterprise. Willa was physically fit as well, but more significant was her talent as an accomplished seamstress. Additionally, she had the ability to read. She lately daydreamed about owning a little shop where, after reading all the latest fashion publications, she would create exquisite gowns for the rich, cultured women of the North.

Heddie interrupted her thoughts, pulling her back to the here and now. "Willa, what are you doin' in this old kitchen with me, child? You bein' awfully clingy today, like you was five years old again. Doesn't Marianne have somethin' else for you to do? There's plenty 'nough servants here to help me with what I's doin'. Maybe you and Laz go take a walk or somethin'. You know he just dyin' to get some time with you!"

"Oh, mamma! Ain't nothin' wrong with me spending some time with you, is there? Can't I be with my mamma?" Willa tried to sound casual, disguising her need for closeness this last day. And she refused to acknowledge the guilt she felt by not inviting her on the journey to freedom.

Since Juniper's passing, Heddie was even more valued at Heavenly. Her life there was as good as life could get for a slave. She was treated with the utmost respect and civility by the Witherells and revered by all her fellow house servants. Duke Henry was forbidden to approach the plantation house and its immediate grounds, so she was safe from the heinous circumstances that took Juniper's life. Even the Missus now seldom appeared in a state of agitation, seemingly reformed by the tragedy (and an occasional dose of laudanum dispensed by Doc Capshaw).

Willa reached over and pulled her mother close in an embrace, deeply inhaling her scent, storing it in her memory for later recall. She held on tighter as if doing so would force back the tears that threatened to give her away.

Heddie broke free, taking her daughter by the shoulders and holding her out at arm's length for questioning. "What is it, Willa? What's got you down, baby?"

The tears disobeyed, running down her cheeks in streams of growing intensity, wetting her face and dripping off her chin. Heddie lifted the edge of her apron, putting the cloth to Willa's face to wipe away the salty moisture. What Willa really wanted was to let the tears flow cathartically. *Stop asking what's wrong, just let me cry.*

Other slave women in the kitchen stopped their tasks and came to the aid of the pair until Willa reassured them that she was simply missing Juniper and feeling sentimental toward her own mother because of it.

"Can't a girl break down and cry when she's feelin' blue and be glad she still has a mother to love on?" After several bittersweet minutes of hugging all around, Willa knew this would serve as a veiled goodbye to these beautiful, courageous black women she'd come to love at Heavenly. Let this serve as her last memory of Heddie. Far better not to have her mother all to herself, tempting the urge to spill the details of her departure. Willa disengaged herself from the women as she quietly, knowingly smiled and backed out of the kitchen doors.

Then it was time to say goodbye to Marianne without saying goodbye. Sorry to deceive her best friend and confidante, Willa dutifully reminded herself that it was far better not to involve her in the plans she and Seth had made. If anyone interrogated her, she could maintain honest, complete innocence. It was the least she could do for the girl who helped her become who she was, the girl who always saw her as an equal, even when forced to have her as a servant.

This would be the most difficult farewell. She bared her soul to Marianne for so many years now, as if they were blood sisters. They were inseparable. Until Gerald came along. But Willa harbored no ill feelings toward him for imposing on their time together. It was natural, inevitable. It also gave her the opportunity to become closer to Seth, as if it were a gift the couple unwittingly bestowed upon her.

She climbed the back staircase to the bedrooms as she had so many times before. But now she ascended slowly, as if savoring the memories that hung over each step. She reached Marianne's room, pausing to take a deep breath and suck in the courage she needed. She knocked softly on the oak door. Her mind flashed to all the time spent behind that door, learning to read in secret, plotting ways to trick Seth, discussing boys in general, crying at growing pains.

Marianne was quick to answer, pulling Willa away from her reverie and back to the moment. "Willa! Come in, my friend. I have something wonderful to tell you! Oh, Willa!" She pulled Willa's arm, urging her into the room and swiftly securing the door behind her.

"It's Gerald! His behavior is so strange lately, Willa. It's as if he has a big secret that he cannot reveal. Oh, Willa! I think he will propose marriage to me very soon! Perhaps he's already asked Father for my hand! Do you think I'm ready for that, Willa? Do you think I am ready to be a wife? Maybe we shall have a lengthy engagement. Oh…but perhaps he will want to wed sooner. What if I'm not ready, Willa? I love him so! I want to be his wife, but what if…"

Willa's best friend would surely collapse, her lungs deprived of air as she failed to pause and breathe. Willa took hold of her shoulders and gave her a light shake. "Marianne! Slow down! My goodness, you'll faint dead away! Then what will Gerald do, girl?"

"Of…of course. Yes." She blew out and steadied herself, taking in slower breaths a few times before continuing in a calmer voice. "Do you think I am ready to be a grown woman? Engaged? A wife?"

"Of course you are Marianne. You are already a grown woman, honey." She pulled her toward the full-length looking glass near the window and stood behind her, arms encircling her waist. "Just look at yourself. You are a woman, a beautiful woman. No girl ever goin' to make a lovelier bride than you, Marianne. And you're one strong woman, too. You'll be the best wife Gerald could ever have and you'll run the house like you were born for it. Don't you even worry 'bout that."

"Oh, Willa…" She turned around to face her sweet companion, tears forming in her deep blue eyes. "You say the most wonderful things!" She put her arms around Willa and held her in an embrace that forced the slave girl's own waterworks. Encircled for several minutes, the two sobbed for different reasons. Marianne shed tears of joy; Willa shed tears for the friendship that was most likely ending forever.

"Oh my goodness, Willa, just look at us," Marianne spoke first, turning her attention to their reflection in the mirror. "We are both crying like two babies. Have I told you that you are the most perfect friend a girl could ever have? I love you more than life, my Willa!"

The heartfelt declaration filled Willa with a swirl of emotions and a new surge of tears. "Oh, Marianne! You know I love you too. I can't bear to think of what my life would have been without you." She squeezed her friend even tighter, burying her face into her neck, breathing deeply her perfume to record it into memory along with Heddie's scent. Her voice became a nearly indecipherable whisper, "I just wish I could be here for you on your weddin' day, honey."

"What do you mean, Willa? Don't be silly, of course you'll be here for my wedding. What are you talking about, Willa?" She broke free of the embrace and looked into Willa's face to question such a comment.

"I...I mean...you know, I wish I could be in your wedding. Part of your wedding, I mean. But you know I can't because...because I am a slave. That's what I mean. I cannot be in your wedding with you. Maybe I won't even be allowed in the church. You know..."

"That is just nonsense! I would die first if you could not be part of my wedding! I..."

"Marianne. You know I can't. Your parents and society and..."

"To hell with them all! Willa you are my best friend!"

"Marianne! You will not ruin your wedding day on my account! And I don't want you getting ideas into your head and worrying and stewing on 'em. You just forget about me where your wedding is concerned. Do you hear me? You be happy, Marianne. I'll be happy too one day. You need not be worryin' about that. Do you hear me?"

"Oh, Willa! What are we to do? Our world is so unfair! Why is it this way? You should have every happiness, too. You deserve that and a wedding like the one I plan to have. We should have our weddings together! Why are my parents, South Carolina, the world...so blind, so ignorant?"

"My wedding? Why would you talk like that?"

"Now don't you pretend! I know you're in love. You can't keep your secret forever, Willa."

Suddenly all of the air left the room, forcing Willa to gasp. If guilt had hands, it was circling her neck, beginning to choke the life from her. She hoped that the dark color of her skin masked the heat she felt rising into her cheeks. It was time to make her exit.

"Yes! I can see it in your face! Look at you trying to hide your feelings, Willa Grigsby! I am supposed to be your best friend and you kept hiding this from me! You and Lazarus are very good at playing along to cover up your love for each other!"

The guilty grip loosened just slightly as Willa knew she was safe from Marianne suspecting a relationship between her and Seth. Better to let her think it was Lazarus for now. Until the next day when she and Seth come up missing and Marianne would begin to assemble the puzzle for herself.

"Just don't worry about me…and Laz. You keep your attentions on Gerald. You hear me? I'm sure the proposal will be soon, Marianne. Just be happy and don't worry 'bout me." She hugged her white friend for what she knew would be the last time and then kissed her on the cheek. "You will always be my best friend and I'm sorry I've been hiding my feelings from you. But I want you to devote your time and attention to Gerald. That's all. I want your life to be joyful. Always know that, Marianne. I love you, my friend. Now if you must know, I'm meeting Laz, so I should get goin' so he won't be worrying about me."

"Alright, then. You go. And Willa, please don't say a thing to anyone about what I think Gerald is planning to do. Please?"

"Of course I won't."

They grinned at each other and nodded in agreement the way friends do when sharing special secrets. Willa made her way to the door and just before exiting, turned around to cast a final reflective look at her treasured companion. Willa knew it was time to gather up what she could in an old burlap sack and head toward the outbuilding.

Chapter 30

With a burdened heart Willa set out to begin her new life with the boy she loved completely. She had no illusions. She understood the danger involved in this life or death venture that could well end with detection by slave patrollers. The macabre scars on her mother's back called to her and she allowed them a place in her consciousness, realizing they might be hers one day soon. Silently she wondered why God chose her to love Seth and him to love her. Perhaps it was simply an unplanned complication. Or maybe it was part of His plan for them and they were truly meant to be together. Regardless, their relationship was a forbidden thing, leaving them no choice but to disobey Josiah and Margaret Witherell, the constraints of Heavenly, the rules of society.

So occupied was her mind that Willa failed to notice she was being followed. Foster stayed several paces behind, waiting for the moment when they were far enough from the plantation house and hidden by the cover of woods. He knew her destination, her motivation. His intent was to delay her significantly, enough to thwart her plans altogether. And in doing so, he would render to his brother a different girl. One defiled, irreparably damaged goods. His gift to Seth for being such an ignorant boy and falling in love with a slave.

Lilith was dead. Questions were being asked in Charleston. Someone saw him at Chateau Dupree, but he had an alibi in the old, ugly prostitute with whom he shared a rented bed that night. Once the investigation began, she appeared to him wanting money. He was surprised how little it actually took to pay her for protecting his story. Never mind, she was a low life without the expensive tastes of someone like Lil. Threatening her life might even have been enough, but Foster was unwilling to take the chance, so he met her meager demands. Small price for a man of his wealth.

Although feelings of love for Lilith seemed to dissolve with the news of her passing, he was full of regret, essentially disgusted that he'd brutalized her. Now that he knew he was capable of killing, he needed to be more careful in controlling his anger. And his lusts. No, Willa would not die by his hands. That was not his desire for her. But, neither was it his desire for Lilith. This time he would have to be careful, make no demands and just get what he needed.

She was getting closer. Just a patch of woods and a pasture. Not yet sundown, the woods posed no threat and would be easy to navigate. As she cautiously entered, she peered around for the sight of wild animals, hoping to avoid anything that might be hungry for the bits of food she'd stowed in her knapsack. She memorized the way through the thickets after several trips with Seth.

But the wolves and feral hogs were the least of her troubles. Foster was far more powerful, more dangerous. He stayed hidden behind tree cover, careful not to disturb underbrush as he continued to track Willa through the forest. Halfway in, he decided it was time to make his move. The thought of surprising his prey excited him and he could no longer contain the emotion.

"What the devil is a good little girl like you doing out in the middle of the woods this time of day?"

Willa jumped, shrieking as soon as the voice registered in her mind. She whirled around to face Foster, wearing a distinct look of terror. Every thought in her brain, every muscle in her body froze in immediate response. *Foster! Foster, of all people to catch me sneaking through the woods*, she told herself, not realizing he had purposely trailed her, premeditating an attack.

"What business is it of yours, Foster? Why do you care where I go?" Commanding herself to be calm, she prayed he wouldn't detect the anxiety in her voice. "I like to walk this time of the evening, if it's any concern to you."

"Do you realize that you're still a slave girl? Slaves have no business wandering around. Or is there someplace in particular you're headin'? Hmmmm...I wonder."

"No!" She answered too quickly, sounding defensive. "No, I have no place in mind. I just like to walk. Clear my mind. Not goin' anywhere. Matter of fact, I'd better get back now..."

As she began to step in his direction, she met with a pointed finger to the center of her chest. He pushed hard to fix her in place. "You sure about that nigger girl? Sure you want to go back? Don't you have someplace to be now? Going to be late for something soon, aren't you?"

He was taunting her now and it was apparent he knew something of her plans with Seth. In spite of this realization, she persisted, "No, got no place to get to. Get out of my way Foster and let me pass. Your sister might be needin' me about now."

"No, no, I don't think so. I think you're going to stay right here. There's something we need to take care of, you and me. I'm going to give you something you think you want from my fool brother. But Seth's too Nancy to give it to you. Come on now, Willa. All you black wenches can't wait to have a white boy."

"What are you talkin' about? You don't know a thing about me, Foster. Get out of my way!" She tried to get past him, but he pushed her down hard to the leafy ground where he instantaneously spread himself on top of her.

She struggled to get free from the weight of his body, but he pinned her with both of his legs on either side, sitting up to straddle her. She began to punch at him, but he grabbed both her wrists and forced them down above her head. He held her, careful not to inflict too much bodily force, involuntary images of a struggling Lilith in his head. Still, his grasp hurt and she writhed beneath him in agony.

"Let loose of me, Foster! You beast, set me free!"

"I'll do no such thing! You listen to me good, black girl! I know what you have planned with my brother. Fools! Running off to the North. Who in the world would let you live in freedom with a white boy? Who do you think cares enough about you to set you free…"

"You don't know anything, Foster! You don't know a thing!"

"Oh, but I do. I've been watching you, Willa. You and that brother of mine. I know what you plan to do tonight. And I'll just say this; you're not going anywhere now. You listen to me, girl." His eyes grew darker and wilder than Willa had ever seen them. "I control you! You do as I say, wench. By God, I've killed for lesser reasons than protecting my witless brother!"

Killed? Willa began to sense something more sinister than anything she'd ever felt, darker than what Juniper must have experienced at the end of Duke Henry's whip. Foster wanted her dead; she sensed it. She began to tremble, her body no longer under her own command.

"Don't worry my dear; I don't intend to kill you. No, I have other plans." He bent down, his face directly over hers. His hot breath smelled of spirits, giving Willa more reason to fear him. He attempted a wet, sloppy kiss, but when she refused to open her lips in compliance, he forcefully opened her mouth with his angry tongue.

She squirmed and he tightened his clutch on her wrists. "Just enjoy this, girl! Give in to me and don't fight it. You struggle and I'll make your life a living hell. Death will seem like a gift to you. And your precious Seth, too. I hear that Duke Henry thinks there've been trespassers hiding in the old storehouse. Said he'll shoot to kill if he catches them. What a pity it would be for Seth to have an unfortunate accident there some time, now wouldn't it! Duke always gets the job done, Willa. All I have to do is say the word."

Foster's words pierced Willa with enough impact to render her numb. He was indeed too powerful as she lay there now motionless. Her will to fight left her body stranded there in the darkening woods while her enemy continued kissing her face, tasting her with his angry lips, working his way down her neck. He understood her immobility as compliance. He had struck the proper nerve. Releasing pressure on her wrists, his hands slid down her body, feeling her curves, pawing at her clothes.

Other than the wicked act of his intentions, no further violence was required on his part. Unlike Lilith's nightmare with Foster, Willa was aberrantly still. She lay silent while he proceeded with the ultimate act of aggression against her womanhood. Separated from her body, her consciousness hovered somewhere in the highest tree as the scene played out below her.

She heard a hoot owl on a branch nearby, but her mind's eyes refused to seek out the creature. She continued to watch below as Foster pulled up the skirts of his victim, slid down her undergarments. As he unbuckled his britches, she knew what was about to happen. He would take from her something precious that was not his to take.

"Ahhh…Willa, that's right. No need to fight me, is there? I knew you wanted me from the start. Settling for my brother, you fool. What were you thinking, girl?" She heard his words, but no longer felt his breath on her as he spoke. She was helpless, unable to acknowledge him in any way. No screaming for help, no squirming for release.

When he was satisfied with his embezzlement of her innocence, he stood up and dispassionately secured his clothing. Calm, cool, as if he raped women on a regular basis and gave it no thought.

"There. Judging by your silence, I must assume that you enjoyed that, my little lover. You may take leave now, but you may wish to straighten out your skirts. Wouldn't want Seth to think you've been tossing about with someone in the woods, would you?" The laughter that followed seemed to pierce the forest, sounding as demonic as he intended it.

Then he left her there, all alone in the quickening dark. She did not feel the ill effects of her tormentor's actions until she returned to her body several minutes later. The night air was turning chilly but she didn't notice, too focused on the stinging physical pain and the turmoil coursing through her soul. As her mind began to recall exactly what happened there under the trees, she began to weep softly, quietly.

She rolled over, holding her abdomen as if she could control the waves of nausea that threatened her. Finally giving in, she sat up and wretched in violent spasms until her stomach emptied of all content. She became silent, curling herself into a ball, making herself as small as she could as if in doing so, she might disappear into the forest floor. What was to be a glorious day for Willa ended before it ever began.

Chapter 31

Seth paced the earthen floor of the abandoned storehouse, wishing that time would match the breakneck speed of his heartbeat, bringing Willa to him and hastening their departure. He earlier chose not to spend his last day at Heavenly making silent goodbyes, instead venturing out to the slave cabins, meeting the missionaries, and discussing their secret plans. He arrived at the storehouse too early, but it did not matter to him. He was too keyed up to be anywhere else, useless to do anything but wait out the time.

He pulled out the pocket watch that once belonged to Grandfather Witherell and was dismayed that only five minutes had elapsed since his last look. He managed to pack a few provisions for the journey that included cornbread, dried meats, and biscuits from the kitchen of Heavenly. His stomach was beginning to grumble in demand of a meal, but he hated the thought of eating already from the supplies which would help Willa and him survive. "Should have gone back to the house for one more meal", he commented out loud to the empty walls of the outbuilding.

Nearing sundown, the anticipation was unbearable as Seth stepped outside and scanned the landscape for his first sight of Willa. Sundown came and went. In the distance, the woods drew darkness in spite of the full moon illuminating the night sky. He knew that Willa would have to pass through those woods to get to him and the thought of her walking through them in the blackness set his nerves on end. He held his watch up to the moonlight and observed the advancing hour, growing more concerned. Should he leave and canvass the woods for her? What if Lazarus and the missionaries came to the shed in his absence and figured he'd changed his mind? What if Willa changed her mind? He knew she was hesitant to leave Heddie, but she assured him she could do it. He decided to wait a bit longer.

At the prearranged time, Lazarus appeared with the evangelists and their wagons. Still no Willa. As the lead wagon pulled up, Lazarus jumped down from the driver's seat. He greeted his friend and master with outstretched arms, but was met with no response. Seth's worried face told him there was trouble.

"Seth, what is it? What's wrong?"

"It's Willa, Laz. She's not here. She never showed." There was a ring of hopelessness to his voice, as if he'd begun to accept the probability that she decided not to leave Heavenly.

"Aw, Seth, I'm sure she be here soon. Maybe she got held up with Marianne. You know how those girls can be. That's gotta be the case."

"Maybe she's changed her mind, Laz. She's decided not to leave with me. She knows how risky this is and I've scared her."

Lazarus put his hands on Seth's shoulders and looked into his eyes. Part of him wanted Willa to have changed her mind about Seth, but the rest of him knew he needed to reassure his master. "No, Seth. She sure loves you. You know that."

"But does she love me this much? Enough to risk everything for me when she'd be better off without me? She should have fallen in love with you, Laz."

"Stop that talk, Seth. You the only one she loves that way. She don't want me."

Just then a tall, rakish man hopped down from the second covered wagon and stepped up to address Seth. "Mr. Witherell, we will need to be setting out soon if we are to keep to our scheduled plans. Is there a problem?"

"It's Willa. She is running behind, I believe. Can we wait just a bit longer, sir?"

"I can give you 30 minutes, son. That will be all. We do have another soul to gather up on the journey yet tonight and if we are too late, we will miss our opportunity. You understand our need to adhere to the schedule, don't you? In the pursuit of saving slaves, we must not tarry and risk detection."

"Yes, sir. I understand your urgency and I thank you for your concern to our plight, truly. I am just going into those woods over there to seek Willa. I fear she may have gotten lost, sir. It is an awfully dark thicket once the sun sets. We shall not be long." Turning to Lazarus, he instructed the slave to light a lantern and accompany him into the woodland.

Soon they picked their way through the timbers, swinging the lantern for illumination, both calling out for Willa. Unknown to them, she had recently collected herself and shambled back toward Heavenly. She was well out of earshot when the woods echoed with her name.

Over twenty minutes later, the search garnered no results, leaving both Seth and Lazarus winded and hoarse. Defeated and hungry, Seth collapsed to the ground. He was too stunned to cry, too disappointed to move. "I cannot believe it, Laz. How could she do this to me? We had plans, Laz. Plans. It was our chance. We may never have this chance again."

"I'm so sorry, Seth. I don't know nothin' else to say."

"Suppose we should hike back and tell the missionaries they've no reason to wait any longer," Seth finally conceded.

"No, Seth. You stay here and I'll go back there. And I'll gather up your things, meet you right back here. You just rest."

"Sure," he resigned, but as Lazarus turned to begin his trip back to the shed, he added, "Laz? Why don't you just go with the evangelists? Get away from Heavenly; get your freedom, my friend. Let something good come of our plans."

Stunned by his master's suggestion, Lazarus paused as if considering then quickly replied, "No, Seth. My place is with you at Heavenly. I got no ambitions 'bout freedom. Heavenly been good to me. Wait here and we go back together."

And that was it. The missionaries continued on to their destination, doing the Lord's work in public and aiding slaves to Northern freedom in secret. The window of escape for Willa and Seth was officially closed.

Chapter 32

As the boys made their way home, Willa was already at the plantation house. She stole quietly inside, making sure she had no witnesses as she crept up the back staircase en route to her sleeping quarters. Her hands tore at her clothing the second she stepped into the room and shut her door. The garments were cast off as if they were suddenly on fire, hurled to the floor in a hateful pile.

Willa rushed to fill her chipped porcelain wash basin with water from a pitcher, not realizing how much of the liquid missed the bowl and dripped to the floor. She dipped a cloth into the water, put it to her face, and began to scrub. She thought of Foster's liquor-infused breath upon her and it made her wince. She dipped into the water again, and then worked the cloth over her body as if she could scour away the memory of his touch, his scent, his filthy violation of her. She was still in pain, still aching from what he did to her.

Her thoughts shifted to Seth and the realization that she failed to meet him for their departure. There was no chance the missionaries would allow him to wait long and by now he had surely given up. Guilt and shame began flooding her soul, drowning her heart. She felt like all the tears she'd ever owned were cried back in the forest. But now there were more spilling down her face.

Willa backed over to the wall nearest her bed and slid down to the hardwood floor. The tears continued and she wondered if Seth was crying as well. She wondered if he would ever be able to forgive her for allowing Foster to overcome her in the woods. She wondered why she didn't fight him off and try harder to get free.

An unexpected knock at the bedroom door interrupted her deliberations. She gasped and then held her breath. Was it Seth wanting an explanation? Willa remained silent as another knock sounded like thunder to her ears. She dared not move. Another knock, followed by, "Willa? Honey, you in there?" It was Heddie.

Suddenly aware that she would indeed see Heddie again, a sense of happiness made Willa leap off the floor and run over to the door. She was just about to throw it open when she realized she was not wearing clothes. "Mama! I'm here! Just a moment mama, I'm changin' into my night clothes."

Quickly she reached into her wardrobe to retrieve a plain cotton sleep gown. She stepped into it, opening the door at nearly the same time.

"Mama!" She reached for Heddie and pulled her close into her arms. Then she buried her face into her mother's chest.

"Girl! What be the matter with you? My lands! You act like you so excited to see me."

"Oh, mama. I'm so blessed by the Lord to have a mama like you, that's all."

"You been actin' strange, girl. All day long. I just come to see if you was alright and now I know you ain't. Must be the full moon, I declare, girl! You just keep on lovin' on mama, that's fine."

If only she could tell Heddie the truth about what just happened to her innocence. But Willa was sure such knowledge would put her mother into an early grave. She hated Foster all the more because his sin also affected her mama. As she held Heddie, she wished to return to the child she was when they first arrived at Heavenly Plantation. That child was now a million worlds away, thanks to Foster.

Chapter 33

Seth's first order of business back at the plantation house was to be sure Willa made it home safely. He could forgive himself for forcing his bold plans upon her only if she was unharmed, only if she had not come to some danger. He would question her tomorrow about her feelings, but he had to be sure she was accounted for in the house. Unable to confront her yet himself, he conspired to send another female up to her sleeping quarters and was relieved to find Chloe in the downstairs parlor snuffing out lamps as the family retired to other rooms.

"I am a bit worried about Willa, Chloe. We were to meet and share an early moonlight walk with Lazarus and she did not show. She may have come down with some affliction, I fear. Would you please go to her room to see if she is present and feeling well? I would go myself, but I don't think it would be proper."

"Oh of course I will, Master Seth. No trouble upon Chloe. You wait right here and I be back in a wink." With that, the slave woman was gone, heading up the staircase. Several minutes later, she returned with the news of Willa's condition.

"Master, she's with her mammy Heddie and you is right about her not feelin' well. She's took to a sniffle and turnin' in early. I 'magine she'll be alright tomorrow if her mammy have anythin' to do with it. She's always good at comfortin' that girl, I say."

"Thank you, Chloe. Thank you for checking on her." He was relieved to know she was inside the house, but strangely unsettled at the same time. Why did she not meet him and at least admit to changing her mind about their plans? How could she be this cold, knowing he would worry, knowing he would be hurt? Perhaps he didn't know her true feelings that well after all. Maybe she didn't love him the way he loved her, enough to forego his comfortable life and wealth to take her away to freedom.

His head began to ache, rivaling the anguish he felt in his heart. He felt weak, wobbly, nauseated. The climb up the stairs to his room was unbearable as he grasped the handrails and held on, pulling himself along. The voice in his head enlightened him. *This must be how it feels to be deathly ill. Nothing to hope for. Only ravaging pain.*

Finally reaching his bed, he climbed in beneath the quilts and fell into a deep, soul-satisfying sleep. Meanwhile in another wing of the great house, Willa's slumber was fraught with hateful dreams and worry.

Visions of Foster haunted her. He towered over her, heaped on top of her, tore at her clothing, thrust himself into her, and filled her with his lusty anger. Again and again. She awaken bathed in perspiration, heart racing like an unbridled thoroughbred. She would sit up, wrap her arms around her chest as if she could will the organ to be tamed. Eventually she would sleep again only to repeat the process. And each time, her nightmare served to cultivate the intensity of her hatred for Foster.

Morning left Willa exhausted and filled with dread and fear of facing Seth. A knock on her door made her sit up in alarm and she sheepishly answered, "Wh…who is there?"

"It's me…Marianne! Willa?"

"Just a moment, Marianne." She got out of bed and ambled toward the door, but suddenly felt entirely naked in the thin old nightgown she wore. How would she manage herself when people looked at her now? Would she feel this bare even when fully clothed? Had Foster stripped away everything, not just her innocence? She pulled a thick woolen blanket around her shoulders in an attempt to banish such thoughts. Then she opened the door to her friend.

"You are sleeping late today, my dear!"

"I am? What time is it, Marianne? I'm so sorry. Are you in need of something? Am I late for…"

"Settle down, girl. It's not that late, but past breakfast. No, you are not late for anything and no, I don't need anything from you. I was just worried when you did not come downstairs. Are you feeling well? Chloe said you were not yourself last evening when she checked on you."

"No," she lied, "I'm just fine, Marianne. Just fine. Worn out, I suppose. Too much sewing work lately."

"Oh. If that's the case then, you have to lighten up and get out of this house. Let's do something today. I fear I've spent so much time with Gerald that I've neglected my dear friend. What would you like to do?"

"No, really, I'm fine and don't you change your plans for me. I'm good here with my sewing, you know I love it. I want to finish some of the gowns I've started for you, for your trousseau. You know that."

"Hogwash, Willa. You need to take some time out for yourself. We need to have some enjoyment. Why don't we go into Charleston and take in some sights? I'll just see if Foster can…"

The sound of her tormenter's name sent a sharp sting down the full length of Willa's spine as she involuntarily began to tremble. Her voice rang a terrifying alarm, "No! No! Please, Marianne, just go!"

"Willa! What is it?" Marianne's light mood turned to panic. She grasped Willa's hands and held on, trying to calm the voracious shaking. "What is it, honey? You act as if you've seen a ghoul."

That's right, a ghoul. An accurate description of your brother! Willa wanted desperately to expose Foster, but she remained silent, looking away, refusing to meet Marianne's eyes for fear her secret would be revealed.

"Willa, say something. What is the matter?"

"N…nothing. Marianne, I feel very sick. All of a sudden…I…I cannot go with you. I…I need to lie down. I…I'm feelin' weak." Her knees became flimsy and gave way to her weight, toppling her to the floor.

"Willa! My Lord! Someone help me!" Marianne was quick to react loudly, her voice wild with distress and helplessness. She fell to Willa's side, applying light slaps to her cheeks to startle her back into consciousness.

Willa responded, just as Seth bolted in through the doorway to see his sister and his love on the floor. "What is going on here? Willa?"

Still worked up, Marianne hastily replied, "I don't know, brother! She just fell down faint like this, but she's awake now…just went out for a few seconds. My goodness, I think she is very ill, Seth!"

"Calm down, Marianne!" he commanded, refusing to give voice to his own anxiety. He knelt, slipping one of Willa's arms around his neck and pulling her up to a standing position. He motioned his sister to hold her up on the other side as they walked her back to the bed and sat her down. Gently he laid her weakened body down and pulled the quilts up around her, staring into her eyes while doing so, asking questions of her in silence.

Seth then turned his attention to Marianne, "Tell me what happened, sister. Why did she faint?"

"No reason, Seth. I must be comin' down with something, that's all. That's it, just getting' sick." Willa answered, feigning a cough, shivering slightly to pretend the discomfort of flu.

"I think that must be the case, Seth. Maybe we should send for Doc Capshaw. Truly. Before she collapsed I was only mentioning that we might do something today and suggested asking Foster to take us into Charleston. Then she went to the floor. That was it."

Foster. There was that loathsome name again. Seth clearly detected that the mention of his brother's name seemed to incite a change in Willa's demeanor as she began to tremble again. Her discomposure was not due to physical sickness at all. There was something else, something unsettling that had to do with Foster.

"Marianne, why don't you get some fresh water and a cold compress for Willa? Maybe find a servant to fix her a bite to eat? Please?"

"Sure, Seth. Alright Willa, I'll be back soon, honey." She kissed the forehead of her ill companion, disregarding its lack of feverish warmth, and charted a course downstairs.

Seth moved to shut the door and then returned to sit on the edge of the bed. Speaking in a forceful whisper, he began, "Willa, tell me what is going on in that head of yours. I saw the look on your face when Marianne mentioned Foster. Is he the reason you did not meet me last night? What happened, Willa? Tell me the truth."

Tears welled up in her eyes. She attempted to look away from Seth, wanting to purchase time enough to halt the emotions. But it was useless. Seth aimed her face back to his and searched two teary eyes, waiting for an answer.

"Seth, I changed my mind", she whispered in reply, "It's just too dangerous, what we were fixin' to do. I can't leave my mama here. I couldn't pretend to be brave anymore. As for Foster", she swallowed hard to help steel herself for the lie, "he's got nothing to do with it. You know how I feel about him. He knows about us and when Marianne talked about us goin' to Charleston with him, well…it was all I could to do keep from falling apart. That's all. What would you expect me to do? And it's true that I'm not feelin' all that well. Kind of sick, I think. I just need to be left alone."

"Of course I understand how you feel about Foster. My own brother makes my skin crawl, too! But I need to be sure that he had nothing to do with you not wanting to be with me. Tell me that's the case, Willa."

"Yes, Seth. He has nothing to do with it." She wondered if he could see the deceit in her eyes, hear it in her voice.

He must have accepted her answer, as he began to re-focus. "How could you change your mind, Willa? Don't you love me enough? I don't understand. We've discussed this, us leaving, your mama, all of it. A hundred times. You were fine until now. What changed you? I don't understand it!"

"Oh Seth, please don't question my love. You know how I feel. It's just that we are both caught up in something that can never be. Even in another place, nobody will accept us, not like we want them to. We'd have to hide our love wherever we go. I can't do that anymore Seth. We need to end this. I'm so sorry…"

"No, Willa. No. We were made by God to be together. You can't give up on us. You just can't!" His own eyes filled with tears as he bent over and began kissing her, boldly unafraid of being detected.

"Seth, stop it! Stop it!" Willa became angered, hands flying up to ward off the kisses, pushing his face away. "Just stop it!" Her mind flashed to Foster's hot, dangerous lips on hers, his disgusting tongue forced on her.

Stunned, Seth pulled back, hurt and humiliation reflected on his face. He wiped at his eyes with the back of his shirtsleeve, trying to regain composure. "What do you want, Willa?"

"Seth, I want to be your friend. I'm not good enough for you to love any other way. You need to find someone your own color, your own kind. You need to leave me alone now. I cannot love you in return, Seth. It has to be this way. Go on. Leave me alone."

It took every ounce of courage, every measure of control to lie to Seth, but it was done. Willa was damaged and he deserved better. As soon as he closed her bedroom door behind him, she knew it was truly over and that Foster had won.

Chapter 34

Over the next several months, Willa's relationship with the Witherells became less familiar. She avoided Seth altogether, afraid she would give in to his love. Instead, she wanted him to resume a life without her. She convinced herself that it was for his own good; he needed to keep company with girls from his own race, his own social class. Girls who were marriageable. Marianne did not even seem to miss her companionship, as Gerald was the center of her world. Willa was also able to stay clear of Foster. He made no other attempt to assault her, as if that one horrible rape satisfied him, extinguishing his lust. The dark, evil secret they shared would remain buried within her and nobody would know her vast shame.

She was growing into her role as a servant, much as expected in Southern households where young slave children were raised with their white counterparts. There was always a period of delineation, where both sides weaned from their former childish relationships. White children would assume command while their black friends would learn subservience. No longer would they look upon each other as equals. Willa became as dutiful as she could, tending even to the needs of Margaret whenever possible.

In those months following the failed attempt to leave Heavenly, Willa also acquired a ravenous appetite. At first she was grateful, as her hunger effectively replaced the desire for Seth's love. But while she didn't seem to gain much weight in proportion to her consumption, there were other changes in her body that caused alarm. She began to realize that something else was at work. Deep within her belly, something craved nutrition, longed for life.

She was pregnant with Foster's child. The thought, when first it struck her, sent her into spasms of nausea. Her abdomen ached as if she had been poisoned, as indeed she felt she had. She wanted to lash out, seek vengeance, and make Foster pay for this tangible manifestation of his sin. The thing inside her was grotesque, dark, unholy.

As the weeks passed however, the repulsive circumstances of her pregnancy were abated by unmistaken maternal feelings. Reasoning that her offspring was a legacy to her parents, she thought less of it as Foster's spawn. It would be a part of herself and her family alone. That seemed to give her comfort and a new sense of hope for her future; a future that she knew could not include Seth.

Still, she felt increasingly lonely now that Marianne was so busy and Seth so distant. Feelings of restlessness overtook any resolution she felt, especially when she considered how difficult it was going to be explaining her condition once her belly began to show. There was only one person she could trust with her secret, one who would be willing to offer a sympathetic ear and possibly some advice.

***

"Hello, Mr. Blacksmith," Willa teased Lazarus as he stopped a hammer mid-swing and looked up at her. "Oh, please don't stop. You have work to do. I just need a word with you when you have a moment."

Lazarus smiled at her, returning focus to a metal piece on the anvil. Holding it with tongs he skillfully aimed his cross-peen hammer and pounded away until he had fashioned a new, gleaming tool. Then he lifted it with the tongs and dipped it into the slack tub filled with cooling water. He looked to Willa with another smile; quickly he'd become a master at his craft and was awfully proud of it.

She grinned, amazed at his skills, yet ashamed of herself for what she was about to ask him to do for her. He wiped his hands on his already-grimy apron and motioned for her to follow him to the side of the outbuilding where they both sat on makeshift stools crafted from tree stumps.

"A word, huh? Guess that's a might better than most get from ya these days, Willa girl!" He snickered, patting her on the arm.

"And just what do you mean by that, Laz?"

"Oh, I just hear from Seth that you all but cut him outta your life. Not speakin' to him and all, that just ain't right, girl."

"You don't know a thing, Laz! It's no business of yours anyhow!" Her words came out louder than she intended, making her sound angry with him.

"Now you wait a minute, missy. Don't you yell at me. I'm your friend, remember?"

Willa lowered her voice to continue, "Listen, I didn't come out here to fight with you, Laz. What I have to ask you ain't easy for me." Then she took a deep breath as if sucking in courage and began, "Laz I'm in some trouble and I can't tell a soul but you. Not my mama, not Marianne, and especially not Seth."

"What? What you gone and done?" His brow furrowed with great concern.

There was no way to relate her dilemma without simply putting it out as quickly as possible. She glanced around to verify their seclusion and then leaned in close to speak in a hushed tone, "Laz, I'm havin' a baby and I need your help."

There it was. The news clung to his ears, rang in his head, but words stuck in his throat as he tried to respond. "Y…you…wha…what? How…who…?"

Placing one finger to Lazarus' lips, she signaled for his silence and repeated, "I need your help." She looked deeply into his eyes now, making certain that her news had truly registered with him.

"I've managed to hide my condition as best I can. Haven't put on much weight, but imagine that'll change soon. Then there ain't no way I'll be able to hide it. But I have a plan." She took his hands into hers and moved in even closer. "You know I love you Laz. As a good friend. And there ain't nothin' I wouldn't do for you. You love me too, and I know you'd like it to be more than friends. Even though you were willin' to help me run off with Seth. That's some kinda love, you know." She smiled broadly at him with pride in her eyes, followed by tears.

"Oh, Willa. You know I love you and I wish things could be different for us. But I understand how you want Seth. Now you have his baby. I…I can't believe it, girl. You in deep now I 'spect and…"

"No, Laz! This baby's not his. That's why I need your help. We gotta say it's your baby. We can be a family now. You and me and this here…" She paused, swallowed the lump in her throat and patted her abdomen. "This baby."

Lazarus looked at her in amazement, not knowing if she was offering a gift or a burden, fearing it was both. His eyes dropped to her tummy where he could see a definite bump. Instinctively he placed one of his hands over the bump, gently moving it in a circle, feeling the roundness. He imagined the child with Willa's eyes and it warmed his heart.

"I know this is a lot to ask of you. Seth will be hurt, awfully hurt. To think that his best friend and I were…were…" She couldn't say the words. "Well, you know…having an affair. Behind his back. He will hate us both, Laz." Willa hung her head low and began to sob softly.

Lazarus took her in his arms and her sobs became more pronounced. His embrace gave unspoken permission for her to release the pent emotions that she shared with no one. The past months of loneliness melted. He had questions, but knew he needed to let her continue to have a cathartic cry first.

When Willa lifted her face to him, her eyes were swollen and red. Lazarus wondered how long it had been since she shed so many tears and silently prayed that she never would feel the need to cry again. He waited for her to speak first.

"Will you help me, Laz? I know it's a mighty lot to ask. We can be happy. I can be a good wife to you and we can make a life for this child." In her mind she rationalized that in time she could grow to love him as she loved Seth. In time.

"Willa, Willa…of course I'll help you. You know that havin' you as my wife would be a dream come true for me, girl. But I know it's not your dream. Can you live with that? Can you?"

"I would never ask if I didn't think I could, Laz."

"But what about Seth? I never did believe you just stopped lovin' him because you were afraid to run off. Seth is mighty hurt thinkin' that and now we goin' to go make him think we been together and made this baby? He's my friend, Willa. And my master. He's goin' be furious!"

"Seth is a reasonable man. We'll just have to convince him that after that…night…that night…" she paused, mentally fighting back images of the horrors contained within the memory of that fateful evening, "that night we planned to run…I decided there was some attraction between us. That's why I couldn't go through with it, why I had to stay. I had to stay and figure out who I loved. And it was you. And you comforted me and we continued to meet in secret. And we got so carried away that we…that we…"

"Made your baby."

"Yes. Our baby." Emotion once more welled up inside and spilled. "Our baby."

Lazarus took her in his arms, wishing it were all true, thinking that if they both recited what she'd planned in her head that maybe it would really seem true. But his mind was plagued with a natural question that begged to be asked of her.

"Willa, who did this to you? Did somethin' bad happen or is there someone else you've fallen for that you can't be with either?"

She pulled away from Lazarus and looked directly into his eyes so he saw both the shame and great pain in hers. Then he knew that someone had taken her against her will, violated her. His first instinct was correct. "Foster? Was it him? Oh, God Willa! It was, wasn't it? That no good, cowardly…"

"Just stop, Lazarus! Just stop!" The mention of his vile name and the revelation of her secret was abhorrent to her. "You can never tell another soul! Never! This will be our secret, Laz. It has to be! Seth will never know. Never!" She became frantic, insistent. "You have to promise not to tell! He needs to believe that we did this. That this baby was made because of our love. Not because of Foster's hatred…violence…"

"Willa, Willa. You have to settle down. Think about your little baby now. Settle, girl." His arms wrapped completely around her frame, effectively calming her, quieting her.

Soon she proceeded by confiding in him, revealing the truth about the night that changed the course of her life forever. He listened intently although seething inside, longing to take hold of Foster and make him pay for the atrocity he'd bestowed upon gentle Willa. After she was finished, he vowed to keep the unholy secret, knowing that Seth would lose his mind upon its discovery and there would be no way to stop him from killing his own brother.

Chapter 35: Marianne's Journal, January 1852

"Dear Journal, if there is anything of which I am certain these days, it is that I am no fine judge of people! I have known my best friend Willa nearly all my life and I thought I knew her well. As it turns out, I don't. Not lately. Something is strangely amiss and I am ill equipped to understand it.

I was understandably a bit upset when she refused to confide in me about her feelings for Lazarus. She simply glowed and bubbled over in love with him. But she denied it. Why would my good friend deny my sharing in her happiness?

But over the past few months, it seems as if she is inside out. That air of bliss no longer surrounds her, so I assume she and Laz had some falling out. But she will not say. She avoids me, actually. And Seth. Sewing seems to be the sole purpose of her life, now. She has fashioned the most wonderful gowns for me! There is no end to her talent with the needle and fabric. But to be perfectly truthful, I'd gladly trade all my new gowns for a few minutes of honesty from Willa.

Even the Christmas holidays held no joy for Willa this year. Typically she becomes giddy at the very start of December and by Christmas Eve she cannot contain her excitement for trimming the evergreen tree. She had no interest in the tree, the decorations, the sugar candies.

All the plans I've entertained for so long regarding our intertwining futures seem doomed. If she cannot share her feelings with me, how can we remain best friends? She regards me in the same way Chloe and Myra, and the other servants regard Mother. But I am not my mother. I am Marianne, her childhood friend. Our relationship as slave and mistress is one forced upon us, a relationship chosen by neither of us. Nor have I ever treated her as my slave. True, she is always helpful to me, but as a friend and not my servant Unless we have to behave that way in front of Mother and Father, and their guests of course. What am I to do? She is so distant.

Seth spends more time with his studies now. I suppose it is high time he started being more responsible and ended with his childhood. He and Lazarus are still bonded together in friendship, unlike Willa and me. I should like to see Seth occupying his time with the ladies, but am sure those days are close!

Mother and Father are doing well, not mixing in disagreeable ways lately, which is good for us all. Foster continues to take on more duties around the plantation and runs many operations in Charleston. There was some distressing talk about him and an undesirable woman in Charleston a while ago. The woman was killed and Foster was questioned because he was an acquaintance. Now, I am not so innocent that I do not understand the nature of his relationship with the girl. He is a grown man and I hear enough talk to know there are places in the city where men such as he congregate and do manly things. But the question of his character in regard to acts of violence? That is pure rubbish! My Foster would never hurt anyone!"

Chapter 36

The dubious task of relating their deceitful plans to Seth was shouldered by Lazarus and not Willa. At least in the beginning. There was no gentle way to tell him, no way to avoid ripping out his heart and throwing it to mad dogs. Seth was almost coming to terms with the notion that Willa was simply too afraid to continue loving him, although his brain was constantly searching for ways to get her to change her mind. He knew she still loved him and that nothing could change that, at least until Lazarus corrected him.

It was a chilly afternoon in late winter. Daniel was scheduled to drive Foster into Charleston to greet an important business acquaintance of Josiah's and accompany the man back to Heavenly. A team of horses was assembled and lashed up to the finest Witherell carriage in an impressive display meant to showcase family wealth and importance. Only one element of the show remained to be placed. Foster. Soon it was determined that he never returned from Charleston the night before, with whiskey the assumed culprit.

Standing in for his increasingly negligent brother was Seth, the perfect young gentleman with man-servant Lazarus by his side. As far as Josiah was concerned, it was time Seth learned a bit of business before sending him off to school, especially in light of Foster's shenanigans that increasingly fueled town gossip.

For Lazarus, this was an opportune time to discuss Willa while they were far from the plantation. There might be questions, confusion, even anger, but unlike Foster, Seth would not disappoint his family with unruly behavior. The return trip to Heavenly would be forcibly civil on account of the visitor and the necessity to maintain the Witherell image. Lazarus could not have planned it any better himself.

Daniel insisted the young men sit in the carriage to keep warm rather than ride atop with him. For that, Lazarus was grateful. Tell Seth before they get into the city, before picking up their passenger, allowing a cushion of time between revelation and his duty to be gracious. As they rode along in comfort, they occupied themselves with meaningless conversation. Seth avoided any reference to Willa, as was customary over the past several months. But soon Lazarus knew he had to take charge and flip the conversation to the inevitable.

"There's somethin' that I have to say to you, Seth. And you ain't goin' to like it. I figure you goin' to find out soon enough."

Sensing the sudden shift in the tone of his servant's voice, Seth leaned forward with interest. "What is it, Laz? You look worried."

"There ain't no easy way to say this, but…I guess I'm just goin' to say it. Seth…me and Willa…we…uhhh…" he stammered, apprehension gipping like icy fingers and altering his speech. He felt exposed and suddenly doubted his ability to lie to his best friend. He felt his temperature rise quickly, his heart beat racing in opposition to the task at hand.

"What is the matter with you? I've never seen you behave like this before, Laz. Are you in some kind of trouble? How can I help you?"

"You could say that. Not exactly trouble, but close enough. What I'm 'bout to tell ya will prob'ly put an end to our friendship, Seth. I'm so sorry, so sorry…" Lazarus looked down at his feet as if there were answers written on the floorboard of the carriage that he could simply read.

"What? What could be that bad? Don't you know by now that we'll always be friends, no matter what?"

"It's Willa. Willa and I are goin' to be married soon, Seth. We are goin' to have a baby." His eyes flashed to his master's for a split second to see reaction and them shot back down to study the floor. Shame mixed with relief now that the words were out, hanging in the airspace between them.

"What did you say? Are you mad, Laz? Why would you say that? How could you say somethin' like that?" His voice grew louder with each question. "Why would Willa marry you, Laz, when she loves me? Don't you know she's just confused and afraid now?"

The rest of the fabricated story had to be told before Seth lost complete control. Lazarus took a deep, bolstering breath and forced his eyes to look into Seth's. "It's true and I'm so sorry. I have to tell ya what's happened. We sure didn't start it out like this, Willa fallin' for me. You know that, Seth. She loved you, sure enough. She still do. But she have to be able to live at Heavenly. She loves her mamma too much to go up north and leave her. And she can't be lovin' you like a husband. You know that."

"No, you got it all wrong. She wants to be with me. She just needs time, Laz. She wants to be with me and have a life and…"

"I'm sorry Seth. We got a baby on the way. We goin' be a family now and that's that."

As if news of the baby was mentioned for the first time, Seth took hold of Lazarus' shoulders and looked directly into his face with complete surprise. "What in the world are you sayin'? You and Willa? She would never lay down with you! She loves me! How could you do this to her? You forced yourself on Willa? Who the hell do you think you are, Lazarus? I thought you were my friend!"

Suddenly his grip loosened and both hands slid down Lazarus' arms until he broke completely free from his servant. His entire frame crumpled in his carriage seat as realization set in. His best friend and his love, an affair, an unborn child. Tears filled his eyes and embarrassed him, challenging his manhood as he wiped them away with a fancy jacket sleeve. He looked away, shielding himself for the first time from the only male he'd ever confided in. His best friend.

The sight of Seth's tears brought an inconsolable sadness to Lazarus as their friendship was tossed away by deceit. He gave Seth some time to compose as much as was possible considering the gravity of the news. When he was certain that Seth could hear more, he resumed his explanatory tale.

"We really don't mean to hurt you, Seth. After that night, the night Willa didn't show, she started talkin' to me. She knew she done broke your heart, but she couldn't leave Heddie. She loved you but can't do what you want. The more she talked to me, the closer friends we got to be. She told me she had feelin's for me too, always had. She said she was real confused 'bout who she really wanted to be with, too. Said she never told you 'cause you had such big plans. She thought she could go with you and forget 'bout me. She was real confused and real sad 'bout it all."

"One time we talked so much that she started cryin' and couldn't stop. I held on to her and told her I'd give her time to decide. She said she had to forget you, 'cause it never would work out. We kissed and then the rest of it just happened. We…"

"I don't want to hear it, Laz! Damn you! How could you do this to me? You were my friend!"

Seth raised his voice again, this time so loud that Daniel pulled hard on his leather reins, signaling the horses to halt. Alarmed, he quickly dismounted, approached the carriage door, and pulled it open to survey the cause of the noise. "What is goin' on in here, you two? Everything alright?"

"No, Daniel. You will have to take that up with your son. As a matter of fact, maybe he should ride on top with you. He has some news, if you don't know it already. Or maybe you do. Maybe everyone does except for me until now."

Lazarus brushed by a baffled Daniel on his way out through the carriage door. "We be talkin' later, Seth. Let's get this cart movin', Pappy."

"You okay, son? You two have a fallin' out? Do I need to give my boy a talkin' to?"

"Not to worry, Daniel. We best keep on schedule into Charleston."

"Yes, sir. We be in good shape. Be there soon enough, Master Witherell."

Seth cried quietly now that he was alone, pleading with God to let this be no more than a bad dream. When the tears finally ceased, he knew he had to come to terms with what was revealed to him. Willa was no longer his to lose. There would be no more waiting for her, she made her decision and she solidified it when she created a child with Lazarus.

Chapter 37

Upon arrival at the plantation, Seth silently questioned why anyone would name it Heavenly. Did his ancestors know some key secret to happiness that they failed to share with their offspring? As the carriage made its way under the thick canopy of moss-draped oaks that lined the drive past the gates of Heavenly, Seth did not feel their usual welcome. He felt cold, disillusioned. Disappointed in Lazarus, in Willa, in himself for letting her have the liberty he thought she needed to recover following their miscarried plans for escape.

The ride back was quiet enough for Seth to reflect, with his father's guest distracted by paperwork after the small talk between them was rapidly exhausted. Seth had no true interest in the family business, always keeping his future life with Willa at the forefront of his mind. Until a few hours earlier, that is. Now he wondered what his life would become. His thoughts now centered on what to say to the woman he loved and assumed would return his love again once the fear caused by the notion of running away subsided.

Lazarus was dutifully at his father's side atop the driver's seat of the carriage, as customary and proper for a manservant. A slave. Seth never considered his friend a slave, but rather a companion who assisted him when his duties as apprentice blacksmith were completed each day. In payment, Lazarus had Seth's total respect and admiration for being such a loyal friend. Where had that respect gotten him? Lazarus seduced his Willa while his back was turned. Willa was carrying his best friend's child instead of his. Unwilling to return love to Seth in that most intimate way, she apparently gave herself freely to Lazarus.

***

Daniel guided the carriage to the entrance of the mansion, urging the horses to stop as Lazarus sprang up from his seat and dismounted. He obediently opened the door to the compartment and poked his head in, bowing low in subservience. "Gentlemen, we have arrived." With a glance toward the guest, he offered his hand, "Sir, I'd be happy to help you out of this carriage." The guest accepted as Lazarus led him down the few steps to the ground where Daniel joined them.

Quickly Lazarus took to his task of offloading the man's luggage, ignoring Seth. He followed Daniel as he escorted the guest to the front door. Soon Daniel returned alone, leaving his son in the house to tend to the man's belongings. Seth was just exiting the carriage when he caught Daniel's eye.

"Come on up here son," the old man urged, climbing aboard and patting the seat next to him. Seth obeyed.

"Now I know what you and Laz were talkin' about on the way into town. He told me. Hope you don't mind, seein' as he's my boy." Seth nodded, head down low. "Why I had no idea you even fancied Miss Willa! That kinda thing don't happen too much around Heavenly, not that I know of. I know there be talk of your daddy and…" He stopped short of finishing his sentence, realizing he had crossed a forbidden line.

"You know he don't mean to cause any pain to you, son. He love you like a brother. What happen between him and Willa took the two of 'em. She musta fell in love with him, too. Could be she love you both, but knew it would never work with you, Seth. You're a fine young man. A white man. She got no business with you. Your mama, now she would just have a fit and die if you run off like you planned and…"

"Daniel! That's enough! You will never utter another word of this to me. Or anyone else. It's over. You would be wise to concentrate on your duties. Get these horses back." Seth slid off the seat and jumped down. He was neither angry nor upset with Daniel. He was simply numb. Before he strode away, he turned to look back at the old man. "Congratulations, Daniel. You will be an excellent grandfather." He meant his words, but felt a flicker of pain in the realization that he would never say that to his own father.

Seth knew what lie ahead. He needed to talk to Willa, although he wanted to hide and never again have to face her. Better to do it now while he still felt empty inside, before he got the chance to think over all of the words Lazarus had spoken to him, before even more anger was allowed to creep in and make him ugly. His knees felt weak and he wondered if he would be able to look her in the eyes. Her eyes used to hold such delight, used to look at him with such passion and love. Would they be different now? Did she save that look only for Lazarus now? He had to know.

***

Willa was easy enough to find. The door to her room was slightly ajar allowing him to see her inside, sitting at her beloved Singer treadle sewing machine, a gift from Marianne. It was there that Seth knew she created beauty from yards of plain, lifeless fabric. Every piece of cloth the woman touched was transformed into something special. Seth cared nothing for women's fashion, but understood that each garment Willa created was embedded with love. He knew that his sister glowed when she wore those dresses, as if made by the hands of an angel. He could not help himself, just standing there in silence and watching the woman he loved at her craft. She hummed like a songbird, unaware of his eyes upon her. She seemed content and for a moment Seth daydreamed about the kind of mother she would be to their children.

And then he snapped back into reality, releasing an unintentional sigh. Willa turned toward him, a look of terror on her face and let out a howl.

"Seth! You nearly scare the life out o' me! What are you doin' there?"

"Just watching you work. That's all. Didn't mean to frighten you, Willa. I'm sorry."

She turned back around to face her cherished machine, carefully rotating the balance wheel toward her, sinking the sewing needle into an expanse of check-patterned cotton. Her feet began a rhythmic pumping on the treadle as she continued with her work, disregarding Seth's intrusion.

"Willa, I must speak with you. Now." There was an unmistakable strain in his voice that caused her feet to pause for a moment and then stop altogether. Slowly she swiveled around to face him.

"What is it, Seth?"

The look in her eyes was as tender as he'd ever seen and if he didn't know better, she looked as if she was still in love with him. It seemed impossible that she could feel any other way after all they had shared in secret.

"Willa, I know about you…" he stammered, finding it difficult to bring the words to his lips. "I know about you…you and Lazarus. I know what you've done."

Her eyes clouded over and filled with tears. She looked away, ashamed to face Seth now. Lazarus was bold in confronting him with the truth, sparing her the deed and paving the way for the conversation she knew was inevitable. "I…I…I can explain, Seth. I am so sorry, so sorry for what I have done. You have to believe me." She found the courage to look at him again, waiting for him to respond.

"How can you say you're sorry, Willa? You betrayed me. With my friend. You both betrayed me. How could you do that?" He suddenly wanted to shake her by the shoulders and demand an answer.

"It was a mistake. The baby. But I can't change that, Seth. We cannot take that back. We should not have let ourselves get out of control. But we are…in love. We are in love. It just happened. I was so afraid of going away with you and leaving my mama. And I knew I was wrong to love you, Seth. And Lazarus is my kind and he's such a good friend and he was there when I knew it was wrong to be with you, and…I guess I've always loved him, too. And there's nothin' wrong with us being in love. We're slaves, both black."

Willa continued to fabricate more lies about her relationship with Lazarus. It seemed to her that the more she said, the closer she was to believing it as truth. Ultimately she hoped to convince herself enough to dissolve memories of the plans she and Seth made just months earlier.

Meanwhile Seth held his head as if his skull was being split in two. But he had to hear the truth from her lips. He needed to hear her admit to loving Lazarus.

Chapter 38: Marianne's Journal, February 1852

"I am now most certain that my ability to understand people has forever abandoned me! Willa and Lazarus are expecting a child! Just when I think they've fallen out for good, I discover that they are more involved than I even imagined. She is no innocent, that Willa! What would result in great shame and scandal in my culture is faultlessly acceptable in hers, so it seems since Heddie is overwhelmed with delight. Daniel and his wife Camille simply bubble in happiness at the prospect of a grandchild!

The wedding will take place soon, so the baby will have a true family. Lazarus did the proper thing in asking both Heddie and my father for Willa's hand in marriage. There is no such thing as a legal slave marriage, of course and that disturbs me greatly. However, my friends' wedding will produce a marriage as blessed as a union can be in the eyes of God. As a child, I honestly never considered that Willa would be denied the type of wedding I expected one day for myself, but as her best friend, I shall do whatever I can to make her day as wonderful as possible. Mother and Father will simply have to agree with my plans.

When Seth heard the news of the baby and the impending wedding, he was furious! Again, I can no longer understand even those nearest to me. I suppose he is being protective of Willa. He and Willa have always shared a certain kinship, as if *she* were his sister. I am mortified even to write this, Dear Journal, but surely he would be livid if Gerald seduced me and we consummated our marriage before it ever took place. Still, he cannot forget that Willa had to have been a willing party.

Oh dear, I am certain he will overcome his anger for the sake of Willa and will welcome the new baby with his entire heart once born. It is almost as if we will have our own niece or nephew to dote upon!

But as I've stated before, Willa and Laz are of a different culture and neither Seth nor I have the right to judge them and their actions. Finally, Willa and Lazarus have admitted to their love for each other and there will be a baby! Although I will lose a part of Willa as my true friend, we will soon be bonded in a new way as wives to the men we love. Our sisterhood will continue into our old age, just as I imagined. Now all that is left is to find a proper wife for Seth and things would be just perfect!

On another course, I am horrified to report that some men have arrived on the plantation asking about Foster and his relationship with that woman in Charleston again. I honestly cannot understand why they think my brother would be involved with her demise and thought they had dispensed with that gossip months ago. She was a prostitute and no more to him. As I understand it, women in her occupation take on many clients in a single day. Is that not dangerous in itself? I have witnessed the businessmen who come to Heavenly to strike deals with Father. They smoke cigars, eat like gluttons, and partake of his whiskey until they are in ignorant bliss. Then I've heard them upon departure order Daniel to take them back to Charleston to be deposited with "the fine whores at Chateau". Who could trust men in such a drunken condition?

The thought of Foster associating with those immoral women is appalling to me, but I understand that he is a businessman. It also disgusts me to think that our own father likely conducts himself in the same manner away from this plantation, taking pleasure in unclean women. Mother has mentioned this to me before during her bouts of anger toward him. She cautions me to stay away from men like him, with only a mind for business and money and women. She tells me that Gerald will be the same once we are married and I argue with her vehemently. Gerald is a gentleman and is truly in love with me. And I am not like my mother, not irate and bitter like her. How dare she accuse him when surely Father acts as he does in part because of her bad temperament?

But enough of this! My intention of writing today was to express both my astonishment and my complete joy about the revelations of Willa and Lazarus. To my dear friends! May they be as happy as Gerald and I, blended in perfect union from here forward!"

Chapter 39

The sun broke through early morning clouds in the usual way on Heavenly Plantation. But this day would prove to be atypical in every other regard as Willa Grigsby and Lazarus Adams prepared to marry, propagating their lie. Marianne insisted on accommodating a celebration fit for white folk and had obtained permission from her parents to host it on the expansive front lawn of the plantation house. A grand reception would follow in the back yard. Both Josiah and Margaret were always quite happy to witness the weddings of their slaves. Such unions usually resulted in offspring, thus the expansion of their property wealth.

It was Sunday morning, the time set aside for worship at the nearby Saint Christopher's Episcopal Church attended not only by the Witherells and other wealthy white families, but their slaves as well. However, the service for the slaves was held in the chapel after the whites vacated the church property. So as not to mix the races, it was as if they recognized two separate Gods even though the same reverend preached both services.

Although slave marriages carried no legal weight, weddings at Heavenly Plantation were performed by a member of the slave community, an elder self-proclaimed minister named Horace Teeter. In an attempt to please their daughter however, Josiah and Margaret had earlier requested that Reverend Wells perform the marriage ceremony for Willa and Lazarus. When he declined, the elder Witherells honored his decision without question. This morning, after her family had already joined the company of other parishioners outside the chapel, Marianne beckoned the Reverend to stay inside with her a moment.

"I must ask you one last time Reverend Wells, to reconsider your position on marrying Willa and Lazarus. Oh, please, sir. My dear friends should be married in a conventional way. You have known them nearly all their lives! They are like Witherell family. Won't you please reconsider?"

"I am sorry, Marianne. You know they have no rights in this regard, just as they have no rights in any other affairs. They are slaves, legally and morally. I know you adore the couple, but I simply object to performing a marriage ceremony for slaves, as usual. My regrets are all I can offer, Marianne. God will bless their union in His provident way."

"Then they have your blessings as well, sir?" Her downcast eyes revealed obvious defeat this time. She could not understand his hesitance, when she knew that other ministers did indeed perform slave weddings on other plantations.

"Of course, so much as I can grant it." Reverend Wells looked at her with what resembled pity in his eyes. No regret. Simply pity. He felt sorry for Marianne and her questionable loyalty to her house slaves. He watched her grow from a baby and thought surely by now she would understand how the world worked. Slaves would always be slaves and at some point she would have to resign to the fact that even her childhood friends would need to be viewed as the property that they were. It was sad that the young woman was so disillusioned and he blamed Josiah and Margaret for allowing her to remain naïve.

As they prepared to leave the church, the reverend paused in the arched doorway, one hand on his hip and the other poised with a single finger extended over his lips as if he was unsure whether to speak the words that troubled him. "Marianne?"

"Yes, Reverend. What is it, sir?"

"I have been thinking about you quite often since your parents began to pursue my services for this wedding."

"Have you changed your mind?"

"Oh, no dear. No. I am sorry, but no. It's just that…well…"

"Sir?"

"May I ask why you insist on treating slaves as if they were family? Mind you, it is commendable to love, but slaves are not to be trusted as though they are like us. They are here for but one purpose, child."

A sudden urge to vomit subdued Marianne before she could speak as sour bile rose from her stomach. Her right hand swung into place over her mouth as she groped for the reverend's arm to steady herself. Prickly heat seared at her face and it burned white hot. He led her to a pew closest to the entrance of the church, sitting her down gently. "Oh my, Miss Marianne! What can I get for you, my dear? A cool drink, a cold cloth?" He hovered over her, fearing the daughter of his most charitable parishioner would faint.

Eying him with contempt, she found the words, "No, Reverend. I am fine. Just shocked at your cruelty toward my friends. It makes me ill the way you speak of them as…as animals! How dare you, sir!"

"Child! May God have mercy on you!"

"No, sir! May He have mercy on you!"

The clergyman's jaw dropped and it was clear that no one had ever challenged him in regard to his ethics. He stared speechless at Marianne, shocked by her obstinacy, waiting for an apology.

"May I remain here for a few moments alone, Reverend?"

"Of...of course. Think about your harshness with me, young lady. Take your time. Mind you, the Negro service will begin shortly."

Reverend Wells abruptly backed away from Marianne, no longer acting sympathetic. He turned and headed out the front door, his heels clacking angrily on the stone floor of the chapel. Once outside he immediately spotted the Witherells. Communicating urgency in his eyes he swept them over to his location aside the stately portico columns built by the hands of local Negro slaves for the enjoyment of the whites who appreciated good architecture.

He spoke first, addressing Josiah directly. "It might do well for you to speak with your daughter about the proper place of darkies in our society. She has a notion that her friends," he winced at the latter word, "have rights. As you know, I will not marry Negros, unlike some of my brethren in the service of the Lord. I refuse to do the unlawful duty, as I have told you, yet your daughter questions me."

"Oh, Reverend, I can assure you we knew nothing of our daughter's request and apologize for her having put you in defense. We shall speak sharply to her," Josiah said.

"Yes, my husband speaks the truth. But you must understand, sir...our Marianne is faultless. She has such a kind heart and her servant Willa is quite special to her. She is young and she will learn in time that this friendship is merely a product of youth. As Marianne steps into a household of her own one day she will see Willa's true value."

"Mind you, we are not simply indulging our daughter by allowing this ceremony for her dark friends. Willa is a fine seamstress, Lazarus an accomplished blacksmith, and they will soon bear a child. A suitable gift to Marianne and Gerald when they wed, I might say." Josiah smiled at himself, proud to have such a couple in his ownership.

Marianne soon joined her parents on the porch, but refused to look at the Reverend as her father added, "Begging your leave, Reverend Wells, we have a wedding to attend to this day. Will you excuse us?"

Chapter 40

It was a quiet carriage ride from St. Christopher to Heavenly with only Josiah and Margaret making polite conversation. The twins stayed behind to spend time with the children of another planter and Foster was out of town. Both Marianne and Seth sulked silently for different reasons.

As they approached the gates of the plantation however, Marianne began to feel lighter. The tree-lined avenue up to the house with its live oaks and their draping of moss looked even more festive today. Closer to the mansion there was a flurry of activity among slaves who skipped their Sunday worship to stay behind and prepare for the wedding of Willa and Lazarus, the couple adored by all who had surprised them with their profession of love.

The lawn took on the life of an outdoor chapel with wooden chairs lined up in symmetric fashion, an aisle formed in the center with end chairs adorned by large billowing bows of colored satin. Grapevines were shaped into a delicate wedding arch covered with magnolia blooms and placed at the bottom of the grand staircase leading up to the mansion's wide veranda.

Other chairs were set up on the veranda itself for the Witherell hosts and their guests, selected white neighbors who would were there to share not in the joy of the wedding couple, but to celebrate Josiah's good fortune. They recognized that although slave marriages were a farce with no legal basis, married slaves were generally happier, willing to procreate, and were therefore less likely to attempt escape. So Josiah's neighbors would come to congratulate him and to partake of the generous spread of food after the wedding.

Between each of the veranda columns was a large wooden basket of multi-colored flowers arranged with greenery that cascaded gracefully over the edge of the porch. Even the front of the massive Big House door was embellished with a wreath of magnolias, azaleas, camellias, and brightly colored ribbons.

The air surrounding the plantation house filled with the delectable scent of roasted hams, turkeys, and other meats. Both the slave and the Big House kitchens were swarming with servants preparing side dishes--collard greens, rice, corn, beans, and salads. They baked assorted cakes and pies, churned fresh butter, and pulled jellies and jams out of storage. Behind the house, cloth-covered picnic tables were scattered about, confirming the magnificent scale of the reception feast.

Not since the wedding of Josiah and Margaret had Heavenly been transformed so dramatically. A passing visitor would never guess this celebration was for a couple of slaves. Some locals might have mistaken the spread for the nuptials of Marianne and Gerald, even though they had yet to announce an engagement.

Daniel drove the Witherell carriage to the front of the house, skillfully halting the horses just in front of the decorated entrance. He jumped down from his seat and quickly opened the carriage door to assist the ladies out of the vehicle. When Josiah exited, he stood transfixed to view the scene on his front lawn, silently wondering what his grandfather would say if he were to witness such elaborate preparations to marry a pair of slaves. He shuttered at the thought of the verbal thrashing that would be his for creating such a spectacle on the Witherell estate. "Oh, what I do to indulge my only daughter", he said to no one in particular, shaking his head slightly and taking Margaret's arm in his so they could stroll up the steps together.

Inside the house, Marianne quickly found Willa so she could begin dressing her for the ceremony, a switch in roles that Willa found amusing. Marianne thought nothing about helping her best friend on the most important day of her life. Slave or not, she was her best friend and was to be honored on this day. Her former irritation with the reverend had eased from her mind so she could focus on Willa.

"Willa! This is it, your wedding day! I do hope you've finished with your dress, my dear. If you had only listened to me and accepted my offer of having one made for you, you would not be here at this moment still at your treadle!"

"No, it is finished," she said in an emotionless tone of voice, not turning to face Marianne.

"Well, let's not sound so delighted, then. My Lord, girl! You sound as if you have just completed a household task. This is your wedding day! Your wedding gown!"

"Oh, Marianne. Don't be so dramatic. You know I am…happy." She still faced her sewing machine.

Noting the hesitation in her friend's voice, Marianne became more concerned. "What is the matter, sweetheart? Are you having doubts about Lazarus? Tell me what troubles you." She placed two loving arms around Willa's shoulders, leaning down to offer a secure, reassuring hug.

Willa carefully unfastened Marianne's arms and stood up to turn around and wrap her own arms around her friend. In a rush of emotions she began to sob, gripping her tighter and holding fast. "Oh Marianne, what have I done? What am I doing? I can't go through with this!"

Marianne pushed her out to arms' length to search her dark brown eyes. Instead of the usual warm, soulful eyes she saw two bloodshot orbs. She had been crying and from her swollen, puffy face it was obvious that she had done so the entire morning.

"My Lord, Willa! What is this about? I thought you were happy, sweetheart. What is wrong? Tell me. Tell me!" She took Willa back into an embrace, letting her cry into her shoulder, wetting her nice Sunday dress. But the dress was the least of her worry as her heart ached for her best friend. "Cry it out. Go ahead, finish with it. Then you are going to calm down and tell me what is happening with you."

The sobbing continued for several minutes until it tapered off to a mere whimper. Patiently Marianne waited for her to quiet altogether before leaning back to look once more into her face. "There, there. That is better. Are you ready to talk?"

"Ye..yes." Willa sniffled and reached into the pocket of her wrinkled cotton work apron to retrieve a handkerchief. She noisily blew her nose as if doing so would also release all the negative emotions trapped within her head. She stalled for words, not knowing how to tell Marianne that she was living a lie, that the wedding was a lie, that she was secretly in love with Seth, and that Foster was the father of her growing baby. She struggled, taking several deep but shaky breaths. The more she breathed in, the stronger she felt until after several minutes the urge to admit the truth lessened within her. She knew she could not back out. Fate was fate; what was done was done.

Better to go through with the wedding, marry her good friend Lazarus as long as he was willing, and keep her child's birth an occasion for celebration when the day came about. No need to bring the devil Foster's name into this. No one but she and Lazarus would ever know the evil circumstances of his or her conception. Her child was blameless and that was the way it would remain. And of all considerations, a relationship between her and Seth was impossible. There would be no good in him knowing the truth. Spare him the hideous details; let him put all the blame on her.

Marianne waited.

"I am so sorry, Marianne. So sorry. I don't know what is running through my head now. I have been cryin' all morning. I must be terrified of becoming a wife. That must be it. What if Lazarus thinks I am a horrible wife? What if I can't cook like my mama? Or his mama? And I am...we are having a baby! What if I'm a not a fit mother? I mean, what if..."

"Just stop right here, Willa. You are worrying yourself for no reason. You will be a wonderful wife and mother! You are making yourself all upset for nothing! Why, look at you!" She took hold of Willa's shoulders and guided her out of her tiny room and into her own bedroom, placing her in front of a full-length mirror.

"Look at yourself! The woman in the looking glass looks horrendous! Look at those swollen eyes and that ashen skin. That ugly old apron and barefoot! She is supposed to be getting married to a wonderful man, the man of her dreams, and the father of her child and future children. He's a blacksmith and a good one. He will provide for her and her children and she will always be proud of him. And she's even made her own wedding gown because she is a talented and magnificent seamstress! And if she does not get out of this sour disposition and let her dear friend Marianne help her get prepared, the wedding shall have to be postponed. And the entire Heavenly Plantation—no, no--the entire community will cry in displeasure at having to wait until another time to witness this fine event!"

"Oh, Marianne!" Willa turned to give her a squeeze of gratitude. "You are so dramatic! Perhaps you should travel to Europe and join the theater. Why are you wasting away in South Carolina?"

The back of Marianne's right hand flew up to her forehead as her head cocked back in one sweeping gesture, tossing a few silken curls free from her chignon. "Oh, my, but you are correct. I am wasting my talent here, you are correct. London calls. I must depart." She strutted toward the door then spun her head around to say, "Good day, my love!" and left her bedroom. Quickly she reentered, shaking her head. "Who was that? Oh, hello Willa. Don't we have a wedding for which to prepare?"

Willa rolled her eyes at Marianne and in doing so realized they were sore. "I think I need to do something about these eyes of mine. Laz will think he is marrying a demon."

"Right you are. I will get a cold compress and you will lie down and rest for a bit. Then I'll work on my own appearance since my maiden has the gall to go getting married today and cannot attend to me." She laughed and headed out to get the compress.

Willa went back to her own room and threw herself down on the bed. Although she was not chilly, she wrapped up in her quilted coverlet. As if it could provide reassurance. Again she drew deep breaths to clear her mind. She knew the day ahead would require all the strength she could muster. How successfully it played out would depend on her own skills as an actress of sorts.

Chapter 41

Willa's wedding dress was delicate pink, made from imported silk originally purchased by Margaret for the construction of a ball gown for Marianne. Once Willa opened the package upon its arrival, she nearly fainted, having never laid eyes on something so exquisite. From that moment Marianne knew she would not be able to wear a gown made from the fabric Willa herself so admired. She told Margaret that she'd changed her mind, preferring instead the periwinkle blue brocade they'd recently bought at Carson's Dry Goods in Charleston. So Margaret cast aside the pink silk and ordered Willa to fetch the brocade and begin the dress. Now Marianne was especially pleased with her decision.

Willa stood in Marianne's room in front of the looking glass, inspecting her dress with Heddie, just before the planned start of the wedding ceremony.

"You look stunning, Willa", said Marianne. "Your skin looks like rich delicious chocolate next to the pink silk. You will simply take Lazarus' breath away."

"You exaggerate so greatly, but thank you. I wouldn't put it in those words, but I guess I look fine." The woman who gazed back from the mirror now was beautiful after some rest and a few cups of tea. Beautiful on the outside, Willa was still feeling uncomfortable on the inside for what she was about to do.

She marveled at the spectacular wedding gown that she had loosely patterned after something she saw in one of Margaret's fashion magazines. The original design called for a tight-fitting bodice, but she had to make it looser with a raised waistline to accommodate the swell of her tummy. A darker pink satin sash tied in a little bow just under her bust line. The same satin was used in the bows that topped her ruffled lace cap sleeves and the ruffled white swag that spread all the way around the full skirt. Her black crinkly hair was twisted into a low knot at the back of her neck and adorned with freesia. On her small feet was a pair of white satin slippers borrowed from Marianne.

"When you're ready, just call for me, Willa. I'll be down in the parlor. Take your time. Don't think they will start without the bride! Heddie, I shall see you outside." Marianne gave Heddie a light peck on the cheek and disappeared through the doorway to give the pair privacy in their last moments as mother and unmarried daughter.

Heddie missed being witness to Willa's earlier distress since she oversaw wedding preparations both outdoors and in the kitchens. This left her with barely enough time to attend to her own appearance, but she managed to look fresh in a white ruffled gown handed down from Margaret's closet. The bodice of the dress dipped lower than she was accustomed and it made her self-conscious as she constantly tugged at it, pulling it well over her breasts.

"Mama, you are just lovely. Stop fussin' with that dress. Why, you look like the lady of the manor now. Step over here and take a look." Willa urged her mother to exchange places with her in front of the looking glass.

Heddie managed a shy smile, although she wanted to burst at the seams. This was her daughter's day, not hers so she was willing to minimize her astonishment at looking so regal. The white dress was a striking contrast to her blackness. It spoke clearly of her African heritage, a tribute to those who lived before her, those who held positions of status in the Motherland. Her mind flooded with the stories passed down from her mother and father who learned the tales from their parents and grandparents. She suddenly felt proud, pulling back her shoulders and standing taller. Her full ruffled skirt billowed around as if she were cradled in a heavenly cloud. Puffed sleeves stood away from her arms as if they were also proud. Suddenly the dipped bodice was a compliment to her, no longer an annoyance.

Willa noticed her mama take on an air of sophistication and was happy for her. The only missing piece was her papa Alfred and her brothers. They should all be standing proudly with her, admiring her beauty. Her heart did a flip as reality poked it with a sharp prong. "Oh, mama!" Willa fought back tears that threatened to reveal her thoughts to Heddie, but it was no use.

"I know what you be thinkin', baby. I miss 'em, too. But this is your day, child. You know that they be with us here, in our hearts." Heddie put one hand on Willa's chest and the other on her own.

"But mama…"

"No, Willa. I will not have you spoil your day with tears. Your papa would not want his angel to cry. Now dry them eyes and think about Lazarus and that baby growin' in your belly. They your future now, child." Unknown to Willa, Heddie's eyes were previously swollen and red at one point in the day when she allowed herself a few solitary moments. She drew in a cleansing breath to put that out of her mind for her daughter's sake.

"Papa and the boys would be so happy for you, girl. Don't you think anything else about the past. From here on it is about you. This day be yours!" She squeezed her child with all the strength she had in her arms. "Now I best be gettin' outside to take my place with Daniel and Camille and you best prepare yourself to become a wife." She put both her hands aside Willa's face and pulled her close to plant a kiss on her forehead, then looked intently into her eyes. "God has blessed you, darlin'. Blessed you indeed. Let's get downstairs."

With one last glance into the mirror, Willa gathered up her skirts and followed her mother down the grand staircase. At the bottom, Heddie called out for Marianne in the parlor and then exited through the front door.

"So, princess…are you ready now? I think we are right on schedule. Willa? Willa? Did you hear me?"

Willa's was busy fluffing her perfect pink gown, feeling its softness against her hands, her mind wandering miles from Heavenly. "What? Oh, I'm sorry, Marianne. This dress…I just never dreamed I would wear something lovely like this. You always let me try on your gowns but we had to keep it a secret. I can't believe the missus let me make this one for myself. Are you sure this is right with her?"

"Dear Willa. Of course it is all right. You know she loves you and cares for you. You are family. You are our Willa."

The look on Marianne's face was so convincing that Willa could easily let herself believe they were sisters rather than slave and mistress. For a few seconds it was bliss to her.

"So, are you ready to go marry your Laz?"

The momentary fantasy of being sisters fell to the floor as Willa snapped back to the reality of what was ahead of her out on the lawn. The wedding. The lie. She cleared her throat, swallowed hard, and answered, "Yes. Yes, I am ready."

Marianne went to the window facing out to the lawn to see if it was time for Willa to make her way outside. Once she confirmed that Lazarus and old Minister Teeter were in place, she returned her attention to her good friend. "It looks as if all that is missing is the bride. It's time for me to go and sit with my parents and Seth. I shall tell them you are ready."

Marianne took a long look at her friend as if she would never again see her. Tears formed in her blue eyes and she quickly batted her lids to dissipate them. She reached out to pull Willa close and kissed her on the cheek. "Oh Willa, do you realize that the next time we embrace, you shall be a married woman?"

Willa felt her throat begin to close on her and experienced the sudden need to gasp for air. Her heart quickened and she felt a flash of warmth spread across her face. She inhaled and exhaled loudly, telling the worry inside to settle down and willing her unborn baby to give her strength. She prayed that God grant her a calming peace and a reassurance that she was about to do the right thing.

"Willa? Are you feeling ill? Is it the baby? Do you need to sit a spell? Let me get you into the parlor. This wedding will have to wait a little longer, until you catch your breath."

Willa put up her hands in protest, gathering her courage. "No. Just give me another moment before you leave me. It is just that…what you said about the next time we embrace. This is it. Our lives will change forever."

"But for the better. You and Lazarus are in love and you belong together, just like Gerald and I. One day we will both be married women." She began to giggle. "Remember when we wanted nothing of boys? We swore we would never become wives. Do you remember it, Willa?"

"Of course I do." She smiled broadly at Marianne, who had lifted her spirits with the memory. "I think I am ready to get married now. Thank you, Marianne. You know I love you."

"And I love you, too. Now I am going to go outside. Lazarus is surely wondering what is keeping you and I don't want him angry with me."

"Very well. Tell them all that we can get started. I'm one minute after you, Marianne. I'll be countin' to sixty."

"That's my Willa." Marianne winked at her and then headed out.

Exactly one minute later, Willa lifted the handle of the big oak door, reminding herself that she needed to keep breathing.

Don't choke on the guilt, Willa. For the baby's sake.

Chapter 42

Outside on the veranda, Willa tried not to look at the white folks gathered there, proceeding down the steps as gracefully as she could. She saw Lazarus looking fine in a brown suit and crisp white shirt. Her first thought was that she was so blessed to be marrying such a handsome and respectable young man. And then a pang of guilt shot through her heart. She was marrying someone who deserved much more than she could give him. Taking her place under the flower-adorned arch, she faced him and as she looked into his kind eyes she wondered if he sensed her guilt.

Lazarus looked at Willa like he was seeing her for the first time. His face lit up like lightning on a summer night. His brown eyes were flecked with gold that sparkled in the sunlight. He felt like he was living a perfect dream, marrying as lovely a woman as Willa, about to be father to the child of an angel. It made no difference to him how the child was conceived. All that mattered was that he and Willa would make a life, structure a real family.

Seated in chairs in the lawn, Heddie, Daniel, and Camille looked unmistakably proud. The love for their children gleamed in their eyes. To them, it seemed that a miracle was taking place, one that could not be squelched by the unholy institution of slavery. They were not disillusioned into believing this marriage would carry enough weight to guarantee the little family would never be torn apart and sold off in pieces. But they silently prayed that God would show mercy on their children and grandchildren. It broke Heddie's heart that her marriage to Alfred was so easily shattered by separation and she secretly envied Daniel and Camille. She prayed every night that Willa and Lazarus would be allowed to grow old together like his parents.

Neither Lazarus nor Willa truly heard the old black minister's words during the wedding ceremony as each floated on a different cloud of surrealism. Willa tried hard not to look at Seth up on the veranda, but instead focused on Lazarus' smooth amber face. She studied the curve of his chin, the gentle slope of his nose, the fullness of his pink lips. She wondered if he would want to kiss her today. She wondered if she would fall in love with him once they were together every day in the same house. He was such a beautiful person that she prayed she would. Her heart filled with admiration for him, but would it be enough to sustain them?

Lazarus could think of nothing but his desire to reach over and take Willa in his arms. Once they were declared married, he would kiss her. He wondered how she would react. Would she go along with it to make the marriage seem real to everyone watching? He wanted her to be his wife in every sense of the word; he wanted them to be lovers, not simply friends. Although he knew this was a marriage for show, he prayed that Willa would come to love him.

Somehow the couple managed to respond to Minister Teeter's request for them to repeat vows and within minutes they were pronounced Mr. and Mrs. Lazarus Adams. They stood facing each other, looking confused as if unsure what to do next. The slaves gathered around them on the chairs in the lawn began to laugh and some shouted, "Kiss her! Kiss her! Kiss her!" Finally Lazarus took Willa's face into his two hands, caressing her gently. Pulling her face toward his, he closed his eyes and fixed a slow, sweet kiss on her lips. She was at first startled, but responded with closed eyes and compliant lips, feeling an unexpected tingle down to her toes. His kiss was different from Seth's, she caught herself thinking.

They kissed again as the wedding guests applauded in approval. Minister Teeter commented quietly, "Well son, you had dis old man worried for a spell." Then he placed a straw broom at the couple's feet explaining that the ritual of jumping the broom symbolized their leap from an old life into the new. Lazarus took Willa's hand in his and together they hopped over the broom, drawing more applause from the guests.

When the ceremony concluded, several slaves gathered around the married couple to offer congratulations as the white guest were ushered into the plantation house to be served cold drinks before the wedding feast. Marianne stayed on the veranda to wait her turn to embrace the pair. She noticed that Seth's face held what looked like a scowl through the entire ceremony and now that it was over, he looked even worse. He stood to go into the house, but she stopped him.

"What has gotten into you, brother? I should think you would be thrilled that your two good friends are making a life together."

Seth looked blankly into his sister's face and did not speak.

"Well? What have you to say for yourself? You seem angry, Seth. I would think you and Lazarus had mended ways since the day you had a scuff with him over Willa. You are much too protective of her, you know. And Laz is a fine enough young man for her…"

"Marianne, it is really no concern of yours!" Seth was quick to scold, but his voice was icy and distant. He shook his head and left his sibling alone on the porch.

"You are just selfish, you know. You can't stand it that your best friend now belongs to Willa and will be taking orders from her from now on!" Marianne's attempt to cajole her brother fell on him as truth, dripping from his heart with enough volume to drown him.

Chapter 43

The wedding celebration for Willa and Lazarus lasted well into the night as black slaves and white aristocrats alike dined on mountains of food and rivers of drink. Music filled the evening air with lightness uncommon to the Negro guests. For one night the field slaves felt almost free, thanks to a house servant's good fortune to marry one of their own, albeit a member of the skilled trade class of slaves since Lazarus was a blacksmith.

The whole scene made Seth feel sick at his stomach as he was forced to listen to all the happy commotion. He retreated to his room quickly after the wedding, but not fast enough to avoid meeting the newlyweds on the lawn. He would rather have died than see Willa look so happy on the arm of Lazarus. He wondered how she so easily fell out of love with him and into the bed of his best friend and man servant. As he watched them approach, he involuntary said the words "best friend" aloud; they tasted bitter and spoiled on his tongue.

"Seth! I am so glad to find you. Thank you for bein' here today, my friend," said Lazarus, patting him on the back. "I know this ain't easy for you, but you are a true gentleman."

"Yes. That I am. Willa, you look wonderful." Seth's eyes evaded Lazarus, cruelly entertaining themselves by looking at the vision in pink silk before them.

"Thank you, Seth." Willa averted her eyes, suddenly feeling vulnerable as if she'd been undressed there in the yard.

"Listen Seth, I hope you have no mind to ruin the celebration for us. I know you're still sore at me, but this be our day. For Willa, please let us be happy."

"Don't worry yourself about me, Laz. I have no intention of standing in front of your happiness. Willa, will you excuse me?" Without another word, he sauntered off to the house without looking back.

Willa felt the fine prickles of guilt poke tiny holes into her heart. She stiffened as Lazarus put an arm around her shoulders to bolster what he knew was a blow to her resolve. "Willa, you knew this was bound to happen. At least he ain't plannin' on ruining this for us. You know the rest of the night needs to look real. Don't let him make you sad, girl. Look at me, Willa."

She looked into her new husband's eyes and he saw the tears as she let herself melt into his chest. Her strained voice spoke her mind. "Will it ever end, Laz? These feelings for him? I don't want to love him, I want to love you. Dear God what have we done, Laz?"

"Shhhhh…no more, Willa. This be a joyous day for us, for your child. For…our child. We done the right thing for us all. Jus' think what would've happened if the truth came out, Willa. We done the right thing by our people and by God. Hush up now, darlin' Willa."

He was right. Under the strange circumstances she knew he was right. A sense of calm unexpectedly washed through her. She sighed in resignation, feeling relieved. She held Lazarus and pressed closer into him. This would work, it had to work.

Chapter 44: Marianne's Journal, April 20, 1852

"My poor, dear brother Seth! He seems almost lost now that his two treasured friends are married and on to their own grown-up lives. He has no entertaining companions with which to share his days and this is forcing him to mature as well. He spends time reading, studying, observing what he can of the business Father and Foster conduct. So serious these days. Almost a melancholy kind of serious, as if his zest for life is snuffed out. Is this simply his normal passage into manhood? Or is he truly disturbed by his friends and their new life together? Envious perhaps?

And Foster. I know that he is not particularly fond of Willa and Lazarus. He has always had so little to do with our colored friends. In fact, he has always been rather mistrusting of our slaves in general, even growing up with Sissy as our nursemaid. Instead of relying on her like Seth and I, he was always running to Mother for this and that.

The gall of him not to attend the wedding though! He knows how I love Willa and how Seth admires Lazarus. He should have made arrangements to be here at Heavenly on that day. Business in Charleston might have waited a day. As soon as he returned the following afternoon, I questioned him at great length. I asked him if he did not love me, his only sister. Why would he not attend the wedding and help us celebrate with Willa, Heddie, Lazarus, Daniel, and Camille? Why, most of the entire county felt compelled to attend, to join with the Witherells and celebrate! He replied in such a venomous way that I scarcely believe he is my brother, my own blood. He called Willa some horrible names, associating her with the lowest of women on this earth because she carried a child before marriage.

I slapped him so hard across his face that my palm stung. He looked at me with eyes so mean that I was frightened and began to cry. I thought he would return the slap but instead he circled his arms around me and pulled me close. Patting me on the back and kissing the top of my head he began apologizing for his remarks. I will never forget his words:

"There is so much pressure in the business world Marianne, that I am often overwhelmed. It is difficult to be the eldest son of such a wealthy, important man as Father and I am under such scrutiny that never desists. You must believe me that I am truly sorry for my ugliness, Marianne. I meant no disrespect to you by being absent from your friend's wedding. And I regret having called her such vile names in your presence. Truly I do. I'm just concerned for you, that she does not influence you. Promise me you will remain honorable, sister. You will honor our family name and be pure when you wed. Promise me."

So he is concerned for me. As always, my dear Foster frets over me. How I love him for his doting and how sorry I am for having taken a hand to him like that. I cannot imagine the burdens he lives beneath while handling business affairs. I am sure I shall never understand the demands placed upon distinguished men like him, Father, and my Gerald who run businesses and plantations. I will forever be grateful to be a woman who never needs worry over involvement in the important matters of men! To become so upset at Foster over not attending a wedding was just wretched of me! It was just a wedding.

Oh, Journal…but what a wonderful wedding it was! My darling friend marrying her secret love. Oh what passion must have smoldered between them and they hid it from the world until it was no longer possible to do so. I often wonder why they kept their romance secret. Even when I asked Willa, she told me in a polite way that I need not have concerned myself. She told me that she was my servant and that her focus should have been on me and not on herself, so her love life was nothing for me to know.

Rubbish! I know her better than that. Neither of us has ever taken her role seriously, even though we both kept up the pretense for the sake of my family, my parents. Any kind of help she has ever rendered was that of a dear best friend simply behaving as such. She helps me with my wardrobe, my hair. I do the same for her, although her needs are not as great as mine in a public sense. She is not constrained to looking the part of a Southern gentlewoman. For that fact, I truly envy her. She is able to live her life without the scrutiny to which I am subjected, even to the point of conceiving a child out of wedlock and not being shamed for it.

Now comes the difficult part. We must learn to live apart, something we have never done since her first days here at Heavenly. Last week she moved out of her room here in the house and has rightly taken up residence in a new cabin built specifically for her and Lazarus. That was my parents' gift to them because they are so well-loved and treasured by our family. With the aid of several of their kinsmen, Daniel and Lazarus built the residence in a few short days without Willa's knowledge. Now Mrs. Lazarus Adams has her own home!

Although Mother strongly cautioned me against going there, I paid a visit yesterday. The cabin is situated well beyond the house slave quarters, closer to the blacksmith shop and about halfway between here and the field slave village. As you are well aware, Dear Journal, I never venture close to the village, close to the area patrolled by that horrible overseer Duke Henry!

The cabin is small, with only two rooms, a fireplace separating them. But I suppose when two people are in love, the volume of space they share is irrelevant. (Could Gerald and I be blissfully happy sharing such cramped quarters, closely surrounded by only our love?) I cannot help wondering how Willa will adjust after having lived in our grand Heavenly house. Lazarus will have no adjustment to make, as I am sure that the dwelling he shared with Daniel and Camille was quite similar.

Willa's beloved sewing machine remains in her room in our house so she will continue to work here on the fine dresses my mother craves. She will also be here each day to see to my needs, according to Mother. My needs are so few compared to Mother's however. It takes all of Chloe and Myra to keep up with her demands, and now Willa is required for her personal wardrobe demands too! But I am happy for that, because it is a great comfort to me to hear Willa in that room sewing away, doing what she truly loves to do.

Back to the cabin…I gathered up as many nice things as I could without my parents' knowledge to help furnish the little home. Quilts and linens, pieces of pottery, rugs, baskets, furniture from the attic, whatever I could smuggle out by nightfall. One evening Old Ned kept watch as his sons Porter and Bailey came over from the slave village to help Lazarus load a wagon. Afterwards, Daniel drove it away. They all risked great peril for me, but I had no other way to accomplish the task. I am proud of myself. Perhaps I am not quite the lady my parents think!

Willa seems pleased with her little place though. She appears to be settled in and calmly awaiting what is next in her life as a married woman, the birth of her baby. The notion of Willa and Lazarus having a baby together still jars me. My little Willa is changed forever, having ventured into the unknown without me, her best friend. She leaped into womanhood without letting me in on her secret.

I long to ask for details, to have her tell me what it was like, the experience of losing oneself to a man. A great mystery of which I shall not partake until Gerald and I are wed, when that first night will unlock for me the secrets to which my Willa has already availed herself. I envy her knowledge and wish I had some inkling of what to expect. Perhaps I will muster the courage and simply ask. Oh, that is for another day…"

Chapter 45

"Get inside, Marianne," Josiah Witherell commanded from the second floor hallway as she emerged from her room. Then addressing two men quickly advancing toward him up the staircase, he raised his voice, "By God, what are you doing in my house? Who are you?" What do you mean barging in on my family? Halt right there! I have a pistol and I will use it!" He confidently waved his firearm at the men.

"We want nothing with you, old man. It's your no good son we want and if he is here we will find him! Do you know what he's done? Do you have any idea of what your damn son has done to our sister?" The taller of the two spewed both words and spit, involuntarily wetting his dark beard.

"What the hell are you talking about?" The short barrel of the pistol was aimed.

The second man began hollering. "He killed our sister, that's what he did! He killed Lilith! Beat the hell out of her! That's what the low life scalawag did!" He was like a rabid dog, foaming at the mouth, his words mixed with a combination of saliva and noxious passion.

Josiah put up his free hand in protest. It was apparent to him that both men were more emotional than dangerous, making it easy for him to wield his authority and intimidate them into submission. If not, and if they were armed as well, he was assured of his abilities as a marksman and had no doubts concerning the outcome of this conflict. Even Old Ned, instead of running for help, stood at the bottom of the staircase, fully confident in his Master, ready to perform the duty of carrying off the bodies of the men should Josiah choose to fire.

"Both of you calm down, dammit! You break in here and accuse my son of murder? Why, I should shoot you both just for principal! I have every right—you're in *my* home and dishonoring *my* name!" He gripped the pistol with two hands now, fixing a precise aim on the temple of the tallest.

"Easy, sir! We are unarmed men!" The tallest backed down a few steps, pulling the arm of his brother. "Our sister was killed and there are witnesses who say your son was the last one with her. We have a right to question him; we've a right to seek justice."

"Justice does not involve breaking into an honorable man's home, fellows! If you seek justice you will do so through the law. My son is innocent and I'll not have you face him! You will do so through the law and we shall see who is in the wrong!"

The other man spoke, "It has been months! We've tried everything we can and there is no law man this side of the Santee who will even listen to us! You have this entire county against us, Witherell!"

"And so I do. Then what makes you think I'll surrender up my son to the likes of you? He is a gentleman, an upstanding citizen, a businessman like you, surely."

"No, sir! He is nothing like us! He is a damned murderer! He killed our sister and …"

Josiah cut him off, "And a fine woman was she. I know who your sister was. What she was. Indeed, someone killed her, but it was not my son. Rather some poor, ignorant customer of hers who did the city some good by ridding it of one strumpet! Now get off my property! Be gone with you both, you…"

Before he could finish, Margaret came charging out of her chambers. She rushed down the stairs separating her husband from the brothers and took aim at one of them. With closed fists she wailed on him repeatedly, beating as hard as she could. "How dare you accuse my son? How dare you! Damned mongrel! Bastard! Refuse! You scalawag!"

She continued to pound the man's chest with her tiny fists while he made no attempt to stop her. Nor did Josiah, who lowered his pistol, anger replaced with near amusement by his wife's efforts to defend the Witherell honor. Soon Margaret was exhausted and stopped abruptly, knitting her bony fingers together and bowing her head as if in prayer. She began to sob while the two men looked helplessly to Josiah. This confrontation was not going the way they had planned.

Josiah shook his head and called loudly for Chloe to come tend to her mistress. Immediately the slave appeared from downstairs, bewildered by the sight of two strangers, her master with a pistol, and her mistress upon the stairway bawling into her own hands. "Y..y..yes, Marster Witherell?"

"Tend to her, Chloe, for God's sake! Get her out of here. We…we gentlemen have business to attend to. See to it that she stays in her room. Margaret, do you hear me? Go to your room. This is of no concern to you."

"Yes, Marster. Come on, Missus Mar'gret. Let's get you some nice hot tea now." Chloe was used to treating Margaret like fragile, easily shattered glass. She put her arms around the woman and guided her gently up the steps toward her bedroom.

Through sobs, Margaret spoke in broken bits. "Chloe, those...those...awful...dreadful men! They speak of Foster. They say...he killed. He killed. Foster killed. My Foster. Not my Foster. Chloe, Chloe..."

"Here, here now Missus, you just calm down now and Chloe tuck you into your room. Make you tea and stay with you. Come on now." The two disappeared down the long hallway.

"Gentlemen, there is no need for such incivility here. Shall we discuss your accusations against my son in private, inside my office?" He gestured toward the downstairs, then tucked the pistol inside his jacket and began to descend, followed by the men. At the bottom of the stairs, he nodded to Ned, who led them into the darkly paneled office in the west wing of the house.

"Brandy?" Josiah offered his intruders. Upon their acceptance Ned fetched the liquid and poured out three small crystal glasses. Both of the men threw back their drinks in haste while Josiah waited for Ned to refill their glasses.

"Let us begin with names. Who are you?"

"Geoffrey and Thomas Hawthorne, cotton mill industrialists. We hail from Newton County, Georgia." The taller one spoke, pointing first to himself and then to the other, each reaching forward to offer a handshake to Josiah.

"Josiah Witherell, as I am sure you know. Please call me Josiah. So, Geoffrey, if I may address you as such..."

"Yes, please. Geoffrey and Thomas."

"Geoffrey, Thomas, tell me about these witnesses from Charleston. What proof do they have that my son was involved in your sister's demise?"

"He was seen leaving Lilith's room the evening she was murdered. He was her last...her last..." Thomas found it difficult to continue.

"Her last visitor," said Geoffrey.

"Her last client you intend to say," added Josiah as if to remind them of their sister's occupation.

"Yes, her client. Look, Mr. Witherell, we know what our sister did. We are not proud of her choices, far from that. But no one deserves to die like that. Not even a woman... a woman who took the risks that she did," Geoffrey finished.

"She was savagely beaten. She died a torturous death and for that we demand retribution. You must understand that, sir. Your son needs to be punished, if not through the law, by other means."

"Did your witnesses see my son raise a hand to this woman? I understand that my son may indeed have been there on the night in question, but from all indication he was quite taken with your sister. You know, he spoke to me of falling in love with her. Imagine that, my son so infatuated with a whore like her!" Josiah laughed, unwittingly insulting the pair, stirring them both from their seats.

"Whoa! Sit down gentlemen! Don't forget who has the pistol here. Have another brandy. Ned!"

The old butler moved from his station by the door to pour more libations as the men obeyed and took their seats. They each downed another drink while Josiah waited for them to cool off.

"Mr. Witherell. Josiah. It seems to us that there is only one civil option here, just one way to settle this dispute. You say your son is innocent. My brother and I say he is not," spoke Geoffrey.

"And exactly what is the civil way of settlement?"

"That would be to challenge him to a duel. We are gentlemen of honor, sir. I know it is highly irregular for the aggrieved to make this request in person, but we feel doubly enraged by this inability to settle the matter by law."

"And which of you gentlemen would be willing to die to settle your sister's honor?"

"That would be me," said the taller Geoffrey. "We wish to settle in this manner and I am most willing to accept the consequence of such an event. My brother and I agree to be satisfied, no matter the outcome. Let your son name the place and the time. I will be there to represent my sister."

"So let it be then. If this will stop these bloody inquisitions from Charleston and now you, let it be then. I shall speak with my son and we will settle this like civil gentry, but be advised that it may be some time before he will be able to do so. The summer is at hand and as customary, we leave these parts for the cool of the ocean. Would you have a mind to wait? I am sure he'll be agreeable to such a contest upon his return."

"As you would have it. Agreed?"

"Agreed then." Josiah stood up and shook hands with both men in turn, then added, "Kindly leave your calling cards on the table and Ned will see you out. Good day, sirs." Swiftly he made his exit from the office, satisfied that Foster would accept the proposed challenge and prevail as an excellent Witherell marksman.

Chapter 46

The knock on her cabin door made Willa giggle. Hadn't Lazarus left just five minutes ago? Or had it been hours? She wasn't sure if she had fallen back asleep or not. Either way, she found it amusing that he would rap on his own door to come back in, his way of gently announcing himself so as not to frighten her and induce an early labor. With what could not be more than a few weeks to go, she was getting used to being treated like a porcelain doll. Even Margaret forbade her from working at Heavenly, insisting she stay home at rest.

Slowly she waddled her wide, swollen self to the door to invite her husband back in. What had he forgotten today? She smiled at the realization that he seemed as pregnant as she, not in size but in mind. In a fog at times, musing about the baby, forgetting the simplest of things.

"Lazarus, Lazarus…" she sang as she pulled open the door. Jolted by terror, she froze when she saw that this was a most unwelcome visitor. She gasped and stepped back several feet, leaving the door wide open, dropping her jaw just as wide.

"Surprise, darlin'," Foster began. "My, you look like you've just seen a ghost! Pale even for a darkie like you. Going to invite me in or shall I stand here and perhaps attract the attention of someone passing by?"

Seconds floated by, so Foster accepted Willa's silence as encouragement to step over the threshold. He pulled the door closed behind him and stood quietly in front of her, surveying the interior of her small cabin. She stared at him with a mixture of disbelief and disgust glowing in her eyes.

"My, my! What a homey little shanty. You've done wonderful things with your décor."

Foster's sarcasm made Willa look away, suddenly ashamed of her little home and not understanding why. Foster did not matter. His opinion was irrelevant to her.

Soon she felt his eyes upon her, surveying her enlarged belly. She looked up and he was wetting his lips in an inappropriately sensuous way.

"Mmmmmmm, mmmmmmm. What a pretty sight you are, just as ripe as a berry. Ready to pop at any minute. Now how long has it been since we've been alone, Willa girl? About nine months as I recollect. That about right?" He waited for an answer, but Willa bit her lower lip hard and looked away.

"Now come on. As shy as you were that night in the woods. Not going to scream are you? Didn't scream that night, as I recall. Look at me." He reached out a hand and gently lifted her chin with two fingers. She looked blankly at him, revealing little emotion as she fought to keep her fears contained within.

His touch sent a shiver down Willa's spine but she was steeled herself and did not pull away. She was terrified for her unborn child and what Foster's impulsive violence might do to him or her. Did he intend to rape her again in her state of maternity? Suddenly she felt warm tears involuntarily roll down her cheeks as he continued to hold up her chin.

"No reason to cry, my dear. I'm not here to hurt you. I swear." He stroked a wet cheek with the back of his hand, smearing the tears into her skin. Reaching into his jacket, he produced a handkerchief. Slowly, but not sensuously now, he wiped the moisture from Willa's face.

"There, there," Foster said as he put a hand to her chest, careful not to touch her breast. "Why, your heart is racing. You must calm down for the sake of our baby."

Our baby? The last phrase sent Willa's stomach churning and she instinctively put her hand over her mouth to contain the nausea she felt rise into her throat. She shuddered, managing to swallow down the bitter taste of the bile.

"Now, now! Don't you worry your little head on that one, Willa. Only you and I know who fathers your little bastard. And you know I shall never tell. How about you, Willa?"

She stared at Foster, unable to speak, yet shaking her head in agreement.

"Good then. Good. Since it looks like the child's birth is imminent, I simply had to be sure. Now I do want to congratulate you on your wedding to that boy. What is his name, Seth's slave boy?"

"It's Lazarus! My husband is Lazarus! And he's no longer Seth's slave. He's a blacksmith. And a fine one! He's nobody's boy!" Willa surprised even herself at her quick defense of Lazarus in spite of the trepidation she felt toward Foster.

"Now she speaks! Got her hackles raised now! Defending her man. Good girl. I take it you are all finished with fancying my brother, then. Is that right?"

"It's no business of yours, Foster Witherell, but I was done with Seth the night you raped me! You put an end to us! You!"

"And you should thank me for rescuing you from that, I would think. How dare you think that you and my brother could ever be together! Here or anywhere else. Not even in the North would a nigger and a white boy be accepted! What the hell were you and dimwitted Seth thinking? You'd both end up dead, so as I see it, I've saved you both."

Willa began to laugh, entertained by Fosters rationale. The notion that she and Seth should be grateful to him for his life-changing violence toward her!

Then she addressed him in the voice of a slave who did not have the upbringing she received growing up in the mansion. "Oh, you be my savior after all! Lordy, I's jus' a dumb little darky who ain't got a clue 'bout my po', sad life. You's done rescued me, Marster With'rell. I's surely grateful fo' dat."

But Willa's mocking tone only activated Foster's anger. "Don't you dare taunt me, girl! With child or not, if I had a mind to do it, I could smother the life out of you! No one would ever suspect me! Imagine your boy coming home to a dead woman, all blue in the face, strangled with her own filthy apron!"

The look in his eyes told Willa that he was serious and quite capable of doing what he said. Her moment of confidence melted as quickly as it had swelled.

"No need for that Foster. Please. Why can't you leave me alone, leave me and Lazarus to our own lives? No one will ever know how this baby came to be. I have nothing to say about you; we have no association now. I serve your sister and I have nothing to do with Seth. There is no reason. Please, just leave me be."

Foster took a deep breath and blew out the air that had fueled his sudden fury. "Smart. Very smart of you, girl. I want nothing of you. Nothing but your assurance that you will keep quiet about that night. So far, you have done well. Not as dumb as I thought actually. Very shrewd for a...a slave. Marrying a light-colored boy. No one will ever know the parentage of our...your child."

Foster reached out with one hand to touch her rounded belly and despite her hatred for him, Willa did not back away. She let him explore its roundness for no reason she could identify. Gently he rubbed small circles over it, his eyes following the pattern as if searching for something.

Then the unborn baby kicked hard right where its father touched. He withdrew his hand quickly, surprised by the sudden jolt. He looked at Willa and she noticed the tears that gathered in the corners of his eyes and threatened to spill. He looked away, snorted as if he had control while throwing back his head to recall the tears. He cleared his throat. Willa understood that he was embarrassed by the show of emotion. Emotion! Soulless Foster had feelings!

"I...I recall my mother. When she was carrying the twins. She let me touch her belly once. The twins were active. My mother was happy. Then. Until they were born. That memory is one of the last I have of her truly content. Never mind."

Foster was quick witted, able to resurrect that memory to cover what Willa sensed was a brief connection with his baby. The child he would never own up to, never claim. For all she knew about him, he would never father a child because he was far too selfish, too unruly to ever hold the love of a woman who would consent to marrying him and bearing his children. She had a strong feeling that he would grow old and die alone. A twinge of sympathy clouded her, but she quickly remembered the night he took her innocence in a sweep of greedy lust and violence.

"Then, I'll take my leave. Good luck with that...child." Foster gathered his wits and exited. Willa heard him kick his horse Heaven's Prince into service and swiftly gallop away. She felt her baby settle in her womb, a sign that it too was glad to have Foster out of their home.

***

On the ride back to the plantation house, Foster's mind was filled with emotions he did not understand. Was it the threat of the impending duel that had him feeling regret for what he had done to Willa, for the child he would never be allowed to acknowledge? Somewhere in his dark heart, he had a longing for her and the baby. And that frightened him to the core.

Chapter 47

It was just after the Witherell's had made the annual journey to Pawleys Island without her when the life inside of Willa began to get restless. One night as she slept close to her husband, she abruptly awoke with a gush of water between her legs. She guessed she'd emptied her bladder since lately the baby's weight was bearing down. But then it struck her! Her bag of water had broken. Not sure how much time she'd have before the labor pains set in, she lay there in awkward silence for a few seconds. *No need for alarm yet.*

She nudged Lazarus gently and he flinched, rolled over, and continued snoring, deep in sleep. Then she grabbed his shoulders and shook him hard. "Laz! For God's sake, Laz, my water done broke. Help me out of this bed. I'm all wet."

"What? What, woman? Oh, no! Oh, no! Baby! Baby! Okay, stay here. Stay here. I go fetch Heddie, I go fetch her. Stay here."

"Lazarus! Calm yourself. I am wet and I need you to help me change this bed. It's not time to have this baby yet. Just help me get changed and dry this bed. We have plenty of time."

The tranquility of her words did not reassure him as he set to flying about the cabin in search of dry bedding and a clean gown for Willa. When he found what he was looking for, she had already gotten out of bed and had it stripped down to the thin, bare mattress.

"What are you doing, Willa? Sit down! Let me do this!"

"Lazarus, I'm not sickly. I'm havin' a baby, that's all. And I'm in no pain. I'll help with this."

"No, you sit. Now!"

She obeyed, amused by his husbandly insistence. He made up the bed and she laughed at his sloppiness, but appreciated his efforts. She was coming to love him, less like a good friend and more like a husband. Not exactly in a romantic way, but as a beloved helpmate.

"Now let's get you out of that wet thing." Lazarus helped pull the cotton gown up past her large belly and over her breasts.

Although they had never been intimate, Willa had lost her sense of modesty once Laz started asking if he could touch her swollen belly. She allowed him that pleasure and even became comfortable undressing for bed in front of him. The sight of her body was comfortably familiar to him now and he never grew weary of its beauty. He could not help but stare at her, wishing that he could touch and caress her in the way a husband should.

"I do love you, Willa. You are the most beautiful woman I could ever hope for."

"Lazarus. I am a huge mess of a woman. Now, give me that dry gown before I get cold and…" She faltered, grabbing at her bumpy abdomen and leaning over, gasping for air. Her first contraction.

"What is it, Willa? What can I do for you? Oh, God! It's a pain, isn't it? It's time now!"

She could not respond. The intense pain took her words as she glanced up at her husband with a twisted look on her face. She blew out a long breath and waited for a few seconds. The pain quickly subsided.

"It's alright, Laz. It's not time. I can go like this for hours. Gimme that gown now."

His fumbling hands helped her into the gown and back into the bed. Within an hour the next contraction gripped Willa and lasted for several seconds longer than the first. Then the pains came quicker, now thirty minutes, now twenty. Lazarus refused to leave her side, sitting on the bed and holding her hand so she could squeeze during the spasms.

"Okay, now it's time to go fetch my mama," she said when the contractions became most unbearable and ten minutes apart. "Go now, Laz!"

"Stay right here, Willa. Right here. I be back just as soon as I can. Stay here, girl!"

"Now Laz, where do you think I'm goin' to go?"

"Okay," he repeated, "stay here!" He threw on an old cotton jacket he kept hanging on a knob by the bed and was out of the cabin in seconds. There was an old mule tied up just outside, put there a few weeks ago for the express purpose of getting him to Heavenly house when the time came to birth the baby. He was a trusted servant, not one tempted to escape on that animal, not that he could go very far and very fast on such an ancient beast.

He reached the rear of the plantation house in no time though. Tying up the mule, Lazarus flew up the steps and began to bang on the door to awaken Heddie, who had taken temporary residence on the back porch for just such an event. Soon she sprang into action, packing up a bundle of clean towels and blankets she had prepared in advance. She wasted no time climbing on the back of the donkey with her goods and as soon as Lazarus mounted, they were off. She held her son-in-law as tightly as she could while he drove the animal on as fast as it would go.

When they reached the Adams cabin, they could hear Willa screaming from inside. Lazarus helped Heddie dismount and then quickly tied up the service animal. Heddie was in the cabin within a heartbeat to find her only daughter writhing in pain on the bed.

"Mama! Mama! Mama it hurts! Help me Mama!"

"Oh, darlin' of course it hurts. But I's here for ya, and so is your husband. Lazarus, best be boilin' up some water, son. Take a deep breath, Willa child. Blow it out nice and slow, like this." She modeled the breathing for her daughter and Willa complied, calming herself through the contraction until she came upon some relief.

By that time Lazarus had the kettle on the fireplace and had rushed back to his wife's side. Heddie reached for one of the clean towels she'd brought and placed it on Willa's forehead to wipe away her perspiration. "Lazarus, go dip some of them rags in cool water, wring 'em out, and bring 'em back here to me. We got to keep this girl cooled off."

"Yes, ma'am." Before moving to the command, he bent over and kissed Willa's head.

Heddie pulled out a length of an old leather strap. "Here, baby. Put this 'tween your teeth and when the next pain come, you bite down. Bite down hard as you can. Okay, sugar?"

Willa shook her head in compliance, beginning to breathing hard again in anticipation of the next agonizing wave of pain.

"How long these been comin'?"

Lazarus answered for her, "Don't seem that long. She woke up in water and then the pain followed 'bout an hour later seems like. Seem like it went on for hours, closer and closer. Your stubborn daughter wouldn't let me fetch you any earlier though, Mama Heddie. She sure is stubborn sometime!"

Willa threw him a hateful look and then became tangled in another tremendous contraction, biting down on the leather for her life.

"I best be takin' a look down there to see where that baby be. Maybe we have a bit of a head by now! Lazarus, you go get on outta here. This is nothin' for you to see. You done seen enough of this girl the way it is or she wouldn't be layin' here like this. Go on, get!"

Lazarus looked at Willa for an answer and she gave him another hateful look, as if he actually was the one who put her in this condition. He wisely decided to step outside and let the ladies do their work.

"Damn you to hell, Foster Witherell. Damn you to hell," he whispered once he was out the door. Although when it came down to the truth, Lazarus secretly thanked the man for creating the circumstances which brought him Willa as a wife, he loathed Foster for the pain Willa was now enduring to bring their child into the world. He was not proud of his secret thankfulness and would never admit it to anyone, especially not to Willa. However, at the current moment, he wanted to see Foster, wanted to spit in his face and curse him for being a rapist.

Lazarus sat down on a tree stump and cried. Willa was paying every possible price for another man's violence and cruelty toward her. Not only was she violated, losing something that can never be replaced, she also forfeited her love for Seth and did the only thing she could think of doing for the good of all, married a man she did not truly love. And Lazarus was a part of the lie, the secret. He knew now more than ever that Willa should have been allowed to run away with Seth when she had the chance. *Yes, damn Foster!*

Then the sound of a healthy baby's cry rapidly pulled him from his thoughts.

*

Chapter 48

"He's perfect, Willa!" Heddie laid a newborn boy in her daughter's waiting arms. "Lazarus! Get in here!"

The cabin door flung open, launching Lazarus into the room where he found his wife and her new son. The smile on his face could not have been any larger if he were indeed the natural father.

"Well, don't just stand there, papa! Dip some of those towels into that boiled water. We have a mess to clean up and a baby to bathe. Go on. There's time for gawkin' later, son!"

Papa. The words stung his ears at first with thoughts of Foster still fresh in his mind. As he was readying the towels though, he had a few minutes to mull what Heddie meant. This baby was his as far as everyone knew. Willa was his wife. He smiled again, this time feeling sure that everything was right, just as God intended for them.

After giving the crying infant a quick bathing, he was put to Willa's breast. The child took to his mama's milk with no urging as if it was something he'd done for weeks. His hunger astounded all of them and Willa was instantly assured that he would grow to be a healthy and vigorous little boy.

"Ramiel. That will be his name. It means, "mercy of God" and that's just what he is. God's been merciful to us, givin' us a perfect son. Laz. Just look at him eat!"

"He's a precious miracle, he is!" Heddie's eyes were on fire with pride and complete joy as she watched her grandbaby nurse at his mama's breast. His tiny jaws filled with milk and he gulped with satisfaction.

"Oh, dear mighty, wondrous God," she began to pray, "thank you for this perfect child. Thank you for your grace, oh Lord and for your mercy. We be the most blessed family, oh Lord. We be surely blessed! Watch over this child, oh God, watch him grow and become the man you intend him to be. And bless these two young 'uns, my precious Willa and Lazarus, as they be new parents. Help them make good and wise decisions 'bout their new son and raise him in a Christian home, safe from the harm of this cruel thing called slavery which we be part of. Spare them from the mis'ry brought to me and my husband, your son Alfred and our boys Sampson and Edgar. Oh, Lord, do them right!"

"Thank you, Mama," Willa whispered. Lazarus nodded in agreement and the three of them continued to watch the hungry infant suck life into his tiny stomach.

When Ramiel seemed to drain one breast, Willa set him to the other. Finally full, he fell into a deep sleep, but Willa refused to lay him down in the bed Lazarus had hewn out of oak for him. "I'll just hold on to him, Laz. Watch him sleep."

"But Willa, I know you're exhausted. You need to sleep, too. Don't want you droppin' our babe and lettin' him roll off on to this cold, old floor."

"Laz. How can I sleep? Look at this fine little man. I just have to watch him a while longer."

Heddie was studying her peaceful sleeping grandson. She took a finger and traced the outline of his face, softly so she would not awaken him. "Oh, he look just like you did as a new baby. But he definitely has Lazarus' ears. And his colorin'. He's not dark like us, Willa. In fact, not even as dark as Lazarus. He'll grow into it though."

The new parents looked at each other in unexpected alarm. Willa's mind snapped back to the day she made the decision to offer Lazarus the proposal of marriage and fatherhood. She considered the fact that he was very light for a Negro and figured that his coloring and hers would make for a fairer-skinned child. No one would question his coloring. No one would suspect that he was half white. She counted on that, planned for that.

As she looked down at her slumbering baby, her gaze was intent. Did his ears really resemble Lazarus'? Did he have any of Foster's features? A painful prick of reality poked at her heart like the thickest of her sewing needles as the color of panic spread across her face.

"What's the matter, honey? Did I say somethin' wrong?"

"N...no Mama. No! I...I'm just thinkin' of Papa and the boys. That's all." She knew that tears would roll any moment and was surprised when they did not come. She held her own against a tide of emotion--part guilt, part panic, and now scraps of memory about their dear family left back at Southwind.

"Oh, Willa...hand Laz the baby and let me hold you."

Willa obeyed, still waiting for a dam of tears to break. Lazarus gently took Ramiel from her and moved himself to the nearby rocking chair that he had also crafted for their cozy home. As he sat down, he was thankful for the comfort of the soft pillow Willa sewed so lovingly to contribute to the project.

Heddie sat down on the bed and encircling her daughter with both arms, she rocked her quietly back and forth. Willa laid her head down on a soft shoulder as finally her tear ducts co-operated with her heart and poured forth a steady stream, spilling their warmth down Heddie's back.

"There, there now, darlin'. I know. I know. Not easy for either of us. Sure wish your papa and brothers could be here now with us, too. But baby, somehow I know that God himself be watchin' over them and givin'"em some kind of sign that we are alright. Some kind of sign that there is a new life and we be doin' fine."

Her words did indeed comfort Willa as she held on to her mama and squeezed tighter in acceptance. Somehow, God would work His miracles and provide this knowledge to her family far away. But more important in her mind at this point, He would also allow her small family here remain intact, with no one ever discovering how baby Ramiel's life was formed inside her. No one would associate him with Foster. Ever.

Chapter 49

The summer following the birth of Ramiel was extremely hot and humid on Heavenly Plantation, but it passed by quickly and without incident. Willa spent her days at the mansion house in her former sleeping quarters, now her exclusive sewing room, fashioning gowns for Margaret and Marianne's fall and winter balls. Marianne had protested fiercely against her mother, first stating her objection to leaving Willa and second to making her toil during the hot season with a new baby.

She had tearfully threatened to stay behind at Heavenly to help their seamstress in whatever way she could. But Margaret eventually won out, convincing her daughter that it would be an important social summer on Pawleys Island and that Gerald was sure to propose at one of their Seaside soirées! Marianne cried for days, hating to leave Willa behind in the late stage of pregnancy, due to give birth to her first child at any moment.

Ramiel was growing fast, gaining weight and strength, nourished in abundance by Willa's milk. During the daytime, she carried him with her to the house where the two of them shared quiet, magical moments together. She worked while he slept in a cradle that had been used by all of the Witherell children, including Ramiel's natural father. After Gabriel and Garrett were born, Josiah had a second cradle made, so this was the older of the two and Marianne had it carried down from the attic without her mother's knowledge. Since it was the old cradle, she figured that Margaret would not mind it being used by Willa's infant.

At first Willa felt a strange sense of guilt by having the baby in the same cradle used by Foster, as if it were a betrayal to Lazarus somehow. Then she consoled herself with the realization that Seth too had used the crib, as well as her beloved Marianne. Her own mama had carefully lifted from the cradle either of the Witherell twins to nurse at her breasts. She smiled, thinking of the little bed's heritage.

Ramiel was indeed a very light-skinned Negro baby. As Willa looked into his face, she knew that the eyes looking back were Foster's. Some of his other facial features were his in a subtle way. One had to look closely, study carefully in order to draw such a conclusion. The thought made her heart race every time, until she once more found solace in the fact that Ramiel's features were also similar to Seth's. She found a sense of comfort in that.

Since she would never bear Seth's children, she had the next best situation here with her new son.

She was getting over Seth; time was healing her and the love she felt seemed to grow dimmer. Occasionally she would reflect upon what might have been if their plan to run from Heavenly were realized, if Foster had not stopped her in the woods. Then she would look at Ramiel sleeping peacefully, so much like an angel. She'd realize that he was the consequence of that night, however horrific his conception. She had to constantly purge that part from her mind.

Lazarus worked hard all day and sometimes into the night. Willa had no idea that a blacksmith would be so busy with his trade, but the plantation was large and the need for tools, barrel supports, horseshoes, and other implements was great. When he finally entered the cabin at the end of the day, he was exhausted, but not too spent to lovingly kiss and hug his wife and hold the baby. His baby. He filled his new role so willingly and authentically that Willa knew she could not have made a better decision than to ask him to marry her.

The couple became husband and wife now in all aspects. Slowly they grew more intimate as they fell into each other's arms at the end of the day. Soon they shared kisses that contained hints of passion. Willa recalled Seth's kisses, the only ones she knew besides the ones Foster had forced upon her. Seth's seemed clumsy compared to Lazarus' kisses. She began to appreciate his physicality and his masculinity. As he undressed one night before bed, she found herself staring at him, studying his perfect sculpted muscles. His arms were bulging and tight, his chest finely chiseled, and his buttocks firm. This was her husband!

Willa felt proud and aroused at once as she made her way the short distance across the cabin floor. She caught his eyes with hers and his held question, as he was surprised by her sudden interest. She put her arms around him, looked into his face and planted a slow, hungry kiss on his lips. He returned the kiss with his own passion, his heart beating fast. *What is happening? Why is she doing this? This is what I've dreamed of.*

They made love for the first time, consecrating their marriage, fulfilling the vows they made to share their lives totally. When they finished, Lazarus gently lifted a still sleeping Ramiel out of his cradle and put him into the bed between he and his wife. Willa began to cry softly.

"Willa? Why ya cryin'? Did I hurt you, honey? I'm so sorry..."

"No. No, Laz." She reached out to hold his chin in her hand. "No, you didn't hurt me. Far from it. I...I am just...happy. I'm happy, Laz. Finally happy. I can't ask for anything more. We have a good life, Laz."

"We sure do, Willa. Sure do."

They fell asleep with Ramiel cuddled between them.

Chapter 50

Fall was approaching as the Witherells returned from their annual vacation at Pawleys Island. The first week back on the plantation was always a time of adjustment where they had to re-assume their usual roles and shed the carefree feelings of summer on an island. It was back-to-business for Josiah, Foster, and now Seth. Margaret and Marianne would attend to household management and a never-ending cycle of social calls and parties. The twins Gabriel and Garrett would begin a new school term.

Marianne could scarcely wait for their carriage to arrive through the gates of Heavenly Plantation. There was news to relay to Willa and Lazarus about her summer marriage proposal by Gerald. There were plans to be made for an engagement party to herald the announcement to society. Most important though was the fact that there was a new baby to meet! How she agonized over the idea of Willa at Heavenly in that tiny cabin giving birth to her baby without her best friend by her side. Was the delivery difficult? Was Willa in much pain? Did she birth a boy or a girl? Is the child healthy? Dozens of questions filled her mind as the carriage rolled along on the road to Heavenly, taking an eternity.

Once they pulled up the long drive to the house, Marianne could no longer contain herself. As soon as the carriage came to a halt, she was the first up from her seat and as soon as the Charleston City Carriage driver opened the compartment door, she was out. Not caring about anything else, she raced up the front steps, pulled open the door and then flew up the grand staircase toward Willa's sewing room where she knew she'd be working. She arrived out of breath and had to pause at the door or risk fainting. She took a few deep breaths, calming herself so she could manage a soft knock on the door that would not frighten Willa or wake the baby who might be sleeping.

She whispered, "Willa? Willa, are you in there?"

The door opened and Willa's face beamed at the sight of her friend. They embraced tightly, enthusiastically, as if they were separated for years instead of months. Finally Willa let go, pulled Marianne into the room, and led her over to the well-worn cradle where Ramiel slept. She waited for her reaction as Marianne peeked down to the baby inside, bundled warmly in layer of soft blankets.

"Oh, Willa! The baby is beautiful! Just beautiful!" Her voice was a high-pitched, excited whisper. "Son or daughter?"

"He's a boy. We've named him Ramiel and he is the most wonderful blessing to us!"

"A boy! Lazarus must be so proud! Oh, Willa, I am so sorry I was not here with you as I should have been." She looked at Willa with eyes of genuine sorrow and regret.

"Don't you go getting' worked up now Marianne. You know that was not a possibility. You have nothing to be sorry for."

"But I truly am, Willa. Tell me, how was the birth? Was it horribly painful? Did it last for hours and hours?"

"To tell the truth, I don't even remember. Not really. I'm sure it was painful at times, but what I recall is that in the end I had this precious little boy emerge from my body. You should have seen Lazarus! And Mama too, of course. She delivered Ramiel herself and made Laz go outside until it was all over. He was so nervous that you'd have thought he was the one havin' a baby."

Marianne put her arms around Willa and squeezed tight. "I am so happy for both of you! You are married to a man who adores you so and now you have his son." Then she held Willa at arm's length to fully scan her over. "You look brilliant, too. Not at all like a woman who just bore a child. I can only hope to look as fine as you after I have my fiancé Gerald's children."

Willa caught the word "fiancé" immediately. "Marianne! He proposed to you! Congratulations!"

"Why thank you, Willa. It happened at the Island during one of our parties, just as Mother predicted. We shall announce it here very soon and I will certainly need your assistance in planning the event. But for now, I cannot wait any longer to hold this baby! We have all the time in the world to catch up on all the happenings of the summer, but Ramiel will only be an infant a short time!"

"Of course!" Willa reached into the cradle, scooped up her beloved child, and handed him off to her friend. In doing so, it struck her for the first time that Marianne came second now that she and Lazarus were closer. She smiled at both the sight of Marianne holding Ramiel and the realization that her husband was becoming her new best friend.

"You look right at home holding a baby."

"I do?"

"Of course you do. You will be a perfect mother, Marianne. Just perfect. You can practice with Ramiel. It will be so wonderful!"

Ramiel slowly opened one eye and then the other, looking up at Marianne. Expecting to see Willa, he was startled by the unfamiliar face of the stranger holding him. His face turned red, his mouth opened wide, and he delivered an ear-piercing wail. Marianne's face responded with a mixed expression of terror and confusion.

"It's alright. He just wants his mama. Probably hungry, that's all. He is quite an eater." Willa gently relived her friend of the bawling baby. Quickly Marianne looked relieved as Ramiel quieted in his mother's familiar arms.

"Don't you worry, Marianne. He'll get used to you. He will."

Willa sat down in the rocking chair that Marianne insisted be installed in the room before she left for summer vacation. Quickly she pulled open the front of her cotton dress to bare a breast to the baby who latched on without hesitation. His appetite was as voracious as ever. Willa saw Marianne look away, embarrassed.

"It's alright to look, Marianne. I don't mind and you know this boy does not. Look how he eats. Your own babies will…" She stopped, suddenly remembering that Marianne will likely have a black wet nurse to do the job of infant feeding. Instantly she regretted what she began to say and felt a twinge of sadness for her friend. The bond between mother and child was so strongly forged during the times of nursing that she could not imagine having it established instead with a wet nurse. She so thoroughly enjoyed her time nursing Ramiel.

The two women remained silent as if a cloud just settled over their conversation and refused to move. Nothing but the sound of Ramiel's urgent suckling. After several awkward minutes, Marianne was the first to speak, albeit in a less enthusiastic voice.

"Well…I really must be getting along now. I'm completely exhausted from the journey. You understand. But…I'll visit again tomorrow. Your baby is lovely, Willa. Just lovely." She glanced down at the nursing baby, smiled, and excused herself from the room.

***

Ramiel went back to sleep after his feeding, allowing Willa to continue sewing without interruption in order to finish a gown for Margaret. It was getting late and she would have just enough time to bundle up her son and return home before darkness set in. She gathered the baby and slipped out of the plantation house without notice.

Arriving home before Lazarus, Willa began to prepare their simple evening meal of ash cakes and ham while the baby continued sleeping. A tap on her door was unexpected, as Marianne was not planning to visit that night.

The thought of Foster's visit while she was pregnant sprang into her mind and she froze.

"Willa? Willa, it's Seth. May I come in? Willa, are you there?"

Seth? Why would Seth come to the cabin? He'd never been there, although Lazarus tried many times after the wedding to invite him there. Did he know that Lazarus was not home? She answered the door with a mind full of questions.

"Seth?" She stood in the doorway just looking at him, studying his face for answers.

"It's getting a bit chilly outside, Willa. May I come in?"

"Y..yes. Of course. Come in and warm yourself by the fire."

"Thank you."

Willa closed the door and turned around to see Seth in front of the hearth warming his hands over the dancing orange flames. His eyes fixed on her for an instant. She was as beautiful as ever with her dark skin and black eyes and he had to look away for fear she'd see desire in his eyes. She looked content. Happy, like she had not missed him at all as her life moved on.

Then he heard a small whimper coming from the other side of the cabin, followed by crying. *The baby, of course*, he told himself.

"Oh. That's Ramiel, my son. Ummm...our son. Lazarus and mine." Willa turned around to go collect the baby from his cradle, the cradle made with love by his only known father. She picked up her infant, cradling him in her protective arms. Walking towards Seth, she turned Ramiel around to allow him to look at the baby. Ramiel quieted and began to smile.

"Oh, God. Willa, he is quite a baby. Look at that smile!"

"Would you like to hold him, Seth?"

Caught off guard, Seth hesitated for a few seconds before answering, "No...I don't think so. I've never really held an infant. The twins were much bigger when I held them. I don't think I should."

"You won't break him, if that's what worries you. Come on." There was something she wanted to see in having him hold her son, something she had to find out for herself. When Seth finally held out his arms, she very gingerly placed Ramiel into them and stood back to watch. Seth looked so uncomfortable that she had to snicker.

"What are you laughing about? I told you I've never done this before." His voice indicated amusement too.

"You look so funny with a baby, that's all. Like you are terribly afraid of him."

"Well I am! What if he cries again? Spits up on me? Starts to choke?"

"Then you hand him over to his mama."

That was permission to do just that. He handed Ramiel back to her as if he were a hot coal. Still, seeing him just briefly with the infant gave her enough time to conclude two important things. One, Ramiel did indeed favor the Witherell looks, even Seth's. And two, she had chosen wisely in asking Lazarus to be father to the child, as he took to the infant so naturally and never for a moment displayed fear or lack of confidence. Maybe now she could forget about her feelings for Seth completely. Completely.

"I'm sorry, Willa. I just wanted to come to you and offer an apology for the way I've treated you and Lazarus. I had no right to expect you to run away with me last year. To make such a life-altering and dangerous decision. I expected too much and I cannot blame you for turning to Lazarus. I'm sure he understands you far better than I ever could since you both come from the same…the same circumstances. I realize that…"

"Seth, Seth! You owe me nothin'. No apologies."

"No, let me finish. Please. I realize that because you are both…both…"

"Slaves. Go ahead and say it. It doesn't hurt me, Seth. I know what I am. It's no shame to me. We are what we are."

"I…I hate these circumstances. The circumstances that kept us from being together, kept us from a life together. But I realize that I cannot know what it is to be like you and Lazarus. My world is different and yours is different. I'll say the same things to Lazarus as soon as he comes home. I want to make amends and befriend you both. I've done so much thinking over the summer and my heart feels mended. I need to know that yours has mended, too. I wish you and Laz such happiness, Willa."

The cabin door swung open and ushered in the man of the house. Lazarus' jaw dropped a bit upon seeing Seth.

"Seth? You're back from the Island. It's good to see ya, my friend!" He rushed over and threw his muscular arms around Seth as if they were two brothers reunited.

Willa let them have time to embrace before declaring that it was time to get supper on the table. She planted a friendly kiss on Lazarus' cheek and handed Ramiel off to him while she went back to preparing the meal. "Stay for supper Seth? It's not much, but you're welcome to it."

"Oh, no thanks Willa. Just let me have a little time to say my piece to Laz and I'll be out of your hair this evening."

The two men took chairs while Willa busied herself with the ash cakes and ham, trying not to listen to their conversation. Finally, it seemed as if life was coming together for her and her little family. She certainly did not feel like a slave.

Chapter 51

Unfortunately Margaret Witherell had taken ill soon after her arrival back at the plantation and was confined to her bed. Marianne was left to planning her own engagement party, with the help of Willa and Heddie. They conspired for weeks on the plans, getting Margaret's approval for this and that only as her health would allow.

Marianne spent considerable time with Ramiel, completely smitten by the baby's emerging personality. She patiently anticipated the day when she could introduce him to Margaret, thinking the baby would make her feel hopeful about becoming a grandmother herself one day. Perhaps she would become pregnant within weeks after her wedding and make that a reality even sooner. She longed for Margaret to be the kind of grandparent that Heddie was to Ramiel, doting and proud. Yes, a grandchild would certainly help her mental state as well.

Just before the Thanksgiving holiday, Margaret was showing considerable improvement and Doc Capshaw lifted her bed restrictions. As soon as the physician left the mansion, Marianne rushed to Margaret's side.

"Mother! I am so happy for you! It's been months and you must be so weary of this insufferable bed and this room! Let me help you up."

"Settle down, daughter. Doc says I must not rush. My legs may well not work as they did before. I should wait until your father or brothers are here to assist me. I'll not want to fall on you, Marianne."

"Oh, nonsense! Let's try!"

"Marianne, no. I said no. Wait on the men. I insist."

"I can get Ned."

"For the love of God, child. Ned is an old man. What good would that do? Then there would be the three of us on the floor!" She laughed and it was music to Marianne's ears to hear such lightness from her.

"Oh, alright. We shall wait. What can I get for you in the meanwhile? A magazine, a book? Some tea?"

"Stop with it, Marianne. I've had enough magazines and tea these past months to fill my lifetime. Don't bother with me. I am just fine and besides, I have servants to bring me such things. Now don't you have some planning to do or are you finished with the details for your engagement party? You know that we can set a date now, as well as a date for the wedding!"

"Oh, of course I have more planning to do. In fact, I can fill you in on everything we've dreamed up so far. Thank goodness for Willa and Heddie or Gerald and I would have to wait until next year to make our announcement!"

"I suppose we should be grateful to them."

Marianne's eyes lit up with an idea. "Mother! You've yet to see Willa and Lazarus' beautiful baby boy! That's easy enough to fix. I'll go get him. Now that we know you are no longer a health risk to him, I'd be pleased to introduce you! Willa is in her sewing room right this moment working on my gown and she always brings Ramiel with her. I shall get him at once."

Before Margaret could voice approval or rejection, Marianne was out the door and flying down the long hallway. Suddenly she was thankful to have shoes on as she imagined herself sliding out of control all the way down the polished wood floors toward Willa's room. She chuckled at the vision in her head. She reached the sewing room and knocked softly.

"Willa, Mother is better!"

Willa opened the door and ushered her in. "That's wonderful news! I am glad. Now take a look at your gown!" She lifted a burgundy puff of dress from a hook on the wall and shook it out to spread its glory over the floor. Layers of satin and moiré taffeta cascaded from a tight-fitted bodice that featured a dramatically dipped neckline and small puff sleeves meant to be worn off shoulder. "It is finished."

"Oh, my! Oh, my!"

"Is that all you have to say for it? All those weeks and weeks of pin pricks and threads tanglin' and treadle pumpin' and..."

"Oh, you be quiet. It is the most delightful thing I've ever seen, Willa. It is perfect. Just magnificent."

"And?"

"And I am going to hug and kiss you!" She did just that while Willa still held on to the gown.

"It is spectacular, my Willa, just spectacular! I knew it would be. May I try it on?"

"I hoped you would."

"Oh, dear! I hurried in here to scoop up Ramiel and show him to Mother. Perhaps I shall do that first and then try on the gown. What do you think?"

"I think you should try on the gown and then we'll both go see your mother with Ramiel. I would like to thank her for letting me help you with your party plans and allowing me to design this gown. She could as well have ordered something from Paris."

"Never! No, you are a gem, Willa. A true gem and Paris cannot compare to you! Someday the entire world will find out about you and we shall lose our exclusivity, I fear!"

"Try on the dress. You may not even like the way it fits."

Marianne gave her arm a playful tug and then the two of them worked at slipping her into the gown. It fit exactly the way Willa intended, as if Marianne were designed for the dress instead of the other way around. She was a regal vision of burgundy richness.

"I will carry my son. I've worked too long on that frock to have him spit up on it."

"Agreed. Let's go."

Willa picked up Ramiel, who was just waking from a nap. *Excellent timing*, she mused as they set off down the hallway.

"Let me enter first to show her your wonderful creation."

"I thought I made it clear that I didn't want to chance my wonderful creation spitting up on you."

"I was speaking of the gown, your other wonderful creation!" The two laughed, resembling the small girls who once roamed the halls of Heavenly house.

"Mother?" Marianne lightly knocked at Margaret's door.

"Come in my dear. Let me have a look at that baby you've praised for months."

"I've something else for you to see first." Marianne stepped inside, drawing up her skirts to fit through the doorway. She fanned out the gown so Margaret could take in its full view. "See what else Willa created?"

Margaret gasped. "My! My! It is glorious! You are so…so…perfectly beautiful my daughter! Come closer."

Marianne approached her mother's bedside and curtsied. Margaret reached out to touch the luxurious taffeta and feel the fullness of the skirts. Then she lifted her hand to Marianne's face and brushed her cheek. "My lovely daughter has grown into a woman. An engaged woman. Oh, my." Her eyes filled with mist.

"Oh, Mother, don't cry."

"These are tears of joy, Marianne. A mother's tears of joy as she sees her own daughter grow into a woman and take on the role she was raised to fill. Gerald is a lucky young man, my dear. A lucky young man to have such a perfect girl like you to marry and mother his children."

"Children. Yes. Oh, that reminds me! Ramiel! Willa! Come in, please!"

Willa cautiously entered and approached, carrying a wide-eyed son. What happened next would remain a blur to both Marianne and Willa forever due to the speed at which it occurred.

"Mother, this is Ramiel Adams," Marianne proudly announced.

Margaret's eyes examined the baby with delight at first until slowly the light in them extinguished. As if vexed by an unseen demon, she shrieked long and loud. Her hands flew up to her scalp and her fingers clamped over masses of beautiful blond hair. She began to tug incessantly until she managed to pull out clumps of it. Next she began to claw into her face with her sharp fingernails, drawing blood.

Ramiel shrieked in response, flailing his limbs as if trying to escape his mother's arms. But Willa kept a tight hold on him, running from the room, down the staircase and out the side door of the house in response to the horror.

Meanwhile Marianne stood there, eyes transfixed on her screaming mother, not knowing what to do, not understanding the sudden fury of the woman.

Chloe was soon in the room, throwing herself at Margaret, attempting to restrain her wild hands and prevent her from continuing the assault on her once-lovely face.

"Ma'am, calm down! Calm yo'self down now! Settle, Miz Marg'ret! Settle! Missy, go fetch Myra. Now! Have her get the laudanum medicines for the Missus! Get on child!"

Marianne stood staring.

"I says, get on child! Do you want your mama to die?"

"N...no. No."

"Bes' get on out then. Fetch Myra."

The spell was somehow broken, allowing Marianne to move swiftly, in spite of the huge ball gown's encumbrance. She found Myra out in the kitchen.

"Myra! Myra! Come quick! Mother needs her laudanum!"

"What, child?"

Marianne repeated her words and Myra sprang into action. After locating the medicine, she coursed back up the stairs and into the sleeping chamber with the precious liquid.

It took Chloe and Myra a good deal of trying to get the drugs into Margaret who seemed all of a sudden to have the sudden powers of a mighty field ox. When she was finally calm and sleeping, Marianne left her and set out for Willa and Lazarus' cabin.

Chapter 52

Willa was safely home, her mind still reeling from Margaret's insane reaction to seeing Ramiel. Fear scorched her nerves. *What just happened?*

After rocking her son, she put him down to sleep and then continued in the chair. Back and forth, back and forth, attempting to repair her singed nerves. Restore calm to her brain. She was not having success with either. Time crawled slowly as she anticipated Lazarus' return from the blacksmith shop. She needed his big arms around her, needed his reassurance that all was well.

Margaret Witherell may have been cleared physically by Doc Capshaw, but mentally she was just as unstable as always, Willa believed. That should be no cause for alarm to her and her little family, and after all, she did not have to live at the Big House any longer. She would talk to Marianne about shortening her time at the house since her work on winter gowns was completed.

Perhaps she could work with Camille and the other seamstresses in the sewing house, stitching clothes for the slaves and other goods needed around the plantation. Christmas was coming and that was the time of year when all the field slaves were given new clothing for the coming year. Although working with the other slaves meant entrusting her son's daytime care to some of the elderly slave women, it would keep them both from being near Margaret and her misplaced wrath.

A knock on the door soon startled her thoughts. She answered quickly, expecting Marianne. Sure enough, there she was. Still in her engagement gown, obviously too disturbed by her mother's behavior to change into her everyday dress.

"Marianne. Come in. You really should not be outside in that gown. I'm sure it's soiled at the bottom. Take it off and I will get you a cotton dress to wear. I'll have one of the wash women clean this for you."

"Never mind the dress, Willa. What on God's earth just happened with my mother? I have never seen her so worked up in all my life! Why would she behave that way? I don't understand it."

"I have no idea, Marianne. It makes no sense to me. All I can say, and I'm sorry for sayin' this, is that your mother is still not well. She may be over her sickness, but she is not well."

"But she's never acted so terribly. Her hair lays in clumps on the floor; her face is scratched as if she's been attacked by a wild animal. But she is the wild animal!" Marianne's breathing was as fast and uncontrolled as the tears that spilled out of her eyes and fell to her once-perfect taffeta dress. The drops left stains that Willa knew would ruin it.

"Marianne! We must get you out of that dress before you wet it completely. Now do as I say and let me help you."

Finally Marianne gave in and allowed Willa to unfasten the laced-up bodice back and slip it down her torso. She supported her while she stepped out of the skirts. Standing in her undergarments, she shivered until Willa produced a common cotton gown for her and then wrapped her in a woolen shawl. Willa shook out the gown and spread it out carefully on her bed.

Then she took a kettle off the fire and poured equal portions of boiling water into two tin cups. She picked several leaves from a canister and dropped them into the hot water, letting them steep for a few minutes before pouring a bit of cooler water over them. Lazarus obtained the leaves from a healer in the slave village before Ramiel's birth, as they were said to have a calming effect when brewed into a tea. However, the baby's birth was not an arduous enough event for her to have needed the medicinal brew. However, today's bizarre events seemed to fit the need.

Marianne sat in front of the spitting fire and stared into its flames as if looking for answers contained within. Soon Willa handed her a cup of the tea and urged her to take a drink. She breathed in the tea's aroma and it seemed agreeable enough, so Marianne obeyed with a tiny sip. She continued sipping while the two sat side by side in silence until Marianne felt more relaxed.

"Perhaps my mother should have some of your tea, Willa, instead of the laudanum she's always given by the doctor. I honestly have no idea why she was so agitated today, but I have never seen her so extreme. She has never attacked her own face, her own hair! Willa, she is a beautiful woman and she would never disfigure herself like this. I cannot understand."

"I'm so sorry, Marianne. I don't know what to say. I don't know why my baby would set her to such behavior."

Unexpectedly, as if someone lit a candle in a dark, black cave, it struck Willa that Margaret's horrific actions might be explainable. Did Margaret see Witherell in the baby? Did she know something about Foster's attack on her? Or did she now suspect that Seth fathered the child? What was it? Marianne did not seem to have any such suspicions and she was around Ramiel quite a lot these days. Willa began to feel sick and stifled the urge to retch long enough to pop up from her chair and bolt out the front door. Outside, she bent over and vomited on the ground.

"Willa! What is it?" Marianne was swift to follow her friend out the door to witness her upheaval. "Is it the tea? My gosh, but I feel fine. Willa?"

"I…I had little to eat today. If I recall, the tea should not be taken on an empty stomach. Maybe you should go now, Marianne. I need to lie down while Ramiel is sleeping. I need to rest."

"I'll do no such thing, I'll put you in bed myself and stay until the baby wakes. Then I'll take care of him while you rest. Now get back into the house."

"Lazarus will be home soon, I'm sure. He'll be comin' soon. Just go home, Marianne. Tend to your mother. Please? I'll get in bed and you can put the baby in with me. Then go home."

Marianne gave in. She lifted her ball gown off Willa and Lazarus' bed, placing it across the chairs near the hearth. Then she tucked in her friend and the baby as requested. Finally she gathered the dress in both arms and walked back toward the Big House.

***

Back at the mansion, Josiah had returned from a short trip into Charleston, weary and wanting no more than to change out of his traveling attire, have a quiet dinner, and then retire to his study. As soon as he opened the front door though, he was greeted by Chloe and warned about the Missus' strange behavior. "Not again, not now", Josiah said to her. "What brought on this bout?"

"Sir, it was a strange thing indeed. Miz Marianne say Miz Willa be here with her baby and the Missus takes one look at him and goes mad. Like the baby be evil or somethin'. That baby look fine to me and Myra. Sweet thing. Angel of a thing, he is. Quiet and not a fussy…"

"Chloe! Spare me the trivial details. What have you done for Margaret? How did you calm her?"

"Dose o'laudanum. Jus' like always. Had to fight to get it down though. She feisty. Pulled out her hair, scratched up her pretty face too. Miz Marianne see it all. Ain't nothin' me and Myra done to her. You can be sure o'that."

"So she sleeps now."

"Yessir. Like a babe."

"That will be all then, Chloe. Carry on with your duties."

"Yessir."

Climbing the stairs to his sleeping quarters Josiah encountered his three youngest sons who confirmed that their mother was still sleeping and that neither was home when the incident occurred. *Talk to Marianne*, they all advised. Josiah silently debated the merits of speaking to his daughter, looking in on his wife, or heading straight to his quarters. His head decided to visit Margaret's room, against the will of his heart.

Without a sound Josiah pushed open her door, careful not to disturb the volatile woman. He tiptoed to her bedside and when his eyes met the sight of her, he nearly lost balance. Margaret's face was pocked with deep scratches to which ointment had been applied. Her scalp showed in several places. "Dear God, Margaret!" he whispered. "What have you done?" He silently prayed that the dose of laudanum was one strong enough one to keep her sleeping throughout the night. He turned and crept out of her room, not bothering to shut the door for fear she would stir. He needed a full night's sleep in order to deal with her drama and he intended to get it tonight.

Chapter 53

The early morning hours at Heavenly were the most precious to Josiah. If necessary he could escape from the plantation house long before anyone noticed. Or he could enjoy the luxury of quiet time in his study to reflect on the past day's dealings or ponder those of the day to come before it would unfold. This day he decided to sleep a bit later, avoiding the inevitable with Margaret. By every indication last night, this was going to be the granddaddy of all her terrible tantrums.

When he finally appeared downstairs he contemplated drinking scotch with his breakfast, but quickly reconsidered, thinking it best to keep a clear head. Perhaps later he might indulge himself, after the worst of the day was over. In the dining room, he was attended as usual by his faithful staff of slaves. He could tell that the previous night was at some time a source of talk among them, for they all avoided looking him in the face.

After a meal of smoked bacon and fresh hen eggs, he gulped down the last of his goblet of milk and set out for the stairs.

"Sir! Marster!" It was Chloe. He paused so she could catch up with him in the hallway.

"What is it, Chloe?"

"The Missus ain't up yet. 'Spect that was a mighty dose of medicine we give to her last night. She still sleepin'."

"Very well then. I shall be in my study. Come get me at once when she awakens." *Ah*, he smiled to himself, *a reprieve*. He strode confidently to his office and closed the door behind him, safe from Margaret once again, but it was only minutes later when he heard the ruckus from above.

"Get out! Get out! Nigger, get out! You touch me again and I will kill you! All of you! Get the hell out!" The sound of glass breaking was unmistakably a vase smashed against the back of Margaret's bedroom door.

"Dear God, be merciful and let that woman have peace," Josiah prayed before exiting his office. Approaching the stairway he had the enthusiasm of a man walking to the gallows. He passed Chloe and Myra on the staircase, each wearing a face of pity for him.

Too soon he was at his wife's door. Opening it, he saw the fragments of a fine cut crystal vase littering the threshold.

She wasted no time bombarding her husband. "You bastard! Bastard! How could you do it again? How could you?"

Recently pronounced well, Margaret threw her quilts aside and pulled herself out of the bed that had been her confinement for months. Standing to her feet was a challenge, but Josiah dared not offer her aid. He waited for her to get her feet firmly planted and watched her amble toward him like a cripple. He felt sorry for her, but wanted to laugh. That would have been his sudden death, he knew, so he kept silent.

She reached his body and lunged at him. Her weak frame was no match to his and she crumpled down to the floor. Again, he offered her no assistance. Margaret grabbed at his legs, pounding her fists into them with the clear intention of harm. He tried to step away, but she held to him. He dragged her with every step.

Unable to get to the bell pull to summon help, Josiah shrieked, "Chloe! Myra! Someone! Help me with this woman!"

"You dirty, unholy filth, you! Bastard!" Margaret continued to punch at his legs, unable to do anything else from her position on the floor.

Chloe came running at Josiah's command, along with old Ned, followed by Myra and Heddie. The four of them managed to get Margaret away from her husband.

"The medicine! Chloe, get the medicine!" Josiah insisted.

Margaret protested, "No, I will not take it. No more medicine! All of you OUT! This is between Josiah and me! Get the hell out!"

"You heard the woman. Go on about your business and leave us now. Margaret, are you willing to settle down and tell me what this is all about?"

She waited for the slaves to clear before she spoke. "Oh, God, Josiah! How could you be so heartless to me? Another bastard child with a slave? Another! How could you do this to me again?" Now her anger had melted into tears that bewildered an innocent Josiah.

"What are you speaking of, Margaret? What child? What slave? I've slept with none of them. None of them, I tell you. Not since Polly and I'll swear to it, by God!"

"Don't mention that name ever again. I will not have you speak of her in my presence!"

"I apologize, but truly I have no clue, Margaret!"

"I saw him yesterday, Josiah. Your son. Your black son. You cannot deny it now."

"What are you saying, Margaret? I think your illness has made you delusional, my dear. Lie down and let me send for Doc Capshaw. Was he not to visit you yesterday? I'll fix his flint for not seeing to you, Margaret!"

"He *was* here, Josiah. He pronounced me well. I am well now, no fever, no illness. I can think clearly."

"And why is it then that you've pulled out your hair and gouged at your face, Margaret?"

She looked at him with contempt in her eyes, unable to account for her behavior. Last night, in her mind it was Josiah she maimed and not herself. Because the laudanum worked so well at dulling her senses, she felt nothing from the lacerations inflicted until now. Her hands touched her face and as her fingers lightly spread out over the wounds she began to weep. Her tears were a salty affront to the cuts, making her wail in pain.

"Oh my God, Josiah, look what you've done to me now. Look at what you've done!"

Josiah poured water into the porcelain basin on Margaret's wash stand and found a cloth to dip into it. After wringing out the excess water, he attempted to apply the cloth to his wife's injured face. She spit at him for his efforts and then managed to deliver a hard, solid punch to his jaw. The blow knocked him back into the wash stand, upsetting the basin. Water spilled to the floor causing him to slip and fall. That was Margaret's chance to pounce upon him. She jumped on top to straddle him and began her assault. Open hand, fists, teeth, nothing was spared to hurt Josiah, who was so surprised by Margaret's unexpected strength that he found it difficult to defend himself.

"Why Josiah? Why? Why Willa? She's Seth's age, for God's sake! She is Marianne's servant! Do you realize what you've done? Do you realize how this affects our children? You bastard! You…"

"Margaret! Stop it Margaret! Stop it!" Josiah rolled side to side, trying to knock Margaret away from him and put an end to her ferocious blows. He finally succeeded and crawled out of her reach until he was clear to stand up again.

"What are you talking about, woman? What about Willa? Explain yourself, Margaret!"

Exhausted from the skirmish, she remained sprawled unladylike on the floor until she caught her breath and pulled to a sitting position. "Josiah, don't tell me that you don't understand me. You bed your daughter's servant, a playmate of your own children! Have you no conscience at all?"

"Margaret! I did no such thing!"

"She showed me your son, Josiah. There is no mistake as to his parentage. He is yours, it is clear. She bore your child!"

"Margaret! Why would you believe something like that? Clearly her lies have upset you, but you can believe me that they are not true! She is lying and I will have her punished before the day is done!"

"She told me nothing Josiah; all it took was for me to look at the child. He is yours, Josiah. I just hope our children never learn of this. Send her away, Josiah. Yes, send her away. Today! And get out of my sight, Josiah. Stay clear of me!"

"Margaret, you are mistaken. That girl bore a child to Lazarus the blacksmith, don't you remember that? She is paired with Lazarus and I had nothing to do with their child."

"Get out of here, Josiah! Take care of your business. Get the hell out of here!"

Shaking his head, Josiah knew that there was only one thing he could do to satisfy his wife. As much as he dreaded upsetting a good blacksmith like Lazarus, he had to send Willa and their son away. Back to Southwind for her. And quickly. He would do it before she had time to talk to anyone about his decision as he did not want to contend with an outraged staff of Negros.

Daniel would not be trusted to transport the pair since he was the grandfather. Instead he'd have Duke Henry gather up the girl and her baby and whisk them away while Lazarus was working. He disliked Duke tremendously, but knew that he could be counted upon to carry out his plans with discretion.

Josiah ordered his stable boy to saddle a horse and in a short time was on his way to the fields in search of his overseer. He found him easily and took the man aside to explain his plan. Duke was too willing it seemed, but Josiah had no choice. Still, he cautioned him that his duty was to deliver the woman and child to Southwind and nothing else.

"Deliver them to my brother-in-law with instructions to put the girl to service in the house. And Duke, if I hear that any harm has come to either, I will deal with you in kind. Am I clear enough on that?"

"Yes. Yes, sir Mr. Witherell."

If Duke Henry did anything sinister to his dear daughter's friend, he would never forgive himself for it. Even an important slaveholder like Josiah had a tremendous heart when it came to his only daughter and it shamed him to have to send away her childhood companion. Under the circumstances however, Margaret would not be satisfied until Willa was gone. He had no idea why his wife seemed so convinced that he had an affair with her that produced a child. How could she think he would seduce Marianne's playmate?

Chapter 54

Willa was preparing to go to Marianne with her request to work away from the plantation house when she heard horse hooves and wagon wheels outside the cabin. Then a man's boots hit the ground. Probably someone looking for Lazarus, who was due to be gone all day on a trip to Charleston with Seth to buy supplies. Whoever it was, she would meet him on the way out. Ramiel was already bundled up in a quilt and tucked into his basket for the walk to the house. She pulled a woolen shawl around her shoulders, lifted the basket by the handle, and turned the door handle. As she stepped outside, Duke Henry was the first sight she saw. She felt the air vacate her lungs.

"Mornin'. Sure been a long, long time, ain't it Miss Willa? Or I should say, Mrs. Willa. That right? You got yourself married, huh? And got yourself a baby there. Let me see it."

She was frozen. Her limbs failed to operate even though she willed her legs to take her back inside the cabin.

"Well, come on now, let's see the thing. I ain't goin' to hurt it." He drew closer to the basket, but still Willa could not move. "Take the blanket off and let me see that baby, now. What the hell's a matter with you, girl? As I recall, you are a feisty one. Been a long time, but I remember that. Ol' Duke remember that. Goin' to talk to me? Show me that baby?"

Slowly, Willa began to thaw and her hand reached to pull back the blanket covering her precious baby, just to satisfy Duke Henry so he would leave them alone. "H...here. Look at him. Then just let us be. Please, we...we want no trouble, Mr. Henry."

"Oh, now look at that! Got some light skin, I see. Who's his papa? Somebody white, I'd say."

"Lazarus Adams. That's his papa. My husband."

Of course Duke knew all about Lazarus and Willa and the baby. Nothing around Heavenly escaped him. Although he'd been cautioned years ago to stay away from the house, Foster had since kept him informed about everything that happened at Heavenly. Even trivial things like slave news. Foster had even hinted that it was his brother Seth who impregnated Willa.

"Sure is a good lookin' child. I mean that. Good lookin', like his mama. You still are a pretty thing...for a nigger, that is." Duke reached out to touch Willa's face and she backed away, pulling Ramiel's covers back into place.

"We need to be up at the house now. Marianne expects us and we don't want to keep her waiting."

"No, no, no. I have me some different orders from the Witherells. They got some plans for you and your bitty one, too. You ain't goin' nowhere near that house today. Or any other day."

Duke laughed out loud, a sound that made Willa shudder. Her heart raced as she tried to decipher the meaning of his words. *What plans? What plans?*

"Let's me and you go back into your little house and have us a talk about that. Whadda you say?" With those words he pulled his jacket to the side to reveal a pistol, sending a clear message to Willa. She obeyed, stepping cautiously backward as Duke advanced toward her and lifted the door handle.

Once inside, his feigned politeness gave way to the Duke Henry she remembered from the day he beat Juniper to death in the Big House. "Now, Willa Adams I give you five minutes to gather up everything your sorry black hide wants to take and then you and that baby goin' to get in that wagon outside and we're goin' to take a ride. A nice, long ride. Five minutes!"

Willa's mind raced in an attempt to grasp his words. She looked at him as if he was not real, only a phantom that would disappear as quickly as it came into view.

"What's a matter with you? Are you deaf, girl? Five minutes! Get your stuff together or you'll take nothing!"

She still could not comprehend.

"You are leaving here, girl. Got orders to take you away. Goin' back to Southwind where you came from. And if you want to take anything like clothes to wear, ya best be getting' it packed up. Right now! Move!"

Willa finally understood that he was serious. This was not simply a nightmare; Duke Henry was taking her from her home. She recalled the night Foster attacked her in the woods, the feeling that she was hovering above in the trees, watching the heinous act play out below her. That same sense of floating filled her as she moved around the cabin, gathering mostly supplies for Ramiel, but a few cotton dresses and an apron for herself. The five minutes dragged in slow motion.

Duke Henry grew impatient with her. Why was she not in a hurry to pack up her things? Did she think he was joking? Was she toying with him, trying him? Finally he withdrew his pistol and with the handle he hit Willa in the head, knocking her to the ground. *It will be much easier this way*, he told himself. She was out cold, limp and easy to move.

He opened the cabin door and looked around to make sure no one was watching before he picked up Willa, threw her over his shoulder and loaded her into the wagon. He pulled out a length of leather cord and tied her hands together. He headed back into the cabin and scraped up the meager belongings she chose, along with the basket and baby. He placed them all into the wagon, hoping that the child would not wake up and cry because he would be tempted to destroy it right then.

From his seat atop the wagon he whipped his horses into motion. Swiftly, Heavenly Plantation was reduced to a spot in the distance behind them.

Chapter 55

Lazarus returned from a successful buying trip with Seth feeling less like a slave and more like the craftsman he was. Although he was not allowed to speak with or acknowledge the vendors by handshake as Seth did, he was introduced as Heavenly's master blacksmith. When he entered his cabin that evening, he did so with an unusual sense of pride and accomplishment. He was eager to share with Willa his day's experiences.

Lazarus didn't worry when he discovered that his wife and child were not at home, even though it was well past the time when they should have returned from the Big House. He understood that Daniel would bring them around once it turned dark. Unconcerned, he settled into a chair and soon fell asleep without hesitation.

It was well into the night when Lazarus finally awoke. Immediately he was surprised that Willa had not sent him to bed when she returned from the plantation house. He stood up, stretching off the discomfort caused by sleeping bent over so long in a hard chair. When he stepped softly to his bed, but Willa was not there. The coverlets were still pulled up; Ramiel's cradle was empty as well.

Alarm spread through him like wildfire over a parched landscape. His mind raced with possibilities. Had his family decided to stay with Marianne? Perhaps Daniel was not available to carry them back home and they stayed at the house. That had to be the case. Or had something happened to one of them along the way? Maybe Willa chose to walk home after dark and was approached by wild animals, or far worse...Foster Witherell. The last thought sent an icy chill down his spine, along with an urgent impulse to go find her and their son.

Now thoroughly in a panic, Lazarus lit a lantern and headed outside, quickly covering the path Willa would have taken to and from Heavenly. He found nothing, no sign of her and Ramiel. Next he scurried to the living quarters for the house slaves to begin interrogating anyone who might have information.

Questioning Myra and Chloe would be first. They always knew everything that went on at Heavenly house, including the comings and goings of its occupants and guests. Lazarus had no misgivings about waking them in the middle of the night because they would understand. They loved Willa and Ramiel perhaps as much as he did.

He knocked with urgency and heard someone stir within. The door was answered by Chloe. "Lazarus? What in God's name you be doin' up here at this hour?"

"It's Willa and the baby, Chloe. They're not home. You see 'em at the Big House today?"

"Sure did, Laz. They was there this mornin'. That is 'til the Missus had one o' her bad spells. Done scared away Willa and the baby. Willa run off like there was no tomorrow!"

"Home? Do you know if she ran home?"

"As a fact, I do. Miz Marianne visited her shortly after. She be upset and frettin' too, just like Willa. Miz Marianne run all the way out there with her ball gown on. Came back in an old cotton dress carryin' the gown in her arms. Don't know what happen to it. Musta got soiled. Sure a pretty gown, it was. Willa sewed it real nice."

Lazarus was losing patience as she prattled on. "Chloe! What about Willa and Ramiel? Did Marianne see her at the cabin? You know what happened? She come back later? To the Big House?"

"No. Sure did not. I was there all day, all the way 'til dark. No Willa."

Now Lazarus was shaking, fear piercing him in the heart that now belonged to his precious wife. His legs turned to gel underneath him and he faltered, having to brace himself against the doorway. "Then...then where? Where could they be? Where am I goin' to look?"

"Maybe she done gone off to your mama and papa's cabin. Since you was gone today she mighta been afraid by herself. Your folks sure to take her in, that's what they'd do."

Chloe's idea did not reassure him at first until he mulled it over, clinging to the door frame. After some time he stood upright on his own again. "Thanks, Chloe. That's where I'll be lookin' now. Sorry to wake you."

"I do anything for you chilluns, you know that. Go on and get now. You find your family, boy."

At Daniel and Camille's Lazarus hit another dead-end in his search for Willa and Ramiel. They had neither seen nor heard from her all day. The senior Adams' began to worry along with their son because there was simply no logical explanation for Willa's disappearance with the baby. Daniel suggested they wait until morning light to begin a more thorough search of the area surrounding the cabin and the plantation house. He convinced Lazarus that it was dangerous for a colored man to be prowling around the property in the dark, not with the probability of Duke Henry or his men patrolling the place.

Rather than stay with his parents, Lazarus decided to return to the cabin, hoping and praying that he would find Willa and Ramiel safely inside.

But that was not to be the case. The cabin was lifeless except for the dim fire still burning in the hearth. He felt helpless and since sleep would not return to him, he lit a candle and pulled out the Bible Marianne had given them for a wedding gift. Willa taught him to read and although he was not proficient, he knew he'd be able to decipher enough to find comfort in the words contained in the Good Book.

He opened the Bible to Psalm 27 and read:

"The Lord is my light and my salvation; whom shall I fear? The Lord is the strength of my life; of whom shall I be afraid?

When the wicked, even mine enemies and my foes, came upon me to eat up my flesh, they stumbled and fell.

Though a host should encamp against me, my heart shall not fear, though war should rise against me, in this will I be confident.

One thing have I desired of the Lord, that will I seek after; that I may dwell in the house of the Lord all the days of my life, to behold the beauty of the Lord, and to enquire in his temple.

For in the time of trouble he shall hide me in his pavilion; in the secret of his tabernacle shall he hide me; he shall set me up upon a rock.

And now shall mine head be lifted up above mine enemies round about me; therefore will I offer in his tabernacle sacrifices of joy; I will sing, yea, I will sing praises unto the Lord.

Hear, O LORD, when I cry with my voice: have mercy also upon me, and answer me."

Then he prayed:

"Oh Lord, oh Lord. Hear me, your lowly servant. I pray you protect my Willa and baby Ramiel. Lord, please don't let harm come to 'em, for they be so weak. Only you know where they may be, Lord and I pray your hands be on 'em and bring 'em both home safe. They both be my world, Lord. Ain't nothin' good without my Willa anymore. Please, please Lord!"

Lazarus began to cry.

Chapter 56

The sun took its time creeping into the early morning sky. An exhausted Lazarus slept well past dawn and was surprised that he fell asleep again in the chair by the hearth. The fire was out, but the unseasonably cool nip to the air went unnoticed as his mind registered that Willa and the baby were still missing. For an instant his brain also lit on the notion that perhaps his wife escaped Heavenly with Seth. Could the pair have rekindled their romance and planned for Lazarus to be away while they got their affairs in order?

No matter what, Willa was gone and he had to find her. He pulled on a coat and set out for his papa's cabin. Upon arrival, Daniel had already assembled a small group of slave men. With the approval of Josiah, they were about to embark on a search of the property. Seth was there as well, so Lazarus' thoughts about he and Willa journeying off together were allowed to dissolve. The weight of suspicion floated from him, but did not bring much relief as other fears continued to bear down.

Seth was visibly shaken by the disturbing news of Willa's disappearance. Although he was not up half the night searching like Lazarus, he looked rough and haggard with red eyes and a defeated expression on his face. He had been crying, but when he saw Lazarus he blinked repeatedly, feigning dirt in his eyes. Laz knew better.

"Laz. I heard the news and came as quick as I could. I want to help. I'll do whatever it takes to bring your…your…family home." Seth faltered as if the word "family" burned his lips as it slid out of his mouth.

"I'd sure be grateful, Seth," Lazarus said, trying to sound sincere while inside he struggled to accept help from Willa's former love. "It would mean a lot to Willa. And me."

***

The search party covered every square foot of the Witherell property, including rice fields and what they could navigate of the swamps. There was no sign of the pair, but also nothing to indicate foul play. It appeared that whatever happened took place swiftly and without incident. They had simply vanished. Questions infested Lazarus' thoughts. Had Willa ran willingly? If so, how did she accomplish such a feat alone? Why would she do it now, just when their marriage was taking on new meaning?

Shortly after the unsuccessful search, Seth took it upon himself to inform Heddie and Marianne about the disappearance. Both women, along with the house slaves were inconsolable. Life at the manor virtually halted as they all clung to each other up, crying in disbelief.

Margaret remained sequestered in her room. The distraught slaves made her feel guilty and she couldn't bear to look at Marianne. She started to question her mandate, but not only for her daughter's sake. Mostly she felt miserable for her own selfish reasons. Although her wardrobe was set for the rest of the winter season, where would she get her gowns for springtime? Would she have to order from New York or Paris? Run the risk having something similar to another planter's wife? Those were the queries plaguing her self-absorbed mind.

She thought about rescinding her command to have the seamstress banished, but decided against it. It simply would not do to have Josiah's bastard in her presence. And she could not fathom the idea of having to look at Willa and think of the deed to which her husband had subjected her. She finally eased herself with the thought that Willa would be working as a seamstress at Southwind for her brother and his wife. She'd only need to send orders there for new gowns. It would not be quite the same as collaborating with her in person, but it would all work to Margaret's favor in the end. Her mood improved enough to rally her out of bed, but when she looked into her mirror she shuddered at the woman with the battered face looking back. She retreated to the comfort of her bed and hid under the quilts.

Josiah remained in his office after his early visit from Daniel to request consent to form a search party. Normally he would never have agreed, but in this situation his approval helped relieve some of his guilt. Even though he knew the men would turn up nothing, at least he'd done his part for them. His thoughts continued to drift back to Margaret's accusations. Where did she get such ideas? Why did she reflect back to Polly after all these years? He presumed she was over all that, had perhaps forgiven him.

He felt sad for Lazarus and his parents. He was fond of the family, as they were all so faithful to the Witherells. Daniel was actually a free Negro who stayed in his service, even though there was no requirement for him to do so. He knew that Daniel's allegiance was due to his desire to stay with his wife and son who were still Josiah's property. But the coachman was free to go and could have cautiously managed to smuggle out his family to meet up with abolitionists.

Daniel liked Heavenly too much and had far more privileges than the slaves, including traveling away from the plantation without supervision and being allowed to search the Witherell property for his son's wife. His daughter-in-law was well on her way to Southwind by now and Josiah wished he could tell the Adams' that she was safe and would be working in the plantation house and not the fields. No need to worry.

Chapter 57

Willa woke slowly, rubbing a tender spot on her head. She felt the crustiness of dried blood, but had no idea how it got there. She was lying on the floorboards of a wagon, moving along a bumpy path. The object in the basket next to her began to cry.

Ramiel! Her precious son was in the basket. She tried to lift herself off the floorboards but was too weak to move. The baby continued to cry while she struggled against an invisible weight sitting on her torso. Her head pounded in pain as unseen hammers splintered away at her skull.

"Shut that thing up! I can't hear myself think! Shut it up right now!"

Willa's eyes shot to the front of the wagon. Up on the driver's seat she saw him. Her worst enemy. It was Duke Henry controlling the reigns, taking her and her child away from Heavenly. It was coming back to her now. The abduction. Duke telling her to get her things together, that he was taking her far away. Back to Southwind he said.

Ramiel kept crying and Willa remained on the floor, unable to move. Now the pain coupled with fear and disgust. She had to find the strength to get up and cradle her son for fear that Duke would hurt, possibly kill him. The overseer continued to holler until she finally managed to sit up, grab the basket, and lift out her son. She assessed the baby before pulling him close, wondering how long she was out and how long Ramiel had cried. He was hungry so she put him under her shawl to conceal her breasts while he nursed. It was difficult to feed him while the wagon bumped along, but she persisted.

The air was growing cool, so she kept Ramiel close and covered them both in the blanket and quilt she hurriedly chose for the journey. Somehow her confused mind remembered that Southwind was far from Heavenly, over into the state of Georgia. The trip would take at least two days. Duke Henry would have to stop during the night and Willa feared he would climb into the wagon to sleep. She prayed that he would sleep up on his seat and not come near her and her son. The thought of Duke so near repulsed her, made her flesh bumpy with disgust.

Toward dusk, the nasty coachmen decelerated his horses, bringing them to a slow walk off the trail to stop in a wooded area. Alerted to the surroundings, Willa was frightened by the seclusion. Duke jumped down from his seat, freed the horses from the wagon, and then secured the animals by tying them to a pair of trees. Willa watched him with eyes that grew ever more suspicious.

Finally Duke came around to the back of the wagon and grunted instructions to her. "Time for you to come on out of there and take care of your business. Better do it fast, just like last time. I'm goin' to watch you. Now hurry up and don't try nothin'."

Willa complied, leaving Ramiel in his basket. After relieving herself, she climbed back into the old wagon with no assistance from the overseer. As soon as she settled down, he climbed in and pulled a few lengths of leather strap from a bundle he'd brought with him. He tied Willa's ankles to some hardware nailed into the sideboards of the wagon.

"There. That should do. You ain't never goin' to get those undone." His smile of satisfaction frightened Willa.

She watched as he stepped down and set to making camp in the clearing near the wagon. He unfolded a bundle and spread it out on the ground for his bed and then built a fire. Soon he hefted his muzzle loader rifle over his right shoulder and disappeared into the thick woods. Fifteen minutes later Willa heard gunshots and shortly after Duke reappeared with a smug look on his face and a dead rabbit dangling from one hand.

He proceeded to skin the small creature and then roasted its meat in the blazing fire. After he had his fill of the meat and some biscuits, he took a long drink from his canteen. He glanced over at Willa and caught her staring, her face fully illuminated by the flames.

"What the hell you lookin' at, girl? Ain't never saw a man eat before?" He began to lick his fingers, one by one, taunting Willa as he savored the taste of the rabbit meat. "You hungry?"

Willa remained silent, looking away from Duke.

"I said, are you hungry? Answer me, girl! I know you ain't too bright, but I'm sure you can understand that."

"Y…yes. Yes, sir."

Without words, Duke then carried the rabbit carcass over to her so that she might gnaw on the scraps of meat remaining on the bones. After she accepted the grimy remains, he then poured a small ration of water into a tin cup and handed it to her. Just as quickly he walked away, not uttering a word.

After gulping down the water, Willa began to work over the rabbit bones. As hungry as she was, she found it distasteful to gnaw on the remains of a wild animal. Still, she needed the nourishment and chewed until there was nothing left except bare bone. She tossed the carcass over the side of the wagon, wiped her hands on her skirt, and then tried to get comfortable for the night while Ramiel continued to sleep. The leather straps cut into her ankles, but she refused to acknowledge the pain. *Stay strong Willa*, she thought to herself.

She bundled up with Ramiel and tried to shut off her mind, trying to stop thinking about the life they left behind at Heavenly. She began to focus on Southwind. Would her papa and brothers still be there? Would she even recognize them after all this time? Would they recognize her? Finally she drifted into a profound slumber.

***

God was merciful and allowed Willa and Ramiel to sleep through most of the long night. When she opened her eyes and sat up the next morning, the scenery had changed dramatically. Acres of cotton spread across the landscape, replacing the South Carolina rice fields. Clearly it was harvest season. Black men, women, and even some children walked down rows of the plants, picking the fluffy white cotton and putting it in sacks they wore over their shoulders.

The night chill disappeared as the sun climbed up the Georgia sky, spreading warmth. Willa noticed that Duke removed her restraints sometime while she slept. She removed the blankets she and Ramiel were covered with and the disturbance made him cry. He had awaken only once during the night to be fed, so she knew it was time again to put him under her shawl to be nursed. He ate for what seemed an eternity and she was glad for that, although she herself was truly starving by now. The meager bits of rabbit from the night before did not register much with her stomach as it growled in protest. She could only hope they were nearing Southwind Plantation where she might be fed.

In the afternoon they reached the plantation, announced by an ornately carved wooden sign hung between two iron posts that read, "Southwind Plantation, est. 1805". The driveway was long and lined with live oaks, just like Heavenly, although there was no moss draped among them. When they pulled up in front of the plantation house, Willa recognized it immediately. She had seen it once as a child. The grand structure was even larger than the Witherell's mansion.

Southwind house was made of rich, red brick. Fluted white columns towered imposingly along the front, reaching up three stories. On the expansive front portico were several white wooden chairs placed into neat groups around small tables. Two stately potted evergreens stood guard by the double entrance doors, each sculpted into perfect spirals. On each white door was a wreath made of greenery and accented with white satin ribbons.

All of window frames were painted white and inside of each hung snowy lace curtains. On the second and third levels, French doors opened out to twin balconies, their carved railings adorned with swags of evergreen, ivy, white roses, and satin bows. The theme for the estate was clearly the color white, as all the outbuildings surrounding the mansion where painted that color as well. The gardens in front were finely manicured, containing meticulously sculptured shrubs and marble statues, interspersed with rose bushes. White roses, of course.

Duke Henry drove the horses around the back of the house and was greeted by a distinguished-looking elder in a butler's uniform.

"Why it's Duke Henry, Josiah's man. Sure haven't seen you in these parts in quite some time. Come sir, off that wagon and we shall go find the Master." The black man spoke in a cultured voice, too white sounding to be a slave, but still obviously in service to the Master. Willa grew up in the white Witherell household but did not think her speech was nearly as white-sounding as his.

"Well, Boston! Good to see you, old boy. Actually, I'd prefer if you'd go fetch the man and bring him to me. You see, got me some cargo here." He pointed to his two prisoners in the wagon, who were originally ignored by the butler.

"Oh, I see. Of course you need to keep watch. I'll get the Master at once. While I am in the house, I'll have the slaves prepare a good meal for you. You must be famished if you've come all the way from Heavenly." He quickly disappeared through a side door, having given Willa just a glance as if she was not the same race as he.

When Charles McAllister came out of the house, Willa recognized him as the last face she saw leaving Southwind those years ago. She came to have nightmares about that face, the one she would always blame for her departure away from her papa and brothers, although he really had nothing to do with it. He was merely making a trade with his brother-in-law.

As Charles approached, Duke jumped down from his seat and removed his hat. He courteously thrust out his hand, which the gentleman accepted. After exchanging a hearty greeting, he remarked, "Duke Henry! My, my! Been quite a while, I'll say. What the devil brings you to Southwind?"

Duke gestured toward the contents of the wagon. "I have a gift for you from your sister and brother-in-law, sir. A good, strong woman, child-bearing years of course. And she's got with her an infant boy. He came from a fine stock male, a hard worker. That boy'll be the same one day."

Charles eyed the pair with suspicion. "Hmmmmmmmmmm. Another pair of mouths to feed, huh? What the hell is on Josiah's mind calling this a gift? Has he gone mad like my sister, too?"

"No, sir."

"Well then, what does he expect from me in return, Henry?"

"Nothing, sir. Slave just didn't work out around the house anymore. She had that there baby and now thinks she don't have to work. Mr. Witherell thinks she needs to be taught a lesson 'bout hard work. Put her in the field and under the thumb of your men. She'll work then. And besides, like I said, she's of child-bearin' age. I'm sure she could whip out some other niggers for you."

"Well. We've had a mass of slave babies born around here. Guess that's what happens after a cold, bitter winter." Charles paused to ponder his brother-in-law's gift and continued, "I suppose one more breeder won't hurt. Don't really trust that Josiah wants nothing in exchange though. I'll give you something to carry back to Heavenly."

Again, he considered for a few moments before reaching a decision. "Hams. Got an excess of smoked hams. Mighty fine hams at that. Go ahead and take these slaves out to the village and when you return, you'll have something to eat and then I'll get one of my boys to load up your wagon."

"Very well, Mr. McAllister." Duke Henry climbed up to his seat atop the wagon and bid the horses to move in the direction of the slave village.

Time seemed to move in slow motion for Willa. She heard Duke's description of her and the situation at Heavenly through a thick fog that garbled her perception of his words. She was being sent to work in the cotton fields and not the Big House? What did she know about working in a field? What about her talents as a seamstress? Surely the mistress here could use her skills, if not inside the house, then with other women in the sewing house. What about her baby? What would become of him while she toiled in the field all day? Who would take care of Ramiel? Who would nurse him? How dare the man call her a "breeder"!

***

The slave village was a considerable distance from the main house, but to Willa it seemed like another insufferable journey. Ramiel began to cry and Duke Henry shouted at them the entire way, agitating the infant even more. When they reached the village Willa was relieved that she'd soon be rid of Duke. He pulled her out of the wagon as she held tightly to her son. An elder female slave addressed him. He told her that Willa was to work in the cotton fields beginning the next morning and that he was on his way to find the overseer to give him the same instructions. Then he gathered up what little Willa brought with her, threw it to the ground, and was gone.

Willa stood motionless, staring at the old woman, not knowing what to do or what to think. Ramiel stopped crying the second Duke left, as if he knew all along that the man was pure evil. The wrinkle-faced woman, sensing Willa's fear and confusion, offered her arms for comfort. Willa accepted and fell into them. She was soft and plump. When she began to stroke Willa's hair and pat her back, she relaxed and knew that this woman, whom she later learned was old Berthie, was going to be her makeshift mama at Southwind.

Chapter 58

Lazarus returned to his cabin at the end of each day and fell into an empty bed, crying for his loss. Just when he and his wife began to live as a true married couple, everything shattered. His dreams were filled with Willa and Ramiel. Some nights they were back home eating meals, laughing, holding each other. Other nights they were being tormented by slave patrollers, being torn to bits by their vicious dogs. On those fitful nights Lazarus woke up bathed in sweat, shaking from a bottomless panic.

He questioned Marianne extensively since she was the last one to see Willa. She told him about the strange behavior of her mother when she saw Ramiel and recalled for him the hasty exit Willa made from the house. She explained that she went to the cabin shortly after to apologize for Margaret's behavior. She mentioned that Willa wretched outside the front door, just after drinking the calming tea, but blamed it on her empty stomach.

Lazarus was originally worried that Willa was ill and wandered off in some delusional state, carrying the baby with her. When they found no evidence of her, he was relieved that she was not lying in pain or dead nearby. Now he began to think that she had indeed found a way to escape from the plantation and perhaps had plotted to do so all along. Perhaps their sudden intimacy was her way of giving him fulfillment and at the same time absolving her own guilt. He had questions. Why didn't she confide in him about the escape? Why didn't she trust him enough to include him in her plans? He reconciled that Willa did not want to involve him in any danger, so she was thinking of him and his best interests.

Didn't she know I would risk my life to be with her and our son? She should have known!

In the days following the searches, Lazarus spent his time mulling over his questions and wondering if Willa and Ramiel were safe wherever they were. He prayed that whoever helped her escape was kind and clever and would avoid detection. His mood lightened when he imagined Willa and the baby living in freedom. Then he would be angry with her for not including him. The anger would turn to guilt. He found that the only way he could stop the incessant churning in his head was to work even harder at his trade. He could easily have matched the output and quality of a dozen blacksmiths!

***

Weeks later there was a thunderous knock on the door early one morning, startling Lazarus from a pleasant dream about Willa. He sprang from the bed, hopeful that she'd come back to him. Instead he found Chloe on the other side of the door. The look of disappointment on his face was unmistakable.

"I know you was wishin' for Willa. I'm sorry, but I have to tell ya somethin'. Will ya let me in? I can't be seen here."

His eyebrows raised and then he opened the door wider so she could enter. "Have a seat, Chloe."

She accepted his offer and sat down on the closest chair, blowing air out her mouth so she could relax enough to breathe normally. It was clear that she'd been worked up about something.

"What's the matter?" Lazarus heart began to beat faster as he feared bad news about Willa and Ramiel. "Tell me, Chloe! Do you know somethin' about Willa?"

Chloe hesitated for a few seconds as if gathering courage, steeling herself for what she was about to say. "Yes."

"Has she been found? Oh, God tell me she is safe! And the baby!"

Chloe could sense the hysteria brewing in Lazarus. "No! Calm down, Laz! Goin' kill yo'self with worry. I got news on where she is. Overheard it in the house, that's why I came here. To tell ya. But you ain't heard it from me. I can't get myself into a stew for givin' you the news."

"No, no! Nobody will know! Tell me, Chloe! Where is she?"

"Well, Marster and Missus was fightin' this mornin'. Like they always do. But this fight was 'bout Willa."

"Why would they fight about Willa?"

"That's what I'm fixin' to tell ya. See, Missus Mar'gret saw the baby just before Willa went missin'. She under some idea that the baby be Marster Josiah's. She think he fathered that baby boy!"

"What? Why would she be thinkin' that? That woman's out o' her head!" As soon as the words left his lips, it suddenly all made sense. Margaret noticed Ramiel's likeness to Foster, mistaking it for a strong similarity to Josiah instead. How strange that the woman saw what no one else seemed to notice. Then Lazarus remembered a story Seth once told him of his accidental discovery of an affair Josiah had with another slave years ago. Their affair resulted in a child and once Margaret saw the baby, she knew instantly who had fathered it. The slave was sent away to Southwind, the plantation owned by Margaret's brother. Lazarus waited for Chloe to confirm his suspicions.

"Yep. She crazy sometimes. But she was throwin' a fit this mornin' and askin' Marster if he done took care of the problem. And that problem be your wife and baby, she say. Marster say he done took care and send them away to Southwind. They be at Southwind, Laz!"

"Oh, Chloe, thank you. Thank you! Least I know they're alive!" He hugged the woman tightly and continued to gush out his thanks to her for having the courage to bring him this crucial information.

"Now I must get back 'fore anybody know I'm gone. Now I leave it to you. Figure some way to get her back, Laz."

Chloe left Lazarus in the doorway, relieved but still not knowing what he could do to bring his family home.

Chapter 59

At Southwind, Willa was adjusting to the life of a field slave. Time seemed to advance slowly for her, marked only by the Sundays when the work load was lifted for the slaves. They did not attend church services on those days, but worshipped among themselves in a makeshift chapel in the woods that consisted of a small clearing with tree stumps as pews. Willa vaguely remembered attending these services as a child. She also recalled the memory of being frightened by the woods because of ghost stories.

Since her arrival she had learned that her father Alfred died shortly after she and Heddie were exported to Heavenly years ago. Everyone suspected it was a broken heart that killed him as he grieved the loss to the point of refusing food and water. Alfred was subjected to constant beatings for his inability to keep pace in the fields, but his body probably registered no pain. He was too consumed by sorrow to even feel it, the slaves told her. Although Willa was distressed to learn of his death, so many years had passed without him that her grief was not as deep as she always imagined it would be.

She was informed that her brother Sampson was sold to another plantation when he was seventeen, because he had become such a troublemaker at Southwind. Although the mystery of Sampson's whereabouts was sure to haunt her, Willa had to smile. Sampson always went against the grain as a child, so she expected it would carry on into his manhood. Wherever he was, she knew that he could take care of himself.

Edgar, or Flash as they nicknamed him, was still at Southwind. Coincidentally he was now a blacksmith like Lazarus, so he lived near a Southwind village set aside specifically for slaves working the skilled trades. When the other slaves discovered he was her brother, they expressed great pride regarding Flash and his successful exit from the village of the field slaves. They had all wished him well, realizing that his life was going to be an easier one.

Willa could not visit Flash since field slaves were only allowed to leave their village to work the fields. However, several slaves promised that they would somehow get word to him about his sister. Willa found comfort in that and the impending reunion gave her a sense of hope. Although she desperately missed Heddie, Laz, Marianne, and the others at Heavenly, she was adapting to her new life. Being able to see Flash again kept her going.

The cotton harvest was long and the picking was difficult. Willa's hands were raw as she returned to the village at day's end. There were many babies at Southwind this season and scarcely enough mature wet nurses and old mammies to take care of them during the day. Willa wished she could be one of the women who got to stay behind to perform that duty, even though she would be forced to nurse other women's children. But the orders from Heavenly, according to Duke Henry, were to have her work the fields.

The slave drivers would randomly assign some of the mothers to stay behind in the village each day. The other mothers would have to take their babies out into the fields with them. Since it was impossible to carry a baby while picking cotton, a long trough was placed at the end of that day's field to serve as a mass cradle. While the women toiled, their babies lay in the trough with no care at all. Swaddled in their blankets, they had no other protection from the sun or rain. Their mothers were allowed short nursing breaks at intervals during the day.

Willa was thankful for the days when Ramiel was allowed to stay at the village, although she missed him terribly. His tiny, smiling face provided the fuel she needed to survive. She struggled through those days with the promise of returning to see that smile. On the days she was forced to put him in the trough, the nursing breaks kept her going.

***

One particularly gloomy day, the slaves watched the skies as a fierce storm brewed while they rode the wagons out to the fields. This was one of the unlucky times when Willa was forced to bring Ramiel with her and she was wholly concerned. The sky showed no signs of clearing, instead turning blacker and more threatening. As usual the babies were laid down into the long cradle. Every mother borrowed extra blankets from other slaves to shield their children from the imminent rain.

Out in the field it was the usual round of picking and stuffing cotton into the cloth bags as the rain held off. Willa was a strong worker, picking quickly and ignoring the pain in her hands. She wondered if she would ever be able to sew again or touch luxurious fabric without ruining it with her rough hands. Still, she filled her mind with visions of the dresses she had yet to create.

The clouds began to lighten and the sky seemed to improve with each passing moment. It was finally time to go nurse the babies when the first drops of rain fell in spite of the kinder sky. It was a slow, steady sprinkle when Willa began to feed Ramiel. When finished, she wrapped him securely and placed him softly into the trough with the other babies. She spread another coverlet over the top of the trough to keep the sprinkles off him.

It was a dry fall season in Georgia. Whenever it did rain, the babies fared well enough under the blankets. They ended up no more than a little uncomfortable by the time their mothers returned to lift them out of the trough.

The section of field being picked that day was the farthest distance they'd ever been away from the trough. All of the mothers dreaded being separated from their infants even more than usual, so they were relieved when the drizzle of rain ended. They returned to their rows of cotton and looked forward to the next nursing break with optimism.

After a few hours back in the field though, the ominous clouds returned, darker and full of contempt, plotting to concoct a violent storm. Willa and some of the other mothers begged the slave driver to let them go back to the babies, but he refused. Willa persisted, pleading to the tall, muscular driver who was every bit as black as she. He responded by pulling his whip from its holder and lashing her across the back. She fell to the ground, mostly from the shock of his actions.

"I say when you be leavin' this field! You hear me, nigga? I'm the Marster out in this here field!"

He whipped her once more and this time she clearly felt the sting of the lash. Willa cried out.

Her first beating.

Two nearby male slaves were told to pick her up and they complied. Willa noticed the knowing look of sympathy in their eyes as they acknowledged her introduction to yet another brutality of slavery. Righted on her feet, she was ordered back to her row of cotton. This time she obeyed. The whip was real and the pain searing down her back was a capable deterrent. Silently she prayed that the rain would hold off until they were safely back in the village.

As she picked boll after boll of billowy cotton, Willa thought about her own mama's experiences with the whip. She recalled the deep scars on her back, remembered times when Heddie returned from a day in the very same fields with her cotton dress shredded and stained with dried blood. She shuddered, thankful that the slave driver had neither torn her clothes nor drew blood. This time.

Soon the sky over Southwind turned darker. It mimicked nightfall, as if someone had just extinguished the lantern of the sun. Rain began to fall, this time without the warning of a sprinkle. It grew in volume within seconds until it poured from the dense, black clouds. Thunder clapped in the distance, followed by bold lightning strikes that temporarily illuminated the darkened fields. The booming continued, closer and closer, with lightning that reached out of the heavens to touch the Georgia earth far below.

Terror gripped Willa as she lost all regard for the slave driver's reprimands and ran in the direction of the baby trough. The ground quickly turned to mud between the rows of cotton, making it a slippery mess. She fell down several times, costing her precious moments as she fought against the elements. By now, the other young mothers joined her in the quest to retrieve their babies. The length of the field seemed to double, triple.

The wind picked up as the storm progressed into the worst ever known at Southwind. Willa pushed on, now battling the gusts of wind attempting to push her down as forcefully as the driver's sharp whip. When she did fall, she clawed through the mud and fought to regain footing. All the while she made little progress. The rain was pelting her in the face, feeling like sharp pebbles pitting her skin. She felt no sensations but the beating of her heart and the adrenaline coursing through her body, propelling her toward Ramiel.

When at last she and the other mothers reached the trough, their horrific screams might have been heard all the way to Heavenly in South Carolina. The trough was full of rain, wet blankets, and babies floating along on the surface of the water. Drowned. Every child was dead.

Willa found Ramiel and quickly put his mouth up to her ear, listening for sounds of breath. There were none. She shook him gently as if to startle life back into his small body. Nothing. She pulled him up to chest and began to rock as she stood there in the storm, sealing off all the commotion surrounding her. She hummed a sweet song and continued to rock. The light that usually flickered in her eyes dimmed to match the color of the stormy sky.

Chapter 60

Willa held her lifeless son during the ride back to Southwind's slave village. After rocking him a while in the field, she carefully bundled him in his wet blankets and got into the wagon without a sound. She didn't cry for fear she would wake him.

As they rode on, the other slave mothers wailed and cursed the rain, holding their babies close as they carried on. Sorrow bored deeper into their hearts and magnified their agony, increasing the cries of pain. It was becoming unbearable to Willa. Such noise, when the babies were trying to sleep!

By the time they reached the village the rain had stopped. The mothers climbed out of the wagons and continued to weep as they were met by the slave mammies and nurses. News of the storm and deaths spread across the village and drew in all the other slaves. Everyone gathered to console the traumatized mothers.

Willa went back to the tiny, drafty cabin she shared with three other young mothers. She began to undress Ramiel as if he was still alive, taking care not to wake him. She pulled off his wet gown and re-clothed him, then changed out of her own soaked garments. Sitting down in a rickety chair, she began rocking her son.

Two of her cabin mates returned, babies in their arms. They were among the fortunate ones who were handed over to the nurses that day. Willa kept rocking, oblivious to the gasps from the women, who knew that Ramiel was dead.

"Willa? Willa? Is you alright? You need to put down that baby now. Girl, he dead."

"Would you like to rock Franklin now, Della? I'm just about to put Ramiel to bed." Willa stood and walked over to her bed, no more than a shabby quilt spread out on a dirt floor and covered with a few tattered blankets. She carefully laid Ramiel down.

"No, Willa. He's dead. Take that baby out of here." the other woman said.

"Are you ill, Lizzie? Why would you say that? Ramiel is sleepin', that's all."

"Oh Lord! She in shock," Lizzie whispered to Della. "Let me take Franklin, Della. Go fetch Polly. She know what to do with this'n." Lizzie put her sleeping daughter Sadie down to her bed of blankets and took Franklin from her. Della wasted no time getting out the door, heading in the direction of Polly's cabin.

It was the same Polly who was stricken from Heavenly long before Willa. At Southwind she'd become something of an apothecary, growing herbs and making potions to cure the slaves of various ailments. Unlike the plantation conjure doctor, she did not profess to have supernatural powers. Instead, she was known for her strong and potent teas brewed to calm and give clarity to the minds of distressed or unbalanced slaves. She lived in a cabin with her daughter Josephine, Josiah's child. Willa had met both of them but knew nothing of their secret connection.

Polly came to the cabin immediately, eager to diagnose Willa's condition and treat it with some of the assorted herbs she carried. Her enthusiasm fell as she saw the dead baby. The child's hands and feet were blue, his body stiff. Willa seemed not to be affected by the sight, flitting around the cabin, straightening this and that, whatever she could do to tidy the appearance of the dwelling and its meager contents. She was humming like this day was like any other where she attempted to carry on in a positive way despite her ill fortune.

Deep sadness filled Polly's heart. She somehow knew of Willa's exile from Heavenly, a situation that mirrored hers. She looked back upon the time she arrived at Southwind and how she so completely relied on her own baby for her self-preservation. She felt a strong connection with Willa, understanding her odd behavior in denying the infant's death.

"Hello, Polly. Nice to see you. Where is that pretty girl of yours? She's always by your side. My Ramiel will probably be like her, by my side. We're so close, that baby and me." Willa looked over to the baby on the blankets and then back at Polly with a proud smile.

"Willa. You listen to me now. That baby be gone. You need to take him out o' here, out to where they's buryin' the others. Goin' to give them a nice service. Men be diggin' the graves just now." Polly knew no way to say it other than to simply put out the truth. Once Willa grasped it, she would settle her nerves with a tea.

"Della, put on a kettle. We goin' to need it soon."

Willa's face showed confusion as she watched her housemates and Polly, not understanding. "Polly? Della? Lizzie? What's goin' on here?"

Polly reached into her sack and pulled out two bags of leaves and a wooden mortar and pestle. She selected several of the herbs from each bag, placed them in the mortar, and began to crush them into a finer blend. Then she transferred her finished concoction into another small bag and tied it with a string. Della gave her a tin cup to place it in and they waited for the water to boil.

"Willa, come sit here with me near the fire," Polly said. Willa complied and the two sat together on stools by the hearth. "Now, I want to tell ya somethin' important. Today when you was out in the field it started to rain. And it rained and poured real hard. All you mamas ran and ran, tryin' to get back to your babies, but it be too late. All of them, Ramiel too, they died in that cradle. They took on water and they died. All of 'em."

Willa's face turned from confusion to horror. "No! No! Why would you say that to me? Ramiel is asleep. He's just asleep." She shot off the stool to go retrieve her baby. She gently lifted him off the quilt, held him up to her bosom, and returned to the stool. After holding him tight for a few seconds, she laid him on her lap.

"Willa, look at him. He done turned blue, girl. He's gettin' cold and he's still as a plank. Willa! He dead, sweet child, he dead."

Still refusing to believe, Willa looked at Polly with hurt in her eyes, tears waiting to spill. "Why are you so cruel to me, Polly? What have I done to anger you?"

"Girl, you ain't angered me none. No, no, no." Polly reached over and guided Willa's chin to face her. Looking soberly into her eyes, she continued, "You know, let me tell ya somethin' 'bout me and you. We come from the same place. We both come from Heavenly, over there in South Carolina." Polly pointed in no direction in particular.

"We both got threw out of the Witherell house. Now I know you got that baby and that's all you got. He be your life, just like Josephine be mine. Josephine…she's Josiah Witherell's girl. You know that? I 'spect yours was his too. And I know how you be feelin', but honey you got to snap out o' this. I'm here to help you. Got some tea for you, make ya' feel better. I'll take care o' you. Me and old Berthie, we take care o' you."

Willa shook her head in confusion as she got up and took her baby back to their bed on the floor. Lizzie took the kettle off the fire and poured boiling water over the herbs in the tin cup she'd put on the sawbuck table. Unexpectedly, the cabin door flew open and a distraught woman emerged, black face almost pale, eyes blood-shot from crying, knees weak.

Lizzie rushed to her side to prevent her from falling. "Caroline! Oh, Lord! Don't tell me that lil' Isaiah dead, too."

"He gone, Lizzie, he gone. My sweet boy, he gone. Took on the water and drown in that trough. Couldn't get to him. Couldn't save my boy. What am I goin' to do? He gone, Lizzie." The poor woman was weary from the weight of her burden and went limp into Lizzie's arms.

Della put Franklin down on his pallet and stood still for a moment, wondering how he and Sadie could sleep through the ruckus. She helped Lizzie get Caroline into a chair.

Willa stood looking at the sad woman with warm eyes that spoke of sympathy for her loss. She went to Caroline and knelt at her feet, patting her legs. "Oh, dear, dear Caroline. I'm so sorry."

Caroline looked down to her cabin mate. "What are we goin' to do, Willa? Our babies be dead. Oh, God! What we goin' to do?"

Caroline bent over to embrace Willa and noticed that her friend's eyes were not red and swollen like hers. She had not been crying. Her face displayed sympathy but not distress. "Willa! Did Ramiel live through the rain, girl? How did he live? All them other babies died. And I know that he was in that trough too. How did he live and not my Isaiah?" She began to laugh, in contempt of her torment. It was a mocking, taunting laugh, as if she could not believe the irony. Her friend's infant was spared and hers was sacrificed! Intense anger spread through her. She reached into Willa's hair and gave it a vigorous tug.

"What are you doing to me, Caroline?" Willa jumped to her feet and backed away from the woman, holding onto her scalp.

Alarmed, Caroline held a clump of Willa's hair in her hand. She moaned and threw the hair to the dirt floor. The other young women came forward to restrain her, but she pushed them away. Springing out of the chair, Caroline bolted towards Willa's bed. When she saw Ramiel's bluish body, she stopped short and gasped. "He is dead! That boy is dead!" she screamed, waking Sadie and Franklin. "He's dead! Dead! Willa he's dead!"

The babies began to wail, summoning Della and Lizzie to their bedsides. Willa sat down on a stool and put her hands to her ears to block the sounds. But there was no quieting them. The baby noises seemed to gain intensity every second. Soon she began to rock back and forth, humming wildly.

Caroline lifted Ramiel off his blanket bed and brought him to Willa. She held him up, forcing Willa to look at his coloring and then she put him on her lap so she could feel the stiffness of his body in death. Soon Willa's screams of terror engulfed the cabin, dampening the sound of the bawling babies.

The tea made for her was cool enough to drink and as soon as Willa's screams ceased, Polly administered it to her. Not long after, Willa fell into a deep sleep, enabling Polly to take Ramiel out to be buried with the other lost babies at Southwind.

Chapter 61

After Chloe's visit, Lazarus' hope was resurrected. He now knew that Willa and Ramiel were safe, taken to Southwind Plantation. They were not lost, not caught escaping by the patty rollers and their vicious mongrel dogs. They were simply on another plantation. Another plantation a state away.

He knew what he had to do. He had to inform Seth and together they would find a way to retrieve his family. Seth had resources that he could use, but maybe instead of bringing them back, he could help them escape for good.

So Lazarus decided to pay Seth a visit at the Big House. When he showed up at the side door of the mansion, he was greeted by Myra. "Mornin' Myra. Seth around here?"

"Mornin' Laz. I still so sorry 'bout Willa and the baby. Sure do miss them chillun. Keepin' yo'self busy 'round that blacksmith shop, that's a good thing. Reckon I can find out 'bout Seth's whereabouts. Come on in here and sit down right here. I'll go see where that young'un be."

Soon Seth appeared, with hope in his heart that Lazarus had somehow found Willa and was calling on him with the good news. He was disappointed when that was not the case, but when Lazarus revealed the details from Chloe's prior visit, he became furious.

"How could my mother even think such a ridiculous thing? It's absolutely preposterous! My father and Willa? Mother has gone totally mad, Laz! There is no amount of laudanum, nor any patent medicine strong enough to cure the woman. My mother belongs in an asylum and I'll see to it that Father does just that with her!"

Lazarus was left in the wake of his frenzy as Seth ran up the grand staircase. When he reached Margaret's room, he didn't bother to knock on the door; he simply opened it with a vengeance and burst in. Just as he suspected, she was in bed, propped up on her downy pillows and looking through her usual fashion magazines.

"Seth! My, my son, what has you aflame? Come talk to your mother, darling."

"How dare you! How dare you, Mother! You've gone mad and this time you've done it! You've gone far beyond reason, you...you horrible woman!"

"Seth, Seth. Whatever can you be talking about, child?"

"Don't call me a child! If you haven't noticed, and I doubt you have, I've grown into a man now. But you've been too involved with having your spells to notice. But I know, I know. You can't be blamed for your mental illness, now can you? No, Mother. There is always an excuse and Father does well to conceal the truth from us. You may well be mentally ill, but you are also a wretchedly evil woman, plotting against innocent people. Plotting against Willa and her son!"

"Oh, dear. Is that what this is all about? Who told you such rubbish?"

"Never mind, Mother. Your secret is out! How could Father go along with your plan knowing he had nothing to do with Ramiel? With what did you threaten him? Did you threaten to expose his affair from years ago?"

"What are you saying, Seth? What…what affair? Now who's gone mad?"

"Don't you pretend with me, Mother. You sent away Polly and her daughter, right before Willa and Heddie came to Heavenly. Sent her to Southwind, to Uncle Charles' plantation. Same place you sent Willa. How could you, Mother? How could you suspect Father of seducing Willa? She's Marianne's friend. My friend. She and Laz have a baby, are a family. How could you? Tell me, Mother!"

Margaret's face revealed the deep hurt she felt inside, knowing that Seth would never think of her the same way again. She might as well have pierced a hole in her heart and lay down to die. Her son's eyes held pure contempt as he stared at her, awaiting her confession. But she remained true to the mother he knew well when she began to sob in her familiar, pitiful way.

"Don't attempt that with me, Mother! I know your ways and they will no longer sway me! Confess and do it now or I'll find Father and persuade him to commit you to an asylum where you truly belong!"

Margaret looked up, wiping away tears. Her dry throat protested and she motioned toward a crystal glass of water on a tray next to her bed. Although Seth was tempted to let her choke, he needed her to explain what she'd done so he handed her the glass. She drank slowly, buying what time she could.

"That is enough Mother! No one is that dry, for land sakes!"

"Seth! Watch your mouth, son. I am still your Mother!"

"In name only, woman. As far as I am concerned. Now tell your story and make it the truth!"

Margaret Witherell sucked in a deep breath of air and began. "Your despicable father was the sire to Willa's baby, Seth. There was no doubt about it. Polly's child looked the same. Same eyes, same skin, same everything. It befuddles me that no one else saw this; it was clear as day. And I could not be near Willa. Will not be near her and her bastard son. She may be the most brilliant seamstress I've had, but that was not enough to keep her here. Not enough to keep the thought of your father and her out of my mind. Just could not keep it out of my mind, Seth. You see? See why she had to be sent to Southwind, out of my sight? You understand, don't you?"

"Mother, you are truly pathetic. You are a blight to my eyes and I am through with you. You sicken me, Mother, and I intend to bring Lazarus' family back to Heavenly! To hell with you and your grotesque imaginations."

Seth turned from her and walked out of the room. As he closed her door he clearly heard his mother weeping and as he moved down the staircase, she began to moan. When she yowled like she was being tortured, Seth could not help thinking that torture could never be enough punishment for his mother's sins.

Downstairs Lazarus waited. Listening to Margaret caterwaul in misery, he knew that Seth had just discovered the reason for Willa's banishment. When Seth soon approached him, he wore a strained look of disappointment on his face.

"She admitted it all, Laz. It's true. Now we have to figure out what we are going to do with this. We need to bring Willa and Ramiel back home."

Chapter 62

The drowned babies were buried in the slave cemetery. Since there were so many, only one long grave was dug into the ground. It resembled the way they had died, in the extended cradle. As if only tucking them in for a night's slumber, all the mothers had placed blankets upon their small bodies before allowing the grave to be covered. Willa slept in her cabin with Polly at her side, aided by young Josephine who insisted on playing nursemaid. Berthie saw to it that Ramiel was properly covered for his infinite sleep. She knew Willa would be distressed that she was not the one to make the final gesture, but her fragile mental state made waking her just too dangerous.

The next morning as the sun arose over the cotton fields, none of the slaves felt its friendly warmth. The events of the day before hung about them like lead ribbons knotted to their souls. All of the grieving mothers were given the day off, not because their owner cared about their grief, but because sending them to the fields would have prompted an uprising among the other slaves. That was too high a price to pay and besides, the crop was getting harvested in record time. One day with a few missing slave women would not impede progress.

Willa woke to see Josephine's face over her. The little girl smiled sweetly and then lowered her lips to Willa's forehead to deliver a soft kiss. "Mornin' Miz Willa. Glad you back."

Looking around, Willa also saw Polly and Berthie. She began to sit up, but the throbbing in her skull sent her back down. "Wha...what happened to me? Polly? Berthie? Where's Ramiel?"

Terror at once struck at her with its cold blade as she remembered the revelation she had before drinking the tea. "He's gone. He's gone, isn't he? Polly?"

"Yes, dear, he be gone. Nana Berthie done covered him all up and he safe now. The baby boy in Heaven now, tended by the angels and the good Lord himself. And we got to be happy 'bout that, child. He with God. No more enslaved, your bitty one be with God."

Sadness shrouded Willa's heart, but now she understood that Ramiel drowned yesterday, the same as all the other babies in the trough. That deadly cradle in the field. She wept quietly, the truth no longer a foreigner. After some time, she dried her tears and thanked the women and Josephine for taking such fine care of her.

After drinking one of Polly's other potions, she felt stronger and wanted to go to the place where her baby was interred. She had to see for herself that the ground was made sacred for the children. It would bring closure and reassurance until a proper slave funeral could be arranged for them.

"Of course you can see it, Willa. I'll take you there to it," said Polly as she gathered up the things she'd brought the night before and led Willa out the door with Josephine following. As she passed through the doorway, she turned and addressed Berthie in a whisper, "You know what to do."

Seeing the mass grave made Willa weak in the knees and she fell to the earth at the spot marked for Ramiel's body. She lay there for a while, sobbing again, pouring out her burden on the already dry earth. Little Josephine put her hand on Willa's back, patting a comforting rhythm with her tiny hands while Polly stood silent admiring her daughter's nurturing ways. When Willa began to pray, both Josephine and Polly knelt and bowed their heads.

"Dear Lord Above, This is the darkest time in my life and I don't understand why it's happened. Ramiel was an innocent baby, not to be blamed for how he came about. I accepted him and found your blessin', but now Lord, I don't understand. But God, you are Almighty and you know your reasons. I must trust in you and hold my faith.

And one day Lord I'll be with my baby again in your Kingdom. Laz and me and Ramiel will be together again, some day in the end. Please keep my baby in your hands, Lord 'til that day. But let my Laz know he's been called up. Somehow, let him know this baby is safe in your Kingdom and that I am just waiting for that day. Amen."

Willa reverently laid a patch worked quilt on the ground above her baby as a tribute to him. It was the one wrapped around him in the trough, as it was custom among slaves to adorn graves with an article last used by the deceased. Polly and Josephine got off their knees and helped Willa to her feet.

As Willa turned around, she received a surprise; this time it was a pleasant one. There before her stood her brother Flash. Willa's eyes grew large and a hand went up to her mouth to squelch a joyful squeal.

"Flash! Oh, dear God in Heaven! My brother!"

"Well stop gawkin' at me and come here, sister!"

The two embraced as Polly winked at Josephine signaling it was time for them to leave the pair. Berthie and some of the others had conspired since Willa's arrival to send word to Flash. Finally his visit could not have come at a more advantageous time.

They spent the day together and Willa told her brother all about their mama, growing up at Heavenly, and her friendship with the Witherell children. She spoke about her life as a gifted seamstress, her marriage to Lazarus, and finally the blessed birth of Ramiel. Then she quietly spoke of the new scar on her heart caused by her son's sudden death.

After consoling Willa, Flash explained how their papa died from heartbreak. It was the same tale she was told by the other slaves at Southwind. Then he talked about his determination to get away from the fields and undertake a profession. When Southwind's cruel overseer Dobbs succumbed to a fatal illness, Flash gained favor with the man who replaced him. The new overseer took interest in the young, determined slave and arranged for his apprenticeship with the blacksmith.

Flash was disturbed that his sister was taken from her new husband and their mother at Heavenly, but he was fully unhinged that she was forced into the cotton fields. When it was finally time for him to return to his side of the plantation, he swore to her that he would find a way to get her into the Big House. If not as a seamstress, then something else that would not be as grueling as field work. They parted with an emotional farewell and the promise of another reunion.

Chapter 63

In South Carolina, the brothers Geoffrey and Thomas Hawthorne were growing impatient with Josiah Witherell. Upon first mention of a duel to settle the matter of their sister Lilith's cause of death, the plantation owner seemed agreeable. Josiah requested stalling the proceedings until the end of summer and notice was sent in writing, as was customary. However, upon their return to Heavenly after that period, Josiah made yet another demand for deferment. The Hawthornes reluctantly agreed, since the Witherells were powerful people and they didn't want to unduly upset Josiah.

But the time had come. The agreement to duel was several months old and the brothers wanted nothing more than to finish this business. If the duel was not soon arranged, they would resort to hiring men to kill Foster. Even Josiah could not prevent such doings if the Hawthorne brothers used hired men from New York or Philadelphia.

As it turned out, those measures were unnecessary. Josiah and his son would meet them just outside of town in a meadow chosen by Foster as the challenged party. In attendance was Doc Capshaw as his surgeon, if needed. One of Foster's Charleston associates, McKenzie Boone would serve as his "second", to act as a witness and monitor the procedures, following a formal Code of Honor that established rules and dictated conduct in such affairs.

Josiah was confident in Foster's marksmanship, but not as assured as Foster himself. He and his father chose Duke Henry to drive their most luxurious landau carriage, since it was risky to use Daniel for the duty. There was too much at stake for Daniel to talk about the event back at the plantation. There would be no need to speak of the duel when it was over. Geoffrey Hawthorne would be taken away in his own carriage, either cold and dead or seriously wounded. The agreed upon end would be the dissolution of accusations about Foster.

The sun was rising above the horizon and Josiah felt strangely empowered by its warmth. He looked over at Foster and gave him a knowing nod of assurance. They rode in silence until they reached the agreed-upon grounds. The four gentlemen exited the fine carriage while Duke Henry stayed aboard the driver seat to watch the proceedings.

Josiah spoke first, addressing the Hawthorne brothers, their surgeon, and the appointed second. "Gentlemen, good morning. Looks like a fine one for a duel wouldn't you agree?"

"Fine indeed. Fine indeed. Let me introduce to you Doctor Lloyd Collier, as well as my good friend Matthew Vaughn," said Geoffrey in a similarly good-natured tone of voice. "You already are familiar with my brother Thomas.

Josiah shook hands all around and then proceeded to introduce his party. "This is Doctor Nelson Capshaw, my son Foster, and his second, McKenzie Boone."

Handshakes commenced in a civil manner, but it was apparent that the Hawthorne brothers were holding back the urge to lash out and attack Foster, alleged murderer of their ill-fated sister. The Code was clear about the behavior of all parties before, during, and after a duel. It was to be orderly, emotionless, and swift. Neat and clean. One principal in the contest would fall and possibly die to avoid dishonor. Either Foster Witherell or Geoffrey Hawthorne.

"Come, Mr. Boone, we have matters to discuss," said Vaughn, speaking of the duty of seconds to set agreed upon protocol.

Meanwhile the rest of the men made light conversation as if this was merely a Saturday morning gathering of acquaintances. Neither principal seemed nervous about this irreversible business that could well shape their fates forever.

Vaughn and Boone addressed each other with complete politeness as they agreed to the details of the duel. Vaughn inspected the pair of weapons furnished by the Witherells. Matching English flintlock dueling pistols, smooth-bore, high caliber, nine inches in length. He then chose one for Geoffrey, his principal. Satisfied, they returned to their men and explained how the duel would proceed.

Josiah spoke to Foster in a still-assured voice, "The best of luck to you, son. Not that you will need it." He removed himself from the established dueling ground. Thomas spoke some words to his brother as well, bolstering his confidence.

The seconds each stepped off the distance of ten paces and put their respective principals in position. Vaughn alerted Boone of his intention to load Geoffrey's pistol; he accepted and likewise loaded Foster's weapon.

With both of the seconds handing off the weapons in the proper manner, Foster and Geoffrey faced each other with muzzles down. Awaiting word to fire, the ten paces between them seemed to shrink. The two marksmen felt as if they could hear the heartbeat of the other, wondering which one would continue to palpitate after the shooting. Each felt empowered enough to think that the man left standing would be him.

There was also the possibility that the duel would instead end in injury. In that case, they would have to deem the matter between them resolved. But Geoffrey Hawthorne wanted nothing of injury for Foster; he simply wanted him dead.

Vaughn spoke. "Gentlemen, it is so determined that an agreement could not be reached between you in the matter of the death of Lilith Hawthorne. Thus a duel will commence in order to settle the honor of both parties. On my command, you will draw your weapons and fire once upon each other. Are we in agreement, sirs?"

Both duelers nodded in unison.

"On my mark... ready your weapons... 3-2-1 FIRE!"

Two blasts rang out, forcing a flock of birds from the trees. The thunderous sound of a hundred flapping wings momentarily caught the attention of the seconds, the surgeons, and the witnesses. Time hung in the air, suspended by thin threads until finally all those distracted acknowledged the two men on the ground, roughly ten paces apart.

Chapter 64

Josiah ran to his son's side with Doctor Capshaw closely behind. Foster was hit. A clean shot though. Straight through him, causing minimal blood loss since the black gunpowder likely cauterized the entrance and exit wounds.

"Foster, you're alive! My son! Hold on, Foster! Doc Capshaw will tend to you. You will live Foster. Do you hear me?"

Foster winced as the doctor began to clean his wound with a strong antiseptic concoction. "We need to move him, Josiah. Quickly!"

Duke Henry had viewed the proceedings from atop the carriage and was already bringing it around. Doc Capshaw wrapped Foster as best he could to prepare him for transport. Then he and Boone loaded him on a gurney they brought in case the duel ended badly.

Josiah was in shock over his son's misfortune. He began to blame himself. Had he not taught him well to use firearms? Where had he failed Foster? Or was Hawthorne that good a shot, a better matched player? He looked over to the other party and noticed that they too looked distraught.

Geoffrey Hawthorne was also hit, but he fared worse. For a moment, Josiah felt relieved, but then he chastised himself for the thought. A man was dead.

Vaughn approached Boone. He was noticeably emotional at the loss of his friend as his voice cracked when he stated, "Sir, are we now at liberty to leave these grounds?"

Boone nodded his consent and shook the man's hand. Thomas Hawthorne said nothing to Josiah and soon the group was gone. The matter was settled, Foster's honor restored. Thomas Hawthorne would now grieve a brother in addition to his sister. Bound by the duel and its Code of Honor, no retribution could be had.

Josiah long suspected that Foster was at fault for abusing Lilith and had probably gotten too rough with her. But he was convinced that it was an accident and not outright murder as the Hawthorne brothers suggested. The duel was fair and although Foster was injured as a result, he had survived.

The landau carriage could seat only four and to make room for Foster on the gurney, Boone had to ride on top with Duke Henry. That left Doc Capshaw to care for Foster, and Josiah to keep his son talking and awake for the short trip. The few miles they had to ride seemed longer to

Josiah who now had to come up with a story to explain how Foster was shot. What would Margaret believe? She was still upset over what she assumed was an affair between him and Willa.

When the carriage pulled up to the side door of Heavenly's mansion, Duke Henry and McKenzie Boone quickly dismounted and went straightaway to lift the gurney. Doc Capshaw grasped his medical bag and followed Josiah to the door, which was promptly opened by Ned. As they all entered, Ned's eyes opened wide and his eyebrows lifted in question.

"What the devil happened to your son, Marster? Do you want me to fetch the Missus?"

"No! No, Ned. That won't be necessary. No need upsetting Margaret. Foster will be just fine. Have one of the other servants make up a guest room and we'll take him there. No reason for Margaret to know we are home. Not yet."

"Yes, Marster. Right away."

Just minutes later a room was ready for Foster at the opposite end of the house, as far from Margaret as possible. Josiah decided to have his son nursed back to health without her even knowing he was home. Since she slept so much lately and scarcely left her room, the plan of deception would be easy to orchestrate. Since he was needed so often for Margaret, Doc Capshaw could come and go without much notice if he used the back staircase.

Once Foster was put into bed, he continued to moan from the pain. The physician gave him a good dose of laudanum and when the drug took him under, he was able to clean the wounds with more care. It would be important to keep the site of injury immaculate to prevent infection. Without voicing this specific concern, Doc Capshaw knew that oftentimes if a bullet didn't kill a man, the ensuing bacterial infection surely would.

When he was finished, Doc gave explicit care instructions to the servants Josiah ordered in to care for Foster. He assured Josiah that by the end of the following week, Foster would be fine; there was no need to do surgery since no organs were hit by the bullet. Josiah, who had held his breath awaiting diagnosis, exhaled in relief. He could easily accomplish his plan to deceive Margaret in the given timeframe.

Chapter 65

After a few days, even with a staff of servants caring for him day and night, Foster began to have complications. He developed a severe case of the chills and could not be made warm. His teeth chattered incessantly, even though there was a roaring blaze in the fireplace of the guest room. The slaves could barely stand to be in the room with such intense heat.

He began to hallucinate. He began to beg for whiskey and then wanted to see Lilith. He spoke of Willa, too, as if she were his lover. At that point Josiah sent for Doc Capshaw, who came immediately to Heavenly. The patient was examined in great detail, but the exam yielded nothing. No information, no reason Foster had taken such a bad turn. He should have been well on his way to recovery by now, given the fact that he was such a healthy young man before the shooting.

Foster's temperature spiked and he lay in a fever, sweating and complaining of being terribly cold at the same time. His breathing grew shallow and his heart rate erratic. Doc concluded that he was in septic shock and advised Josiah that it might well be a grave condition.

Enraged and full of unfamiliar emotions, he ran out of Foster's sick room, sprinting downstairs and out the front door. Doc Capshaw followed as Josiah muttered under his breath, cursing the slaves for not keeping Foster's wounds clean. Then he turned on the doctor, blaming him for somehow being negligent.

"You incompetent bastard! You call yourself a physician? You swore my son would survive. A simple, clean shot through. That is what you said. I relied on you, Capshaw! You filthy liar! Fraud! It's no wonder Margaret fails to improve under your care. Now Foster! I should have you hanged..."

He all but foamed at the mouth like a rabid dog, spewing insults and threats upon the doctor. In return, Doc Capshaw did nothing, understanding Josiah's need for release.

Finally Josiah went in the house, withdrawing to his office. Inside, behind the closed doors he sank into his leather chair and broke down in tears. His firstborn might not survive. All the years of grooming Foster to take over the family businesses one day! For nothing. Second in line would be Seth and Josiah was not sure the boy had it in him. Margaret would blame him for agreeing to the duel. He blamed himself for having Foster visit Chateau Dupree that first time. If he had not met Lilith she would be alive and there would not have been reason to duel. What did he do to deserve such tribulation?

***

When Foster's symptoms persisted and would not be relieved, Josiah knew he had to tell his family. If his eldest son died suddenly, how could he live with himself if he didn't let Margaret say goodbye to him. His other children were likely to disown him as well, especially Marianne. So Josiah instructed Ned to gather all of them except Margaret for a meeting in his office. Something he had never done before.

"I've called you together to discuss your brother Foster. He is not away on business, as you all believe. He is in this very house, in one of our guest rooms. Foster is gravely ill and so I want you all to spend some time with him in what may be his final days."

Marianne's face turned pale. Just when she seemed ready to collapse, Ned was quick to act, bringing her a glass of cool water. After taking a few refreshing sips, she began to question her father. "How did he take to illness, Father? How long has it been? How long has he been here at home without our knowledge?"

Seth added to the inquisition, "Are you sure this is so serious? What does Doc Capshaw say? Why can he not be cured?"

Gabriel and Garrett stared at Josiah for answers, too shocked to vocalize their questions. Although they were not especially close to Foster, they loved their brother in spite of his indifferent attitude towards them.

Josiah took a deep breath and then paused for several seconds before he finally spoke. "There was an argument between your brother and some gentlemen. The men felt slighted by your brother and so they challenged him in a duel."

Marianne gasped and put her hand to her mouth to muffle a shriek of alarm.

"Foster is such a fine marksman. Absolutely first-rate, as you know. We had no doubt he would prevail. And he did; the other man was fatally shot. Foster was only wounded and since the bullet did not damage any organs, he was expected to recover quickly."

"Then what happened, Father? What happened? Why did you not tell us sooner? Is he going to die?" Seth asked.

"We don't know what happened, Seth. Doc thinks it is some type of infection. I ordered round-the-clock care for him, but somehow an infection entered his body. I did not alert you all because Foster was expected to heal

256

quickly; I had no intention of worrying you needlessly. He may die and I want you all to be with him. So you will do that and when you are finished, your mother will see him."

"Then we are saying goodbye, aren't we Father? He is going to die, isn't he?" Garrett voiced the concerns of his twin as they both began to sniffle.

Josiah Witherell never to showed emotion around his children and saw tears or other signs of grief as a mark of weakness. This time however, he could barely contain the rush of sensations coursing through him. With a wavering voice he answered his youngest sons, "Y…yes, boys. I'm afraid that Foster will…"

Before he could finish his sentence, Marianne began to cry. Josiah took her in his arms and held her tight as he held back his own tears. Seth was the only one not struck by the urge to weep. He tried to summon tears, but they would not come. Turning away to avoid notice of his family, he hid by burying his head in his hands.

The scene continued for some time until Josiah dried Marianne's tears with his hands and then cleared his throat before speaking, "Now, you must not let Foster see you like this. Pull yourselves together now. Be strong. Gabriel and Garrett, can you do that? Marianne? Seth?"

"Yes sir," they collectively answered.

"Twins, I'd like for you to see Foster first. Of us all, you've not known him as long. Spend some time with him. When you are finished, get Seth so he can have his turn. And then Marianne will go. Are you ready boys?"

"Yes, Father." The boys dried their wet eyes and followed Josiah upstairs and down the hallway to the guest room, leaving Seth and Marianne alone.

"Oh, Seth. What are we going to do? Foster is dying! Our brother…is dying." Again, tears erupted form her blue eyes. Seth took her into his arms and patted her back as her grief increased.

He was miserable for his sister, but found it difficult to identify what he felt for Foster. It was not exactly grief. He and Foster never got along, never had the close relationship that he thought brothers should have. Marianne was Foster's favorite sibling and he let Seth know it every time he could with his constant mocking and taunting. Seth was not sure he even loved him - certainly did not respect him — and something inside said that Foster finally got what he deserved.

Suddenly Seth knew that he couldn't handle seeing Foster, could not lie to him about loving him and feeling bad for his injuries. He let his sister out of his arms and without speaking a word to her, ran out of the office.

Perplexed by his behavior, Marianne figured that he was overwhelmed by sorrow. Instead of running after Seth, she left the office to await her turn upstairs.

***

The twins spent less than half an hour with Foster. When they met Marianne in the hallway she told them about Seth's hasty exit.

"Shall we go find him?" the boys asked in tandem.

"Please. He may have left the house and rode out to Lazarus' cabin. That is likely where you'll find him. Go on, I will take my visit now and Seth can come in later."

The boys ran off, not only to find Seth but to escape close proximity to Foster and the possibility of having to visit with him further.

Marianne breathed deep and pulled back her shoulders to gather her courage. She wondered how much more grief she could bear with Willa and Ramiel missing, Foster dying. Silently she prayed that God would show mercy and let this be the last of the hardships facing the Witherell family. Her heartbeat quickened as she walked into the makeshift hospital room to see her beloved brother.

He was as pale as the sheets on which he lay. Sweat beads dotted his forehead and were being wiped away by Myra, who was in on the secret. Marianne walked up to her and asked to take over the duty and she nodded in consent, handing her the cool cloth. Josiah neared the bedside, told her that he would give them some privacy, and then left the room with Myra.

"Foster? Hello there, brother. What have you gotten yourself into this time? Do I need to become your guardian to keep you from trouble?" She tried to be light. No need to weigh him down with her sorrow; perhaps he did not know the gravity of his condition. "Can I get you some water? Or anything else?"

He managed a weak smile. "No. Nothing you can get; nothing you can do." His voice was frail, his words faint. He motioned Marianne closer and when she was near his face he continued, "I'm dying dear sister."

"Oh, no Foster. No. You will recover. Don't forget how strong you are, brother. You are not going anywhere. Gerald and I plan to have you in our wedding. Surely you haven't forgotten that. Silly Foster."

"Marianne, listen to me," he nearly whispered. "You have to hear me out. I am dying. I can feel it in my bones, my muscles, every place."

"No, Foster! I will not have you saying that to me!" Marianne began to cry, unable to hold back as she'd planned to do in his presence.

"Sister, please. There are things you need to know about me. I am not the perfect brother you've always thought me to be. I have to confess my sins to someone and you are the person I am closest with."

He paused to take a deeper breath and coughed a few times, alarming Marianne when he brought up blood. She quickly reached for a cloth and noticed there were other bloodstained rags on the floor. This was not the first time he'd coughed blood. Gingerly she wiped his mouth and when she was finished and he regained control, he began again.

"I have done horrific things, Marianne. Horrific things. I deserve what is now my fate."

"Shhh. Just save your strength Foster so you can fight harder. Please."

He disregarded her. "I've killed a woman named Lilith, a prostitute in Charleston. Beat the life from her. That is why I dueled with her brother. I killed him as well. These are unforgivable sins as it is, but there is more and it concerns this family."

Marianne wasn't sure how to respond, but her dropped jaw displayed astonishment from hearing Fosters confessions She became mute when she tried to speak her protest against his words and had no choice but to listen to his raspy voice.

"I am so sorry Marianne. So sorry you have to hear this. You know that I've always taunted your friend Willa, but you didn't know it was due to my interest in her. Lust for her." He took a deep breath. Letting the air rattle in his weak lungs before continuing.

"Seth and she were in love and planning to run from Heavenly together. The night of their set departure I followed Willa into the woods." Now his eyes filled with tears of regret. He faltered, waiting for his frail body to fortify itself before he made another revelation.

"There I...I took her womanhood. I stole it from her...and...and I left her alone there. The baby she bore is mine, sister. I attacked her to get at Seth, to take away something that might have been his, and to fulfill my lust for Willa. Seth had no knowledge of my actions."

Fosters voice continued to tail off with every word from his lips. He grew fainter with every deliberate breath he drew, but persisted with his confession. "You must tell Seth. Tell Mother and Father what I've just revealed to you. All of it. I...I don't have long and I cannot leave this world without releasing this weight from my conscience. Please, I...I beg of you. Mother...sent...Willa...away. Thinks the child...the child...is from...Father..." He coughed more blood into the cloth, soaking it thoroughly.

Foster caught hold of Marianne's hand and weakly pulled at her so she would get very close. "I...love...you...Mari..." Those were the last words to leave his lips.

By the time Josiah arrived back in the room, he knew he was too late to render any help. His eldest was gone.

Marianne leaned over Foster's body, her face buried in his neck, her arms holding tightly onto his torso. "No, Foster, no Foster, no, don't you leave me! Please, Foster!" She repeated as if dying was his choice and she could suddenly reverse his decision. Her voice cried out in the most melancholy tone Josiah had ever heard and it broke him into a million pieces.

He moved to the foot of the deathbed, knelt down, and covered his face in his hands to begin his own brand of grieving. He sobbed without sound, tears running into his palms to preserve his male dignity.

Chapter 66

Once the brunt of their misery seemed to subside, Josiah and his daughter examined Foster to verify his passing. His eyes were closed, his chest did not rise and fall; there was no pulse. They looked at each other to confirm what they knew and then embraced. The deep sorrow returned and this time Josiah cried as much as Marianne, not worrying that he might appear weak. When they separated minutes later, Marianne occupied herself quickly. She took a clean cloth, dipped it in to a wash basin, and began to wipe her brother's face to clear away traces of blood and perspiration.

Now Josiah would have to confront Margaret. He would have to tell her about the duel and everything that led up to Foster's death and she would blame him for it all. Since she did not get the chance to see Foster during his last moments, Josiah was doubly sure she would condemn him to hell. He stood for a while, just watching Marianne work, contemplating his duty and soon decided to leave out the information about Foster's involvement with the prostitute's death. He'd simply say that the duel was over a business matter and reassure Margaret that he died to defend the family honor. But it was questionable what comfort that would bring now.

He instructed Marianne to get a servant to send for Doctor Capshaw and the undertaker. At that point, he put her in charge of informing the rest of the family since she was now the eldest, next in line to handle family duties such as this.

Then Josiah set off to apprise Margaret. When he arrived at her room, he found her sleeping. Near her bedside he contemplated his following move, tempted to simply escape and let the dire news wait. Hovering for several seconds, he finally decided it would be prudent to wake her.

"Margaret? Margaret?" He nudged her gently and then shook her a bit when she did not respond. "Margaret!"

"Wha...what, Josiah? What the hell is it?" She sat straight up and gave him a look of sheer hatred, wasting no time becoming angry.

Josiah poured her a glass of water and handed it to her as gently as he could. "Please take a drink, Margaret. I must tell you something that is very serious and you must remain calm."

"I am not thirsty. Get to the point. I hope you woke me for some good reason!"

"Margaret…there's been a terrible accident. I've come to tell you…that…"

"Accident? Who was in an accident Josiah? Tell me! Stop stuttering and tell me!"

"It's Foster. He's been shot and…"

"Oh, dear God! Dear God!" Margaret climbed out of her bed so fast that he had no time to finish his sentence as she bolted out, headed for Foster's bedroom. Josiah ran after her, but when she found the room empty she turned back to him with her eyes ablaze. "Where is he, Josiah? What have you done with my son?"

"Margaret, Margaret, you must calm down and I will tell you. Let's get back to your room and I will explain it all."

She refused to move. "Margaret, Foster was shot in a duel. Defending the Witherell honor."

"To hell with the Witherell honor! There is no honor to defend! His father is a wretched whoremonger! I hate you Josiah! Hate you!" She pelted Josiah's chest with her fists repeatedly. He let her continue. Certainly she was relieving the bulk of her anger and would be spent by the time he delivered the rest of the news.

He waited until she slipped down to the floor crying and then sat down on the hardwood with her as she calmed.

"Where is he? I need to see him, take care of him. My son."

In one quick breath he said, "He is dead, Margaret. From infection. There was simply nothing that could be done. Our son is gone and you need to take hold of yourself and not upset the children any further. Can you do that, Margaret?"

Looking into Josiah's eyes were the eyes of a demon. Margaret did nothing at first but glare at him with their sudden darkness. Her breathing was heavy but controlled and he knew there was a storm like no other brewing within his wife. He took advantage of her silence to pull up off the floor and put distance between them. Before he could back away too far however, she was up and had her bony fingers around his throat.

"Damn you Josiah! It's your fault! Everything wretched that's happened to this family is your fault! You killed my son! You killed my son!" She managed to push Josiah to the floor with strength he didn't know she possessed. She was on top of him. Her fingers never let go of his neck during the fall, pressing into his windpipe and cutting off his air. As he struggled to be free of her, she clung like a wild animal.

After a good while, Josiah managed to regain control, rolling her over and pinning her wrists to the floor. Now he was on top of her, restraining her as he coughed.

Margaret howled like a wolf in a trap, arousing the attention of Chloe who was just entering the house. She ran up the stairs towards the ruckus and found her owners on the floor in a tussle. Gasping, she yelled even louder than her mistress.

The Witherell children, teary eyed and ruddy-faced from grief, came to the aid of Josiah. Holding down their mother, their father was able to break free and stand to his feet. Margaret continued to kick at him from the floor. It took Seth, Marianne, and Chloe to keep her down until she weakened.

Finally, the wild demon appeared to exit Margaret Witherell and she stopped fighting. Recent anger all forgotten, she said, "I need to see my son now."

The family guided her to the room as Chloe followed, not knowing anything about Foster's passing until she saw his lifeless body. The dutiful slave then fell to her knees and began to pray silently, rocking back and forth in a spiritual rhythm.

Margaret was unusually serene as she took Foster's hands in her own and then reached down to place a tender kiss on his cheek. Tears began, but they were controlled. No wailing, no cursing God or Josiah.

Chapter 67: Marianne's Journal, November 29, 1852

"The last several weeks have proven torturous for me, my family, and our entire household. It started with Willa and Ramiel's disappearance. Lazarus worries himself sick with wondering where they have gone. He, Seth, and Daniel have searched everywhere, but have turned up nothing. No sign of them. I fear greatly that I will never see my best friend again, but cannot help thinking that she is somewhere headed for freedom. Freedom in which to raise her son. Her son, and Foster's son.

Foster is gone, having died in a tragic way defending the Witherell family honor. Or so Father explained. But I know the truth.

The funeral was peaceful, held in the church with Reverend Wells officiating. All of our house slaves were invited to attend, but only a few actually did. It seems as if my dear brother Foster had made some enemies in his short life.

Do not misinterpret, Dear Journal. I truly loved…still love Foster, but I know now that he had faults. And by all measure his were unforgivable. He told me on his deathbed that he dueled with the brother of a prostitute because he had killed her. Her brother was defending *his* family honor, even if for a strumpet of a sister. All those gentlemen who found their way to Heavenly over the past year were correct in questioning Foster's behavior. The woman's brothers were correct when they charged into our home last spring and accused him of murder. I struggled to understand why my dear brother would be accused of such a crime.

On his deathbed Foster revealed something even more disturbing to me. First he claimed that Willa and Seth were in love. Now all of the peculiar secrecy surrounding her love for Lazarus can be explained. She was not in love with Laz. It was Seth all along! My poor, poor Willa! Pining away for Seth and unable to love him but in secret. And her baby! Foster's baby. His baby by a forced attack on my best friend. My Foster. A cruel rapist as well as murderer.

Oh God, it is as if my world has grown dark. Everything I believed about Foster was a lie. His hateful attitude toward Willa was to cover up his desire for her. And then he took her against her will. How could she have come to me with her sorrows? She could not because I would have thought her a liar! My brother was a saint in my eyes. Now far, far from that.

Foster is buried in the Witherell cemetery just beyond our back lawn. Mother visits him nearly every hour, sometimes crying, but oftentimes wailing for him. It is a miserable sight to see her out there. So distraught. She has no idea who her son was, what evil he'd done.

Now that the funeral is over, it is time for me to share Foster's deep secrets. But shall I reveal his murderous acts? That has yet to be decided and I will think upon it for a day or two. I wish my parents no harm.

How could Mother blame Father for parenting Willa's son Ramiel? Did Father even deny it? Why send her away? And where did they send her? They both need to know that the baby is their grandchild. Or does Father already know the truth? Too many secrets in this house. Too many lies.

December 5, 1852

I had to speak to Seth, to confront him about his feelings for Willa. Would he lie to me as well? No. He fully admitted that the two of them were in love for quite some time and did plan to run off together.

Then I had to tell him about Foster and what he did to Willa. Suddenly it all made sense to him, how she turned away, avoiding him and taking up with Lazarus. Their relationship was a lie, one designed to protect Seth and cover for Foster. It occurred to me that she must have been terribly afraid of Foster and I wonder if he threatened her life, or possibly the life of the baby. Or even Seth. I feel sick even thinking of the possibilities and the notion that Foster could be even more malicious. Was he the reason she left Heavenly without notice? Most likely. I pray that wherever she is, she somehow feels a sense of weight being lifted off her shoulders. Perhaps she will sense that there is no longer danger here and she will return, or at least find way to send word to confirm her well-being.

Seth cried for quite a while and I did my best to console him. He misses Willa even more now, knowing that her heart may still belong to him. Then suddenly his face brightened and he told me that he knew of Willa's whereabouts. She's been at Uncle Charles' Southwind all along!

Here is the good news: Seth and Laz were planning to get Willa back, but plans were put on hold when Foster died. They wanted to wait until after the funeral to activate their scheme. He did not tell me exactly what they had plotted and I am truly not concerned because now it does not have to happen. Once I tell Mother about Ramiel's father, she will surely agree to bring them both back to Heavenly!

I have decided not to inform Mother of Foster's other crimes. There would be no purpose in upsetting her. Her eldest son is gone and there is no reason to further disparage his name, although if he were still living I would have no qualms about doing that. I have taken Foster off the pedestal I'd placed him on all my life. It saddens my heart and when I visit his grave, I shed tears of disgrace for him."

Chapter 68

Margaret was understandably despondent after Foster's funeral. Her eldest son was dead and although she never felt he was an angel in life, now he was canonized by her in death.

But Marianne and Seth were not at her room to enlighten her about one of her deceased son's crimes. They knocked on the door and it was opened by Chloe. They could see that the inside of the room was dark; heavy curtains sealed sunlight from the windows. It was Margaret's tomb of mourning. The tomb from which she emerged only for graveside visits. It was as if the rest of the family was dead to her as well.

"Oh, chilluns, your mama ain't in no mood for this. No visitors, not even her own flesh n' blood. Not now. Best be goin' on your way."

Chloe began to shut the door on them, but Seth stuck his foot in to prevent it from closing. "Not so fast, Chloe. Our mother needs us now more than ever. We have some news for her and were waiting until she was more stable to tell her. We won't be but a few minutes. Please, Chloe." Both he and Marianne knew that the slave woman would do anything in her power to protect her mistress.

"Oh, alright. But don't you be upsettin' her or you have to answer to me, I tell ya."

Next to their mother's bedside, the pair found Margaret lying still as a corpse, with her eyes wide open in an eerie gaze. Marianne parted the curtain on the nearest window just slightly to let in a peek of sunshine. Margaret's eyes squinted from the violent assault of light. Marianne didn't care; she wanted to be able to see her mother's reaction when she heard the news.

"Mother?" Seth called out, but she remained still, didn't even blink her eyes. Instead she stared up at the ceiling. "Mother, please look at me. Marianne is here, too, Mother. We have news. Please look at us."

Nothing. It was as if Margaret had gone deaf. She continued to stare up and whatever she saw had her in a deep trance. Marianne tried to get her attention by putting her hands upon her shoulders. She shook her gently. "Mother, it's Marianne. Can you hear me? Please, Mother. We have some information that might bring you hope."

"Is it Foster? Is he alive? Is my son alive? Oh, my Lord! He's alive!" The grieving woman's eyes lit faster than a lantern on a dark night and she quickly sat up in her bed. "Oh, my children!"

"No, no, no, Mother! It's not that. Foster is gone. I'm sorry, we are all sorry. Mother we buried him. You remember that, don't you?"

The disfiguring twist of pain on Margaret's face was as fresh as if she'd just received the news of his death. She began to wail, burying her face into a pillow. "No, no, please not again. Please not again."

Chloe was at once inside the door. "Now, you two! I told you not to upset the Missus. Now you gone and did it. You best get out now and let me get her settled. Go on!"

Seth had no more patience, could not ride the crest of one more of his mother's emotional tidal waves. "Foster has a baby, Mother! Willa's son is Foster's child!"

The wailing ceased and Margaret's tears stopped short. She was positively not deaf now. "What did you say, son?" Her eyes fixed on Seth, darting back and forth and questioning him as if he were playing some sort of trick on her.

Marianne answered. "Foster has a child. His son is Ramiel, Willa's baby."

"How can that be? Why would he...why would he..."

"He raped Willa, Mother. Your perfect son raped my friend. That alone is unforgivable! But then you sent her away, along with your own grandchild, Mother!" Marianne had not planned to get confrontational with her, but the anger poured out so freely that she could not rein it in.

"Marianne! How can you say that about your dead brother? God rest his soul! You tarnish his name, Marianne! He would do no such thing. Not to any woman, especially not a slave! He was raised in better conditions and would never do such!"

"Mother, it's true. I am sorry for raising my voice at you, I truly am. But you must believe me. Foster admitted this to me as he died. He wanted to clear his conscience. He wanted to die in peace, Mother."

Seth added, "Mother, to what purpose would Marianne fabricate this tale? There is nothing to gain by telling lies about Foster. You know how much she adored him."

"Seth is right. What could I gain? I speak the truth, Mother. We cannot change the circumstances. It is done. Your grandchild waits at Southwind. Do you even care? Would you not want to have a part of Foster return to Heavenly? A bit of Foster lives on. How could you refuse his child?"

A multitude of confused thoughts and emotions whirled in Margaret's brain. When her hands went up to her head, Marianne was ready to restrain her for fear she would pull hair as she did the day she met Ramiel. This time however, Margaret simply held onto her scalp as if she were experiencing the pain of a severe headache. When she finally looked up at her children she wore remorse on her face.

"I have done something truly abysmal, haven't I? But I thought your father... I thought he and Willa... Oh, God. Marianne, I sent away your beloved Willa and... and... my grandchild. My Foster's little baby. The baby who resembles Foster, not Josiah. My, God!"

Several minutes passed as Seth and Marianne let the revelation soak into their mother's psyche. Then they watched her transformation from sniveling, distraught soul to rejuvenated madwoman.

"We must get them back at once! I will not have them with Charles! My grandchild must live at Heavenly! My Foster! My firstborn! His baby! Get your father! Send for Daniel!" Margaret was out of her bed, flapping her arms, and turning about like she'd just been set on fire. "Now! Get going now! Seth! Marianne! What are you waiting for?"

The Witherell pair obeyed and went off in search of Josiah, leaving Chloe to deal with the animated Mistress of Heavenly.

***

Twenty minutes later Josiah was at his wife's side listening to her gush on about Foster's son and the fact that they were grandparents and that Foster was alive in some way.

"Margaret! Calm down, woman! Do you realize what you are saying? Have you gone fully mad? The child is Negro, Margaret! What the devil are you thinking? That he will be a Witherell? No mulatto will be living in this house as my grandchild! Foster's mistakes are of no concern to us, Margaret!"

"How can you say that Josiah? You heartless bastard! He is Foster's child! Foster's blood runs through his veins! Our son lives on through his child. My God, Josiah! You are the mad one! If you do not send Daniel to go after him, I swear I will...I will..."

"What will you do, Maggie? What power do you have to do anything against me, Maggie?"

"You will stop calling me Maggie! Do you understand, Josiah? What I will do if you do not send for my grandson? Why, I will kill myself. I will do it in a most public way. At a ball perhaps. And I will make it the most horrific scene that society has ever known! And I will blame you before I commit my gruesome end! Then how will your society friends see you? Someone who has driven his own wife to the grave. I swear it, Josiah! I will make you the most despised man among all the planters in South Carolina!"

Josiah knew that she was serious. Margaret would do something that drastic, that dramatic. He considered his reputation, and then conceded to her. "Alright, Margaret. This time you win. I will send for Willa and her son. I will allow the boy to be raised here as Willa's son while she works here in the house as your seamstress."

"But I will not have it publicly acknowledged that he has Witherell blood. You may dote upon him within these walls, but I'll not have you breathe a word of his parentage outside of Heavenly. Do you understand? If you do not, I just as well may kill you myself, woman."

"Have it your way, Josiah. You may stay clear of both me and the child for the rest of your life. Just bring him home to me. Do it quickly."

Josiah shook his head, not believing what he'd agreed in order to pacify Margaret. He left her room, setting out to make the promised arrangements.

Chapter 69

Josiah quickly summoned for Daniel and Lazarus, giving them orders to go to Southwind the following day. He did not discuss the matter of Foster parenting Willa's baby. No need for them to learn of the Witherell muck. He told them that he and Margaret had a change of mind. His wife simply could not work with dress designers in the city and did not want to deal with Paris or New York. Willa's gowns were the only ones she desired and she was sorry to have sent her away.

Josiah even apologized for Margaret's unbalance and her misguided belief that Josiah fathered her child. He explained that he was embarrassed for his wife. He vehemently denied any involvement with Willa, but she would not let it rest until Willa was banished. He also lied and told them that he planned all along to return Willa and the baby once Margaret cooled off.

It was agreed that they leave early the following day, accompanied by Seth. Even Camille would be given a pass to leave the plantation. Soon Josiah sent the two men away to prepare for their journey and Seth decided to follow. When the three reached Daniel's cabin, Lazarus pulled Seth aside.

"Seth, I know all about Foster and Willa. I know what he did to her the night before you was to run. She told me all of it, not too long after. She asked me to marry her, 'cause she didn't want you hurtin' all the time. She couldn't tell you 'bout your brother for fear you'd go out n' kill him. She was so scared, Seth."

"So, you were never in love, Laz?" Seth looked bewildered and hopeful at the same instant.

"No...no we wasn't," he lied. His mind filled with thoughts of the intimacy he and his wife shared before her disappearance. His heart ached, but he had to do the right thing.

"Seth. She was yours first and you're the one she loves. Our weddin' was to cover over what your brother did to her. Had to make an excuse for her bein' with child. But it's out now. Seth, she's rightly yours."

"Laz, don't say that. I'm sure she loves you now and has forgotten what she felt for me. She's probably thinking of you right this minute. And she will be with you soon, my friend. Besides, we both know that there's no future for Willa and me. If you'll remember, she's black, I am white."

"I know that, Seth." He rolled his eyes. "But I been thinkin'. Thinkin' real hard on this. Before Foster died, we'd been plannin' to get Willa and Ramiel. Bring 'em back here. Now we've been given the blessin' to do it. But Seth…is what you want? Do you want her back here a slave and you still in love and not havin' her? You are still in love, ain't you?"

"Lazarus, she is your wife now. If I have any love still in my heart, I just have to let it go. She is your wife, not mine. You two are happy, even if you say there is no love between you."

"She loves you. Always will. I can't keep her now that the secret's out about the baby. Can't do it. It ain't right, Seth. Just ain't. Now I been thinkin', like I said. Been thinkin' 'bout how you two can be together. You gotta run, Seth. We can all run. Been talkin' to some of the fella's that come through to shoe their marster's horses. There's somethin' called the Underground Railroad. They help slaves escape. We can all go. Me, Willa, Ramiel, my folks, and you. Why you'd be a bonus to us bein' a white man. Maybe get us supplies and things and not raise suspicion."

"I've heard of it. It's dangerous, Laz. Do we really want to put Willa, the baby, and your parents through that?"

"It's the only way, Seth. The only way. Think 'bout it tonight."

"I will. I will. Are you sure about this?" Seth's heart began to beat faster at the idea of taking Willa to freedom up North, perhaps Canada.

"Sure as anything. See you in the mornin'."

Seth returned to the Big House with a million questions filling his mind. In his bed he tossed about, unable to find sleep as he thought of Willa,. He longed for her sweet kisses, the ones he'd lived so recently without.

Dawn couldn't come soon enough for Seth, but when a hint of pink finally appeared over the horizon, he dressed like a warrior on a mission. He rifled through his chest of drawers to find clothing for the trip. Not just an extra set, but several. He'd made up his mind.

He left the house with a heavy heart and would have liked to say goodbye to Marianne and the twins. No time. He took one last look at the mansion house as memories of his childhood flooded his consciousness. It was difficult, but he kept moving in the direction of Daniel's cabin.

The carriage Josiah let them use for the journey was far from the wagon used to transport Willa to Southwind. This one would keep them comfortable, as Josiah Witherell would not have his second son troubled by a poor ride. Inside, there were cloth sacks of clothing, food, and supplies. The significant amounts were more than necessary for just a few days travel. It was clear that the Adams' were busy overnight.

Seth greeted Camille, who was also in on the plan. He understood what a sacrifice this was going to be for the elder Adams'. They both loved

Heavenly and never dreamed of leaving its borders. But there would be no way for them to explain returning to it without the young people.

The journey began with little discussion. Lingering at Heavenly would weaken their resolve so they rode away as quickly as possible. Distance increased their collective optimism. To make the most of the daylight, Daniel drove the horses for many hours and then rested while his son took the reins. Twice along the way they were halted by slave patrollers who questioned either driver atop the carriage, closely inspecting Daniel's free papers and Lazarus' pass. However, once Seth stepped from the carriage, the dubious men backed off, withdrawing their angry dogs. Seth grew more confident that their escape plan would work.

Before dark the co-conspirators were nearly out of South Carolina and well away from Heavenly. They rested the horses for the night, built a fire, and ate a good meal packed for them by Heddie. Seth thought of her while he ate his fried chicken and tears filled his eyes. His heart longed to reunite Willa with her mother, but that was not to be. Suddenly he was discouraged. Would she even want to be with him now? Maybe she'd prefer Lazarus and want Seth to return to Heavenly without any of them. Or maybe she would simply want to go back to the plantation and be with Heddie. He tried to envision all of the scenarios, knowing that only one of them would play out.

Chapter 70

After sleeping in the carriage bundled in blankets for comfort, it was soon daylight again and time to move. Although there was less distance to travel on this leg of the journey, time dragged slowly for Seth. The closer they got to Southwind, the more his nerves felt scorched, as the fire of anticipation burned throughout his body. The remaining trip was agonizing, but he imagined that Lazarus was feeling just as anxious. He was, after all, relinquishing to Seth his wife and the son he considered his own.

"Laz," he finally spoke, "are you sure this is what you want? Willa with me... uh, if she'll have me, that is? We can just go back to Heavenly and to the way it was before Willa and Ramiel left. You're a fine blacksmith, the best my father's ever seen. You'll be giving up that as well. Please think about it."

"I've made up my mind. Seth, she's goin' to want you back. You think I wanta live my whole life with a woman who can't get your ugly face out of her mind?"

Seth laughed at his friend's remark.

"Besides, I can work someplace else one day. If I'm that good, ain't nobody goin' to refuse work to me." Then Lazarus became stone serious, looking Seth directly in the eyes. "You know I love Heavenly. Right, Seth?"

Seth nodded.

"And your father gave me a chance to do somethin' more useful than work the rice fields. He been real good to my family, Seth. And I'll never forget that. No, sir. But I'm still a slave and I belong to your family. Who knows if I might end up on the auction block one day? Now, I'm not just doin' all this for you and Willa, Seth. I'm doin' it for me, and my mama. We've never had freedom. You don't know what it's like to be owned by another man. But it does somethin' to ya. Even though we be treated right, there's a mess of darkies out there in the fields who ain't. They get the whip, live in fear of it. If the Lord blesses me with another family someday...children, you think I want that for them? My own blood?"

"Of course not, Laz. You deserve better, deserve your freedom. Camille deserves to be free like Daniel."

Lazarus smiled a grin that spread wide across his face. "Yeah. That sounds right nice."

***

When the carriage finally pulled up to Southwind they were greeted by Boston, the well-cultured old butler. Seth climbed out of the carriage and introduced his party and their intentions. Boston acknowledged him and no one else then withdrew into the mansion to inform his master. A pleasantly surprised Charles rushed out and greeted Seth with a warm, enthusiastic handshake. Then he stepped back to take in a full view of his nephew.

"Seth! Oh, my how you've grown since last I saw you! The cooks at Heavenly must be superb. It is a delight to see you so unexpectedly! But oh, my goodness. We received word of Foster's passing and I am so terribly sorry. You must be miserable, Seth. Just miserable. Charlotte and I were in Europe, so we have just recently learned the news. How is my sister managing? Tell me, Seth."

"Uncle, she is delicate, as can be expected. She experiences grief more deeply than anyone, you know."

"Of course. Will you accept my sincere condolences? We've already sent word to your mother and have promised to visit Heavenly in the spring. So then, what in the world brings you to Southwind this time of year?"

"I'm actually here on some business for my father. I am here to retrieve Willa Adams and her infant son. Mother and Father gave me money for exchange, since her removal from your house leaves you without the talent of an excellent seamstress."

"Seamstress? Where did you get that idea, my boy? In my house?"

"Yes, sir, as my father requested. He was specific about her occupation and she was to work in that capacity, Uncle."

"I received no such request. As I recall, Mr. Henry was specific in stating that your father intended to teach her a lesson about hard work. Apparently she was careless with her duties and the cotton field would afford her the opportunity to understand what hard work was about. Did he not tell you that?"

"My father assured me that Willa was to work in the house! Where is she then, Uncle? Direct me to her at once!"

"Don't get upset, young Seth. What is she to you but a slave? Come now son, let's go in the house first and visit. Aunt Charlotte will have a conniption fit if I don't invite you for a meal and visit. Tell the driver and your other Negroes that I'll send someone out to take them to the slave village to find the girl."

"No! I mean, thank you, Uncle Charles, but we are in a bit of a hurry. You see, Willa is such a fine seamstress that Mother insists we return her immediately. We try to do everything Mother requests these days, she's in such a fragile state."

"Ah, I see. Well then, let me call for someone to take you all to the village. I will have the cooks prepare some things for you to take for the journey back. Are you sure you won't stay here and let your slaves go get the girl? You have no business in the slave village. You've not been around cotton pickers. They are a tough breed. Hmmmm…but I do imagine the girl will be changed and willing to work harder by now." Uncle Charles chuckled, rearing back his head, as if proudly responsible for Willa's conditioning.

"I will be fine, Uncle. I can handle myself. Please give my regrets to Aunt Charlotte for not staying. Thank you."

Soon a rather broad-shouldered young Negro man emerged from an outbuilding after being summoned. He greeted the Adams' with a nod and spoke to Seth. "You lookin' for someone out there?" He pointed to the west side of the property.

"Yes. Her name is Willa. Willa Adams. And her son is Ramiel. Do you know of her? Can you take us to her?"

"Sure I do. I can take you right to her. You must be Seth, the Master's nephew. Mind if I get up there with the driver so I can tell him where to go?"

"No, please do. And yes, I am Seth. How did you know my name?"

"I'm Edgar. Edgar Grigsby. You can call me Flash," said the broad-shouldered man, his mouth forming a king-sized grin displaying his teeth.

Seth wanted to embrace him. Willa's brother was standing before him. She wasn't alone after all. He then wondered if her father and other brother were still there at Southwind. He soon introduced Edgar to Lazarus, Daniel, and Camille. After his visit with Willa, Edgar knew who all of them were to Willa. He knew about Willa's lingering love for Seth and her marriage to Lazarus.

***

It was Saturday, so the slaves completed work early and were allowed to return to their village. Willa's cabin was at the center of a long row of cabins. The dwellings were four deep, and at least twenty wide. Eighty cabins held at least four slaves apiece, but some as many as ten with young children included. Daniel stopped the carriage at the near edge so they could walk to where Willa was housed.

Seth wanted to run, but restrained himself since he depended on Edgar to guide him. Edgar walked at a smooth, steady pace with his head held high. Seth was pleased with the air of dignity with which he carried himself, thinking that he surely kept Willa safe. Lazarus lagged behind with his parents, excited to finally get to see his wife and her son, yet his gut churned knowing he would soon release them to Seth.

When Edgar knocked on the cabin door, Willa answered and threw her arms around his neck. As she looked over his shoulder, she caught sight of Seth first. Then she saw Lazarus and her in-laws behind him. The joy she felt seeing her brother was eclipsed by seeing the trio. She had hardened herself to the idea that she'd never again see a face from Heavenly. But now here they were. Was she dreaming again?

She cautiously approached them as if they were vapor ready to dissolve in the air if she moved. Lazarus rushed over and took her in his arms for what he imagined would be the last time. He clung to her, kissing her face, but avoiding her lips. They both cried, releasing the deep sorrow of separation. There was so much to tell him, but before she could speak he whispered in her ear.

"Willa, you know I love you so damn much. I do anything to be with you. But honey, secrets come out and we got to talk. You, me, Seth. Just remember, I love you. Always will."

Lazarus broke free from their embrace, leaving her confused. Seth stepped in as Laz backed away. "Willa. God, I have missed you." His voice broke and he could not continue. She looked into his eyes and saw his love for her, like a flame burning slowly, surely. Fresh, like it was before Foster took her innocence in the woods. She was more confused and looked away, looked to Lazarus. He nodded as if giving her permission to feel something for Seth, to let her acknowledge the light in Seth's eyes with the light of her own.

"Willa, I still love you. I never stopped. And I know about Foster and why you married Laz. I understand it now. And we're here to take you and Ramiel away from here."

The mention of her baby's name tore at the deep wound of loss covering her heart. Willa slumped to the ground with a weighty sigh. As soon as the tears fell, Camille hurried to her side and offered motherly arms of comfort. No questions, just comfort.

"Oh, Camille! Lazarus! Ramiel is dead! My son is gone...he's gone."

"Dear God, Willa! What are you sayin', darlin'? What are you sayin'?" Camille brushed the hair back from Willa's forehead and kissed it, rocking her back and forth. "Lord, Jesus!" Ramiel was her grandson, the pride and joy she thought was of her own flesh through her son.

"No! He can't be, Willa! He can't be!" Lazarus dropped to the ground to hold his wife and his mother. The three of them continued while Seth and Daniel looked on, not knowing what good it would do for them to join the huddle on the ground. Seth wanted to pick up Willa and be the one to soothe her, but it was not yet his time, his place.

After Willa calmed, she explained how Ramiel died. The account of his death enraged the travelers, especially Seth. He was angry at his parents for sending her away to Southwind, and angrier with Duke Henry for having her put out to work in the fields. *The lying bastard!* Seth entertained the notion of returning to Heavenly just to find Duke. He would force his evil face down into a horse trough until he drowned and died the same horrific death as baby Ramiel!

Seth had to walk away in an attempt to calm the storm welling up inside of him. Willa watched him traipse off by himself, aware that he was fuming, filled with hatred for Duke Henry and possibly his own parents. Then, while she and Lazarus were alone, she learned about Foster's death and his final moment confessions to Marianne.

"Don't you see, Willa? Now there ain't no need for us to pretend to be married. You know it wasn't lawful anyway."

"But Laz, we're happy together. Even before Ramiel. We were happy. Didn't you feel it when we were together, when you touched me and I touched you for the first time?"

"I felt it. A man hafta be a damn fool not to feel that, Willa. You know I love you. I love you so much it hurts sometimes. But I know who your heart's with. It's Seth. And Willa, I want you to be happy. Even if it's not with me. And we always goin' to be friends, the three of us."

"Laz, don't." Willa wanted to protest, but her heart was not in it as much as her voice was. She was beginning to love Laz, but feared that it was in resignation that she felt that way. Resignation to the cold fact that a relationship with Seth would never be acceptable. Society would never allow it.

"I release you from this marriage, Willa. I want you to tell Seth that it's alright for him to love you. Or he won't let himself. He'll keep bein' stubborn like always. Tell him Willa. Soon as he gets back here."

"Oh, Lazarus! Me tellin' him that just makes no difference. He is a Witherell. I'm a slave. We're back where we started. That's never goin' to change!"

Soon Lazarus began to detail the plans they'd schemed in the few days before the journey. He and Seth, along with his parents would find a way to meet up with the Underground Railroad. Seth was white, indeed. That would prove to make it plausible. He'd be privy to information that only whites could access. It would work.

When Seth returned with a cooler head, Lazarus revealed what he discussed with Willa. It would now be Seth's turn to speak with her and make things right between them. They'd obtained Lazarus' blessing. And Seth needed to believe that they would finally have the blessing of God Himself.

Epilogue, Olivia

On the last page of the journal, Marianne wrote…

"April 2, 1853. Dear Journal, It has been many months since Seth disappeared, along with Lazarus and his parents Daniel and Camille Adams. They went on a mission to retrieve Willa from Uncle Charles' plantation in Georgia, but they never returned. Mother and Father, of course, were infuriated. Not only have they lost another son, but four of their most treasured servants.

Soon after, Father sent a search party to look for them. They turned up nothing. Mother and I fear the worst, that something dire had happened. Father seems certain however, that Willa and the Adams' are runaways and have done something terrible to Seth in order to break away from him. Father hired bounty hunters, but even as they scour the country, so far they are unsuccessful.

Early this very morning a post was delivered to me. The letter wore no markings to indicate its origination, but it was from Seth. I am pleased to report that he is well and that he, Willa, and the Adams' are safe. However, I fear that this may well be my last communication from my wonderful, brave sibling.

(Seth Witherell's letter was affixed to the journal page. The paper on which it was written retained the distinct pattern of tears, sometimes smearing the ink in places.)

"My Dear Sister Marianne,

By now I am certain that Heavenly is all a bloom with the glory of springtime. When I close my eyes I see it and I miss it more than my words can describe. I long for you in even greater proportion, Dear Sister.

I know it has been several months since we were last together, and I sincerely apologize for the way this must appear to you. I'm sure you have spent considerable time worrying about us. Please be assured that Willa, Lazarus, Daniel, Camille, and I are all in fine condition. Please assure Heddie that Willa is well. And please take to her Willa's love.

I will simply say that we were compelled to leave Heavenly. After Foster's passing, the truth was told to you about Ramiel. The marriage of Willa and Laz was one borne to cover the truth and protect the child. And to protect me because Willa was sure I might have killed Foster myself. I am aware that you also know Willa and I have loved each other for many years. Please understand that this is why we did not return to Heavenly, for the love we share is great and something that our society will not accept. But now we are free.

Perhaps one day the world will be different and we will return to Heavenly, but until then please do not forget me, sister. Know that you are in my thoughts each day, as are Garrett and Gabriel. Of course I still think of our parents, but the evils they inflicted on Willa are still fresh in my heart and I find it difficult yet to forgive.

I also must tell you that Willa's baby Ramiel died before we made it to Southwind to save them. The months since are difficult for Willa. Nightly she grieves for him as I hold her in my arms for comfort. Pray for her, Marianne. Pray that her heart heals with the passage of time.

I know that Mother's own heart was set on seeing her grandchild. Please do tell her that anything left of Foster died when she sent Willa to Southwind. Now Mother has nothing of him.

I love you, my sweet sister. Until we meet again, I am forever your loving brother, Seth"

"Somehow I must go on with my life, my heart heavy and my head full of knowledge I must somehow keep inside until the proper time to reveal it.

I imagine that as soon as Mother hears this news, she will surely collapse. Father will want to send more hunters far north to track down his wayward slaves, along with Seth. He may severely reprimand Willa, Lazarus, and Camille. His property. And although Daniel is a free man, he will have him prosecuted for his part in the escape.

He will force Seth back to resume the role of Foster in running his businesses. Now I add these new burdens to those already besieging me, and I think perhaps this news might best be kept secret. I resolve to share it only with dear Mammy Heddie.

I should be well prepared to keep secrets, as that seems to be the hallmark of the Witherell name. I finish this journal entry with a prayer for the peace and security of Seth, Willa, and the Adams'. And I pray that one day I shall see my brother and best friend again."

Olivia

For better or for worse, this is my heritage. My ancestors were slave-holders and I knew that all along. I always saw my mother as a direct extension of them; a racist who stubbornly refused to live past what I assumed was a purely Southern-bred prejudice. I swore I would never be like her, but I had no clue that her bigotry was influenced by something else—an attack. Can I forgive her now?

I think of Foster's attack on Willa Grigsby. So similar to Mother's, reverse the skin colors. Willa never held the entire white race at fault. Even in dire circumstances, she seemed too strong for that. Apparently Mother was not. I sit here and reflect on all the precious years we wasted, me defending Anthony and her refusing to accept him. Her intolerance seemed so criminal, especially where her own daughter and son-in-law were concerned.

Now I know, but I still don't understand. Why did she write me a letter to read only after her passing? How could she have gone to her grave without making peace with me and accepting Anthony into our family? I'll never know.

I do know that I live in a different world, far removed from the one known by ancestor Marianne. I wonder about the fate of Willa and Seth and whether they stayed together, grew old together as Anthony and I will. Suddenly I feel so blessed that my husband and I only had to endure Mother, a woman who was inextricably shackled by her secret. Bound up like the Witherells by the many secrets once shrouding Heavenly Plantation.

ABOUT THE AUTHOR

Teresa Robison enjoyed writing as a child. While her classmates groaned when their teachers assigned book reports, research papers, and essays, Teresa had to hide the spark in her eyes and the giddiness in her voice. From adolescent poetry to short stories, writing was a creative escape for a shy little girl who tried to keep her voice under wraps.

As Teresa became a working adult, she always gravitated to the jobs that allowed her the freedom to express ideas. She worked in administrative positions where she could write company policies and employee handbooks, then "graduated" to marketing work where her blood truly began to boil. Ad copy, catalog descriptions, marketing collateral, company newsletters.

Then, one day after reading a book titled "To Be A Slave" (by Julius Lester), she was especially angered by one account of particular cruelty. It was the story of infanticide carried out on a plantation where there was a surplus of slave babies. Teresa knew that she had to craft a story and that this "scene" had to be woven into its fabric. Two years later, her first novel, "The Secrets of Heavenly," was born. Now she hopes her voice will be heard.

Teresa, known as "Teri" in her private life, resides in Indiana with her husband Karl. The couple has two adult children, daughters Kayla and Abbey. Teresa currently works as a trainer/facilitator, teaching career skills to adults, as well as writing training curriculum.

The author welcomes any comments or questions at her email address: **write.tr@gmail.com**, and encourages you to leave a review for this book at Amazon.com: **http://amzn.com/B00B40B0LI**

Made in the USA
Charleston, SC
14 March 2013